DeLore's

Confession

&

DeLore's Confession

Paulette Crain

Oak Tree Books

Oak Tree Publishing Inc.

New Orleans

British Columbia, Canada

1999

ℰℬ

Oak Tree Books

Oak Tree Publishing Inc.

New Orleans

ℰℬ

White Rock, B.C.

Canada

Library of Congress Cataloging-in-Publication Data
Crain, Paulette, 1942
DeLore's Confession / by Paulette Gaston Crain
p.   cm.
ISBN 1-892343-00-2
I. Title
PS3553.R259D4   1998   98-18982 CIP
813'.54—dc21
Printed in the United States of America

First Edition

10 9 8 7 6 5 4 3 2 1

This book is printed on acid-free paper.

BOOK DESIGN BY ANTHONY MORELAN

PHOTO BY LYNN SEQUOIA ELLNER PRODUCTIONS

Oak Tree Publishing Inc.

www.previewbooks.com

ℰℬ

ॐ

This book is dedicated to
my beloved parents

Wortham & Carmen Gaston

ॐ

$\mathcal{A}$cknowledgments

When embarking upon your first novel, if you are fortunate, many people come into play. Without them this book would not have been possible. I sincerely thank you all.

First to my two dearest friends, Renée Trudeau and Renée Wrede who tirelessly edited each page of a lengthy manuscript. To Patrick Shannon and Renée Trudeau who helped me become a bit more computer literate. At times, I'm certain they wanted me to simply disappear. To my book collaborator, Sandy Gelles-Cole, who had the insight to change the title from Prism to Delore's Confession. To my good friend, Pat Ladd: Your suggestions were right on. And to my agent, Billie Johnson, who stoked my confidence.

Finally, to my family who, even through the disappointments, were always supportive and kept me believing in myself. But especially to my husband, Des, who endured the journey with love and assurance.

વ્ય

DeLore's Confession

Prologue

The old mansion of Belvedere slowly emerged through the evanescent fog. A lonely sailboat glided through Raccoon Straits between Tiburon and Angel Island, making its way toward Belvedere. The Golden Gate, bridging the gap between Sausalito and the steepled city of San Francisco, lay shrouded.

A woman leaned heavily against the railing of the Corinthian Yacht Club, looking toward the old mansion. It had been five long years since he had summoned her to that forlorn house. A house she had dreamed of entering. To refurbish and bring back to life. She, Ashley Winthrop, the renowned designer and renovator of vintage houses. How could she have known the evil that awaited behind those magnificent walls?

Those past horrifying years had now forced her to do the unthinkable. With one deep breath, she drew the cool dampness into her lungs. Her task at hand, she slowly yet determinedly withdrew, stepping backward across the deck. Ashley Winthrop disappeared into the fog.

ॐ

Chapter One

Ashley could hear the screams of a child.

"Mommy! Mommy!" she cried, her fists pounding against the wall.

Collapsing onto the floor, Ashley drew herself into a fetal position and stared across the room—yet seeing nothing but the images of her dream. It was that same horrifying dream she had lived with since childhood.

But it was different this time. Why had she screamed? *What* had she screamed?

She forced her mind back into the dream.

She is a small child, sitting in the back seat of a car. The car is advancing slowly up a narrow cliff road. Protruding from the banks are enormous oaks that seem to reach out to her.

On and on she travels through the tunnel formed by the branches of the oaks. As the car moves onward, the branches thicken. She can feel the density close in on her; desperate, she reaches out and opens the car window. She can almost taste the fog as it brushes past her face.

The pounding of the waves roars like thunder. Frightened, she quickly closes the window and leans forward into the darkness. She screams out, calling someone's name. It is then she feels it: a cold and evil presence. Consumed with fear, she shrinks back into the leather seat as the car continues up the winding road.

Without warning the fog has cleared. She gasps as a massive facade of stone and mortar rises up before her. Slowly the car passes through iron gates. The car door swings open, and she finds herself standing alone with only the deafening roar of the sea. Desperate to find her way, she becomes aware of the gnarled branches of the giant oaks. Quickly she turns, stumbling along the aged cobblestones.

The magnificent house looms again through the mist. She is entranced as strangely she thinks, this house must have always been there, just as she is seeing it now. Time has not marred the delicate features of its leaded windows that have withstood decades of encroaching ivy.

Her eyes focus on the limestone terraces framed by marble balustrades. She feels suspended between the past and the present as she fancies the tall French doors swinging open. Then, almost without thought, she looks up at the round window high above her. The light from the slate roof dims as the dark clouds inch past. The once-glistening window withdraws into darkness. Her legs seem incapable of movement. Terror fills her as a wave of cold air sweeps past. It forces her toward the massive doorway framed in intricate carvings of marble and stone. As she approaches, the doorway vanishes. Far off in the distance she sees a man. He seems to loom over her, holding a woman in his arms. The woman is naked and lifeless.

Seized with panic, she struggles to run, realizing with horror that she is running toward him.

Chapter Two

"Ashley Winthrop, you are stark raving mad. I can't believe what you just let walk out that door." Stanley threw his head back in exasperation.

"Stanley!" Ashley exclaimed, tired of his relentless babbling. "If you don't give this infernal fixation about my sex life a rest, I swear I won't be held responsible for your sudden demise!"

"Sex life? Ha! You wouldn't know a sex life if it reared up and bit you on the ass." Stanley traipsed across the studio through a maze of eighteenth century furniture in his all-too-familiar operatic rantings. "Mr. and Mrs. Victor Winthrop are pleased to announce the long awaited marriage of their daughter, the renowned designer, Ashley Winthrop. After her torrid affair with a George II walnut armchair, she is, at last, settling down with a William and Mary walnut chair, circa 1690."

Ashley laughed in spite of herself, then turned her attention back to an ancient Chinese porcelain vase. She stared at it, the dream from the previous night gnawing at her. Why had it been different? It was that ominous round window. It had not been in her dream before last night. And she had screamed out something. Why couldn't she remember the words?

Ashley Winthrop was a renowned designer and an authority on vintage houses. A classic beauty, tall and slender, with long chestnut hair, she possessed an air of sophistication, of unapproachability. At the age of forty, she still had not married. Her parents chided her for being too independent and too much the perfectionist. But neither independence nor perfectionism had caused her to remain single. She simply wasn't interested.

Why she felt this way was a mystery, even to Ashley. But she didn't spend time fretting about it. She lived only for her work.

"Ashley," Stanley called from the front office. "Pick up the phone. It's Shelby, she's about to bust a gut."

"Hi Shel."

"Meet me at Sam's in twenty minutes. You're not going to believe the news I have for you."

"What news?"

"Never mind. Just be there."

Ashley heard the click at the other end. She slouched back in her chair with a sigh.

පා

It was only 11:15, and Sam's had yet to fill with its noontime hordes. This famed restaurant was a true phenomenon. People would stand in line for hours while the other restaurants along Tiburon's shoreline held only a handful of customers. But at this hour, few tables were occupied.

Ashley snaked her way past an array of tables and several hopeful pigeons to where Shelby sat anxiously at the far end of the deck.

"All right. What's this news I'm not going to believe?" Ashley could see Shelby's excitement. But then, everything excited Shelby.

"You're not going to believe it! Her short black hair danced about her face.

"No, I guess I won't," Ashley said, a soft smile forming on her lips. She looked into Shelby's big brown eyes, seeing the familiar animation.

Shelby's eyes darted from side to side.

Ashley rested her chin in the palm of her hand. "Well?" she whispered. "What is it I'm not going to believe?"

"Guess what haunted house is about to be occupied?"

Ashley pretended to think. "Gee Shelby, I don't know. I've seen a lot of haunted houses."

Shelby leaned further into the table. "The one you'd give your soul to decorate!"

"No!" Shelby had captured Ashley's attention. "You can't be serious. The DeLore mansion?"

"Yes, the DeLore mansion. And guess what?"

"What?"

"It seems that a certain Mr. DeLore, supposedly the great-great-grandson-or-something of the original owner, is moving in."

Ashley looked out past the Corinthian toward Belvedere. The old mansion could barely be seen through the heavy branches of the cypress.

"How do you know?"

"I'm in real estate, dummy. Besides, Connie over at the Landmark Society told me. I was afraid you had already heard."

"Not a word," Ashley said, looking out toward Belvedere. "Is he there now?"

"I don't know, but we could find out."

Ashley looked at Shelby anxiously.

"Well?" Shelby grabbed Ashley's arm and pulled her from the table.

Winding their way through the narrow, escalating roads of Belvedere, they finally rounded the bend at the top, and there, behind enormous wrought-iron gates and concealed almost entirely by a giant cypress, stood DeLore House.

The old mansion was thought to have been built around the early 1800's and had been vacant as long as anyone could remember. Its block walls struggled to be seen through the encroaching ivy, revealing random patches of a faded ocher coloring. Its slate roof still clung on valiantly, defying decades of abuse; its chimneys stood tall, commanding respect. It was a magnificent piece of architecture. Six French doors encased in stone cornices were terraced behind stone balustrades. Weathered shutters clung precariously to the second and third story wall, while the fourth floor dormers rose high and eerie. At night, the blank windows would reflect the moon's beam streaming through the branches of the old cypress. Ravaged by time, yet maintaining the aura of power, the estate intimidated.

Transfixed, Ashley and Shelby left the car and walked across Golden Gate Avenue. Suddenly, another car rounded the bend. The driver slammed on his brakes and laid on his horn. Ashley and Shelby came instantly back to life.

"Jesus Christ!" the man screamed. "What are you day-dreaming idiots *doing* ?" He quickly sped out of sight.

Ashley fell against one of the stone pillars supporting the tall cast-iron fence, struggling to regain her composure.

Shelby, not shaken by the near miss, hurled a few choice words after the man. "He's a goddamn maniac," she grumbled, as she rushed over to Ashley. "Are you all right?"

"Damn," Ashley moaned.

"Come on." Shelby grabbed Ashley's arm. "Let's see if this DeLore guy has moved in." Shelby peered through the cast-iron rails. Ashley jerked her arm free. "Shel, if Mr. DeLore has moved in, I'll contact him like the professional I am, not snoop around his house like some half-wit."

This situation reminder her of the days when she and Shelby had been in high school. Shelby would drag her out at night to creep around old houses that were supposedly haunted. Ashley loved old houses. Sneaking around them in the pitch dark, however, had never appealed to her.

"Look! Shelby gasped, ignoring Ashley's comment. "Over there. He's here all right. What kind of car is that, anyway?" She pressed her face against the rails.

Under the portico was a 1950's white Jaguar convertible with red interior. It had a long protruding hood with large rounded fenders.

"It's a Jag," Ashley replied with authority, "probably early to middle fifties. They're gorgeous cars; I've always thought I'd like to own one."

"You do own one," Shelby said.

"No I don't. My car is a '77, not a fifty-something. There's a big difference."

"Yeah, yours is always in the shop. I wonder if Mr. DeLore has the same problem. If he does, the two of you would have something in common."

"Never mind," Ashley said sternly. "Let's get out of here. She quickly headed back to the car.

Seconds later, Shelby came flying across the street, yanked open the car door and flung herself in.

"What is it?"

Shelby threw the car into gear and roared out onto the road, barely making the turn around the bend.

"Jesus! Slow down." Ashley braced herself against the dash.

"I saw him, Ash. It was him."

"What?" Ashley was horrified. All she needed was a prospective client catching her in the act of spying. "Slow down!" she bellowed.

"You don't want him to see us, do you?" Shelby jerked the steering wheel to the right. The Cadillac screeched around another hairpin turn.

Ashley shook her head in defeat and gripped the dashboard. "We have every right to be on these streets. Now stop it, you're acting crazy."

Shelby let off the accelerator and glanced into the rearview mirror.

Ashley slumped down into her seat. "He didn't see you, did he?"

"I'm not sure."

Ashley began to laugh. There was nothing more amusing than Shelby evolving into one of her chronic, frenzied states. "Why don't you go back to your office and take a Valium?"

"Very funny."

❧

Belvedere Designs was located in an old English-style cottage overlooking Belvedere Cove. San Francisco could be seen in the distance. It was a prime piece of real estate. Ashley was grateful that Shelby had found it for her. The main floor was the design studio. Ashley had converted the top floor into her private residence. Decorated with exquisite antiques, her home was both lovely and austere.

"I'm back, Stanley," she announced as she stepped through the door. She walked past his office and through a large room displaying fine European antiques. Every important period was represented. There were pieces from the Empire, Regency, Victorian, and Neoitalianate periods. A casual browser looking for a quick bargain would have been put off by the prices, for these were important pieces.

Ashley's office was at the far end, to the right of the main room. It had small leaded windows overlooking the cove with French doors opening onto a balcony shared by the main room.

"Michael called," Stanley said, walking back to Ashley's office. Stanley, in his late twenties, had fair skin and small delicate features. This gave him a youthful appearance despite his thinning hair, which he wore long on top but neatly trimmed around the neckline.

Five years earlier, Stanley had walked right into the office of Belvedere Designs. He had graduated from design school a year before and had been working for a small studio in the city. He threw her a sales pitch about his talents and showered Ashley with copious flatteries. She had been so amused by his antics and impressed with his tenacity that she offered him a three-month trial period. Five years later, he had gained her friendship as well as her respect for him as a designer. He was now a partner in Belvedere Designs.

"Wish that hunk of a twin brother of yours would call me." Stanley made a low moaning sound. "What a waste."

Ashley gave a preoccupied smiled. "Oh stop," she said. "What did Michael want?"

"Certainly nothing of interest to me," he pouted, turning and crossing the main room to a 19th century Italian buffet cabinet with mirrored sides that had just arrived. He began rearranging a romantic 19th century cast-bronze sculpture, fussing until he was sure that it reflected just so in the mirror. "Something about your mother's birthday dinner at Ernie's tomorrow night. I didn't think you and your mother got along."

"We don't," she said matter-of-factly, admiring the sculpture. "It's stunning, isn't it?"

"That it is," he agreed. "I'd say one of our better purchases."

"And I know just the house for it."

"You're absolutely right," he said quickly. "That French villa in the city. The one in Pacific Heights. It's perfect."

"No, not Pacific Heights, the one out there," she said, pointing to the top of Belvedere. Ashley grinned, noting Stanley's confusion, and looked back at the piece slyly. "It was made for that house. Don't you think?"

"What house? We're not doing a house up there."

"If I have anything to say about it, we will."

Stanley looked at Ashley suspiciously. "All right, Ashley. What's going on?"

"The old DeLore mansion," she said with studied nonchalance, inspecting the intricate designs in the mirrored buffet. "It seems a certain great-great-grandson is here from France. He's moving in."

She turned to see Stanley's astonished look. "Close your mouth, Stanley," she ordered. Patting him on the shoulder, she walked back to her office where her French writing desk stood piled high with an array of papers and fabric swatches. "We're going to write to Mr. DeLore and request an audience with him."

"I don't believe my ears. How did you hear?"

"Shelby told me. Connie at the Landmark Society told her."

"That's amazing." Stanley turned and glided back toward his office. "Simply amazing," he murmured again just as the front door opened. A very tall, elegantly dressed man stepped through the door. Stanley froze in mid-stride.

"May we help you?" Stanley's words were barely a whisper as he gazed into the man's face. Ashley had not heard the man enter. She was on the phone with Michael, discussing their mother's birthday dinner.

"Yes," the man answered, "very possibly you can. My name is Tryn DeLore. I've just moved into one of the houses up on Golden Gate Avenue." He spoke with a dignified yet indiscernible accent.

The man looked down at Stanley with cerulean eyes that had already rendered Stanley paralyzed. A slight smile graced the man's face as he continued. "I'm told by the Landmark Society that your design studio is the best. That you specialize in vintage homes." He turned away, seemingly amused, and strode among the numerous antiques on display.

"Yes," Stanley blurted. "Uh, we've done some of the most prestigious homes in the Bay Area, and the DeLore mansion, it's—well, it's always been a favorite of mine."

Mr. DeLore lifted his walking stick and pointed across the room. Stanley caught a glimpse of a gold ring. It looked like the head of a jaguar with deep-set ruby eyes.

"That buffet," Mr. DeLore remarked, "a handsome piece. And the bronze sculpture. Nineteenth century Italian, aren't they? Very handsome indeed."

"Yes, yes they are," Stanley agreed, trying not to stumble over his words or feet. His eyes were now glued to this incredible-looking man. Mr. DeLore looked to be at least 6'5". And dressed in a dark linen suit. Stanley had already noticed what looked to be ruby-studded cuff links.

"My associate and I were just admiring them," he said. "They were delivered today. In fact, we were just saying before you arrived how perfect they would be for your house."

"Is that so?" the man replied imperiously, turning to glare at Stanley.

Stanley caught his breath at DeLore's reaction. Grasping for an explanation as to why he and Ashley were discussing his house, Stanley began to grope for words. "Huh, uh, over at the Landmark Society,

Connie?" he stammered, his hands flailing in all directions. He had now lost what poise he had mustered.

"Why, yes, of course, a nice woman, Connie. She mentioned your studio." With this Mr. DeLore turned, again pointing to the buffet with his gold-handled walking stick. "You and your associate are quite right. They are splendid pieces. My foyer is in need of such a piece, and that bronze sculpture, it is magnificent. Quite right."

"Oh, Ashley," Stanley called, as she emerged from her office. "This is Mr. DeLore. My associate, Ashley Winthrop," he announced, pleased that he was the one to present Mr. DeLore to her.

"Mr. DeLore," she said, crossing the room with her hand extended. "I have *so* wanted to meet you. Your home has always fascinated me."

As she approached, DeLore jerked backward. Ashley noticed this and dropped her hand. She studied his eyes, realizing that she had never before seen a man that she would actually consider beautiful. His dark, full, shoulder-length hair was swept back in soft waves. His dark lashes framed lapis eyes that stared down at her. "It's a pleasure to meet you," she continued, and turned in an awkward fashion. "I see you were admiring the Italian buffet and the bronze sculpture. Did you say you had a place for them in your foyer?"

Mr. DeLore staggered, then reached out and grasped the back of a large chair. His eyes were wide and glaring. He hurriedly crossed the room and all but fled the studio.

Ashley and Stanley were left standing in the middle of the room. Stanley gazed at the front door, his mouth agape.

Ashley collapsed into a velvet Louis XV fauteuil. "What did I do?" she asked, dumfounded.

"I haven't a clue," Stanley sighed. "But he's the best looking thing I've ever seen, except maybe that brother of yours. Stanley rested his chin in his hand and tapped the side of his face in concentration. "Now that I think of it, he rather reminds me of Michael. Oh, I hope you didn't scare him off for good. I'd hate to think I'd never see that hunk again. One thing's for sure," Stanley laughed. "I won't have any competition from you." He quickly looked at his watch. "I've got to get out of here. Have an appointment in Sausalito. Why don't you call Connie and get the lowdown on Mr. DeLore?" Stanley then breezed out the door.

Ashley sat for several minutes, perplexed, not only by the man's bizarre reaction but of his profound beauty. What had she done, she wondered, to strike such fear into those beautiful eyes? She reexamined the moment.

'Mr. DeLore, this is my associate, Ashley Winthrop,' Stanley had said. And all she had said was that she was fascinated by his house. How could that have triggered such a reaction? Or, she suddenly thought, had he seen her today, peering through the gates at his house?

As she rounded her desk, a vision of his face formed in her mind. He was more than physically attractive, more than dignified in demeanor. Inexplicably, she wanted to be near him, to feel him next to her, to touch that beautiful face and feel her finger tips on his full lips as she drew closer to him. She could almost feel it happening.

The phone's ring pierced the silence. Ashley straightened with a start, looking around as if she thought someone was watching. She fumbled for the receiver.

"Ashley, it's Connie over at Landmark."

"Connie, yes," she mumbled. "I was just about to call you."

"Does that mean you've already met our Mr. DeLore?"

"Yes," she said. "It was the strangest thing though. The minute Stanley introduced us he gave me this horrid look and practically ran out of the studio."

Connie chuckled. "I will admit, he is unusual. A little eccentric maybe. But so handsome. He probably just had a lot on his mind. I wouldn't take it personally. I'm sure you'll hear from him. Why, he's living up there without electricity. I told him that Belvedere Designs was the best."

"I appreciate the referral, Connie. Maybe I'll send him a note. By the way, what do you know about him, anything?"

"Only that he came here from France. He doesn't seem to have a French accent, though. What do you think?"

"I don't know. He never spoke to me."

"Well," Connie said. "All I know is that for years the London Historical Society has had an arrangement with us to oversee security for DeLore House."

"Ash," Shelby called as she trekked through the studio. She was following a silver-gray miniature Schnauzer who trotted straight into Ashley's office and leaped into her lap. His greeting consisted of a long high pitched whoooo, and a series of grunts that accompanied the erratic movements of his hind quarters.

"Schatzi! Connie, I've got to run, let me know if you hear anything from our Mr. DeLore. I think I'll still drop him a note."

"Gee Shatz," Ashley praised, hanging up the phone, "you look fabulous, this must be your week with Aunt Roberta."

"That's right," Shelby said. "Gotta get him spiffied up for his all time favorite person." She sighed and sank down into the chair. "Loyalty is not one of your strong points, is it Schatz?"

Schatzi jumped down from Ashley's lap, twisted and turned and grunted back to Shelby for more pats and kisses.

"Where's that cute Stanley?" she inquired, stroking Schatzi's tiny head and pointed ears.

"He had an appointment in Sausalito. He'll be back around five."

"Have you told him about our Mr. DeLore?"

Ashley smiled, "Yes, Shel, I told him."

"Did you tell him we went snooping?"

"No."

"Why not? He'd have loved it!"

"Because. Mr. DeLore dropped by before I had a chance."

Shelby practically vaulted onto Ashley's desk. "You don't mean it! When?"

"Just a few minutes ago."

"He was just here?"

"Yes."

"Well?" she pressed.

"Well, what?"

"For Christ's sakes, Ash. What did he say?"

Ashley squirmed. "He talked with Stanley. I was on the phone with Michael about Meno's birthday dinner." Ashley, for no apparent reason, had called her mother, Meno, since childhood.

"Yeah, we're taking her to Ernie's," Shelby said. Margaret Winthrop had become as much Shelby's mother as Ashley and Michael's. Shelby's father had died shortly after her birth, and Ashley's parents, Victor and Margaret Winthrop, friends of Shelby's mother, Natalie, had taken both Natalie and Shelby into their home. Then, when Shelby had just turned thirteen, her mother was diagnosed with an inoperable tumor. There was little the doctors could do. Natalie's wishes were to spend her remaining days at home. Michael and Ashley would sit with Shelby on the stairway outside Natalie's room. Holding Shelby's petite body in their arms, they would try and comfort her while she sobbed endlessly for her mother.

"Why?" Shelby would cry, her face buried against Ashley. "Why does God have to take my mother away?"

With no comforting answer, they tried to assure Shelby as best they could.

"We'll never leave you," Michael and Ashley would say, kissing Shelby's wet face.

And through the years, as different as Shelby and Ashley were—Ashley tall, elegant and sophisticated, buried in her work, and Shelby petite, vivacious, the social butterfly—the two women were inseparable. Michael was Ashley's only sibling, so she had always pretended that Shelby was her sister.

And Shelby loved Margaret Winthrop as though she were her real mother. Ashley, however, had never formed a close bond with her mother, which had resulted in years of petty bickering.

"What did Mr. DeLore say!" Shelby pressed.

"He said he was interested in that buffet out there," Ashley replied irritably. She intended to leave it at that. She had no intention of stoking Shelby's imagination. There was no telling what Shelby would conjure up if she got wind of Mr. DeLore's strange behavior.

A prime example was when Ashley had landed her first big design project in Pacific Heights, a very prestigious area of San Francisco. By Shelby's account, you would have thought Ashley had been commissioned to redecorate the White House. Shelby contacted every newspaper within a forty mile radius. A rather impressive layout appeared in the San Francisco Chronicle a week after the design had been completed. Ashley's phone hadn't stopped ringing since.

"Schatzi, my Schatzi," Roberta cried, walking through the door, her arms stretched out in a big welcome. "I've missed you." Roberta, an adorable, petite little blonde in her mid thirties, was a flight attendant. She had once worked part time managing one of Shelby's apartment complexes in the south bay town of Cupertino. During that time, Roberta fell head over heels in love with Schatzi. From then on she was known as "Aunt Roberta". Schatzi was in high gear, grunting and singing his woooo whoooo's in a tenor vibrato.

Roberta said her hellos, indulged in a moment of chit chat, then whisked Schatzi off to Los Gatos with a promise to return him in a few weeks.

Shelby again had Ashley alone and quickly resumed her probing about Mr. DeLore's.

"Come on, Ash. I want details. What's he look like? What was he wearing?"

"Give it a rest, Shel. The man simply stopped by to talk about his house. He's handsome and dresses like anyone else. He wore a suit. You know, a suit?" She strode back to her office and rounded her desk, fumbling with a few fabric swatches. Shelby stood in the doorway, tapping her foot.

"What?" Ashley slid down in her chair.

"Well? Did you get the job?"

"Not exactly," Ashley mumbled, fidgeting with some papers.

"What does that mean?"

Ashley sighed a long sigh. "He saw a few pieces he was interested in." Just as the phone began to ring, she looked up at Shelby and said matter-of-factly, "When Mr. DeLore decides he wants my services, he'll ask."

Shelby stared at Ashley suspiciously. "That doesn't sound like you. Since when have you lost your aggressiveness?"

"I haven't," she replied reaching for the phone. "Oh, hello, Jeff."

Shelby's ears perked up when she heard the name. Jeff Montgomery was one of the most successful men in the Bay Area, making a near fortune developing office parks in Silicon Valley. Shelby moved in closer. Ashley looked bored.

"Jeff," she persisted. "I'm sorry. I'm going out of town tomorrow on business."

Ashley looked over at Shelby as if to say, "Don't you dare start hassling me."

"I don't think so Jeff. My work takes up most of my time."

Ashley hung up the phone and went back to her papers as if there had been no conversation.

"You're impossible," Shelby wailed. "Jeff Montgomery is not only sexy as hell, he's got class!"

"Then why don't *you* date the man?" Ashley replied calmly.

"Because, he's not interested in me. It's you he's interested in. Though God only knows why. I wouldn't blame him if he never called you again."

"Hopefully, he won't," Ashley said, reaching for a book on 19th century furniture.

Shelby headed toward the doorway then turned back. "I don't know why I stood up for you all those years we were in school. It didn't bother you one bit, did it, everyone making fun of you? I just never dreamed that your weird asocial behavior would last this long. My God, you're forty years old and still more interested in antiques than men."

Ashley looked up from her book with a bored expression. "And you're forty-one and still flitting from one man to the other."

"Never mind," Shelby said, shaking her head. "By the way, I've had a pot of mulligan stew simmering all day. You're welcome to come for dinner."

"No date tonight?" Ashley said, her sarcasm evident.

"I haven't been asked."

"Oh really. Since when has Bob quit asking?"

"He hasn't. He's out of town. You want to come for dinner or not?"

"Not tonight, I think I'll just curl up with a bottle of wine and throw a salad together. But save me some stew."

"Have it your way," Shelby said, and she was out the door.

ఴ

The thought of Tryn DeLore would not go away. She felt as if she could reach out and touch him.

Holding the pen in her hand, she pondered her words.

Dear Mr. DeLore,

It was our pleasure to meet you today. My associate and I would be honored to have the opportunity of discussing the restoration of your home.

We have, for many years, admired the DeLore mansion, and feel that we could maintain its authenticity while recapturing its youth.

We look forward to hearing from you.

My best regards,

Ashley Winthrop

Stanley had already come and gone, giving Ashley's note his approval. As she put it into the mail box, she prayed that Mr. DeLore would respond, and soon.

Ashley locked the front door and climbed the stairs to her apartment. Crossing the living room, she opened the French doors to the balcony and looked across Belvedere Cove. The sun had long since dissolved into the horizon. The myriad lights atop Belvedere glittered in the night's sky. San Francisco with its greater panorama of lights lay in the distance like a constellation. She could see little of the old mansion. It stood dark, concealed almost entirely by the giant cypress.

She wondered. What could he be doing, all alone in that big house? A house that had long ago seduced her from afar. Would its owner do so as well? A warm sensation came over her as she crossed the balcony toward the railing, drawing closer to the source of her thoughts. Then she noticed it. A glow of light coming from one of the dormer windows on the fourth floor. Faint and distant, yet she could still see its movement. From one dormer to the other the light appeared. Then finally it vanished. Ashley leaned into the railing.

These feelings were so foreign to her. She clutched her arms tightly and closed her eyes. Had it finally happened? After forty years, was she now to experience desire and passion? Her body no longer felt dead. It felt strangely alive, like a candle that had stood dormant for decades then brought to light by a tiny flame. The warmth of that flame seemed to spread through her, as though she were experiencing a miraculous rebirth.

Chapter Three

*H*er wrists and ankles are strapped down tight. Her throat . . . she can't breathe. Struggling to scream for someone to help her. Then the hands come. Touching her. Cold and invading, they search her, while, off in the distance, a glowing flicker of light reveals a tall, dark figure. His eyes penetrate; his presence seems to exist in a dimension far away. Moving almost imperceptibly, it is as though he orchestrates each movement of the hands. Pain rips through her body.

Ashley bolted from her pillow as the dawn breeze swept gently through the opened window of her bedroom, sending the lace curtains swaying.

Frantically she clutched her knees, glaring out across the room. The antique walnut dresser, the Victorian night stand, the rose-colored oil lamp. Where am I, she thought, feeling strangely removed from her surroundings. That wallpaper, its cabbage-rose pattern drawing her in like one of those magic paintings that change shape as you study them. It seemed to grow more familiar right before her eyes.

Suddenly, a cold gust of wind swept through the room. Ashley pulled her knees closer as she watched her silk scarf, draped over the gold cheval mirror, dance moth-like through the air. She followed its waltzing journey as it came to rest on the Persian rug. She felt as if she were seeing it for the first time. It was familiar yet different.

The room seemed to be taking on an atmosphere of timelessness. The sounds around her became muted, past and present seemed to converge, curving around her. Her lips parted, whispering the words, "Thornton Square".

As suddenly as it had come, it had gone.

Her bedroom was again filled with the sound of a distant fog horn. Ashley felt exhausted, and sat frozen to the bed. Then mindlessly she reached for the phone, pressing one of the programmed buttons.

"Shelby," she gasped.

"Ash?"

No response.

"Ash! What's wrong?"

"I don't know."

"What do you mean?"

"I'm not sure."

"I'll be right there!" Shelby slammed down the phone and tore out of her house. She was scaling the stairs to Ashley's apartment within minutes.

Shelby bolted across the living room. "Ash!" she cried, stopping just inside the bedroom door. Ashley was sitting on the side of the bed, her hand clutching the phone. She looked up, dazed, as Shelby knelt down beside her.

"Ash, what's happened?" she said, touching Ashley's face.

Ashley looked down at Shelby, her eyes distant, her hand falling from the phone. She rose from the bed and crossed the room to the window. The cool October breeze brushed softly against her face, fanning her long hair. Her cotton gown moved in slow delicate motions around her. Ashley reached up, trailing her fingers across the leaded glass of the window. Shelby quietly approached.

Ashley then turned, walking back toward the bed. "I'm sorry Shel. I didn't mean for you to come rushing over here." She sat down again on the side of the bed.

"Don't be ridiculous. Now tell me what's wrong and don't say 'nothing.' " She latched onto Ashley's arm.

Ashley pulled away and began fussing with the bed. "It was this dream I had."

"Dream?"

"Yeah. Really, I didn't mean to scare you. It sure as hell scared me, though," she laughed, walking toward the dressing room as though nothing had happened. Noticing the clock, she said. "I have an appointment in the city. Oh, and don't forget, we're supposed to be at Ernie's by six. That's four trips across the bridge. I hope Meno appreciates it." She disappeared into her dressing room.

"Ashley," Shelby called, reaching out as if to reel her back. But the words stuck in her throat. "Hey, I'll drive to Ernie's tonight."

18

"Thanks, I'd appreciate it."

After finishing her shower, Ashley stood in front of the dressing table. Inspecting her reflection, she gathered her chestnut hair into a twist. Her complexion was flawless, her eyes a brilliant green, framed by full dark lashes and symmetrical brows. Her lips were full, turning up at the corners, creating the illusion of an eternal smile. When she was a young woman, her height of five foot ten had been devastating, rendering her a moving target for cruel jokes. But as her body developed, so did her sensuous beauty; now she clearly had the last laugh. And at age forty, she still looked half her age.

Examining her watch, she found that she only had three hours to prepare for her mid-day appointment and get across the Golden Gate Bridge. She scanned her closet, finally choosing a black and gold mid-calf skirt and a gold silk blouse. After pulling on her black leather boots, she grabbed her purse, stopping momentarily to gaze at the cheval mirror. Its reflection showed the Victorian three-quarter canopy bed. She gazed deep into the mirror, feeling somehow drawn to it. Finally she turned away and started down the stairs to her office.

"Ashley, my sweets," Stanley crooned from the foot of the stairs, "you look ravishing." He watched her descent. She displayed no recognition that he was within twenty feet of her, much less that he had just paid her a compliment. "Ashley, what's wrong?" She turned, hesitating, then finally looked directly at him.

"What?"

Stanley gently placed his hand on her shoulder. They were exactly the same height. "Are you all right?"

"Of course," she replied, patting his cheek. "Why?" and she strode across the room through a maze of antiques and plopped down at her desk. "What are you talking about?"

"I'm talking about the way you looked right through me."

"I'm sorry Stanley. It's just that I have a lot on my mind. I didn't mean to ignore you." She proceeded to rummage through several stacks of folders. "Now where is that Hollingsworth file?"

Stanley slumped into the doorway, concluding that the conversation was going nowhere. "So, do you think we'll hear from that gorgeous Mr. DeLore?" he asked, turning to leave.

Ashley paused, then reached for the phone. "We'll hear from him."

"My, aren't we confident," he muttered, heading back toward his office.

෨

Ashley sat quietly in the front seat as the car sped across the Golden Gate. Her appointment at the Hollingsworth home had been stressful. All she wanted was to go home and turn in early. She sighed, not at all looking forward to Meno's birthday dinner. She often felt that if she never saw her mother again it would mean precious little. Ashley had always been daddy's little girl. Margaret had never showed outward resentment to this, although Ashley was certain it had caused arguments between her parents.

And poor Shelby, robbed of her parents so early in life. She was forever jabbing at Ashley. "Why are you so unable to love your mother?" Shelby would anguish, the distress of losing her own mother painfully evident.

But Shelby didn't understand. How could she? Victor and Margaret had taken her in—were her parents now—and besides, how could she understand Ashley's feelings when Ashley couldn't understand them herself?

Turning onto Montgomery Street, Shelby found a parking spot within walking distance of Ernie's Restaurant. Victor and Margaret Winthrop had been regulars at Ernie's since first moving to San Francisco from New Orleans. Ashley and Shelby had fallen in love with the famed restaurant after seeing the Alfred Hitchcock movie "Vertigo". Several scenes had been filmed in the upstairs dining room.

The owners, Roland and Victor, greeted them warmly, and showed them to the lounge where Michael was waiting.

"Hi, Michael," Shelby greeted enthusiastically. "Dad and Meno not here yet?"

"Not yet," he said, giving her a big hug.

"You look tired, Ash," Michael said, scrutinizing her. "You all right?"

"I'm just fine," she snapped.

Michael and Shelby looked at each other.

"I'm sorry, Michael," Ashley apologized. "I've have a lot on my mind with work and all."

"Work is always on your mind," he said casually. "How about a double Stolie, rocks, extra olives."

"Please." She turned, walking toward a secluded table off in the corner. Shelby followed, after putting in her order for a margarita.

Several minutes later, Margaret and Victor Winthrop arrived. Everyone said their greetings, wishing Margaret a happy birthday. As always, Shelby was her exuberant self, Michael was warm and loving, and Ashley was merely polite.

The evening went beautifully and without incident with raves to the chef for superbly prepared rack of lamb. Then Shelby mentioned Ashley's possible client. Margaret and Victor exchanged stern glances.

"Who did you say?" Victor asked.

"Tryn DeLore, he's the heir to the old DeLore mansion in Belvedere. Haven't you ever heard of that old place?"

"No," Margaret replied abruptly.

"It's marvelous. French architecture, isn't it, Ash?" Shelby asked.

Ashley was staring at Margaret.

"Ash," Shelby repeated.

"What? Oh, yes . . . French," Ashley said, glancing back to Margaret.

"I know that house," Michael said. "You're right, it is French with a little Italianate influence thrown in." Michael was an architect and had worked with Ashley on several restorations.

"Have you met this man?" Margaret asked, glancing Victor's way.

"Just briefly," Ashley replied. "He came into the office yesterday. He hasn't asked for our services yet. But the Landmark Society gave us an excellent reference."

"I'm sure you'll get the job," Margaret said, patting Ashley's hand.

Ashley flinched and withdrew her hand.

"Oh, by the way, you two," Michael said, motioning to Ashley and Shelby. "I'm taking the boat up to Bodega Bay this weekend. Met a new girl I wanna impress," he said teasingly. "I could use some extra deck hands. And you're welcome to bring someone along."

"You go through girls like I go through panty hose," said Shelby.

"You're one to talk," Michael and Ashley said in unison.

Shelby just smiled. "I'd love to go yachting. I don't have anything pressing this weekend. In fact, I haven't had a pressing engagement for at least a week."

"How about you?" Michael said, turning to Ashley. "You could use a few days off."

"I don't think so. I've got too much work to do."

"Ashley always has too much work to do," Shelby said.

"Don't start," Ashley warned.

"Oh, come on, Sis, you said you were overworked. It'll do you good to get out of that damn studio."

"I'll think about it."

"Don't count on it, Michael," Shelby laughed. "Ashley's interested in antiques, not men."

Ashley's face went cold. "Damn you Shelby! I've had enough of this. You're older than I am, and I haven't seen you walking down any aisles lately." Ashley turned to Michael. "And you're nothing but a forty year old playboy. You've *never* been serious about a woman." Ashley bolted from her chair and traipsed out of the room, leaving everyone completely stunned. Victor quickly left his chair, catching up with her in the hallway. As he reached out and took her arm, she turned and pressed her head against his chest.

"Ashley. What's wrong?"

"I don't know," she sighed, tightening her arms around his waist. Even with Ashley's height, Victor towered over her.

"What do you mean, you don't know?"

"I guess I'm just tired. I haven't been sleeping very well." Ashley took her arms from around Victor's waist. "Sorry," she said. "I'm a little on edge. I didn't mean to cause a scene."

"Ashley," Victor said, taking her shoulders. "Look at me."

Ashley reluctantly looked into her father's eyes, seeing the concern and thinking how much she loved him. She looked at his thick white hair and full brows. They too had turned snow white. But not even time could take away the beauty of his face, the gentleness behind those deep blue eyes. Her father was truly the love in her life.

"Tell me what's wrong," he demanded.

Ashley reached up and kissed Victor, managing a smile. "Dad, please. Don't make a federal case of this. It's stress, that's all. Stanley and I have some very important deadlines to meet. I didn't mean to ruin Meno's birthday."

"You haven't ruined anything," he assured her. "I'm just concerned about you."

"And I love you for that. But I'm fine. Honestly. Now come on. Let's go back."

Victor followed Ashley back to the table where she offered no apologies to her mother.

"I'm sorry, Michael," she said. "It's P.M.S., you know how I get."

"Michael laughed out loud. "I'm used to it," he said. "You've chided me for my womanizing as much as I have for your terminal chastity."

Ashley glanced over at Shelby. "I didn't mean to snap at you, Shel."

"I know," she smiled, bouncing back in her usual way.

After dessert, which consisted of a beautifully decorated carrot cake and French vanilla ice cream, everyone said their good-byes, again wishing Margaret happy birthday.

"Ashley?" Margaret said as she and Shelby were leaving the table, "Let me know if you get the DeLore account."

Ashley didn't buy Meno's interest in her business, but she managed a smile.

"Ash," Shelby said as they drove back to Belvedere, "did you notice Dad and Meno when I mentioned Mr. DeLore?"

"Yeah."

"What do you think that was about?"

"Oh, probably nothing." But secretly Ashley did think her parent's reaction to hearing Tryn DeLore's name was peculiar. They were always so proper. The non reactors.

Ashley slumped in her seat. With a yawn she closed her eyes. I'm probably just imagining it, she concluded.

Climbing the stairs to her apartment, Ashley's thoughts went again to Tryn DeLore. Pulled to the window, she opened the French doors to the cool night air. She approached the railing and looked out across the cove. Who are you? she thought, noticing a faint glow coming from one of the second story windows of the mansion. She wondered if he was alone.

Again a warm sensation came over her. She felt weak and strangely vulnerable as though she were losing control of her body. Her mind suddenly filled with thoughts of desire, along with a compelling physical need. The experience was disturbing, almost frightening. She lowered herself to the floor of the balcony and wrapped her arms around her shoulders, feeling that her body belonged, not to her, but to someone else.

"Tryn," she whispered.

ဆ

The next morning had already brought several calls from prospective clients, while there was a scattering of customers in the shop. Ashley came walking through the door just as the last customer was leaving.

"Mrs. Vance," she greeted. "It's good to see you."

"And you, my dear," the woman replied, her feathered hat covering the entire left side of her face. Abigail Vance was little more than five foot one and was as wide as she was tall. Her festive hat gave the illusion of an extra inch or two in height, while adding to the enormity of her stature. She looked like a throwback from the 1800's. Her house was filled to the brim with priceless antiques. There wasn't a week lost without Mrs. Vance perusing Ashley's inventory for fear of missing something.

"Find anything of interest today?" Ashley inquired.

"Well, my dear," she said, resting her chin in the palm of her hand. "I must say, that Italian piece over there has caught my fancy."

"I'm afraid I already have someone interested in it."

Stanley quickly emerged from his office. "I'm sorry, Mrs. Vance, I had completely forgotten."

"Don't give it a moment's worry, Stanley dear. I need another buffet like I need another hat. If it does become available though . . . well, I just might find a little spot for it."

"You'll be the first to know," Ashley assured her.

"I would appreciate that," she said, turning back to the buffet. "It is a mighty handsome piece." She looked back at Stanley, waved good bye, then gently patted Ashley's arm. "Well, my dear, gotta run, meeting with the Landmark Society today about that wonderful old DeLore mansion. Did you know it was occupied?"

Ashley smiled. "Yes, Mrs. Vance. We're in hopes of doing the renovation."

"I should say. It's a grand old place. Can't seem to remember when anyone's ever lived there." She looked up at Ashley with a shy grin. "It's haunted you know. Seen many a strange goings on there from my third floor window." Mrs. Vance's eyes narrowed to a squint. "Last year I saw a woman walking along the lower path. Plain as day I saw her. And that's not all. I've seen strange light coming from the fourth floor dormers."

"Probably just a reflection." Ashley said reassuringly.

"It was no reflection dearie, it was candle light, and I've seen it more than once." Mrs. Vance gave Stanley an uncertain glance as she reached up and began fiddling with her hat. "You know," she said, "I hear this new occupant is the great-great-grandson of the original owner. We want to learn its history and put it in our historical brochure. I do hope this Mr. DeLore will want to cooperate. That house is such a fascinating old place. Simply a gem."

"It certainly is," Stanley agreed. "I'd love to get my hands on it." He turned with a wave to Mrs. Vance and went back to his office. "Would love to get my hands on DeLore," he muttered.

"Have you met this DeLore fellow?" Mrs. Vance asked Ashley.

"Only briefly, he came in the other day. He's the one I'm holding the buffet for."

"Dear me," she said, covering her mouth with a gloved hand. "So our mystery man is my competition."

"I'm afraid so," Ashley whispered.

"Well, I must say, he does have good taste. Hope he knows what he's getting into with that house," she warned with a wink and a nod. "Better run now, dearie," and she was out the door, waddling down Beach Road.

Ashley stood in the doorway, reflecting on Mrs. Vance.

Later that afternoon, Michael called, inviting Ashley to dinner at the Corinthian. He was in Sausalito meeting with a client, and said he would be finished around six. She accepted.

Michael was waiting as she entered the Corinthian's lounge.

Framed in rich mahogany, pictures of magnificent sailboats dating as far back as the late 1800's graced the walls. The bar ran along one side of the room. The parallel wall boasted a large cabinet filled with trophies of past decades. A handsome stone fireplace flanked the trophy cabinet. Two sofas filled a corner of the lounge, and several small tables were placed throughout. The large picture window revealed the skyline of San Francisco.

They settled into chairs close to the window and ordered wine while thoughts of her dream the previous night spun through Ashley's mind: That metal table, the hands moving across her body. A cold dread passed through her. No, she thought struggling to push the vision from her mind. I won't think about it.

She turned and looked out the large picture window toward Belvedere. The old mansion could be seen much clearer here than from her apartment. Except for a scattering of fog, the night was clear. Through the old cypress she could see light coming from the first and fourth floors. There are probably hoards of antiques stored in that attic, she thought. He must be moving some of the furniture from the attic to the other rooms. She slumped back in her chair and sipped her wine, fantasizing about the mansion.

She was walking up the long stone walkway. The grounds, once turned back to nature, had been cleared and manicured. The lawn was a dense green. The old cypress had been cleared of decades of malignant growth. It now stretched its sloping, hovering limbs in a vibrant rebirth. Around the base of the cypress, a courtyard, once lying in ruin, had been restored. A large semi-circular limestone garden seat flanked by winged lions sat on moss-covered bricks. The house had been cleared and painted. She stopped momentarily, thinking that she actually preferred its aged appearance. It had, in its refurbishing, lost its character. Now it looked like any beautifully built home. No, she thought, she could not rob this glorious house of its years. Bringing back its youth would destroy it. It needed to be lived in, cared for, loved. That would restore its vibrant beauty, not the cosmetics. Only a few repairs here and there out of necessity, but nothing more.

"Ashley," Michael said nudging her shoulder.

"What?" She looked up at Michael dazed.

"Where were you, off on another planet?"

"Close," she said, looking back toward the house.

"Okay, Sis, give. What's on that brilliant mind of yours?"

"It's that obvious?"

"It's that obvious."

"I was just thinking about the DeLore mansion. I really want that job."

"And why wouldn't you get it?"

"I don't know."

"Think positive," he said taking the seat across from her.

Ashley fumbled with her wine glass. "That's not what's bothering me."

"It's not?"

She looked at Michael. "No. It's this dream I had the other night."

"Dream?"

"Yeah. It was weird."

"What do you mean?"

She sipped her wine, then described the dream.

Michael slumped back in his chair and listened intently.

"Wow! That's a hell of a dream."

"But it wasn't just the dream," she said. "It was after I woke up. I felt like I wasn't really in my bedroom. The furniture was the same, it just felt different. And the wallpaper seemed so familiar. It was like it had always been there. But that didn't make sense because I had just bought it. I don't know," she sighed. "Maybe you're right. Maybe I do need to get away."

"Damn right you do. You're too wrapped up in that studio. No wonder you're having nightmares." Michael shook his head. "Why don't you turn everything over to Stanley, go see Uncle Buzz in New Orleans and start writing that book you keep talking about. I can help Stanley out if he gets in a bind. What do ya say? You can write about old houses instead of working on them."

"I can't, Michael."

"And why not?"

"Because. If Mr. DeLore decides to restore his house, I don't want to be off in New Orleans writing a book. You know how much I've always wanted to get my hands on that place. And now, well, it looks like there's a chance."

"All right. I know what getting that project means to you. Actually, I'd love to see inside that house." He looked up toward Belvedere.

"I know. That's just about all I can think of lately."

"Then why don't you call the guy. Where's your aggressiveness?"

"In the note I have already sent him," she countered. "I just hope he doesn't think I'm desperate for the job."

"Well . . . aren't you?"

"Of course, but he doesn't need to know that."

"Tell me," Michael said. "What is this DeLore guy like?"

"Gorgeous," she blurted.

Michael glared at Ashley in stunned disbelief. He had never, ever, heard his sister refer to a man this way. He had actually heard passion in her voice. He tried but failed to hold back a smile.

Ashley immediately realized what she had said but ignored Michael's amusement. "In fact," she said, "he looks a little like you."

"That handsome, huh?"

Ashley began studying Michael's face. He had the same full lips, satin smooth skin, and piercing blue eyes. In fact, she contemplated, if his hair were longer, it too would fall into soft full waves.

"Well, I can't wait to meet this guy. But right now I'm starving."

The view from the Corinthian's dining room was even more spectacular than the one from the bar. The city seemed to rise up in the distance. The Bay Bridge spanned across the water connecting San Francisco to Oakland as though stippled by millions of stars.

Ashley indulged in grilled salmon while Michael couldn't resist the veal Marsala.

"They sure made the right choice with that dish," Michael praised, as he and Ashley walked through the lounge and out into the night air.

"How about a nightcap," Ashley said. "I have a bottle of Remy Martin just waiting to be opened."

"Don't tempt me. I'd love to, but I've got to get back to the city. I just landed the Blanchard account. That design is going to assure me another fortune," he laughed. "You going to let me know about this weekend?"

"Michael, I'd really like to, but . . ."

"But nothing. A vacation might be out of the question, but a couple of days off on the weekend—come on, say you'll go. In fact, why don't you call your Mr. DeLore and ask him to come along."

"Don't be ridiculous."

"Why? Even a gorgeous man couldn't resist my beautiful sister. What's the matter, you afraid my sixty-three foot yacht isn't impressive enough?"

"It's rather small."

"I suppose. He probably has a two hundred footer in the Greek Isles somewhere."

"Probably."

"Shit!" Michael cursed, approaching his car.

"What's wrong?"

"A goddamn flat. And my spare is flat."

"Now how did you let that happen?"

"Never mind."

"Well, guess you'll have to stay with me tonight after all."

He slouched against the black BMW. "Is that Jag of yours running?"

"You start giving me a rash of shit about my Jag and you can go sleep at Shel's."

"Lighten up, Ash. I'm only teasing. Besides, I love your Jag."

"Then keep quiet about it."

"Don't get so testy," he said, pulling her to his side. "By the way, what kind of car does your Mr. DeLore drive?"

"You don't want to know." Ashley reached out and opened the door to her car.

"Why wouldn't I want to know?"

"You just wouldn't. Now get in."

"Don't tell me," he laughed.

"What?"

"A Jaguar. Your Mr. DeLore drives a Jaguar."

"Well, so what? It's a classic, Michael. Nineteen fifties or so."

"My, my, our mystery man does have class."

"Yes, as a matter of fact, I think he does."

After two Remy Martins and more conversation, they both went to bed. Michael was in the guest room across from Ashley. It was a classic looking room: golden tan walls accented with a dark green overlay. The process gave the illusion of old stone. The row of leaded windows was swaged in antique tapestry. The cherry floor was covered partially by an oriental rug of burgundies and golds. Placed against the center of the far wall stood a mahogany sleigh bed. Adjoining the room was a large bathroom of black and white marble. A claw foot tub was at one end, and a large open shower at the other. A pedestal sink with porcelain fixtures stood in the middle. Ashley always kept the bathroom stocked with an array of toiletries. Michael brushed his teeth, undressed, and was asleep in minutes.

Except for the distant sound of a fog horn, the night was still. Michael tossed and turned. He dreamed erratically, then finally moved into peaceful slumber.

He woke just before dawn. Lying under the heavy blankets, he listened intently. The sound was faint but steady, like a moaning cry. He sat up slowly. The glow of the street lamp reflected off the prisms of the beveled windows, bathing the room in soft, colored light. The door to the bedroom stood slightly ajar.

"Ashley," he called. No answer, just that faint sound. Throwing the covers back, he left the bed and peered out into the living room. In the distance, the skyline of the city still held on to its brilliance. The living room lay in shadows. He searched the room with his eyes for the source of the sound. Again he heard the moan. And then he saw her emerge from the shadows and cross to the far end of the room. She reached out and pushed open the double doors to the balcony as her gown rippled under the wind's gust.

"Ashley?" Michael hurriedly crossed the room. "Ashley?" he called again but with no response.

Just as she reached the railing she collapsed. Michael caught her in his arms. Anxiously, he carried her to the sofa. "Ash," he whispered brushing her hair from her face. Slowly she began to open her eyes.

"Michael?"

"I'm here, Ash. You were walking in your sleep."

"Sleep?" she murmured, a frown creasing her forehead. "But--but it was so real. I was there."

"Where? You were where?"

"That house. That man. I kept running toward him, not away. God! it was real."

"The same dream from when we were kids?"

Ashley pushed herself to a sitting position. "Yes . . . but it was never like this. If I didn't know better I'd swear I was there."

Michael sat down next to her. "What do you think it means?"

"I don't know," she sighed looking over at Michael. "Maybe I'm going mad?"

Michael laughed. "Who are you kidding? You've been mad for years. The way you love to snoop around old houses. And all these antiques," he said, scanning the room. "Ash, you don't live in the present, you live in the past. You've surrounded yourself with it."

"Because I love old houses and antiques? That's why I'm having nightmares? Don't be ridiculous."

"You don't just love them, you're obsessed with them. You'd rather occupy yourself with old mansions and furniture than you would, say, cultivate a relationship."

"Michael, don't start. You aren't any better."

"At least I have a social life. You have old relics."

"You're a womanizer," she protested.

"No comment. Look," he said, resigned. "The sun's up. I'll make the coffee."

"Oh, no, you don't. I can't drink that mud you call coffee. I'll make the coffee. Go take your shower. You've gotta get that tire fixed. Remember?"

"Don't remind me." He disappeared into the bedroom.

Michael and Ashley drank their coffee and indulged in hot bagels topped with cream cheese, tomatoes, a minimal scattering of red onions and a generous portion of Jalapeños.

Michael borrowed Ashley's car and left to have his tire repaired. Ashley went downstairs to her office. But she couldn't work. Her mind was cluttered; she found it impossible to concentrate. Her thoughts drifted back to the dream. Why had it suddenly seemed so real?

"Miss Ashley," Stanley called, walking through the front door.

"In my office," she replied hesitantly, quickly pulling herself together.

Stanley strolled into Ashley's office. "So, anything exciting happen since yesterday?"

"Not really," Ashley replied smiling and thinking how child-like Stanley looked.

"Thought maybe you might have heard from the divine Mr. DeLore," he said then turned, striding back toward his office. "Still hanging on to that buffet?"

"Of course."

"Michael," she heard Stanley say. "Where did you come from?"

"I had a flat tire last night. Here's the mail." Michael tosed it on Stanley's desk.

"Ashley's in her office," Stanley motioned, glaring down at the stack mail.

"Thanks."

"What a waste," Stanley moaned.

Michael stood in the doorway of Ashley's office. "You wanna drive me back to my car? It'll be ready in a few minutes."

"Sure, I can't keep my mind on work anyway," she said, leaving her desk.

"Ash," he said, planting his hands firmly on her shoulders. "Have you thought about seeing a doctor?"

She looked at Michael grimly. "You mean a psychiatrist?"

"Well, yes. Any other suggestions?"

"No. But I'll think about it. Come on, let's go get your car."

"Ashley!" Stanley yelped, as they approached the front door. He sprang from his office, knocking a stack of papers off his desk.

"What!" Ashley said, startled.

Stanley reeled himself back in and handed Ashley a small cream-colored envelope trimmed in gold. The handwriting was beautifully scrolled. There was no stamp. On the back flap, embossed in gold lettering, was the name Tryn DeLore.

She read aloud.

Dear Miss Winthrop,

Please forgive my rude behavior and sudden departure. I am afraid I was not myself. I had been struggling with a bout of flu. It was most inconsiderate of me to expose you and your associate. I trust that you are well, however, and that we may discuss the renovation of DeLore House.

If you are free Friday evening, it would be my pleasure to offer you a glass of wine and show you the house. My chauffeur will call for you at seven. If you find that you are not available, please deliver a note to my house.

Regards,

Tryn DeLore

"My, my, Miss Winthrop," Stanley mocked. "So he's concerned about our health. He sounds gay to me."

"Stanley, for Christ's sake, you think everybody's gay."

Stanley squeezed his eyes shut.

"He sounds like a stuffed shirt to me," Michael said. "And look at that handwriting. What's with this guy?"

"What's with you two?" Ashley retorted. "Can't a man have class without being accused of either homosexuality or stuffiness?"

33

"Come on, Ash," Stanley said. "Really, that's the most pretentious thing I've ever seen."

"It most certainly is not." She gave Stanley a steel glance and turned on her heel. "You're just jealous that he didn't ask you."

"Where are you going?" Michael called after her.

"Stanley can take you." She disappeared into her office.

"Well," Stanley said, turning to Michael. "She's right, I'm jealous as hell."

Ashley buried herself in her office for the rest of the day. Determined to impress Mr. DeLore, she pulled from the shelves every book she owned on French and Italian architecture. She would not allow him to intimidate her, at least not about her work. She knew she was one of the best. She had studied architecture, traveled extensively throughout Europe, renovated and restored some of the most significant homes in San Francisco; she knew her craft. What she didn't know was how she would handle herself with this man she had been fantasizing about since their first meeting.

Chapter Four

The old George III clock chimed at the stroke of seven. The thought of again seeing Tryn DeLore was frightening. She smiled, sighing heavily, her reflection from the gold cheval mirror staring back at her. "He's already started his intimidation," she muttered, inspecting her outfit. She had chosen a long winter white wool skirt with buttons down the front, a rust colored silk blouse, and soft leather boots. How many buttons should I leave undone? She pushed her leg through the opening of the skirt. Don't want to look too provocative.

Ashley jumped as her door chimes rang loudly.

"Stop," she scolded herself. Unconsciously reaching for her scarf, she draped it around her neck then grabbed her jacket and fled down the stairs.

Opening the front door, she found herself looking into the eyes of an older, yet dignified-looking man.

"Mademoiselle Winthrop. My name is Maurice." He nodded, tapping the brim of his hat. "I am Monsieur DeLore's chauffeur."

"It's nice to meet you, Maurice."

"And you. Shall we go?"

"Yes." She stepped out, closing the door.

Ashley stopped short when she saw the black 1950 Jaguar Mark VII saloon.

Maurice reached down and opened the back door. "Mademoiselle."

"Thank you," she said, and slid into the back seat. The soft leather felt good to her skin.

As Maurice wound his way up the narrow road toward Golden Gate Avenue, Ashley gazed out through the passing trees. Is this really happening? she thought.

"Have you been with Mr. DeLore a long time, Maurice?"

"Yes."

"Does he plan on staying in California?"

"A while."

Well, Maurice is certainly not the chatty type, she mused.

The Jaguar sedan continued its uphill journey, then rounded the bend where she and Shelby had almost been run over. They entered through the gates and passed under the old cypress. Maurice parked the sedan next to the Jaguar convertible. Maurice opened the door and offered his hand. The butterflies fluttering in her stomach had now turned to angry moths. Ashley breathed deeply as Maurice led the way along the stone terrace, past the French windows. Thinking she detected a soft glow coming from behind the windows, she wanted to turn and look, but something kept her from it. Maybe it was the ghostlike shadows that she glimpsed from the corner of her eye.

As they approached the front door, Maurice opened it and gestured her in. The sconces emitted a soft glow, throwing shadows against the dark walls. In the distance, she could barely see the outline of a staircase. It seemed to be very wide, curving upward to the left.

"Mademoiselle."

Ashley turned abruptly. Maurice was standing in the double doorway.

"Monsieur DeLore will be down momentarily. He asks that you wait in the parlor."

"Thank you," she said forcing a smile.

"I apologize for the lighting."

"Please don't. I find it soothing."

"Would you like a glass of wine?" he asked, walking toward a marble buffet.

"Yes, thank you." She turned to inspect the molded cornices encasing the windows. There were heavy rod insets at the top. What drapes they had held were now gone. Probably rotted with age.

"Your wine, mademoiselle," Maurice said, holding out a light baluster wine glass. Ashley took the glass, marveling at its beauty.

"Will there be anything else?"

"No, Maurice, thank you."

Maurice nodded and left the room. Ashley's eyes followed his departure, as the thought of Tryn DeLore entering those double doors nearly paralyzed her.

She quickly turned her attention back to the room, noticing the marvelous sculptured walls. What was left of the inlaid covering was faded and partially eaten away. It looks like silk, she thought, going over to inspect it. Yes, a rose colored silk, now bleached with time. How incredible this house must have been. How incredible it was, still. The ceiling was at least fifteen feet high, bordered in a massive sculptured molding. It displayed random sculpturing throughout. The baseboards were sienna marble. In the center of the ceiling hung an enormous crystal chandelier, encrusted with decades of candle wax. Again she looked at the double doors. "Stay calm, Ashley," she said softly. "You're a professional designer, expert in antiques. You've done this a hundred times."

The last words had just left her mouth when the doors opened.

"I'm sorry to have kept you waiting," said DeLore. He walked toward her with a sophisticated confidence.

She thought she felt her heart stop.

"I can't think of a more elegant place to be kept waiting," she managed.

"You look stunning," he said and gently took her hand, bringing it to his lips.

She noticed the ruby-eyed jaguar ring, as his eyes met hers.

"Please accept my apology," he said. "My behavior at your studio was unacceptable." He released her hand, smiling. "It seems I am forever apologizing."

"It's quite unnecessary," she said, noticing that he was staring at her scarf.

"Good," he said hastily. "Apologies become tiresome, and we have more significant matters to discuss"

"Yes," she responded without thought. Finally she pulled away from his stare. "This wine," she said, "It's excellent. Is it a California?"

"No," he replied, walking past her. "It's a La Montrachet. I brought it from France." Pouring himself a glass, he turned. "Here's to the restoration of DeLore House." He lifted his glass.

"Just like that?" Ashley looked surprised.

"No. I check my references thoroughly."

"I see." She lifted her glass. "Then here's to DeLore House."

"Are you ready to see the rest of the house?"

"Yes," she said anxiously. "I've been waiting for fifteen years."

"That long?" he said amusingly "Then by all means." He lead her through the double doors and into the shadows. "As you can see, my only sources of lighting are candles and oil lamps. I do plan on bringing electricity to the house. But that will only be for certain necessities. The lighting will stay essentially as it is. I much prefer it over electric."

"I agree," Ashley said.

"Everyone seems to be consumed with conveniences these days. Quite frankly, I find them boring." DeLore began lighting the sconces behind the staircase. The entire entrance came into view. The stairway seemed to rise up and unfold. Enormous in width, it swept upward, curving gracefully to the left, then winding to the right and opening onto the second floor. The heavily carved balustrades encased the circular hallway that held entrance to five large rooms.

"Do you want to maintain the same decor throughout the house, Mr. DeLore?" Ashley asked as she climbed the stairs at some distance behind. He was moving too fast. She could have stayed just in the entrance hall for hours.

"Please." DeLore turned in mid-stride. "Let us cease with formalities. I prefer that you call me Tryn."

Startled, she responded hesitantly, "Of course." DeLore was several steps ahead, towering over her. A lock of hair had fallen over his forehead. Again his eyes locked onto hers. She stood paralyzed, yet wanting to touch him as she had in her fantasy.

DeLore continued up the stairs. "This house must remain as it was after my great-great-grandfather built it. That is to say, I want to maintain the same decor. I will authorize structural repairs. But nothing more than what is of the utmost necessity. Otherwise, it's to stay as it is."

DeLore stopped and turned back. Ashley clutched the banister. He smiled, holding her with his eyes. "You might find me difficult to work with."

Determined to ambush his intimidation, she said. "You will not find me difficult."

He continued holding her with his gaze as though she had not spoken. "Only one of the bedrooms have been arranged. He then lead her to the second floor landing. "With the exception of Maurice's room, of course.

The others are as I found them. Cleaning this house has been quite an undertaking for Maurice."

"I'm sure it has." Ashley replied.

A large sitting area stood at the top of the stairway, adorned with gilt-framed paintings. Antique sofas, tables and chairs filled the room. As they walked toward the bedroom, a French bronze of a young girl caught Ashley's eye.

"She's beautiful," Ashley remarked, stopping to admire the piece.

"Yes," he replied, gently touching its surface.

"You certainly have good taste in antiques."

"I am an expert in European art," he said, his hand sliding from the base.

Oh really, she thought. Pompous, too.

Ashley scanned the portraits as she followed him through the sitting area. "Are these your ancestors?"

"They are," he replied, stopping just short of the bedroom door. He turned abruptly. "I am not accustomed to taking ladies to my chambers on such short notice." His tone was serious, but his face less somber.

"I am quite accustomed to it, Tryn." She pushed the door open and walked past in confidently, thinking how good it felt to say his name. I will not let this man daunt me, she thought, finding herself suddenly overwhelmed by the room. In front of her were tall Palladian French doors overlooking a long, wide balcony, beyond which San Francisco loomed—a priceless piece of chiseled art. The room was a large rectangle. To the far left stood an exquisite marble fireplace. A tall mirror framed in beveled mirrors hung above. Like a portrait, Ashley's reflection filled the face of the mirror, while the beveled frame surrounded her with kaleidoscopic color. A roaring fire blazed inside the fireplace.

"That's an unusual mirror," Ashley remarked.

DeLore walked past, watching her through the mirror. "It's been in my family for centuries. It was brought here when the house was built."

"When *was* this house built? No one here seems to know."

"1803."

"1803? But—there was nothing within miles of here."

"Precisely."

"It must have been an arduous project."

"It took twelve years."

"You mean they started construction in . . . 1791? But why here?"

Tryn crossed the room and opened the French doors. "This was a beautiful and peaceful island then."

"Your family left Europe to find beauty and peacefulness?"

"Europe?" Tryn turned and faced her.

"Isn't your family from Europe?"

He smiled knowingly. "And yours, I'd venture to say."

"You know what I mean." Ashley wanted to slap the smirk from his face. "Then where *is* your home?"

Tryn's face turned somber. The oil lamps cast a rich glow across his face. His dark blue shirt hung loose over his broad shoulders and draped his wide chest. The billowing sleeves gave him the appearance of an eighteenth century prince soon to be king. Again, she imagined herself swallowed up in his embrace. He walked toward her. She tried to speak.

"My home is here now," he replied then looked away. "My wife died several years ago."

Ashley suddenly felt nervous, embarrassed for even bringing up the subject. She wanted to apologize but before she could speak he turned and glared at her. His face had become cold and lifeless.

"There were no children." DeLore drew closer. So close she could almost feel him. His eyes were again piercing hers as though he could read her thoughts. She felt suspended, unable to move.

Quickly, she caught her breath and turned away. "I'm originally from New Orleans," she said, bringing her wine glass to her mouth and forcing a sip.

"New Orleans. An exotic city."

Ashley took another sip of wine, though it was more of a gulp.

"You need a refill," DeLore said, retrieving her glass. He crossed the room to where an Italian giltwood and marble side table stood.

Ashley watched as he poured the wine, feeling suddenly overwhelmed as she waited, yet again, for him to turn and face her. She breathed deeply.

"Maurice is preparing the solarium," she heard him say. "I thought the view there would be nice for dining."

"Dining?" She forced the breath from her lungs. DeLore was now standing within inches of her.

"Yes. You will join me, won't you?"

"I'd . . . yes. I'd love to."

"Good. Now, why don't we sit down and further discuss the restoration of DeLore house." He motioned to the sitting area in front of the fire.

"These arm chairs are marvelous," Ashley said needing to sound professional.

"I trust that Maurice has cleaned them to your satisfaction. I'm afraid there is much left to do."

"I could recommend a cleaning service," Ashley offered.

"That won't be necessary."

Ashley quickly drew her attention back to the chairs. "These are exquisite," she said inspecting the wood. "William and Mary, circa 1690."

"You do know your craft."

"I'm an expert in European antiques," she stated authoritatively.

"Then we should get on quite well."

There was momentary silence until Ashley noticed the cello leaning against the far wall. She stared at it, then rose and walked toward it. DeLore watched her curiously.

"Do you play?" he asked.

No respond. She lifted her hand, trailing her fingers along its surface.

"Ashley?"

"What?"

"The cello. Do you play?"

"Play?".

"Yes. Do you play the cello?"

She turned to him with a dazed look. "No."

"It's my favorite instrument. I've played for years."

"Play it now," she pleaded.

Tryn studied Ashley.

"Please," she said, almost childlike.

As DeLore played, Ashley stared heavily into the fire, stroking her scarf. He watched her curiously.

"Ashley," DeLore was, again, next to her. He pulled her from the chair to face him. "Ashley," he repeated, seeing her vacant stare. Quickly he pulled the scarf from her neck. His hands caressed her face. Gently, he touched his lips to hers. She responded, opening to receive him.

Then suddenly, she pushed away, feeling strangely removed. What's happening? she thought. Feeling awkward and embarrassed, she fumbled with her hair, which had fallen from its clasp, cascading around her shoulders. "What happened?"

"I kissed you," he answered confidently.

Ashley eased slowly down into the chair. DeLore knelt beside her and took her hand.

"I thought you wanted me to kiss you. I would never have taken such liberties otherwise."

Ashley turned from DeLore. "What did I do to make you think that?"

"How do you explain it? It was the way you looked; the way you didn't resist."

Ashley lowered her head. "I feel so foolish."

"There is no need for that," he said and retrieved her hair clip from the rug. She reached for it but DeLore caught her arm. "Don't. Let me."

"All right," she consented.

"You must be starving," DeLore said, escorting her to the door.

She reached back and lifted her scarf from the chair.

Maurice had prepared an elegant candle-lit table draped in white linen. The kitchen remained antiquated, so Italian food was brought in from Servino's, a popular restaurant in Tiburon. Maurice's presentation of silver candelabras and fine china was elegant.

DeLore relentlessly questioned Ashley about herself. After dinner she realized she had told him her entire life's story. He, however, remained a mystery, having evaded her questions skillfully.

"So your brother's an architect," he said as they climbed the stairs to the third floor.

"The best," she said feeling strangely more comfortable with this man. "He's helped me with several of my restorations."

"I would like to meet your brother. There are a few out buildings I need to construct."

42

"He would be honored, I'm sure."

"Good. Why don't you have him come by tomorrow afternoon."

Ashley remembered that Michael was taking his boat to Bodega Bay for the weekend. Maybe she would ask Tryn to join them after all. No, on second thought, it was too soon.

Too soon? she mused, almost feeling his embrace. If only she could remember, could feel him kissing her. All she remembered was pushing him away.

There were two stairways leading to the third floor, each at a far corner of the second floor. They curved slightly toward the center. Each side held two large bedrooms. Centered between the bedrooms and running front to back was a stone wall with detailed carvings. Tryn reached out and slid open a small panel, behind which was a brass lever. He lifted the lever and a portion of the wall opened into darkness. Tryn went into the darkness and opened another panel which held a long brass lamplighter. He moved around the room, lighting the wall sconces. The flames brought into focus a magnificent room with crimson walls and elaborate portraits, French and Italian furnishings throughout. The floor contained inlaid sienna marble. On the east wall, a handsomely carved limestone fireplace seemed to rise up out of the floor. A massive gilt-framed mirror hung above the mantel. Ashley looked up at the heavily sculptured ceiling that rose some twenty feet.

"The ceiling," she said. "It looks like the work of Robert Adams. Is that possible?"

"Quite accurate. I'm impressed."

"I'm amazed." She looked at Tryn, who was now leaning against the mantel. "It's as though time has stood still here. The walls, the paint; it hasn't faded. These chairs, they look new."

"This room is pristine. I don't think it was ever used."

"But why? Why would your great-great-grandfather have such a magnificent room designed and then not use it?"

"We would have to ask him, and we are too late for that."

Ashley ignored the comment and strolled past him. Arrogant bastard. "Are these your ancestors?" she asked, scanning the wall of all-male portraits and noticing that each subject clutched a gold-handled walking stick.

43

"Yes," he said, amusedly watching her.

She also noticed that each man wore on the little finger of his left hand, a gold jaguar ring set with ruby eyes. She suppressed comment and continued her inspection of the room. The furnishings were mostly French, Louis XV and Louis XVI. A large gilt console table with eagle supports stood under the mural walls at each end of the room. They were flanked with heavy crimson damask drapes. One mural was a sweeping scene of mystical female bathers, the other a dark forest under a desolate sky. She studied both murals in silence, then inspected the rich fabric that framed them. It was silk damask, draped and fringed. The weighty folds were looped back with fat cords and tassels the size of pineapples. They were like new.

"I can see you won't need my services here," she said, crossing to the center of the floor where a large family crest of Winged Lions had been designed. Between the lions was an ornate candelabra with the letter 𝔇 inscribed on the base. How magnificent this room was.

"Are you ready to see the rest of the house?" Tryn was again beside her.

"The house?" Ashley could feel the warmth of his hand on her arm. "Oh—yes, of course."

With the exception of his bedroom, the rooms on the second and third floors had not been disturbed. The furniture lay hidden under heavy tapestries. The attic, she learned, held very little except for a few priceless paintings. He made it clear that no one was allowed there. Downstairs were five large rooms: the parlor, two reception halls, a library, and a large dining room. A hallway led back to the kitchen. Just off the kitchen was a small but adequate servants' quarters. There were two entrances into the solarium: one through a wide hallway leading from the kitchen; the other through the back of the entrance hall.

The house was beyond what Ashley had envisioned. She had restored some magnificent homes, but words to describe DeLore House failed her. She feared the magnitude of what she would see tomorrow in the daylight. Some of the oil lamps had not been working, and it had been difficult to see the rooms properly.

"Do you mind the convertible?" Tryn said, helping her with her jacket.

"Not at all. What year is it, '54?"

"You know your cars, too. Is there anything you aren't an expert on?"

"Very little."

"I see."

As the car passed through the gates, Ashley felt Tryn release the clasp from her hair.

ꝏ

Ashley lay in bed thinking back over the past several hours. She wanted to reach out and recapture the night. On the other hand, she wanted to run, as far and as fast as she could. Where were these strange feelings coming from? She thought back to the day that Tryn had walked into the studio, and that night as she stood out on her balcony. Never had she experienced such desire. It had slowly consumed her, leaving her body with a strange hunger. But why, after all these years? Why this man?

She dimmed the lamp beside her bed as Tryn's words echoed in her mind. "You are an exciting woman, Ashley Winthrop." He had smiled, almost pulling her to him with his eyes. He had then said good night and left her at the door.

Dreams invaded her sleep.

The room was large. There was no door, just windows covered in heavy fabric. The tall ceiling was filled with dozens of crystal chandeliers. Tiny little flames flickered. The ceiling seemed to move with their shadow dance. Suddenly, the chandeliers began to sway above her. Back and forth they swayed, faster and faster. The prisms knocked against each other with a piercing, tinkling sound. Louder and louder it came. She pressed her hands to her ears. Frantically looking around, desperate to find a way out, she began running toward one of the windows, reaching out for the draped window. But the faster she ran the farther the window moved into the distance.

She was surrounded, now draped by fabric on all sides. She began pushing her way through, but layer after layer confronted her. Her breathing was labored; her heart seemed about to pound out of her chest. Frantically she reached out, and with a slow sweeping motion, she began falling through the heavy crimson fabric. She seemed to glide through the air ghost-like as he swept her up in his arms; down and down.

Ashley bolted from her pillow screaming.

"Where am I!" Her body was seized with fear. Then slowly the reality of her bedroom came into focus. Her mind rushed back into the dream. The chandeliers; she could almost hear the incessant clanging. She felt the desperation to run, to get out. And the drapes; that heavy, endless mass of fabric. And then, the weightlessness. She felt him surround her, pulling her slowly down. His presence, she knew his presence.

Why couldn't she remember him now?

"Ashley," she heard Stanley calling.

She glanced at the clock. It was only six-thirty. What was Stanley doing here so early?

"Ashley!" Stanley was now banging on the door.

She grabbed her robe from the chair. "I'm coming," she yelled. "For Christ's sake, stop that banging." Ashley threw open the door. "What!"

"What hell! What was all that screaming about?"

Ashley ignored the question and traipsed across the living room to the kitchen. "What are you doing here at six-thirty in the morning?"

"I have a seven o'clock appointment. What was that yelling all about? I thought you were being murdered."

"Only in my dreams. You want coffee?"

"Of course I want coffee. What do you mean, only in your dreams?"

"I mean I had a dream, that's all. I woke myself up screaming. Haven't you ever done that?"

"No, not really. I enjoy my dreams," he said, making himself comfortable on the sofa.

"I bet you do. You want a bagel?"

"Love one. Are you going to tell me about the divine Mr. DeLore?"

"You don't want to hear about his house first?"

"I don't give a damn about his house, now give."

"You have a one track mind," she said, handing him a cup of coffee.

"Yeah, when it comes to a piece of change like that."

"Well, that piece of change, as you put it, is pompous, arrogant, narcissistic, and charming. Did I leave anything out?"

"Yes, gorgeous. And right up my alley," Stanley beamed. "I'm sure he's gay. When are you going back? I want to go."

"Dream on, Romeo," she laughed, walking back to the kitchen for more coffee. "He is no more gay than I am."

Stanley laughed. "No, you're sexually deficient."

Ashley just smiled.

"I'm going back there today," she said. "You're welcome to come along. If you promise to behave." She refilled his cup and handed him a bagel.

"Behave?" He sunk his teeth into the warm bread.

"Who are you meeting at seven?"

"A new client from Santa Rosa. I'll be finished by eight thirty. What time are you going up there?"

"Around nine. He wants to do minimal restoration. And I agree. I think we should keep it as close to original as possible. Do you know that construction began on that house in 1791?"

"1791! You can't be serious. Belvedere was nothing more than an island then. Probably inhabited by Indians, for Christ's sake."

"I know. It took twelve years to build."

"That's weird," he said as the door chimes rang out.

"There's your appointment."

Ashley worked in her office while Stanley met with his client. She called Michael and told him about her meeting with Tryn and that he wanted Michael to help design some of the out buildings. Michael wasn't about to cancel his boat trip, but agreed to meet with Tryn Tuesday morning. Ashley begged off going to Bodega Bay. Under the circumstances, Michael let her off the hook.

Stanley appeared back in her office around 8:45, anxious to accompany Ashley to DeLore House. She was on the phone with her father.

"I'll be fine," she was telling Victor. "In fact, I feel marvelous. I got that account I was telling you about. You remember, the old DeLore estate."

Silence.

"Dad?"

"What do you know about this DeLore?" he asked.

"Nothing much. Just that he's moved here from France. He's an expert in European art."

Again silence.

"Dad, sorry to rush. I have a nine o'clock appointment with Mr. DeLore. I don't want to be late."

"No, of course not," he replied. "Oh, honey. This guy DeLore."

"Yes?"

Victor paused. "Never mind. I'll talk to you later."

Ashley hung up the phone, wondering why her father seemed so preoccupied.

Minutes later, she and Stanley were headed up Beach Road in Ashley's car. The gates were open and Maurice was clearing off the old courtyard around the cypress. Ashley drove past and waved. He nodded perfunctorily, returning to his chores.

"Who was that?" Stanley asked.

"The chauffeur."

"What's the chauffeur doing cleaning up the yard?"

"He does a lot of things for Mr. DeLore."

"Mr. DeLore, huh. Not Tryn? Pretentious bastard."

"Shut up, Stanley." Ashley parked the car behind the old Jaguar Saloon. "For your information, we *are* on a first name basis."

"Look at those cars," he said.

"They're beauties, aren't they?"

"This guy sure knows how to live."

"Wait till you see his house."

"Ashley," Tryn called, walking across the terrace. "You're right on time."

"You remember my associate, Stanley," she said. "He was anxious to see your house."

"Stanley. Why, yes." Tryn held out his hand.

"Good to see you again," Stanley said. "Ashley tells me you were not well the other day." Stanley shuffled from one foot to the other.

"Pardon?".

"You said in your note you had the flu." Stanley shuffled nervously.

"Yes, the flu. Now, if you'll excuse me, I have an appointment in San Francisco."

"Certainly," Stanley said, trying to sound dignified.

"Oh, Ashley, if you have no other engagements, there are some things I'd like to go over with you. Say, the Corinthian around seven?"

"I . . well, certainly."

"Good." Tryn headed toward his car.

"The Corinthian?" Stanley said. "He already belongs to the Corinthian Yacht Club? How did he manage that?"

"I have no idea."

Stanley was rendered speechless, as Ashley pulled him from one room to the next. She had saved the best till last. The ballroom would be the pièce de résistance. Stanley had been set on seeing Tryn's bedroom. But Ashley said no, that it would be invading his privacy. Stanley sulked through the rest of the tour.

"Stop acting like a child, Stanley. Now come on, I've saved the best till last."

"I've already missed the best," he pouted.

Ashley ignored this as they walked down the hall to the ballroom. "You're not going to believe this," she said, pushing open the panel and lifting the brass lever. Stanley stood in the doorway as Ashley took the lamplighter and went from sconce to sconce. His mouth dropped open.

Stanley slowly walked into the room, muttering to himself. He stopped abruptly.

"What's the matter?" Ashley said, as she finished lighting the last sconce.

"I don't know." Stanley looked around the large room. "It . . . feels strange."

"Strange?" Ashley walked toward the fireplace. "Are you crazy? This is the most spectacular room I've ever seen." The words had barely left her mouth when she noticed the cello leaning against the mantel.

49

She lifted her hand and let her fingers glide across the rich wood.

"This room gives me the creeps." Stanley turned abruptly to leave. Ashley remained by the cello, trancelike.

"Ash, let's go."

Silence.

"What's the matter with you!" Stanley glared across the room.

More silence.

"Damn!" he cried, and sprinted across the floor.

"Ash! Let's get out of here." Ashley remained fixed to the cello. Stanley frantically took her by the shoulders. It was then he saw her distant stare. "Ashley. For God's sake, what's wrong with you?" Suddenly he found that he was shaking her. "Ashley," he pleaded, then pulled her to him, wrapping her in his arms. He didn't know what to do. Only that he wanted to get out of this horrible place.

"Monsieur?" Stanley jerked around. Maurice was standing inside the doorway. "Is there something wrong?" he asked calmly.

"You're damn right there's something wrong," Stanley blurted.

Maurice walked toward them. Ashley pushed Stanley away with a gasp. She stared at him. "What happened?" She reached up and began rubbing her forehead.

Stanley took her arm, "Let's get out of here."

"Mademoiselle," Maurice said. "Why don't you come now to the kitchen. I will get you a glass of water."

"Yes, thank you Maurice. I think I will."

The kitchen was sublimely antiquated. A mass of oak and copper, it drew its water from large cistern tanks. There were two ice boxes. One was not much larger than a modern refrigerator, the other took up a third of a wall. Across the room was a cast iron wood stove. A large stone fireplace stood at one end. The wide hearth was covered with heavy kettles. In the center, overhung by an enormous iron rack with hanging pots, stood an oak draw-leaf refectory table. It looked to be mid-17th century, about twelve feet in length and five feet wide. Six heavy oak chairs lined both sides.

Stanley had seemed to calm. "People sure knew how to live back in those days," he said, eyeing Maurice suspiciously. "Who needed modern conveniences, folks had servants to pamper them."

"Oui, Monsieur, DeLore House had many servants." Maurice handed Ashley a small bottled water.

"Where did they live?" Ashley asked, wondering how he would know. "The servants' quarters could only house five or six."

"There are three small out buildings in the back. Are you feeling better now, Mademoiselle?"

"Yes, thank you." She smiled at Maurice weakly.

"Very well then, I'll be going back to my chores."

"He's a strange one," Stanley whispered, looking after Maurice as he disappeared through the swinging door. He looked back at Ashley with a grimace. "What in the hell happened to you up there? You scared the shit out of me."

Ashley was looking out across the kitchen. What a marvelous room this would be to renovate, she mused, suddenly noticing the old stone floor. Wonder how far he'll let me go with it? Surely he wants a more workable kitchen than this.

"Ashley!" Stanley howled. "For Christ's sake."

"What?"

"I don't believe this." Stanley rolled his eyes. "What in hell is going on?"

"Look Stanley. I have a lot of work to do. Why don't I take you back to the studio. I'll be a while."

"Are you crazy? I'm not about to leave you in this house. It gives me the creeps."

"The creeps? Stanley, what's gotten into you?"

"That room," he blasted. "It felt . . . I don't know. Evil."

"Stop with the dramatics."

Stanley glared at Ashley. "Dramatics!" He bolted from the chair. "And another thing." He glanced around the kitchen to make sure Maurice had gone. "That Maurice guy; I don't trust him. He's got beady eyes. And what a pompous tight ass."

"Maurice is a dignified man."

"I didn't say he wasn't, I said he had beady eyes and a tight ass. I don't trust people with beady eyes and tight asses."

"You're impossible."

&

Stanley sat at his desk, wondering if he should tell Michael what had happened. He couldn't get the incident out of his mind. And that room. It made his skin crawl just thinking about it. He glanced down at the answering machine. He pressed the play button and took down the messages. There had been one from Ashley's mother, who rarely called, and another from Shelby. Both wanted to know about Tryn DeLore.

&

The sun was setting; dusk crept in slowly. The tide rushed in through the Golden Gate as if angered, sending swarms of white caps threatening what few boats remained in its waters.

Ashley stood by the stone balustrades feeling the rush of the wind against her face. To the west, the fog was making its journey across the bridge and into the bay. The city would soon be shrouded, its brilliance lost for the night.

The terrace doors to Tryn's bedroom stood open. She heard him enter. The wind was stronger now, sweeping, lifting her hair. She could feel his presence slowly consuming her. Could almost taste him as he drew closer.

"Ashley." His voice sounded strangely distant yet dangerously close.

She turned. The sight of him took her breath, the breeze moving his dark hair about his face. The intense eyes. And the elegance of his movements as he reached out and pulled her to him. He held her face in his hands, his lips touching her. She could feel his warm breath on her face.

He took her shoulders and turned her around, covering her neck with his hands, then her face. She felt faint as he trailed his fingers across her lips then pulled her deeper into him. She now felt his strong chest, his arms surrounding her. His hands were now finding their way inside her blouse. She could feel the buttons releasing. His hands smothered her breast. She couldn't breathe. She knew she was going to faint as he began to unbutton her pants, then slide his hand between her legs. She collapsed into his arms.

He lifted her and carried her to his bed, placing her gently on the silk damask counterpane. Very slowly, he began undressing her as he caressed her body with his lips. She now lay naked. The room was deep in shadow, lit only by the soft glow of the lamplight. He then stood over her, undressing. Afterward, he pulled her from the bed, holding her naked body against his. She could feel his chest moving with each breath. Feel the strength of his hard penis against her. His lips urgently caressed her mouth, taking her, searching her as he lifted her back onto the bed.

She felt his mouth on her breast, his hands moving down her body. And then between her legs—kissing, exploring, spreading her legs as he explored her. She moaned in pleasure, wanting it never to end.

"You are my first," she whispered.

"Yes," he said, "I know."

He entered her, slowly, gently.

Why did she feel no pain? Only suspended, as though time had reached out and cradled them in its arms.

The room seemed to whisper in distant voices.

Chapter Five

Michael and Shelby had returned to the Corinthian late Monday from their boat trip to Bodega Bay. Shelby stopped in at Ashley's office the next morning, bombarding her with questions about Tryn DeLore.

"Come on, Ash," Shelby said, rooted in the doorway. "When do I see DeLore House and meet this mysterious client of yours?"

"Don't you have houses to show?" Ashley said irritably.

"No," Shelby retorted.

"Well I'm busy," she said nervously rummaging through her files.

Shelby remained in the doorway looking wounded.

Ashley left the filing cabinet and went back to her desk. "What?" she said, glancing up at Shelby.

"Nothing." Shelby turned to leave.

"Come back here," Ashley said. "I'm sorry. It's just that I have a lot on my mind. Michael and I are going there around one o'clock. You're welcome to come."

"Great. I'll be back at 12:30." Shelby pranced across the studio and out the door.

Ashley slumped down in her chair, thinking that her body had never felt so alive.

Everyone arrived at DeLore House just after one o'clock. Maurice was busy with the arduous project of clearing the grounds.

It had been years since Michael had driven by the old mansion.

"It's magnificent," he said as Ashley drove through the gates.

Shelby was rendered speechless.

Ashley stopped the car just behind the sedan.

Michael left the car and peered through the window of the Jaguar sedan. "This guy does have class."

"Are you a lover of Jaguars, Michael?" Tryn was standing at the end of the terrace, his gold handled walking stick firmly in hand.

Michael looked up. His face suddenly went blank.

"I'm Tryn DeLore," he said offering his hand. Ashley has told me a lot about your work."

Michael gathered his wits. "It's, it's nice to meet you."

Michael and Tryn were the same height, their features similar. Although Michael looked older. Tryn had a certain maturity in his mannerism, as well as an intriguing eccentricity. His words were articulately spoken, and his presence demanded respect, causing him to appear wise. This coupled with his youthful appearance left one with a disturbing sense of mystery.

Shelby had emerged from the car and was walking toward the terrace.

"Oh, Tryn," Ashley said. "This is Shelby Kincaid, a dear friend of ours."

Tryn turned from Michael.

Ashley heard the gasp. She looked up to see Tryn glaring at Shelby.

Tryn then stepped back and awkwardly turned to Michael. "Are you available for the rest of the day?" The words seemed to gush from his mouth.

"Why . . . yes," Michael replied.

Tryn took Michael's arm. They quickly disappeared around the back of the house.

"What's the matter with that man?" Shelby said.

"I don't know," Ashley replied, looking thoroughly confused, She then remembered that same reaction when she was first introduced to Tryn. But she wasn't about to stir Shelby's overactive imagination. "He's eccentric," Ashley said. "Who knows what he's thinking? Let's go, I've got work to do."

"He's the most gorgeous eccentric I've ever seen," Shelby said, following Ashley across the terrace.

"Yes, isn't he."

After meticulously studying each room, accumulating mounds of notes, and overwhelming Shelby with a tour of the house, they went to find Michael and Tryn. They located them out in one of the servants' cottages discussing the design of a three-car garage, a pool, and a pool house.

"May we get in on this?" Ashley said, standing in the doorway.

Tryn didn't acknowledge her but continued his conversation with Michael, who seemed not to have noticed her at all. Moments later Tryn looked briefly toward Ashley. Shelby was standing next to her.

"Michael and I will be awhile," and he turned his attention back to Michael as if no other conversation were needed.

The sun was just setting over the Golden Gate. Ashley stood on her balcony sipping a glass of wine.

Only a few days ago, she thought, her life had followed the same path it always had: busy days full of endless decisions, phone calls, trips several times a year to Europe, and an occasional night out. As fulfilling and predictable as one's life could get. And now, this strange man, Tryn DeLore, appeared out of nowhere, pulling feelings from her she had never experienced. Why had she stayed at DeLore House that day, waiting for him to return? She had done it without a thought. Had walked up those stairs and into his bedroom as though drawn by some strange, invisible force. Those lost moments when he had first kissed her—why couldn't she remember them? And the next day while showing Stanley the ballroom. She only remembered entering, then Stanley's arms around her.

Maybe I do need a rest, she mused.

"Ashley," she heard Michael call from the living room.

"Out here," she answered.

He appeared in the doorway. "We need to talk."

"Did Tryn say anything about what happened today?" she asked.

"What?" Michael responded as if he had no idea what she was talking about.

"You saw his reaction when I introduced him to Shelby. Did he say anything about that?"

"No, why?"

"You didn't find it strange?"

"I don't remember anything strange. Look, I'm not here to talk about DeLore. It's you I want to talk about."

"What about me?" Ashley slouched against the railing.

"I've talked to Stanley. He told me what happened yesterday."

"Happened?"

"You know exactly what I'm talking about. When you two were at DeLore's."

"Damn Stanley!"

"That's not all."

"Now what?" Ashley glared at Michael.

"He told me about that dream you had the other morning. He said you woke up screaming."

"Michael. Don't start." She raised her hand. "Look, I promise to take some time off. But right now, this DeLore project is too important."

"Not if it lands you in some mental institution."

"Cease with the dramatics Michael." She turned away, sipping her wine.

"I'll tell DeLore."

"What!" Ashley jerked around, spilling her wine down the front of her blouse. "You open your mouth and I'll never speak to you again."

"I'll take my chances."

"That's goddamn blackmail!"

"And don't think I won't do it."

"Damn you!" She stormed back into the living room. "You bastard!"

Michael stood on the balcony with a wounded look.

Ashley pushed her fingers through her hair, "You know I didn't mean that." She went to him and folded her arms around his neck. Michael responded instantly, pressing her to him. Ashley lifted her head and touched her cheek to his. Her body was now flooded with that strange, restless sensation. As their eyes met, the reality of being in her brother's arms hit her. She instantly pushed away. Michael caught her arm.

"Stop it, Michael," she said, pulling free. "What's gotten into you?"

"Me? What's gotten into you?"

"Never mind," she said, not wanting to further the conversation. Maybe she only imagined it.

"I have been thinking about making a trip to New Orleans to get away—clear my head and talk shop with Buzz. But I can't just walk out on Tryn."

"I don't expect you to," he said, relieved that she was finally giving in. "You can have everything scheduled within a week's time. You said yourself the project was more of a restoration than renovation. Besides, Stanley's here and I'll be up at DeLore House most of the time."

"I'm only going to stay in New Orleans a few days, though. I'll go crazy with nothing to do."

"You're going crazy now. Besides, you can take Miss Mary Harper for her afternoon strolls, and antique shop for DeLore."

"Mary Harper bit my ankle the last time I took her for a stroll."

Buzz Harper was an old family friend who owned Harper's Antiques in the French Quarter of New Orleans and Harper's Design's on Magazine Street. He too was a celebrated designer. The Winthrops had lived in New Orleans a short time before moving to San Francisco. Buzz had helped Ashley make connections on the West Coast, but was forever urging her to leave the Bay Area and return to the South.

The next day Ashley went to review the plans with Tryn and schedule her workmen.

"I'll be in New Orleans for a few days, consulting on a house," she explained, handing Tryn the schedule she had planned.

They were standing by a large partner's desk in the library. Tryn took the papers and put them aside. "Am I to understand that my project is not your highest priority?"

Tryn's question threw her off guard, and she was finding it difficult to answer. It was then that she saw the restlessness in his eyes. Before she could utter a sound he had taken her into his arms. She cried out softly as he clutched a handful of her hair and jerked her head backward. His mouth came down on hers hard and hungry. She suddenly lost all sense of time and place. He lifted her into his arms and carried her to his chambers.

The next morning Shelby drove Ashley to the airport.

"What's going on with that gorgeous DeLore guy?" she asked.

"What?" Ashley was blankly staring out the window.

"Tryn DeLore. Is he still acting weird?"

"Huh." She glanced briefly at Shelby then back to the window. "Ask Michael."

৪০

Toulouse Street was shaded as the lazy afternoon sun fell beyond the horizon. Shortly the gaslights would take on their flickering dance, creating a mysterious glow. The tall hurricane shutters and impermeable double doors were overhung by sweeping wrought iron balconies. Their rafters were lined with lush ferns and flowers of many hues in rows of hanging baskets. The Quarter, with its moss-covered bricks and mystical gas-lit courtyards, seemed to harbor ancient secrets, stirring a sense of curiosity in the passersby.

Ashley approached the green double doors of Harper's Antiques. From inside she could hear the piano. She stood by the entrance picturing Buzz in her mind: his long silver hair that he always wore pulled back in a pony tail, his narrow face and pearl white teeth. She could almost see him smiling, just the way she knew he would. Ashley turned the heavy brass knob and entered Harper's. It held an exquisite display of European antiques. Across the room, lying on a swaged and tasseled Louis XVI sofa, was Mary Harper, Buzz Harper's toy spaniel papillon. Her brown and white fur glistened under the lights. She was oblivious to Ashley's arrival, remaining undisturbed.

Buzz was lost in his music and had not heard Ashley walk in. He was a talented pianist and had taught Ashley to play as a child. But work had taken precedence over the piano.

"I miss playing the piano," she said, running her fingers across the polished wood.

Buzz looked up. "My precious," he said, and quickly raised his six-foot-four frame from the piano bench. He greeted her with long, outstretched arms. "You are more beautiful every time I see you."

"What?" Ashley suddenly realized that she had been staring at the piano. She immediately threw her arms around his neck, planting a kiss on his delicately featured face.

"It's so good to see you," she said.

He kissed her forehead. "You don't come to see me enough. I still think you should buy a place here in the Quarter."

"If I didn't adore San Francisco you could bet I'd move here. Bugs, humidity, gaslights, courtyards, Mardi Gras and all." With her head tilted back to meet his eyes, she whispered, "But especially you."

"I wish you would. And I have just the place," he added with a wink."

She patted his chest. "Don't tempt me."

"Victor and Margaret should never have left New Orleans. You belong here, not in San Francisco. Buzz walked to the rear of the shop. "A glass of wine?"

"Love one," she replied, turning back to the piano.

"I can still remember the first time Margaret walked in my shop," he said, uncorking the wine. "That was over thirty years ago. She had seen one of the chandeliers through the window. Nothing would do but for her to have it. Five minutes later, you and Michael and Victor walked in. I'm not crazy about children in my shop, but honey, I melted when I saw the two of you." Buzz walked out of the back room with glasses in hand.

Ashley was sitting at the piano, her eyes glazed, her hands caressing the keys.

"Why don't you play something?" Buzz said.

"Play?" Ashley studied Buzz's face, then looked down at the keys. "It's been too long." She hurriedly left the piano, taking the glass of wine. "Maybe I'll practice a little while I'm here."

"A splendid idea. Now, my sweets, how about Commander's Palace? I've made reservations."

"My favorite. Is Les going to join us?" She eased down on the sofa next to Mary Harper. The little papillon darted her an uncertain eye, then finally scooted closer, resting her chin on Ashley's leg, as if to say, "I'll allow you to pet me now."

"Les is in Charleston working on a historic home."

"I don't trust you, Mary Harper," Ashley said, petting her cautiously. "I was hoping I'd get to see Les while I was here."

"You will. He'll be back in a couple of days."

Ashley smiled. "How long have you two been together?"

"Ten years," Buzz replied. "Best thing that every happened to me."

"I imagine Les feels the same about you," she said.

"I'm not so sure about that," Buzz laughed. "I am rapidly approaching the big six zero. He's still in his thirties."

Mary Harper suddenly let out a growl. Ashley jerked her hand away.

"Mary Harper," Buzz warned. "You mind your manners." He reached down and lifted the imperious creature from the sofa. "Let's get you home," he said, nuzzling her fur. "Ashley and I have dinner plans."

Commander's was elegant as usual. After a leisurely dinner and several attempts to convince Ashley to buy a place in the Quarter, they headed back to Buzz's home on Chartres Street. Buzz pulled his '85 Rolls up to a pair of tall black-green doors. Ashley got out and opened the doors, revealing an old brick driveway, its crumbling brick walls adorned by numerous gaslights. In the distance, the flowing sounds of a waterfall enveloped the courtyard Ashley knew to be full of lush green ferns, banana trees and a brilliance of gloxinias, bulging from strategically placed black urns. Securing the Rolls in its proper resting place, they walked through the door and up the tall staircase to the formal entrance.

Softly, in the distance, she heard the piano. As Buzz reached for the brass knob, sounds began to drift around her. The door seemed to take on a life of its own. When it opened, the room was flooded in light. Ashley's body seemed to float into the light, moving as though drawn toward the piano at the far end of the room. Seated at the piano was a woman, her hands moving gracefully over the keys. But the melody sounded strangely distant. The vision was shrouded in a mist of blues and greens and reds, and swirls of deep lavender. Again, as in her bedroom that morning, Ashley felt a sense of timelessness.

"Jenny," she said and reached out toward the woman. She then lowered her hand and uttered the words "Thornton Square."

The next thing she knew, Buzz was sitting next to her, calling her name. He looked confused, almost frightened. Why was he looking at her that way? She turned away, suddenly noticing the parlor. The ornate plaster moldings separated the cobalt ceiling from floral walls. The intricately-carved marble mantel was adorned by two gold urns balanced majestically at either end. Above the mantel hung a large gilt-framed mirror. To the right stood a naive painted screen of century-old castles, encircled by a bastion of moats and stone arches, with voluminous clouds suspended over soft, green meadows. In front of the screen stood two Louis XV grands fauteuils upholstered in a deep burgundy velour.

Why were these furnishings so familiar?

Ashley looked back at Buzz in wonderment.

"Ashley?" he asked, "Who is Jenny? What is Thornton Square?"

"Jenny? Thornton Square?" she whispered.

Ashley looked at Buzz as though she didn't understand the question. "What?"

"You called out the name Jenny," he replied. "Then you said Thornton Square."

Ashley slumped into the brocade pillows lining the back of the sofa. "What is happening to me?"

Buzz turned her to face him. "Honey," he said. "Now don't be angry. Michael told me about your dreams. He and Shelby are worried about you."

Ashley suddenly grew anxious. "They haven't told Dad have they?"

"Victor? I don't think so. Look, angel, Michael just wants you to get some rest. He thought coming here, getting away from all the stress, would help."

"But it hasn't. It's getting worse."

A lot worse it seemed. As though it were following her, whatever it was, all the way to New Orleans. She had felt it when she first arrived at Buzz's shop. Had felt drawn to the piano somehow. And now, in his house, she couldn't even remember walking through the door.

Ashley rose from the sofa and crossed the room to the fireplace. "Jenny—Thornton Square. I said that?"

"Yes. You walked to the piano bench as though there was actually someone there. You said, 'Jenny.' Then you turned away, looking frightened. You said, 'Thornton Square.'"

"Somehow it seems familiar." Ashley laid her hand on top of the mantel. "I know this mantel." She turned, studying the furnishings. "The things in this room. The rug, the chairs, the vases . . . they're familiar."

"Of course," Buzz said. "I had just bought them the last time you were here."

"No, it's not that kind of familiar. It's like I've known them all my life."

Buzz paused for a moment, then said, "Honey. Would you consider seeing someone?"

"What?"

"I have a dear friend. He's studied hypnosis for many years. He's very respected in the field."

❧

St. Charles Avenue, lined with Neo-Italianate and Greek Revival houses, had witnessed decades of electric streetcars carrying their riders noisily down its center. Buzz and Ashley drove past the streetcars, then turned off St. Charles into the cluster of mansions and headed toward Prytania Street where David Clarendon maintained an office in his home. Buzz turned his Rolls into the driveway of 2343 Prytania.

Heavy wrought iron gates led up to a century-old mansion of Ecole des Beaux Arts design. As the Rolls came to rest just short of the portico, Ashley opened the door and walked toward the front lawn. She seemed to focus on a round, intricately carved, stone-framed window that sat centered on the third floor. Her arms hung limply at her side, her eyes fixed on the window. Seconds later, she wrapped her arms around herself, shaking violently. She called out, "Stefan . . . no!"

Buzz bolted across the lawn, snatching her up in his arms. Then, whatever it was that had her in its grasp seemed to let go. She looked at Buzz. Her face blank. "What are we doing out here?"

Trying to distract her, Buzz laughed, "You wanted to get a good look at this magnificent house, to put it in your words. Now . . . if you've seen enough, why don't we go inside? That's even more spectacular."

Buzz took Ashley's arm, guiding her to the front steps. Before he could ring the bell David had opened the large door. He held out his arms in a big "welcome." His five foot eight, one hundred and ninety pound frame occupied most of the doorway. His short black hair framed a jolly little face, partially concealed by a black beard sprinkled with gray. He was dressed in dark gray slacks with heavy cuffs, a turtleneck that was searching for even a hint of neck, and a paisley smoking jacket. Untraditional as he appeared, he exuded gentility and compassion. Ashley at once felt a sense of security.

David took her hand. "Ashley, Buzz has told me a little about why you have come here," he said, leading her through a long narrow entrance hall. As they approached the staircase, Ashley froze. Ten feet wide, its cherry treads were lined with an exquisite oriental carpet and framed by a thick wooden balustrade. The banister coiled like a snake at the foot of the stairs. A carved medallion clung to the ceiling, displaying a twenty-arm, three-tiered gaslight chandelier.

Horrified, Ashley glared at the banister. She turned to David and said in a whisper, "I have killed my husband. I will never see my child."

Buzz and David looked dumbfounded. Ashley fled from the house, collapsing on the front lawn.

Chapter Six

As Ashley fought to gain clarity, the massive armoire slowly came into focus. The bedroom lay quiet except for the soft hum of the ceiling fan. She struggled to recreate the events from the day before, suddenly remembering David Clarendon yet nothing of being inside his house. She only remembered David Clarendon greeting them at the door. She did remember the hospital, waking up in the emergency room with Buzz and David Clarendon hovering over her. There was that woman doctor who had examined her, found nothing, and released her. So they left the hospital with orders for her to rest. Then Buzz told her what had happened, that she had run from Clarendon's house and had fainted on the front lawn.

She suddenly thought back to Tryn. Of how she had been drawn up those stairs and into his bedroom. It seemed more dream than reality. As though she had not participated, only watched from a great distance. Nothing could have kept her from him that night. God, how she wanted his touch, his scent, the feel of him taking her. The hunger was so powerful. Like one hungers for food, weak from starvation after an eternity without nourishment.

Ashley slowly propped herself up on one elbow, wondering why she felt so groggy. Then she remembered the sedative.

Carefully lifting herself off the bed, she walked over and pushed opened the drapes. An elaborate wrought-iron gallery overlooked a courtyard of lush plants and shaded ferns. She unlatched the doors and swung them open to the flowing sound of the waterfall. The cool air felt good, bringing her some semblance of life. In only a matter of months, she thought, the thick hot air would converge, becoming unbearable under the blazing sun, forcing a retreat into the cool, air conditioned rooms. She could almost smell the fragrance of the earth after a summer's shower, weaving its essence through her senses.

Buzz's footsteps echoed down the hall as he walked from the hardwood floors to the antique rugs. He entered the room and walked up behind her, wrapping her in his arms.

"Good morning, my precious."

She rested her head against his chest. "Good morning, Uncle Buzz."

"Angel," he said. "You haven't called me that since you were a child."

"I feel like a child," she sighed.

Buzz held her close as they looked out across the rooftops of the French Quarter, taking in the early Louisiana morning.

"Why do you feel like a child?"

She clutched Buzz's arm. "Because I'm scared."

"No, you mustn't. We'll get to the bottom of this."

"That's what I'm afraid of."

"Does that mean you don't want to see David today?"

"No, I'll see him."

"Good. Now come over here and sit down." Buzz led her to the edge of the bed. "Do you remember what happened last night?"

"Last night?"

"Yes. I found you in the parlor playing the piano."

Ashley searched her memory.

"You were playing Lakmé. Quite beautifully, in fact."

"What?"

"Lakmé." It's a classical piece by Léo Delibes."

"I've never heard of Lak—whatever it is. Besides, I couldn't have played the piano. It's been too long."

"Then how do you explain it?"

Ashley ran her fingers through her hair. "I can't." She looked at Buzz in defeat. "I can't explain any of it. I came here to get some rest, yet it's got worse."

"Maybe it's here we'll find the answers."

Buzz began filling in the details of what had taken place at David Clarendon's. Ashley listened in stunned disbelief. Killed her husband? What husband? She looked at Buzz in horror, then buried her head in his chest.

ର

David Clarendon had converted a second floor bedroom of his grand old mansion into an office. An oriental rug covered the portion of the office where a large partner's desk stood.

Buzz and Ashley sat in chairs facing the desk. David eased his short rotund frame into his leather chair.

"Buzz has filled me in on your dreams and these recent visions," he began. "But I need for you to tell me anything else that you can remember. What might seem the most trivial detail could be important to understanding your experiences. Now, let's go back to when you were a child. Buzz said you were born here in New Orleans." David shifted slightly as if to find a more comfortable position.

"Yes," Ashley replied. Clarendon's jolly face and apparent sincerity were easing her tension, if only slightly. "My brother and I. Michael is my twin brother."

"No sisters?"

"No, well, not really. It's a little complicated."

"I'm listening."

Ashley told Clarendon about Shelby.

"So yes," she replied. "I guess you could say I have a sister. I love her like a sister."

She thought back to Meno's birthday dinner. Why had she been so irritable with Shelby? Shelby had always needled her about her non-existent love life. That was nothing new. And it was also Shelby who had come to her rescue during those horrid teenage years when she was made fun of and whispered about for her asocial behavior.

"Ashley," Clarendon smiled. "Tell me about these dreams. How far back do they go?"

Ashley told him about the dream she'd been having since childhood, then about the dream she had only a few nights back. The horror of being strapped to that metal table.

"This was the first time you had ever had that dream?" he asked.

"Yes."

"What had happened that day? Was there anything out of the ordinary?"

She thought back, but the days seemed to run together.

"Buzz says you two are in the same business. Were you working on a particular project?"

"Yes," she remembered. "I hadn't started the project; I was hoping to restore one of the old mansions nearby. The owner had come into my shop."

"Did you know the owner?"

"No. He had just moved from France."

"Did anything unusual happen?"

"Unusual? I don't think so." Then she remembered Tryn's strange behavior. But he had explained that. Then she remembered the same behavior toward Shelby. She had no explanation for that.

Again, just thinking about Tryn sent that strange excitement through her body. She could still feel him next to her, see his lapis eyes as they bore into her.

"Ashley," Clarendon said.

"What?"

"I asked you how you felt about this man."

"Felt?" Ashley squirmed in her chair. "I don't know what you mean."

"Did you feel comfortable with him?"

"Of course. Why wouldn't I?" she said sternly. Why was he asking her this?

Clarendon scribbled a few notes on his pad.

"Ashley," he said. "Could you come back tomorrow? I'd like to do the hypnosis then."

Ashley glanced at Buzz.

Clarendon rose from his chair and walked around his desk. Leaning against it, he folded his hands over his large belly and smiled. "I know it sounds a little frightening."

Ashley shook her head. "At this point, I'd try most anything."

"Good," Clarendon said. "And Buzz, I'd like for you to come too."

"You couldn't keep me away."

Ashley slid her arm around Buzz's. She would leave David Clarendon's house the same way she had entered—with her eyes closed.

Ashley stood out in the front room of Harper's Antiques inspecting several shipments that had arrived from Europe. But all she could think about was Tryn.

"I have a few calls to make," she vaguely heard Buzz announce.

Buzz walked to the back room and called Michael. He described Ashley's meeting with Clarendon and the incident at the piano the night before.

"Michael," he said. "I found her at the piano playing a classical piece like a professional. She has no memory of it. None of this is making sense!"

"No, it isn't," Michael said, sounding a bit preoccupied.

"I'm going to keep her here until we get to the bottom of this," Buzz said.

"Good idea," he agreed readily. "Tell her the DeLore project is under control."

"The DeLore project?" Buzz asked.

"Yeah, it's her pet."

"Sounds interesting. "Who's DeLore?"

"Tryn DeLore. He's from. . . . ."

"France," Buzz interrupted.

"Why . . . yes, how did you know?"

"I've been buying containers of antiques from a Tryn DeLore for years. Michael," Buzz said pensively, "does DeLore know that Ashley is with me?"

"I don't think so. Why?"

"I'm not sure. Let's just keep it that way. I'll call you tomorrow after Ashley's appointment. Oh, and by the way. I'm playing a bit of cupid with Ashley."

"Cupid?" Michael laughed. "Don't waste your time."

"I already have. They're in the front of the shop now, and from what I can hear, carrying on a divine conversation. Scott Trudeau is perfect for Ashley. I've known his family for years."

"My sister is immune to men."

"Just leave her to me," Buzz said.

As Buzz hung up the phone his thoughts went back to DeLore. He thought of the furnishings in his parlor. He had bought every piece from DeLore, and paid handsomely for them.

But what connection could DeLore have with Ashley? As far as he knew, DeLore was not one of her European contacts. He had never mentioned DeLore to her. He wasn't sure why, he just hadn't?

"Scott," Buzz called, emerging from the back room of the shop. "What brings you here?" But knowing full well that his description of Ashley would lure any healthy male for an introduction.

"Wanted to drop by and say hello to you and Les."

"Les is in Charleston. He'll be sorry he missed you. So, business still good?"

"Can't complain."

"I see you and Ashley have met," Buzz said, eyeing her conspiratorially.

"Yes, we have," Scott said. "Where have you been keeping her?"

"If it were up to me, right here in New Orleans. I'm afraid she prefers the west coast."

"I'm from the San Francisco area," she said. "A small town across the bay."

"Not Sausalito, by chance?"

"No, Belvedere. It's across Richardson Bay from Sausalito."

"What a coincidence. I'll be in Sausalito next week opening a new store. How about dinner one night?"

"Why, yes," she said without as much as a thought. "I would like that. I have a shop much like Buzz's. You might enjoy seeing it."

Scott said that he would and asked how long she would be in New Orleans. Buzz chimed in, saying it would be several more days. Ashley glared at him. Scott quickly suggested that they all meet at Arnaud's the next night for dinner. Buzz readily agreed. Ashley smiled, knowing full well what he was up to.

"You said you were opening a new store?" she asked Scott.

"Yes, Trudeau's has been in my family for years. Are you familiar with it?"

"Trudeau's Haute Couture? I never miss it when I come to New Orleans. And you're opening one in Sausalito?"

"Yes," he said proudly.

"That's going to be a strain on my pocket book," she laughed, noticing a certain sparkle to his eyes.

"Well, maybe we could work out a volume discount," he said with a wink.

Scott apologized for having to run and reconfirmed their dinner date for the next night.

ಜಿ

David Clarendon's house was more beautiful than she had remembered. The intricate designs of the black wrought iron fence framed the grounds. Buzz drove through the gates, stopping just under the portico. She held tightly to his arm as they walked toward the porch. Its gallery was supported by eight Corinthian columns. Before they reached the steps she stopped, clutching his arm and looking up at the round attic window. Her body became suddenly rigid. Buzz urged her toward the porch and climbed the dozen steps to where David Clarendon awaited. They followed him through the long hallway and up the staircase.

"Ashley," David said, leading them through the second floor gallery. "Do you feel more comfortable about the hypnosis?"

"Comfortable? She hadn't been comfortable since she and Buzz had driven into the driveway. "No, not really."

"Well, that's to be expected. It's only normal to be a little apprehensive about something you've not experienced. But your willingness to go through the process is what's important."

"I'm as willing as I can be," she sighed, settling into the soft leather chair. "The sooner we get through this the better."

Buzz sat next to her, holding her hand.

"I know these dreams and visions are disturbing, but once we start digging into this puzzle and putting the pieces together . . . well, you just might not find them so disturbing after all."

"If you say so."

Clarendon smiled his reassuring smile. "Now," he continued. "Hypnosis isn't an exact science, in fact, it's not a science at all. There is still much that needs to be studied and learned. Not everyone has the ability to be hypnotized, but from what I've learned about you, you could be a good candidate."

Ashley hung on to Clarendon's every word. This genteel man had managed to ease her apprehensions. But then, she had guessed he would. How could he hypnotize her otherwise?

"Well," she sighed, looking at Buzz, then back to Clarendon's bushy face, "Let's get this over with."

Ashley was escorted to a small room. Before her stood a cubicle of dark, heavy glass. Inside was a leather recliner with a pair of earphones lying across the back. Ashley sat back in the recliner, noticing a small screen in the ceiling. The screen had intertwined black and white geometrical lines in a three dimensional pattern.

David gently placed the earphones over her ears, giving her a reassuring smile.

Ashley settled into the leather recliner, trying to stay calm. She could hear David's voice distantly coming through the earphones.

"Ashley," he said, "I want you to close your eyes and take a deep breath. Deeply now, then let it out slowly, sending with it all the tension in your body."

Ashley responded willingly.

"So relaxed Ashley," David's voice was soft and distant. "So relaxed now that you will be able to close your mind to everything except the sound of my voice. Listen to my voice. Concentrate. Feel the words. Obey them. Do you understand?"

"Yesss."

"There is a screen above you. Open your eyes, gaze at it. Do not take your eyes from it."

Ashley opened her eyes to a dark room with a lighted screen overhead. Inside the screen were geometrical lines moving like waves, entwining continuously.

"The screen is moving into your mind now. The lines are moving in and out of your memory; deeper and deeper. Go with them. They will show you your memories."

David and Buzz watched Ashley on the monitor above the cubicle. So far, she seemed relaxed and undisturbed.

After a few moments of silence, he began again.

"Relaxed, you are so relaxed. Your body is weightlessly floating. Only your mind can see. Do you understand?"

Barely parting her lips, she answered, "Yes."

"We are going on a journey. You will follow a long, narrow path. There will be intervals along the path, doors that you will open. These doors will represent moments in your life, moments that I will ask you to reveal to me. But remember, this time you are not a participant, only an observer. Nothing can harm you. Do you understand?"

"Yes."

"You are walking down the path now. Do you see it?"

"I see it."

"Good. Up ahead is a door. On the other side of the door is when you were very, very young. Open the door now, and remember, you are only an observer. Have you opened the door?"

"I see flowers. Louis is there. He's helping me plant the flowers."

"Who is Louis?" he asked, glancing at Buzz. Buzz shook his head.

"Louis is my friend."

"How old are you?"

"Three."

"Where do you live?"

Silence.

"Ashley, do you know where you live?"

"In a big house."

"Where is your house?"

"Manchester."

"Manchester what?"

"Massachusetts."

David and Buzz looked puzzled.

"What is your name?"

"Ashley Winthrop."

"Where is this house? Do you know the address?"

"I can hear the ocean."

"All right Ashley. I want you to move farther down the path to the time that is in your childhood dream. Are you there?"

"I'm walking up the stairs. They're hard and shiny. I'm looking for my mother. The hallway is dark, but I can see the big doors at the end of the hall. They're open, slightly. I'm calling out for my mother. She doesn't answer. I can see her robe lying over the chair."

Suddenly Ashley jerked upright, clutching the arms of the chair. She sat stiff, motionless, her eyes wide.

"Distance yourself Ashley. Distance."

"A man! He's carrying my mother. He's taking her behind the wall. Mommy!" she screamed. "He's killed my Mommy!"

"Ashley," Clarendon said sternly. "Relax. I want you to relax now. You are calm and relaxed, moving away now, continuing down the path."

Ashley fell back into the chair.

"Now, Ashley. I want you to find the door to Jenny. And remember, only observing. You will not be afraid. Have you found the door?"

"No," she said. "It's not there."

"Why? Why isn't it there?"

"Because. It's, it's . . . " Ashley lifted her hand. "It's back there."

"Is the door behind you?"

"Yes, behind me."

"Turn around then. Go and find the door."

"It's so far. I can barely see it."

"Keep going, you're almost there."

"No, it's too far. I feel heavy. The wind, it's so strong. Pushing me back."

"You can reach the door, Ashley. Reach for the door. Push through the wind. Open the door."

"It's so beautiful," she whispered.

"What's beautiful?"

"Winthrop House."

"Winthrop House?" Buzz looked at David.

"Ashley, do you know what year it is?"

"I'm not sure. 1900, I think."

Buzz let out a muffled gasp. David continued. "Tell me what you see."

"A woman. She's sitting at a piano. And a man. He's playing a cello."

"Are you the woman?"

"No."

"Who are you?"

"Ashley Winthrop."

"Who is the woman?"

"Jenny Winthrop. She's playing the piano. She is sad."

"Buzz whispered to Clarendon. "Ask her what she's playing."

"Ashley, do you know what Jenny is playing."

"The piano."

"No, Ashley, the name of the piece. What is the name?"

"I'm not sure."

"Try, Ashley. You must try to remember."

"She stopped playing," Ashley blurted. "She's talking to the man."

"What is she saying?" David asked, abandoning his previous question.

"Christopher. She called him Christopher. She's crying. He's trying to comfort her."

"Why is she crying?"

"I don't know. The words. I . . . I can't make them out. She's getting up now. They're leaving the room. She's pregnant."

"That's good, Ashley. Can you tell me about the man, Christopher. Is he Jenny's husband?"

"Husband? I . . . I don't think so."

"What is Christopher's last name?"

"Last name? I think . . . Winthrop."

"All right, Ashley. Now I want you to look carefully at the room. Tell me what you see."

"A large screen. With clouds and a green meadow. In the distance is a castle. There's a moat around the castle. To the left of the screen is a fireplace. There are two gold urns, and a large gold mirror."

"Ask her to describe the piano," Buzz whispered.

"That's very good Ashley. Now I want you to look at the piano. Can you describe the piano?"

"It's a grand piano. It's shiny; browns and golds. I can see the chandelier reflecting from its surface."

"Go to the keyboard now and read the name."

"I'm not sure. I think it's 𝕲 . . . 𝖀 . . . .𝕬𝕽𝕯.

Buzz whispered to David. "She's just described the furnishings in my parlor."

David breathed heavily.

"All right, Ashley, we're going to move on now. Just watching though, not participating. Where are you?"

"The attic." Her voice suddenly deepened.

"Distance yourself. Just tell me what you see."

"It's Jenny. She's naked. The men, they've strapped her to a table."

Ashley's breathing was now erratic. She clutched the sides of the chair and screamed, "Stefan!" Then she collapsed into silence.

David quickly instructed her that on the count of five she would wake up refreshed and would remember everything.

"How do you feel?" David asked, leading her back to a chair in his office and easing himself into his leather chair.

Ashley rubbed her forehead. "Strange."

"Do you remember what you saw, what you said?"

"Yes. But, who were those people? And that house. I called it Winthrop House." She looked at Buzz. "That furniture," she said. "It was the same furniture that's in your parlor." She turned to Clarendon. "I don't understand what's happening? That woman. I called her Mommy." Ashley's face twisted in confusion. "Who is Jenny?"

"I'm sorry," Clarendon said. "I didn't know about your mother." He turned to Buzz. "You didn't tell me Ashley lost her mother as a child."

Buzz looked baffled.

"I didn't know I had," Ashley said.

"Possibly, this could mean something else," Clarendon said. "We can't be sure . . ."

"No," Ashley interrupted. "It happened just as I said." She looked at Clarendon, her eyes all but piercing right through him. "My mother is dead. I know she is."

"Well," Clarendon admitted nervously. "Your memories certainly seemed real, and obviously trapped in your subconscious. We've just got to find out why. I certainly understand why you would suppress that particular memory. But that's not all we're dealing with here." Clarendon smiled reassuringly. "I've had many cases of repressed memory. Each has its peculiarities, but most do have resolutions. And in your case I know someone who might be able to shed some light on this. Ever hear of Dr. Will Taylor?"

Ashley shrugged, as if exhausted from her ordeal. "The writer? Who hasn't?"

"I thought so. But Will is not just a writer, he's a genealogist and a professor of history. He hides out at some obscure university up the road in Hattiesburg, Mississippi, of all places. S.M.U.? M.S.U.? U.S.M.? It doesn't matter. At any rate, we were at London University together back in the dark ages and, despite himself, he has emerged as one of the world's leading genealogists. A real hot-shot. Charges a bundle, if one can lure him out of his lair. I'll ring him tonight and see what I can do."

Ashley stared at the floor, a frown creasing her forehead.

"Do you object to our bringing Taylor into this?"

"No," she replied. "It's just . . . I'm afraid he might be too good at what he does. He just might find the key to Pandora's box. I know his reputation. My father introduced me to his books a long time ago. He and Taylor have the same publisher. My father writes law books."

"I see," Clarendon said. "So you know Blake Sheldon."

"Not really. I've only met him a few times. But he's been my father's publisher since he wrote his first book twenty years ago."

Buzz reached over and took Ashley's hand. "Maybe we can solve this whole thing by asking your father about this Winthrop House."

"No!" Ashley said emphatically. "Absolutely not."

"But why?" Buzz asked.

"How can you ask me that? It's obvious that Dad has lied to me all these years. To me and to Michael. And I'm going to find out why."

Ashley turned to Clarendon. "Lure that hot-shot professor out of his lair. We'll see if he is worth all that big money he charges."

ဢ

Ashley was silent as she and Buzz left David Clarendon's and headed back to the Quarter. She felt that her life had been turned inside out, as though she were seeing it from a distance, its fragmented edges exposed. Winthrop House, she mused. Could that have been the house she saw in her childhood dream? The same house where she had walked down that long corridor to her mother's bedroom? Was Winthrop House in Manchester where she said she had lived? If it was, then that would explain why Buzz's furniture had seemed too familiar. But why would her father have lied, having her and Michael believe they had been born in New Orleans? And who was Jenny? And why, or better yet, how could Clarendon pull memories from her of a woman who had lived at Winthrop House back in the 1900's? Memories surfacing from her childhood was one thing. But from almost a hundred years ago? She slumped down in the leather of the Rolls. Stefan. She had been terrified of him. Jenny had been terrified. Ashley cringed at the thought of him. She realized he was the one in that horrifying dream she had had a few weeks back, where she was strapped to that metal table. She had never had that dream before. It was even more terrifying than her childhood dream that had suddenly surfaced after all these years. But it wasn't *her* strapped to the table. She now knew it was Jenny. And Stefan. Who was he? Why would he do such a horrible thing? But the most disturbing thing was that possibly her father, the man she had adored her whole life, knew her mother had been killed. And all these years he would have her thinking that Meno was her real mother. She couldn't bear to believe that.

Massachusetts. Was that where she and Michael had been born? Well, there was one way to find out. She would call Baton Rouge, Louisiana, and Boston, Massachusetts, and ask for a copy of their birth certificates. But did she really want to know? If she had been born in Massachusetts and not Louisiana—if she actually saw this in black and white . . . no, she wouldn't allow herself to even think about that now.

Chapter Seven

The silver Rolls pulled into the carriage way of the old Chartres Street courtyard. Buzz closed the tall double doors and quietly followed Ashley up the stairs. Neither had spoken about her session with Clarendon.

As they entered the foyer, Ashley cautiously advanced into the parlor. She studied each piece: The French sofa, the two velvet grand fauteuils, the gilt urns, the painted screen. She walked to the mantel, ran her fingers over the intricate carvings, then turned and crossed the room to the piano in the far corner. Gliding her hand across its rich surface, she sat down, momentarily caressing the keys. She pressed her fingers into the ivory. Buzz stood by the parlor doors as Ashley began to play Lakmé.

Moments later, she lifted her hands, held them in mid air, then slammed them into the keyboard. The room reverberated like thunder; her body collapsed against the piano. Buzz was immediately at her side.

"I felt her pain," she whimpered, "her sadness."

ဆ

Three hours had passed since she had sat at the piano, Ashley noticed, glancing at the old clock across the bedroom. Her thoughts went to Jenny. Who are you, she pondered despairingly. Why are you torturing me? How strongly she had felt Jenny's pain. She wondered. How had Jenny died, and why did she feel so close to her? What was it that connected them? Was it Winthrop House?

Once again she envisioned the long journey Clarendon had taken her down that dim corridor. She was that child walking down the corridor, in the distance the tall double doors slightly ajar.

She had walked down that corridor. Had seen her mother's lifeless body clutched in the arms of a man. Just like in her torturous childhood dream. Except in her dream there was no corridor, just that man with no face, holding a woman's lifeless body. Was she seeing it for the first time as it had really happened? Not a distorted dream?

And now she knew why she had been running toward the man.

"My precious," Buzz said as he approached the doorway, Mary Harper cradled in his arms. "You have a dinner date in one hour. I suggest you not keep the gentleman waiting."

Ashley looked up at Buzz with a start.

"Yes ma'am," he announced, ignoring her surprise. "Arnauds at eight sharp."

She tried to clear the cobwebs from her head. "What do you mean, 'I'? What happened to we?"

"My darling, something's come up," he said sheepishly. "I'm sure you'll be fine, though. Scott's a perfect gentleman."

Strange, she thought. She was actually looking forward to being alone with Scott.

&

Scott and Ashley left Arnauds around ten and drove downtown to the Top of the Mart for a nightcap. Most of their conversation had been centered around Scott. Ashley had questioned him relentlessly, learning that he lived on Palmer Street, not far off St. Charles in the same house he grew up in. His mother and father had divorced when he was eight. Scott stayed with his father and had begun working in the family store when he was fifteen. Trudeau's had not been the high fashion haute couture it was now. Scott had changed its image in the late seventies shortly after his father's death. He had a knack for merchandising and an elegant sense of style. Trudeau's had seen a twenty percent increase in gross profits within the first year, attracting an entirely different clientele.

Ashley listened intently as Scott talked about his plans to open other stores, finding that she loved watching him, his expressions, that ever present sparkle in those sleepy brown eyes. His dark brown hair was neatly trimmed and combed back from his narrow face. His mouth turned up slightly at one corner as if he were anticipating a smile. It was almost childlike, yet there was a disturbing masculinity that drew her closer, taking her in gradually. She had begun to feel a subtle yet definite attraction toward him. It seemed to blossom, to unfold, the longer she was with him. And being with him now, here, overlooking the Crescent City—she was glad Buzz had not joined them.

As these thoughts flowed through her, they were abruptly shadowed by her memories of Tryn. Her body flooded with warmth, her heart began to race. The memories of him seemed to move outside of her. It was as though that night when Tryn had first taken her was replaying itself. On stage for all to see.

"Ashley?" Scott said touching her shoulder.

Ashley flinched, "I'm so sorry about your father," she blurted. "My father and I are very close. I can't imagine how awful it must have been for you to lose him."

"Why . . . yes, it was."

He must think I've lost my mind, Ashley thought still struggling to push Tryn out of her thoughts.

Scott reached out and took Ashley's hand. "Now that you know my life's story, I'd like to know who Ashley Winthrop is."

The touch of Scott's hand seemed to calm her. She wanted to latch onto it. "Well, let's see," she said, managing composure. "I'm forty, single, a lover of antiques. Buzz and I are both restorers of vintage houses. He's taught me everything I know."

"I doubt that."

Ashley smiled, feeling suddenly awkward.

"And I'd never guess you to be forty. You look twenty."

Ashley smiled. "Thank you, but compliments aren't necessary."

"It wasn't a compliment." He smiled. "So, how do you know Buzz?"

"I used to live here. I was born . . ." she hesitated, realizing suddenly that she was no longer certain where she had been born. In a matter of eight short hours she was not certain of anything.

"You were born where?"

"What? Oh, I'm sorry. I just remembered; I need to call my brother. He's helping with one of my restorations."

"There's a phone in the hall," he said, motioning toward the door and looking concerned.

"No, that's all right, I can wait till tomorrow. Right now, though, we'd better call it a night. This cognac is putting me to sleep."

"I hope it's the cognac and not the company," he said, taking one last sip.

"It is," she smiled, thinking of his southern accent and how Shelby would approve of him. "By the way, do you have any plans for breakfast tomorrow morning?"

"What did you have in mind?"

"Cafe Du Monde. I haven't had beignets since I arrived. I love those evil donuts."

"Is eight-thirty too early? I'll swing by and pick you up."

"Eight-thirty is fine," she replied.

It now dawned on her that she had actually asked Scott for a date.

Ashley heard Mary Harper's soft growl from the upstairs bedroom as she unlocked the front door. She took a deep breath, uncertain of walking through the parlor alone. Had these furnishings been part of her home at one time? That time when she was a small child, planting flowers with Louis? When she walked down that long corridor looking for her mother?

Her mother. She labored the thought. The image in her mind was so vivid—her mother's lifeless body, carried by that faceless man. The wall sliding shut. She could still see it. She had stood in the doorway frozen as she watched her mother disappear behind that wall. Then she had run to the wall. Yes, that's what had happened. It was crystal clear now. She could almost feel the motion, her little legs running across that enormous room. She could feel herself slamming into the wall, her tiny fist bashing against the hard wood. Screaming, screaming for her mother to come back. Then her tiny body, exhausted, crumpled to the floor.

"Oh God!" Ashley cried, falling to the sofa, tears streaming down her face. Moments later Buzz was beside her.

"Honey, what's happened?" he asked, pulling her to him.

"I remembered," she sobbed.

"Remembered?"

"I remembered being there, seeing that man holding my mother." She turned to Buzz, her face covered in tears. "I was there. I was that little girl. I felt it this time." Ashley stared into Buzz's eyes. "I know what happened afterward."

"You do?"

82

Ashley told Buzz in vivid detail how she had run across the room after her mother and how the wall had closed in front of her.

"You didn't remember this during the hypnosis," he said.

"I'm certain," she said glaring. "Margaret is not my mother."

"Ashley!"

"I don't think I ever felt she was. I've never felt close to her."

"But what has Margaret done to make you feel this way?"

"I don't know." Ashley pushed herself from the sofa. "But I'm sure as hell going to find out."

Buzz gently took her arm. "That man. The one carrying your mother. Did you see his face?"

"No, he has no face" Ashley placed her hand on Buzz's shoulder. "Poor Uncle Buzz. Are you sure you want to get involved in this?"

"Don't be ridiculous, I love mysteries," he said, attempting to lighten the moment.

"Yeah," Ashley crossed the parlor, looking back at Buzz. "Margaret Winthrop is not my mother," she said emphatically, disappearing around the corner. "See you in the morning," she called back. "And make sure I'm up by seven, Scott's taking me for beignets."

Mary Harper attempted a growl from inside the bedroom as Ashley passed by.

"Scott," Buzz muttered. "Splendid," and he turned off the light.

ಬಿ

Buzz called Michael the next morning and filled him in on Ashley's session with Clarendon.

"This is outrageous," Michael said. "What in hell is happening to her?"

"I don't know. But she's convinced that Margaret is not your mother, and that your real mother was killed when the two of you were children."

"That's absurd. Don't tell me you believe this."

"Michael. I don't know what to believe. But Dr. Clarendon is one of the best. Ashley's in good hands."

"A hypnotist? I'm not so sure."

"You can count on it."

Buzz then asked Michael if he had any memory of a man named Louis.

"Louis who?"

"I don't know. He was just a man Ashley talked about during her hypnosis."

"I've never heard of him," Michael said impatiently. "Look, why don't I just ask Dad about this Winthrop House."

"No, Michael. Ashley is adamant about that. Let's wait a while longer. She's going back to see Clarendon tomorrow. Oh, and another thing. Have you heard of Dr. Will Taylor?"

"I don't know. I don't think so."

"He's a genealogist and a famous writer of family history. He and Victor have the same publisher."

"So?"

"Well, Clarendon is going to contact Taylor. He thinks Taylor can find out more about this Winthrop House. If it existed and who's lived there."

"You really do believe this stuff, don't you," Michael let out an arduous sigh.

"I don't know what to believe, Michael. But I'm keeping an open mind. I suggest you do the same?"

"All right," Michael capitulated.

Buzz hung up the phone not feeling, in the least, comfortable with his and Michael's conversation.

ಌ

The sweet smell of beignets hovered inside the open-air cafe. Engulfed in his music, the old black man seemed oblivious to the world around him. He played the rhythmic music of the French Quarter through his saxophone. The same music he had no doubt played as a young boy, walking the Quarter and entertaining tourists for change. The locals no longer heard his music. It had long since blended into the everyday, familiar noises that were the flavor of New Orleans' Vieux Carre.

"There's something very special about this place, isn't there?" Ashley was saying to Scott.

84

"I think it's special. I've lived here all my life and still find it charming."

"And the history." Ashley gazed across the open-air cafe. "I've thought for a long time that I'd like to write a novel. New Orleans is the perfect setting. Ghostly and mysterious."

Scott chuckled. "A ghost story?"

"Of course," she smiled, thinking how she loved his laughter. "Know any haunted houses?"

"Isn't that more up yours and Buzz's alley?"

"We restore old houses, not necessarily haunted houses."

"Now that you mention it," Scott recalled, "there is a house uptown. On Camp Street. It covers the entire block between Amelia and Antonine. It's known as the Fink Asylum. I'm surprised Buzz hasn't mentioned it."

"I am too," she said. "It sounds eerie. An asylum?"

"That's what it's always been called. I don't know why."

"Who lives there?"

"No one. It's vacant."

"Vacant? That's odd. I can't imagine why Buzz hasn't mentioned it. He's not one to let grand old houses sit around vacant." Ashley looked thoughtful. "Why don't we do a little snooping. I'd love to see it."

"And I'd love to go snooping around old houses with you. How about my house, tonight, for dinner."

"Your house is haunted?" she asked, forcing back a smile.

"I'll let you be the judge of that. Say around seven?"

Ashley smiled, biting into another powdery beignet. The thought of spending another evening with Scott excited her, that unfamiliar excitement that had only recently surfaced. But why did it seem different with Scott? There was no obsessive, insatiable hunger like with Tryn. This was a gentle, more satisfying emotion.

How much she really did love this old Vieux Carre, she thought, walking down Toulouse Street toward Harper's past the Hotel Mason DeVille. It was a small but quaint hotel, one of the oldest in the Quarter. Tennessee Williams had stayed in one of the courtyard cottages when he wrote A Streetcar Named Desire. She smiled as she passed, thinking of him tucked away in one of those bungalows, overlooking the back courtyard.

Entering Harper's Antiques she noticed that Buzz had just made a sizable sale. He thanked his two customers and promised delivery to their home in Chicago within two weeks. After they left, Ashley immediately questioned him about the Fink Asylum.

"Never heard of it." he said abruptly.

"Now that's a first," Ashley said. "An historic New Orleans home that Buzz Harper's never heard of?"

Buzz pretended to be preoccupied with a three-tiered bronze centerpiece, so Ashley reluctantly dropped the subject.

"I'm having dinner at Scott's house tonight," she announced, hoping to regain his attention.

Buzz's demeanor took a sudden change. "My precious," he said looking up from the bronze piece. "That's wonderful news."

ⅎ

David Clarendon led the way up the wide spiral staircase to his office. This time her eyes remained open as she clutched Buzz's arm and cautiously took each step. Whatever it was about the staircase that was so disconcerting, she had to fight it, not let it take over as it had that first day.

"Ashley," David said, easing into his leather chair and taking a note pad from his desk. He thumbed through several pages, thoughtfully. "I've talked to Will Taylor."

Buzz and Ashley looked anxious.

"Your Winthrop House does exist. And is most probably the same house of your childhood dream. It's in Manchester, Massachusetts, just as you described. It's on the Atlantic. You did hear the ocean. And Will has been interested in the house for years. But he's been working on a lengthy British research project, and I'm afraid it's kept him quite busy. He'll be wrapping that up soon and is anxious to help us. The only other thing he could tell me was of a rumor that it was the oldest structure in Manchester, although there are no records as to when it was built."

"Did he say if anyone lived there?" Buzz asked.

"He doesn't know. But he's anxious to start research on the place. He's uncovered some pretty dirty skeletons with his digging. Ruffled a few feathers."

"I know. I've read his books." Ashley looked sullen. "Afraid I'm next in line. But ruffling feathers doesn't bother me. I need the truth."

"Are you sure the truth is worth disrupting your life for?" Buzz asked.

Ashley grew stern. "You damn right it is."

David quickly assured Ashley that, if anyone could unravel this mystery, Will Taylor could. He informed her of Will's request to learn as much as possible about Jenny Winthrop. The kinds of things that were beyond the reach of a professional genealogist and historian.

"How do we do that?" Ashley asked.

"I'll need to hypnotize you again."

Ashley's body stiffened.

"Ashley, I . . ."

"I know," she interrupted. "Let's get on with it."

Ashley reluctantly settled into the small cubicle. David then took her down the distant and painful path to Jenny.

Soon, Ashley began to whimper, then cried out. "Don't! Don't take her baby!"

"Whose baby?" David asked.

"Jenny's."

"Who's taking Jenny's baby?"

"Those awful people. They're telling her . . . I don't know."

"Are you at Winthrop House?"

Hesitation. "No, I'm at Bartlington Hall. In the servant's quarters."

"Where is Bartlington Hall?"

"London. It's in London. Something has happened to Jenny's family. Those people, they're taking her away, she's screaming for her baby. Wait, she's giving them something."

"Who?" David said. "Giving who something?"

"It's a locket." Ashley stopped for a moment and reached out. "A gold locket with tiny pearls in the center." She brought her hand back to her lap. "She's telling the woman that's holding her baby—she wants her baby to have the locket. The woman's taking it. She's leaving—disappearing down the back stairs. They're taking Jenny now, out the other way. She's sobbing. I can't stand it!"

"It's all right, Ashley. You must try and distance yourself more. We need to find out what happened to Jenny. Can you help us do that?"

"I'll try."

"All right then, can you tell me what year it is or how old Jenny is?"

"I'm not sure, 1887, 88. Those people, I think they were telling her she was too young, that she couldn't take care of her baby."

"Is Jenny married?"

"Married? No, I don't think so."

"What is her last name?"

Silence.

"Think, Ashley. What is Jenny's last name?"

"R . . .", hesitation, "Arden," she blurted. "Her name is Jenny Arden."

"Good. Very good. Now, can you tell me where they took Jenny?"

Ashley's restlessness escalated.

"Distance, Ashley," Clarendon warned. "Where are you now?"

"Nine Thornton Square." Her voice was deep and jaded.

"Where is Nine Thornton Square?"

"In London. Oh God, it's horrible. The men—they make her do awful things."

"Do you see Jenny?"

"Yes, she's in this beautiful room. She's lying on the bed crying, calling someone's name. Stefan, she's calling for Stefan. Someone's coming in the room. It's a woman. And a man. He's walking toward her. Jenny is running to him. It's Stefan. He's saying that he's going to take her away with him, that they're going to be married. She's so happy."

"Ashley," David asked gently, "Who is Stefan?"

"A wonderful man. He's going to save Jenny from that horrible place. He's going to marry her, take her home with him."

"Take her where, Ashley? Where is home?"

"The United States."

"Ashley, tell me about Stefan. Who is he? Where does he live?"

"Stefan Winthrop. He lives at Winthrop House."

David looked at Buzz. "I think we have what we need. I don't want to keep her under any longer."

Ashley walked from the cubicle, stopping just short of David's desk. She gazed down at the floor. "Why?" She looked up at David. "How can I know these things?"

David took Ashley's arm. "Come over here and sit down."

Buzz and Ashley settled into the two chairs across from David's desk.

"How much did you tell Will Taylor about Ashley?" Buzz asked.

"Everything. And he's very interested. In fact, he said he'd take the case pro bono."

ജ

"What are you thinking?" Buzz asked as he turned onto St. Charles Avenue.

"Thinking?" she replied, looking out at the old mansions as the car swept past. "That I haven't called Michael since I've been here."

"Michael? There's no need. I've talked to him. Your DeLore project is progressing nicely."

"Have you told him about all of this?"

"Yes."

"And?"

"He's concerned about you."

"You told him not to tell Dad? Didn't you?"

"Yes," Buzz said, patting her hand.

"Michael must think I've lost my mind."

Buzz didn't respond.

Ashley slumped down into the leather seat. "Why wouldn't Dad tell us the truth?"

"Precious, there's no use in second guessing any of this."

"Why isn't Michael having dreams or memories? We're twins. Why is it only me?" Ashley glared at Buzz. "What if Michael isn't my brother."

"Ashley!"

"How do I know?"

89

"Honey, of course Michael's your brother. I don't want to hear any more of that talk."

"I am going to find the truth. I don't care what it takes."

༺༻

Scott and Ashley sped down St. Charles in his Lincoln Continental past the streetcars and nineteenth-century mansions, then turned onto Palmer. Lined by a gallimaufry of houses, it too offered long ago architectures of clapboard, stucco, and brick facades. Scott turned into the driveway.

"What a lovely house," she said, gazing up at the modest three story structure.

"Thanks," he replied. "Lived here all my life." Scott walked around and opened her door.

"Victorian Queen Ann. It doesn't look very haunted to me," she smiled, taking his hand. "It looks loved and cared for."

"It is," he said, escorting her up the dozen steps and onto a curved porch supported by three columns at each corner. To the left of the porch was a three story octagonal tower with patterned wooden shingles. The door was typically New Orleans with heavy leaded and beveled glass. "My father loved this house. He treated it like a fine piece of art."

As they approached the door, the beveled glass caught the dance of the gaslights on either side, radiating a kaleidoscope of color.

"San Francisco may have its views, but it will never capture the essence of New Orleans." She looked at Scott. "Or the people. This city has a way of seducing you."

"Yes. Doesn't it." He turned and unlocked the door.

Ashley stood behind him, wondering about literally being seduced in New Orleans. The thought brought back the memory of Tryn and that overwhelming hunger. Her body, once again, seemed to come alive. She leaned against the doorway and took a long deep breath. Scott pushed the door open and turned on the lights. Ashley took another long breath and walked in.

"It's beautiful," she said, entering the moderate sized hallway. The staircase spiraled all the way to the third floor, interrupted only slightly by an entrance to the second floor. The plaster walls were the shade of wheat fields just before dusk. The floors were planked with cherry wood.

"Look around," he said, motioning her into the living room. "I have to get Jocque and MacDougle."

"Who?"

Scott laughed. "I'm a dog lover too. They're my Scotties and almost as spoiled as Mary Harper."

"Should I be concerned?"

"Not in the least. They'll fall all over you."

Ashley noticed a subtle smile as Scott disappeared down the hallway.

Turning toward the living room which was decorated in dusty rose, she walked across the two patterned carpets covering part of the cherry wood planks. The thought of Tryn still haunted her mind, and that hunger, she couldn't shake it. As she forced her attention out across the living room she realized that her hand was resting on her breast, her fingers gently circling her nipple. Quickly she took her hand away, hiding it behind her like a naughty child caught in the act. Her eyes darted around the room frantically, but there was no one there. Ashley let out a long sigh of relief, feeling overtly foolish. Determined to wipe all thought of Tryn from her mind, she focused her attention on the antique furnishings. They were mostly empire style. Yes, she thought, very handsome. Masculine. Not overly expensive, but in good taste.

Ashley kept her focus on the house and the furnishings as she walked through the living room and into a small study. One wall was lined in bookshelves, the other featured a dark green marble fireplace. Above it hung a portrait of a man and a young boy. The man was seated in a high-back leather chair with the boy standing at his side. At the man's feet were two black Scottish terriers in plaid coats.

This must be Scott and his father, she thought, stepping closer to get a better look. Tears came to her eyes as she thought of Scott's father, and the thought of her own father came to her. She pictured his tall and elegant physique, those piercing yet loving blue eyes. And that perfect face, as though sculptured down to the finest detail. Not even time, working its subtle deterioration, had yet to take away his good looks entirely. His body still held its height and masculinity. She wondered how it would feel to be held in his embrace, smothered in his passion. She quickly turned from the portrait, realizing that she was fantasizing about her own father. The thought frightened her.

She then thought of Margaret. Somehow, she reflected, Margaret must have lured her father into this life of deceit. For whatever reason, Margaret was to blame, not her father.

Ashley forced these disturbing thoughts from her mind and continued browsing around the library. There were pictures of Scott from infancy to college. She saw that he had graduated from Tulane University and had received a master's degree in Business. His diploma read: Bradley Scott Trudeau. What a wonderful name. She loved the sound of it. Just then two Scottish terriers came racing into the room, running in circles, barking at the top of their lungs. Then they stopped and plopped themselves down in the middle of the oriental carpet with their tongues hanging out.

Ashley was leaning against the bookshelf in laughter, as Scott walked through the doorway. "Well, I see you've met Jocque and MacDougle."

"Yes, I guess I have." She knelt down between them. "Now, which one of you is Jocque and which is MacDougle?"

"Jocque has the green plaid collar, MacDougle the red. MacDougle has a slight weight problem." Scott looked up at the portrait. "They are the great grandsons of Brandon and Maize."

Ashley stroked their long black beards. "Well, I must say, you two have the same aristocratic quality as your great grandparents." Jocque and MacDougle nuzzled in closer.

"It looks like my pups have taken to you," Scott said, as he placed two long-stem glasses on the small bar that was just to the right of the doorway. "That's a sign of good character."

"Your pups are very wise," she said, sliding onto one of the bar stools. The Scotties were stretched out at her feet.

"To a beautiful lady who looks half her age."

Ashley lowered her eyes and smiled, thinking how good it felt to be near Scott. "I wouldn't mind looking a little older than twenty." She then tipped her glass to his.

"Let me help with something," Ashley said as they left the library for the kitchen.

"All right. You can make the salad while I dazzle you with culinary skills."

"That sounds interesting," Ashley said.

"It could be." Scott smiled and pointed to the refrigerator. "You'll find the salad fixings in the bottom drawer."

"Where did you learn to cook?" Ashley asked, as she ran water into the bib lettuce.

"Self taught," he replied, pointing to a row of cookbooks lining a portion of a small counter top. "My father had no interest. I was the odd man out. It's called survival."

Ashley looked back at Scott lovingly, as he sliced through several cloves of garlic with deft speed, realizing that she had been waiting an eternity for this man. She wanted to consume him, wrap herself in his masculine gentleness. She turned from the sink, her hands still wet from the lettuce. Scott stood at the chopping block, diligently working. Ashley leaned back against the counter. She watched him, and all the while wanting to touch him. Wishing he would take her as Tryn had done. Yet that debilitating hunger that had consumed her with Tryn wasn't present with Scott. She felt consumed. Oh yes. Passionately so. But a peaceful and loving passion.

Ashley's reverie was suddenly broken. She could feel the softness of Scott's face next to hers. His arms straddled her as he braced himself against the counter, his hands still covered in garlic. She was lost momentarily in the shock of feeling him. And then her body went limp, as he gently pressed his mouth on hers. She tried to lift her arms to embrace him, but they had lost their strength. Never could she have imagined what she was now experiencing. His gentleness, his smell. Nothing had ever felt so good.

Scott smiled and pushed himself back. "I'm glad I met you, Ashley Winthrop."

"Me too," she whispered.

"Are you hungry?" He turned his attention back to the chopping block.

"Hungry?"

Scott had prepared Orange Roughy with a sherry prawn sauce, roasted potatoes and a Boston bib salad with a creamy vinaigrette dressing. Ashley praised the meal excessively. Jocque and MacDougle had not left Ashley's side since their first meeting, following her every step.

"It seems that my pups have forsaken me," he said, walking out into the courtyard.

Ashley was a few steps ahead. She turned, bringing the glass of cognac to her lips.

Scott hesitated, noticing the subtle change that had suddenly taken her. He remained still, at a distance, watching her curiously. How beautiful she was, he thought, her long chestnut hair cascading over her left shoulder, caressing her breast. Her hair glistened with each dance of the gaslights. Her tall, slender body held a grace and elegance that had captured him the first time he had laid eyes on her.

"Make love to me," she whispered pleadingly. Her eyes had now taken him, caressing him as he walked toward her as in a dream. The brandy snifter he clutched fell from his hand. He reached out and took her glass, releasing it onto the moss covered bricks.

She could vaguely hear the distant sound of the jazz saxophone through the intercom as he carried her up the stairway. His closeness, his scent; it was as she had envisioned. She wanted to smother herself in him.

Scott carried her down the long hall toward a curved double doorway. The doors were partially open, revealing a sitting room of Empire and Queen Anne-style furnishings. The room had a subtle glow from the dancing flames, coming from the marble fireplace. At the far end of the room stood a rice-carved four poster bed.

Scott lowered Ashley to her feet. Gently he swept her hair from her face and touched his lips to hers. With a murmured, "yes," she took him into her arms, their mouths hungry.

His hands were touching her now. Within moments she stood naked and feeling his gentle kiss on her stomach, then down to the soft patch of hair between her legs. He lifted her onto the bed. Her breasts now revealed for him to see, to caress. Her legs begged to be spread. She desperately wanted to open herself for him.

He stood over her, still clad in his ivory sweater and brown slacks. Then he sat down beside her, brushed a fallen strand of hair from her face, and gently ran his fingers across her lips. His hands followed the curve of her face and down her slender neck. He stared intently at her, then pushed her arms over her head. Again his hands moved down her body, as his mouth found her nipples. He sucked her gently, discovering her with his tongue.

She was gasping in the pleasure, suddenly feeling his teeth on her hard nipples. She screamed out, begging him to enter her, needing it desperately. He ignored her pleas. Again his mouth urgently found hers. They tore at each other—Ashley begging for him. Then suddenly he put his arm beneath her and turned her over. She felt his hands caressing her back. With lingering strokes his hands found the crease of her buttocks. Gently, exigently, he fondled her wet sex. Ashley clutched the sheets, almost ripping them from the bed, while he continued to explore her. Then he parted her legs slightly. She felt his mouth, his tongue. She gasped aloud.

He rose from the bed and began to undress, taking his time while his eyes gazed at her. She knew he was taking pleasure in making her wait.

It was then that she felt Scott's naked body. She wanted desperately to see him, to touch him as he had touched her.

She felt him kneel down between her legs, spreading them wide apart. She moaned in an agony of pleasure as his fingers stroked her soft wet crevice. He caressed her knowingly, while she begged for him. Then finally she felt his knees pressing hard against the inside of her thighs as he spread her further, lifting her to her knees. He entered slowly, filling her.

In only seconds Ashley's body came alive with orgasm. He pulled out suddenly and quickly turned her over, thrusting deep inside her. Ashley wrapped her arms and legs around him as he entered her again and again.

Scott fell exhausted. Arms and legs entwined, they lay clutched to each other as the lazy fire cast shadows on the ceiling. Their breathing was soft and comfortable, as they drifted in and out of sleep. The jazz from the intercom filled the room with languid euphony.

"Did this really happen?" Ashley asked, breaking the silence. Scott reached over and gave her a lingering kiss, then sat up against the back of the bed, keeping her in his grasp.

"It did."

Ashley snuggled into the soft curly hair of his chest, wanting to feel nothing again but the serenity of this moment. She looked up, seeing that Scott was staring across the room, the reflection from the fire dancing in his eyes.

He drew her closer.

ॐ

Where was she? she thought, as fear seemed to hover over her. In desperation she looked around. Off in the distance she could see Scott through the murkiness spiraling before her. She tried to call out, but her throat was paralyzed. Then suddenly, she heard his voice. Why was he so far away? she thought, straining to see through the heavy cloud.

She gasped. Smoke! She struggled to comprehend what was before her. Again and again she screamed, but her screams failed to penetrate the darkness. Fear raging inside her, she tried to force the cries from her throat.

She could hear him calling her. How desperately she wanted to answer. Oh please! I'm over here. Please help me. Stefan!

Ashley awoke with a jolt, her body drenched with sweat.

Scott was holding her. "Ashley," he said. "It's all right. You were just dreaming."

She wrapped herself around him. What is happening to me, she screamed inwardly. Scott gently lowered her back onto the bed. "It was only a dream," he said, kissing her face.

"You must think I'm mad," she said, trembling.

"I find your madness beguiling. Would you like to tell me about the dream?"

"I'm not sure I can," she whispered. "It seems so vague now." She looked away. "I was in this building. There was smoke all around me."

"There's nothing to be scared of now." He held her close.

"I'm sorry, I don't usually act so unbalanced." Unbalanced? She had been acting unbalanced for the last week.

"Don't be silly, you had a bad dream. That's all." He kissed her cheek, cradling her in his arms. The hot embers from the fireplace exuded a bright orange glow.

His nakedness sent a surge of desire through her again. Why was she feeling such emotion after a near lifetime without it?

Chapter Eight

Shelby was sitting in her real estate office going over several pending contracts, wondering if she should call Ashley. It had been several days now since Ashley had gone to New Orleans. Michael had told Shelby about the dreams. And for Ashley to suddenly abandon her prize DeLore project . . . well, there was more to this than just dreams. She had been trying to find Michael since yesterday, but no one seemed to know where he was.

Shelby picked up the phone to call Buzz. As she dialed the last number she thought she heard a noise coming from the front office. She looked at her watch and wondered who would be coming in at such a late hour.

"Hello," she called out. Shelby's office was located in the far corner of the building which made it impossible for her to see the reception area. Just as she heard Helen announce, "Mr. Harper's residence," she saw a figure pass her doorway. "Hello," she called again, mindlessly placing the phone on the desk. "Who's there?" She walked to the door and peered down the dark hallway but saw nothing. The other three offices lay in darkness. Maybe I just imagined it, she thought, turning back to her desk and realizing that she had not hung up the phone. She could hear Helen's voice coming from the receiver.

Before she could get to the phone or even utter a sound, she felt the force of something tight wrapping around her throat. She gasped, trying desperately to scream, but her throat grew tighter as she fought for air. Frantically yet helplessly, her arms thrashing about, she felt something being forced over her head. "No!" she cried, fighting desperately, the thing around her throat sinking further into her flesh. And then came blackness.

The phone was carefully placed back in its cradle.

The streets of Tiburon were virtually empty. No one paid the least attention to the car as it pulled away.

৪১

The bedroom lay dark and still, empty in its silence. Michael gazed out toward the distant lights, the darkness concealing his nakedness. He heard footsteps. His senses heightened.

The wick of the oil lamp suddenly ignited, piercing the darkness, filling the room with its eerie shadow-dance. The nebulous figure moved into the fiery glow of the lamp. His smooth, taut skin seemed also to ignite, glowing within the restless flame.

"Come closer, Michael." His voice was deep yet whispered. "Come closer to the flame."

Michael drew a long, agonizing breath as a rush of desire swept over him. He felt strange and awkward. His sex ached. The pleasure of it seemed exhausting, unbearable. Why was he standing here like this? Naked, and desiring another man. It was insane, preposterous, that he would have these feelings. How had he let it happen? Why was it happening?

Slowly, Michael entered into the fiery dance of the lamp.

"Good, Michael," he said. "I want to look at you." He paused while he regarded Michael's body "There is beauty in what I see. It makes me want to touch you, to feel you in my hands. Fondle you. But I will wait for these pleasures. I will first take you with my eyes, feel you, taste you, and fantasize of all the things I will do to you."

"Yes," Michael whispered, surrendering to the hypnotic gaze.

"You are my virgin," he said. "You have never been with a man, have you, Michael?"

"No," he answered, as if obeying a command.

He then pressed his cheek against Michael's and whispered, "I will give you pleasures far beyond your wildest dreams. Show you things you cannot even imagine. And I will watch you squirm in bliss."

Slowly, deliberately, the figure withdrew. "I see that I have already given you pleasure." A smile rising on his lips, his eyes met Michael's. "You are hard."

"Yes," Michael whispered.

Again he drew close. Michael could feel the strange man's presence drawing him in, luring him. Michael wanted to open his arms in surrender.

"How young and handsome you still are," he said, stroking Michael's face. He ran his fingers down the strong jawbone, following the contour of his chin. Then he gently glided his fingers across Michael's soft, eager lips. "How tragic, for such beauty to deteriorate. He lowered his hand, gliding his fingers down Michael's neck and across his chest. "There is still strength in this healthy body. I can feel its power. How pathetic for one to lose it. To slowly watch it lapse into decay."

He lowered his hand and clutched Michael's hard penis. Michael flinched, gasping in its rapture.

"Tryn," he sighed.

ↄ

The next morning Ashley sat quietly as Scott drove down St. Charles Avenue toward the French Quarter. She suddenly felt a strange foreboding that something terrible had happened. Minutes later, they pulled up in front of Buzz's house.

Buzz greeted them with a somber face.

"Could you stay a minute?" he asked Scott.

"Of course," he replied, seeing the grave expression on Buzz's face.

Ashley felt paralyzed. Her fears had been real. Something terrible had happened.

"Buzz. What's wrong?"

"I'm afraid I have some distressing news."

Ashley felt her heart suddenly stop. Scott reached over and took her hand.

"It's Shelby, honey."

"What?" She glared at Buzz. "What do you mean?"

"She's in the hospital."

"Hospital?" She squeezed Scott's hand.

"Honey, Shelby was assaulted."

"Assaulted?"

Buzz hesitant. "She was raped."

"No! Oh God! No." Ashley burst into tears. "Why? How!"

"Nobody knows," Buzz replied gravely. "She was found in a ravine somewhere between Sausalito and the Golden Gate."

Scott turned to Buzz looking somewhat confused. Buzz realized that Scott had no idea who Shelby was.

"Ashley and Shelby grew up together."

"She's going to be all right, isn't she?" he asked.

Silence.

"Well . . . she is, isn't she?" Ashley said anxiously.

"They're not sure. She—she still hasn't regained consciousness."

"She's unconscious!"

"I'm afraid so."

Ashley pressed her face into her hands. "When did it happen?"

"Last night. They found her this morning."

"I have to go," and she started for the hallway.

"I'll go with you," Scott said. "I have to be in Sausalito in a couple of days anyway."

Buzz looked at Scott and managed a smile.

Ashley went to Buzz and put her arms around him. "I couldn't bear it if anything happens to Shelby."

"Shelby's a fighter," Buzz reminded her.

"I know."

"My prayers are with her." Buzz took Ashley's face in his hands. "Promise me that you will come back as soon as possible."

"We'll see," she replied. But coming back to New Orleans was the last thing on her mind.

છ

Buzz called Belvedere Designs to inform Stanley of Ashley's arrival. He had not been able to reach Michael who was working at the DeLore Mansion and wasn't expected back that day. The new receptionist told Buzz that Stanley was out working with a client in Santa Rosa. She assured him that she would give Stanley the message when he returned.

Scott and Ashley arrived at San Francisco General Hospital around five. As they entered the private room, they saw Margaret sitting next to the bed, her head resting against her arm. She was clutching Shelby's hand, crying.

Ashley stood in the doorway, her eyes filled with tears. She felt Scott's comforting hands on her shoulders as she walked toward the bed. Shelby lay still and silent, her face swollen, her head wrapped in bandages. This can't be Shelby, she thought, this lifeless body. She reached down, taking Shelby's hand.

"Ashley," Margaret said, startled, her face puffy from crying.

Ashley ignored Margaret.

"Oh, Shelby," Ashley sighed, tears streaming down her face.

Scott quietly went to Margaret. "I'm Scott Trudeau," he said. "I'm a good friend of Buzz Harper's."

Margaret graciously took his hand. "It's nice to meet you." She wiped the tears from her face. "Buzz is a dear friend of ours. I'm Margaret Winthrop, Ashley's mother."

"I'm so sorry about Shelby," Scott said, thinking how much Ashley resembled her mother. "Ashley told me how close they are."

Margaret smiled "Yes," she sighed, turning back to Shelby.

Ashley was now sitting on the side of the bed, talking earnestly to Shelby as though she could hear every word.

"You're going to be all right," she said. "You're a fighter. Do you hear me? A fighter. That animal couldn't have taken that from you. You can't give up. I won't let you."

Ashley ran her fingers over Shelby's bruised and swollen face. "Oh, Shel," she sobbed. "I love you so much." She finally looked at Margaret. "What did the doctor say?"

"He's not saying much, honey. Just that every day she stays like this is one more day of lost hope."

Stop calling me honey, she wanted to scream. "He actually said that! That's cruel, it's absurd!"

"Well, he didn't put it in those words. He didn't have too."

"Well, it's not true."

That night Ashley insisted on staying at the hospital. She'd be damned if she was going to let Shelby die. She would talk her back to life if she had to.

It was close to nine o'clock. Ashley had been talking endlessly, desperate for even a small sign that Shelby knew she was there. Whatever it took, she was not going to let her die within this cataleptic darkness.

The phone's ring jolted her. She quickly reached out, hoping it was Michael, not Meno, the last person she wanted to talk to. She couldn't understand why her brother hadn't been by or called.

"Hello," she answered. "Scott."

"Hi. Just thought I'd see how you're doing."

"I'm still having trouble believing this has happened."

"I know. I'm here if you need me, though." He gave her the number of the Casa Madrona. "I'm in the Petite Boudoir," he laughed, hoping to lighten her gloom.

She managed a slight tone of amusement. "You're kidding."

"No. That's what they call it."

"I know. I designed it."

Scott laughed. "Now why am I not surprised?"

"All the rooms were designed by different designers," she said. "I was involved in a big restoration at the time, so I chose one of the smaller ones. How do you like it?"

"Better if you were in it."

"I wish I could be."

"I hope you're planning on getting some sleep," he said. "You're no good to Shelby if you get sick."

"I'll do my best. Would you do something for me, though?"

"Just name it."

"I'll need to go to my apartment some time tomorrow."

"I'll be at the hospital first thing in the morning."

Ashley hung up the phone and looked over at Shelby. Nothing, just stillness. She leaned back in the chair and closed her eyes, feeling Scott next to her. Even in his absence she could still feel him, his gentleness, his passion as he swallowed her up in his embrace. He was taking her completely.

That night her dreams were strange and dark, filled with terror. She could see Shelby running down a long corridor.

Running and running, then disappearing into a forest of tall eucalyptus trees. Faster and faster she ran, stumbling on the stripped bark scattered on the forest floor. Her screams echoed through the endless maze of towering trees. Suddenly the trees began to sway. Undulating as they melted into a swirl of mist and fog, rising up from the ocean's depths. Shelby's faceless body appeared, slowly spiraling up through the eye of the swirl, then down again her twisted body slamming against the massive trunk of the eucalyptus. Her agonizing screams tore through the forest as her body, twisted and torn, lay sprawled on the forest floor. Ashley screamed out, feeling her body being pulled downward, heavy hands invading her. Desperately she fought to get free of this forceful presence, but the more she struggled the stronger it became, squeezing the life out of her.

Ashley bolted upright at the sound of the phone. Where was she? The persistent ringing forced her from the rollaway bed and to Shelby, hoping that she was wide-eyed and alive. But nothing. Shelby lay still, her eyes shut against the world.

Clumsily, Ashley reached for the phone. "Michael? she said. "I almost didn't recognize your voice. Where in the hell have you been?"

"I've been working," he said irritably.

"How can you work at a time like this?"

Silence.

"Michael? What's wrong with you?"

"Nothing's wrong with me," he said irritably.

A long sigh. "Tell me what happened," Ashley said. "Where was Shelby when this happened?"

"We're not sure. She could have been at her office. A couple of hikers found her."

"Hikers! What do you mean, hikers? Found her where?"

Hesitation.

"Michael. Stop it. Found her where?"

"By the eucalyptus trees. Just below Spencer Avenue in Sausalito. Her head had been covered with a heavy cloth and taped around her neck."

"What!" Ashley suddenly thought of her dream: Shelby's faceless body, the eucalyptus trees, the bark on the forest floor. "Couldn't the bastard even look at her while he raped her!"

Michael didn't respond.

"The police sure as hell better find out who did this," she said, looking over at Shelby. The nurse had just walked in and was checking the monitors as she had done off and on through the night. "That Goddamn bastard," Ashley blurted.

Silence.

"Michael."

"What."

"We've got to talk about Meno. I can't stand being in the same room with that woman."

"Ashley, for God's sake. You really believe this stuff, don't you. This hypnosis thing."

"Of course I believe it. But it's not just that. I remembered things after hypnosis. I actually remembered being there. I saw our mother."

"Then you know what she looks like?"

"Looks like? No. I just know it was her."

"Then it could have been Meno."

"NO! The woman in that man's arms was dead."

"How can you possibly know that? It could—"

"Michael." She cut him off. "Winthrop House is not a figment of my imagination. It exists. We know that."

"We?"

"Yes. A friend of Dr. Clarendon's, a Dr. Taylor. He's a famous writer, a genealogist and professor of history. He knows of the place. It's in Manchester, Massachusetts, just like I said it was. Michael, these dreams are real. And I can't explain how I knew my mother was dead. I just knew."

"All right Ashley," he conceded.

But Ashley knew she hadn't convinced him of anything.

"I hear you've been seeing some guy named Scott?" Michael said. "Is my sister suddenly getting horny after all these years?"

"What!"

"Well, you did spend the night with him. Didn't you?"

"What's gotten into you," Ashley said incredulously.

"You don't want to tell me about it?"

"No!"

"Too bad. I'd love to hear it. In detail."

"Shut up Michael."

"Sorry. I didn't mean to ruffle your feathers."

Ashley was bewildered. Michael had never talked to her this way. "What's happening with the DeLore project?" she asked, wanting to change the subject.

"DeLore? Huh, It's . . . the restoration's fine. You don't have to concern yourself with it."

"I don't? Why?"

"Stanley and I have it under control. They're already running electrical lines, and a phone line. The plumbing's next. Stanley's talented. And he has your good taste."

"Then Tryn hasn't asked about me?" The thought of going back to that house and seeing Tryn frightened her. Just thinking about him gave her that feeling of being out of control, vulnerable to the influence he seemed to have over her.

"Not a word," Michael replied. "Stanley has a lot more time now that he's hired Karen. You'll like her. She's good with the customers. So," he asked, "when do I get to meet your new love?"

"I'm not so sure I want you to," she said. "But if you'd show a little more concern for Shelby and come to the hospital you'll meet him."

"He's here?"

"Yes. He's opening a store in Sausalito."

"How convenient."

"Good-bye, Michael," she said, determined not to prolong the conversation.

Ashley sat next to Shelby, massaging her arms and legs. The nurses had advised that keeping Shelby's body stimulated and repositioned was very important. She had just turned Shelby onto her side when Margaret walked in.

"Hi honey," she said to Ashley, walking to the other side of the bed.

Ashley began rubbing Shelby's back as though Margaret had not spoken. Margaret reached out and touched Shelby's face. Tears began to well in her eyes.

"I'll never forget," she said, glancing over at Ashley, "when you were lying here much like this, so still and lifeless."

Ashley flinched.

"You were only seven. So young and fragile. You had come down with pneumonia. Your fever was high. The doctors couldn't seem to get it down. I would sit by your hospital bed for hours, bathing you in cold compresses."

Margaret wiped the tears from her checks, her gray-and-auburn hair clumsily twisted at the nape of her neck. Several strands had fallen, now clinging to the side of her tear-streaked face.

"I prayed and prayed," she continued. "Then, that last day, you had been delirious. Just before you woke up you called out, 'Mama'. You had not called me that in a very long time. And you haven't since."

Ashley nervously straightened Shelby's gown.

"I would not have been able to go on if I had lost you," Margaret said. "You were a gift from heaven. You will never know what you mean to me." Margaret looked into Ashley's sullen face. "You never have." She bent over, kissed Shelby gently on both cheeks, and left the room.

Moments later, Scott walked in. Ashley was sitting by the bed, staring into space.

"Ashley," he said, gently taking her shoulders.

"What?" She turned, gazing up at him as though he were some stranger.

"Honey," he said.

"Scott," she blurted, letting out a long sigh. She rubbed her forehead, still thinking of what Meno had said. "I'm a little foggy, I guess."

Scott looked over at Shelby. "I know how horrible this is."

"Yes," she said, "you would, wouldn't you," thinking of Scott's father and wishing that Scott would just take her in his arms.

"Tell me about Shelby," he said, as he scooted onto the bed. "What is she like under all that darkness?"

"A real firecracker," she said, smiling down at Shelby's lifeless form. "Full of life and curiosity. Everybody's friend. Just look around this room. Have you ever seen so many flowers?"

"No, I haven't." He took Shelby's hand. "My name is Scott. It's nice to meet you. Ashley tells me that you'll be well soon." He released her hand and leaned down, kissing her gently.

It was then that Ashley noticed Shelby's hand move. Only slightly, but it had moved.

"Scott!" she cried. "Her hand."

Scott looked down at Shelby's hand. It lay still.

"I saw it move. When you kissed her. Only a little, but it moved."

Scott rose from the bed and pulled Ashley to him. For a long moment he just held her close.

Ashley pressed her face against his chest, thinking how safe he made her feel. He was actually giving her a glimmer of hope.

"I talked to your mother," he said finally.

Ashley stiffened. "What?"

"She was outside in the waiting room. She said she would stay until you got back."

"Then we'd better go." She reached over and kissed Shelby. "I'll be back."

❧

As Scott and Ashley pulled up in front of her studio, Ashley noticed Tryn's Jag parked a short distance away. Ashley tensed.

"What's wrong?" Scott asked, noticing this.

"Wrong?"

"You're shaking," he said pulling up to the curb.

"It's nothing. I'm just tired. Didn't get much sleep last night. You know, the nurses coming in and out."

"Are you sure?"

"Of course. Don't look so serious." She reached over and fumbled with the door handle.

Scott followed Ashley to the studio door. Her body shivered as a cold dread swept through her. She breathed deeply and entered the studio.

Stanley had cleared away several pieces of furniture, making a small reception area. There was a large French writing table and chair just to the left of the door where a young woman now sat with a phone and an appointment book. A gold four-arm candelabra that had been converted into a lamp stood at one corner of the desk. The effect was charming yet professional.

The woman looked up as Ashley and Scott entered. Ashley stopped in mid stride.

"I feel like I'm in someone else's studio," she said, viewing Stanley's handiwork. She studied it, then turned. "You must be Karen." Karen was pretty, her face sweet and delicate. She wore her golden brown hair in a Gibson Girl style with soft strands falling loose around her face.

"Yes, and I'd know you anywhere," Karen said, rising. "Stanley has described you to a 'T.'"

"I'm sure he has," she smiled accepting Karen's hand. "Oh," she said, turning to Scott. "This is Scott Trudeau."

"Nice to meet you, Karen."

"And I'm delighted to make your acquaintance as well, sir."

"Scott's a friend of mine from New Orleans."

"New Orleans, that's right," she said to Ashley. "Stanley said you were originally from New Orleans." Karen sighed. "The mystical city. I love it there. Except during Mardi Gras. Then it's wall to wall drunks and naked people. Most of whom are not very attractive."

"You're too kind, Karen," Scott laughed. "I think grotesque would better describe it."

"You're right. I'm afraid there are some people better left dressed."

"Karen, isn't that Mr. DeLore's car out front?" Ashley said.

"Yes, it is," Tryn said, walking from the back of the studio, his gold-handled walking stick tapping the planked floor as he approached.

Ashley froze.

"It's good to have you back," he said, drawing closer to her.

She could feel her heart pounding as he reached out and stroked the side of her arm.

"Michael and I have missed you." Tryn seemed vaguely and inexplicably amused. He glanced over at Scott. "You will approve of the progress Michael and your associate have made in your absence," he said to Ashley, while still holding Scott in his gaze.

Then he turned and pointed his walking stick toward the back of the studio. "I'd like the buffet delivered tomorrow morning, Karen." He turned back to Ashley. "You're right, it's perfect for my foyer." Again he looked at Scott. Ashley noticed his deep glare. It was surreal, hypnotic, as if he were looking through Scott, not at him. Then he smiled politely and left the shop.

Ashley stood immobilized. She felt as though she had been transported to some other place. But no. The surroundings were the same. Scott, Karen, the antiques were the same. She looked toward Stanley's disorganized office. Yes, she reassured herself, it's all the same.

Scott walked over, taking her by the shoulders. "What's wrong?" he asked. "You look like you've seen a ghost."

"What?" she murmured, staring into Stanley's cluttered office.

Scott looked at Karen in dismay, then back to Ashley. Karen lowered herself into her chair.

"Honey," Scott said. "Why don't you go upstairs and lie down?"

"Lie down?" she frowned. "No, I have to get back to the hospital." She turned to Karen with a disjointed gaze. "Hum, I huh," she motioned toward the stairs. "I need to get some clothes."

"Sure," Karen replied.

Ashley smiled. "I'm glad you're here."

"I'm glad to be here," Karen said.

"Your apartment is impressive," Scott said as he followed Ashley into the large living room. "And that view!" He walked toward the French doors that opened onto the balcony. "The view alone is worth a million dollars," he said, crossing the balcony to the railing. Ashley walked up beside him. For a moment neither spoke.

"Who was that strange man?" Scott asked casually, breaking the silence.

"He's a client," Ashley replied. She looked out atop Belvedere. "He lives up there," pointing to the old cypress. "It's the oldest house in Belvedere. I've wanted to restore it since the first time I saw it."

"Does he always act so weird?"

"Yes, I guess you'd say he does." She turned to Scott. Reaching up, she took his face in her hands. Gently, she put her lips to his. He responded, taking her into his arms. Then he lifted her from the balcony and carried her into the bedroom.

That familiar passion that had taken her so completely the night Tryn had claimed her virginity, rushed through her like a thunder bolt. She pulled Scott to her suddenly, her mouth smothering his; probing. She was taking charge, just as Tryn had done, her hands finding their way inside his shirt, ripping it open. Feeling the strength of his bare chest she sucked at his naked skin, while her hand released his belt and unzipped his trousers. She then knelt down, devouring his sex with an insatiable hunger.

This time she would make Scott beg as he had made her. She pushed him onto the bed, then slowly finished undressing him. Again she took him into her mouth, only to stop again. She stood beside the bed looking down at him. Running her eyes across his body, she carefully and determinedly removed her clothing. For a moment she just stood there, smiling into his eyes. Forcibly she pulled him from the bed and onto the floor, pushing him inside her. She brought him to an exhausted orgasm.

Tryn had taught her well.

℅

When Scott and Ashley returned to the hospital Margaret had gone. Victor was talking with Dr. Hopner. Ashley drew close to Scott as they approached. A strange feeling had unexpectedly come over her. She looked at her father, feeling a sudden rush through her body. That same rush she had felt while standing in Scott's study that night, thinking of her father. Seeing him in her mind as she had never done. She saw him, not as her father but her lover.

Victor turned to Ashley. "Dr. Hopner, this is my daughter Ashley."

"It's nice to meet you, Ashley."

Ashley gazed into Dr. Hopner's bearded face, her mind dazed.

"Doctor?"

Victor put his arm around Ashley. "Honey?" he said "Are you all right?" Ashley pulled away with a gasp. Victor looked stunned. "Honey, what's wrong?"

"Nothing," she said, struggling desperately to compose herself. "I apologize. I haven't had a lot of sleep." She turned to Dr. Hopner. "I'm upset. That's all," and she went to Shelby.

"I can't stand seeing her like this," she said.

"I know," Dr. Hopner replied, placing his hand over the bandage that covered most of Shelby's head. "She's making a miraculous recovery, though. I never expected her to come this far. And so quickly."

Ashley reached down and gently ran her fingers over Shelby's swollen and bruised face. "What exactly has happened to her?" she asked.

She's suffered an injury to the brain. It's affected the part of the brain that involves conscious activity or the maintenance of consciousness—in particular, parts of the cerebrum, the main mass of the brain."

"How severe is it?"

"There was massive intracranial hemorrhage. We have relieved as much pressure as possible. The good news is that she's breathing on her own and the bleeding seems to have subsided. Considering her injuries she's come a long way. It's quite incredible."

Ashley took Shelby's hand. "I can't just let her lay there and die." She looked at Dr. Hopner, thinking what a kind face he had. She studied his neatly trimmed beard and sincere eyes. "There must be something I can do."

"Yes there is," he said. "Talk to her. Genuinely talk to her." He gave her a reassuring pat on the shoulder, then went to the far corner of the room where Victor and Scott sat talking. "I wish there was more I could do," he said to Victor.

"Thank you, Dan, I know you're doing everything possible. We aren't giving up hope."

"I can see that. And that's just what might get her through this." He turned and left the room.

Scott had introduced himself to Victor and told him about his and Ashley's recent meeting. Victor was visibly delighted with the news that his daughter was actually seeing someone. They talked a little about Buzz, then about Scott's business. Ashley was talking on and on to Shelby about the things they used to do as children.

"Remember all those creepy old houses you used to drag me through?" she was saying. "I always pretended I didn't want to go. But I loved it." Ashley sniffed, wiping away tears. "And those cemeteries. We must have explored every cemetery in the Bay Area. I wasn't as crazy about that as you were, especially when you would round up a bunch of our friends and sneak around the graves telling ghost stories. You were always the one with the scariest stories. Remember? Oh, and remember the time we had that slumber party and Dad appeared in the window with the flashlight shoved into his mouth? His whole face was glowing. We all ran screaming from the room, even you."

On and on Ashley reminisced. "And the time you talked me into sneaking out of the house to see the midnight movie down on Union. 'Invasion of the Body Snatchers.' I'll never forget it. Dad thought someone had snatched us. When we got home the police were everywhere. I'm surprised Dad didn't lock us up for good."

"You have a very special daughter," Scott said to Victor.

"Yes," he agreed quietly. "I do."

"She's very determined."

Victor leaned back into the vinyl chair. "Lack of determination has never been her weakness." He turned to Scott. "Thanks for being here for her."

"I wouldn't be anywhere else," Scott replied.

&

Ashley slept on the roll-a-way bed next to Shelby lost in a dream world.

She was walking through the fog. The night air was cold, finding its ways through the openings of her coat. Shivering, she tucked her collar under her chin. As she advanced she could hear the restless stir of the sea. Then slowly the fog began to swirl, turning to mist. And there, only feet away she saw it. A tiny headstone. She approached the stone, bending down to read the inscription. But there was none, just a tiny stone with intricate carvings. She reached out and trailed her fingers over the face of the stone. It felt slick and cold. At that moment, she felt a sudden and most powerful presence. She looked around her, as though searching for something or someone. It was then she noticed the full moon brightly shinning through the tangled limbs of a large oak tree. Its branches reached out, gnarled, sinuous, and barren.

"You must go back." A gentle voice said.

"Ms. Winthrop. Wake up. "Ms. Winthrop."

Jolted from her dream, Ashley found herself staring into the animated face of one of the night nurses.

"Your sister," the nurse said. "She's awake. She's conscious."

"What!" Ashley bolted from the rollaway. "Shelby?" she called, hovering over her.

Shelby opened her eyes.

"Oh my god. Shel." Tears went streaming down her face.

Shelby looked at Ashley blankly.

"Shel, it's Ashley," she said, searching her face for some sort of recognition. Anything. But there was nothing, just a cold, vacant stare.

"It's going to take time," the nurse said. "She still has a ways to go. It's a good sign though."

"Yes," Ashley said. "It is." She bent down and kissed Shelby's forehead.

"Thirsty."

"What!" Ashley said, startled.

"Thirsty," she repeated, this time a little louder.

"I'll be right back," the nurse said, and hurried out the door to refill the water pitcher.

"Thirsty."

"I know, honey," Ashley said. "The nurse is getting you some water."

Shelby reached up and touched her head. She frowned and lifted her other hand.

"You had an accident," Ashley said lowering Shelby's arms. "You've hurt your head."

114

"Accident?"

"Yes, but you're going to be fine. Just fine."

Shelby closed her eyes tight. "I don't know . . . " she sighed.

"Here's your water," the nurse said.

Ashley gently lifted Shelby off the pillow, giving her a small sip of water. Shelby took the water, coughing with the first few sips. Then she gulped the rest of the cup.

"You were thirsty," Ashley said, lowering her onto the pillow. "Are you hungry?"

"I don't know," she said. Her voice was now clearer. She looked at Ashley as if studying her face. "Who are you?"

The nurse saw the sudden look of disbelief in Ashley's face.

"Shelby," the nurse said, "this is your sister, Ashley. She's been very worried about you since the accident. Do you remember your sister?" The nurse turned to Ashley with an assuring look.

"My sister?"

"It's all right if you don't remember," Ashley said, seeing the fear in Shelby's eyes. But you will. I'll help you."

Shelby closed her eyes, her tears running onto the pillow. "I'm scared," she whimpered. "I can't remember."

"No," Ashley said. "Everything's going to be all right. I promise."

Shelby grasped her head. "But I can't remember."

Ashley took her wrist. "You will," she assured her.

Shelby looked up at Ashley, that incredible look of fright still on her face. "But I don't know who I am."

The nurse intervened. "I know you're scared. But memory loss is not uncommon. It doesn't mean it's permanent." She patted Ashley's arm and whispered. "I'll call Dr. Hopner. He's not going to believe this." She gave Ashley a reassuring smile.

Shelby looked up at Ashley. "Where is Scott?"

Ashley's mouth dropped.

છ

It had been a week since Shelby had regained consciousness. Dr. Hopner was utterly baffled by her speedy recovery. Frankly, he had not given her much hope of recovery. He had no scientific explanation for it.

He was calling it a miracle and released Shelby into the hands of Victor and Margaret with explicit instructions as to her care. She had regained most of her strength in the past seven days. But it seemed that the only memory that lingered was of Scott touching her and talking to her while she was still in a coma. She remembered every detail of that moment.

Scott's store on Bridgeway was now under renovation. He had asked Ashley to design the interior. Between spending time with Shelby and working on the plans for Scott's building, Ashley had worked little on DeLore House. She had gone there a few times. Tryn had been away both times which gave her a sense of relief. Her relationship with Scott was growing stronger. There were times when she wanted to simply blurt out the words, 'I love you.'

But the thought of seeing Tryn again was still haunting her. She feared what would happen if she had to face him. If she felt him touching her. It made her restless and fearful that the power he seemed to have over her would cause that uncontrollable hunger to surface.

Chapter Nine

avid Clarendon pulled into the long driveway of Chelsea Farms, Will Taylor's Hattiesburg home. Situated in the middle of six acres, its sweeping lawns were lined with a forest of tall pines. Two energetic chocolate Labradors leaped from the side door of the house in anxious pursuit.

"Darby Mole, Molly Mole," he yelped, overcome by their zealous greeting. "Where is that molish daddy of yours?" David lifted his suitcase and trudged up the walk and through the side door with Darby and Molly at his feet. He could hear Will upstairs, yelling at the top of his lungs. "Sounds like a storm's brewing," he said. "Come on girls, let's go take a look."

After braving the stairs to Will's office, David stood in the doorway, panting furiously. He watched as the distinguished Dr. William Banks Taylor III roared at the unfortunate person on the other end of the phone line.

"This is going to be a treacherous weekend," David announced to Darby and Molly, who were now sitting happily at his feet.

"That arrogant old coot!" Will howled. "That blisters my ass! My puppies are worth more dead than that old fuck is alive. You tell Hoot Bluestone to stick it. You hear me? Stick it. Straight up his rickety old ass. And if he tries this shit with me again I'll sue his worthless ass."

Will slammed the phone down, sending a stack of papers crashing to the floor. "That limp dick old fart," he grumbled, bending down to retrieve the papers.

"I say, old fellow," David called in his best English accent. "A bit cranky are we?"

Will glared toward the door, still fumbling with his papers, then let out a high-pitched giggle. "Where did you come from?" he snickered. He ran his hands through his thick salt and pepper hair which seemed to take direction, studiously falling back into place. "You weren't supposed to hear that," he said, raising his eyebrow. "Not good for my image."

"And what image is that?" David questioned, leaving the doorway and patting Will on the shoulder. He set his suitcase down and threw his briefcase on the couch.

"I have two. That was one of them. "Good to see your scrubby old face," he said, slapping David on the back. "Just seeing you puts me in a good mood."

"Jolly Good." David grunted, falling into the couch.

"Old boy," Will said, "that belly of yours is growing."

"The air in this room is growing," David growled. "It stifles my lungs."

"Then go sit by the window. I can't talk about this Winthrop thing without a cigarette."

"Never mind," David conceded, knowing it would take an act of God to lift him from the couch.

Will reached for a lighter among his cache of lighters, lit a cigarette, and walked to the bookcase. "I owe you one," he said, pulling a file from the shelf. "This Winthrop thing's a doozie. A real mystery."

David squirmed on the leather cushion.

Will walked back with the folder, leaving a trail of smoke in his wake. He plopped down in the chair behind his desk, which was stacked three feet deep with papers.

"For Christ's sake, Will, how do you find anything in that pile of rubble?"

"Rubble!" he wailed. "For your information, these are very important papers, eighteenth-century shit. So hush up. Don't start hounding me about my desk," and he began sorting through the folder. "You want some coffee? A bourbon? A beer? A joint? Some pussy? Anything but food, considering that gut."

"No, I'll have a drink later."

"You'll need a drink later."

"Then get on with it."

"Keep your shirt on," Will ordered, rummaging through his notes.

David bore further into the soft leather cushions, sighing heavily.

Will rearranged his papers as though putting them in order. "Now," he said, eyeing David, who looked like a small hippo buried in a mound of leather. "You comfortable, old boy?"

"I am," he said petulantly.

"Good." Will reached for his glasses. "Let's see. It was around 1896 or thereabouts. Seems there was a nasty little scandal at Bartlington Hall, the home of Lord and Lady Arundel of York. An incredible place. I've seen it." He eyed David. "You listening?"

David opened one eye.

Will went back to his notes. "Lord and Lady Arundel had two sons, Harold and Charles. Charles was an avid collector of art. He became quite wealthy. But Harold—Harold was the black sheep. Reckless and flamboyant; the prodigal son and a notorious womanizer. Sort of like you, David," Will laughed.

David gave Will a hostile stare. "Get on with it."

Will took a long draw from his cigarette. "Harold was also a chronic gambler. That shamed his parents and eventually plummeted them into bankruptcy. A wealthy banker bought the place, lock, stock and barrel. He willed it to York's Historical Society. It's open to the public now."

"That's absurd," David scowled. "How could his parents allow him to get away with that? It's outrageous."

"I agree. But from what I could dig up, Harold's mother worshipped the sorry ground her son walked on."

"David rested his head back into the couch. "Are you going somewhere with this tale of woe?"

"You wanted to know about Jenny, didn't you?"

"I'm ready now."

"Fuck you. We shall do things at my pace, on my terms, or I'll send your ass back to sin-city empty handed."

"Christ, and I thought you were surly twenty years ago, back when you terrorized those grad students in London. At least I'm comfortable." David settled deeper into the soft leather.

Will laughed and turned the page. "From what my sources in London tell me, Young Harold, who was probably twenty at the time, took a fancy to your Jenny, who was only fourteen. She lived with her mother and father at Bartlington Hall. Her father was in charge of the staff. Jenny and Harold met secretly. Now that I've seen Bartlington Hall I can understand how. You could bury yourself in that place and never be found. Anyway, Jenny became pregnant, but before she confided in her parents, they were killed. Their wagon overturned one day during a storm. Soon after, Jenny went to Harold and told him she was pregnant."

"She actually thought the slime would marry her?" David said.

"Of course. She was fourteen."

"This guy sounds like you, Will." A smile worked at the corner of David's mouth. "A real Don Juan. How many wives have you had?"

"Two, and that was two too many. Fuck'em, are you interested in my wives or what I have in this folder?"

Conceding, David lifted his hand.

Will went back to his notes. "In a word, abandonment. That little bastard went running to mummy. Jenny had her baby at Bartlington Hall, and the rest Ashley revealed under hypnosis. They took the baby away. No one knew what happened to Jenny until now. And we still don't know about her baby. Ashley said Jenny was at Nine Thornton Square when she was rescued by Stefan Winthrop and brought to the states. Isn't that right?"

"That's right." David grunted and pushed himself off the back of the couch. "Nine Thornton Square. What is that place exactly?"

"Exactly? I don't know, exactly. And you can bet your ass I have access to the best sources, and to the best historians. All I can tell you is that it's the address of a very prestigious men's club in London. After hearing what Ashley had to say, though, I have a pretty good idea. I'd like to know how they've kept the thing under wraps this long."

"And how long is that?"

"Make a guess?"

"I wouldn't know."

"Neither does anyone else. Don't have any idea when the thing was built. I don't know anybody that belongs. I don't know anybody who knows anybody who belongs. Whomever they are, they drive through the gates in closed cars. You never see them. Hell, I just thought they were a bunch of eccentric old farts. Now it makes my skin crawl. It looks like Jenny was only fourteen or fifteen when those bastards got her. How they get away with it is beyond me."

"Have you seen the place?"

"Bet your ass. It's smack dab in the middle of London. Stands behind tall iron gates. A huge four-story brick building with heavy ornate moldings. Gaudy if you ask me. No one has though."

David collapsed back into the sofa. "What about Winthrop House? That's where this Stefan Winthrop supposedly took her."

"Yeah." Will scratched the back of his neck. "Winthrop House. I know as much about that place as I do about Thornton Square. Can't find a thing on it. I had Donald Severn, a professor friend of mine at Boston University, do a title search. Absolutely nothing. It's the damnedest thing. You'd think the place didn't exist." Will shook his head in defeat. "It does, though. Donald drove up there. Said it was amazing. A huge place overlooking the Atlantic. He asked around town and found out that some old man lives there with his servants. Louis is his name." Will looked over at David. "I'm going there in a couple of weeks. I'd have my ass out of here tomorrow if I didn't have this other commitment."

David looked thoughtful. "How about some company?"

"Company!" Will exclaimed. "You?"

"And why not me? This is my case."

"You'd better think about that, old boy. Are you sure we could stand each other that long?"

"We'll manage," David responded with finality.

જી

Three months had passed, and the renovation of Trudeau's Haute Couture was nearing completion. Even the onset of Christmas hadn't slowed the construction. Scott had been genuinely impressed with Ashley's gift of design and had turned the entire project over to her. Most of Ashley's nights were spent in Sausalito with Scott. As far away from Tryn as possible. She had virtually turned the DeLore project over to Stanley and Michael.

Trudeau's was evolving into a focal point of curiosity. Passing tourists would stop in wonderment as workers labored with plaster moldings and stone balustrades. Chandeliers were hung, indirect lighting set in place, and a marble fountain with circular seating was erected in the center of the main room. There, you could relax with a glass of wine and shop at your leisure. And there was a waiting list for the two upstairs apartments.

Management and sales positions were filled. Merchandise and display fixtures arrived. After three short months, the grand opening was a week away. Ashley had sent invitations to everyone she knew from San Francisco to Tiburon, and beyond.

Shelby, although still with Victor and Margaret, had miraculously recovered from her injuries, which was still baffling Dr. Hopner. She had sporadic flashes of memory, but nothing sequential that pieced together who she was. The frustration of it was taking its toll. She would frequently lapse into depression, staying locked inside her room for days, eating only when Margaret begged her.

Ashley and Scott made a point of spending at least an hour each day with her. It was obvious that Shelby looked forward to their visits, especially Scott's.

Before long though, Shelby had become receptive to moving on with her life. She was now seeing a psychiatrist and dealing with her memory loss in a more positive way.

Surprisingly enough, she showed interest in going back to work, spending a few hours a week at the office. Shelby continued to live with Victor and Margaret. She had not found the courage to move back into her house, surrounded by unrecognizable things they said were hers.

Margaret and Victor owned a beautiful Victorian home on Washington Street in Pacific Heights, an exclusive area of San Francisco. It had beautiful gardens and a large patio overlooking the bay.

It was early afternoon. Shelby was sitting on the patio taking in the warm sun and reading a book on real estate. She looked out across the bay to where she had once lived. When they would tell her about her past, it was like hearing about someone in another time. She looked out toward Tiburon.

"You were the best real estate agent in the area," they had said. How could she not remember that? And Bob. They said she dated him. And she must have. He wouldn't stop calling her. But talking to Bob made her feel weird. She had still not found the courage to look at photo albums or read letters she had once written. She couldn't even look at the picture of her mother, the one they said she kept by her bed in her house in Tiburon. It was an odd sensation, thinking of looking at a strange woman who was supposed to be your mother. Shelby wondered why they hadn't mentioned her father. Surely there must be a picture of him too. She closed her book and settled back in the lawn chair. *Did I ever have a husband?* Then she realized. *I don't even know how old I am.*

"Shelby," she heard someone call. She turned to see Scott and Ashley and a blonde woman holding a small dog. The dog squirmed out of the woman's arms and went running across the patio, landing in Shelby's lap.

"Schatzi's missed you," the blonde woman said.

"Missed me?" Shelby looked addled. Schatzi grunted and turned in circles while planting kisses on Shelby's face.

"Looks to me like he knows you," The blonde said, sitting down in one of the lawn chairs. Shelby looked over at the woman. "I'm supposed to know you, aren't I?"

The woman smiled. "Roberta."

"Roberta," Shelby repeated, turning her attention back to Schatzi. "Your dog and I seem to be pals."

"No," Roberta said. "It's the other way around. Your dog and I are pals. He visits me a lot."

"My dog?" Shelby's face suddenly lit up. "Really?"

"Really," Roberta said. She reached over, giving Schatzi a pat. "I hope you'll still let him visit. He's my best buddy, but he's your baby and he loves you."

"Of course." She looked at Roberta curiously. "Were we friends?" Schatzi was now pawing at her hand, wanting her to keep up the petting.

"I used to work for you," Roberta said. " Between trips I helped manage your apartment complex in Cupertino. I'm a flight attendant."

"I have apartments?"

"Not any more," Ashley interjected, sitting down next to Shelby. "You sold them a few years back."

"Did I make a profit?"

"You did. And bought your house in Tiburon."

"Good business decision," Scott pitched in.

"You're a born business woman," Ashley said. "And the best realtor I know."

"I'm not feeling so businesslike right now," she said, tossing her book on the glass table. "Schatzi, you might be better off with Aunt Roberta. I'm kind of out of my head these days."

Ashley and Roberta stared at one another.

Ashley turned to Shelby. "Did you hear what you just said?"

"What?"

"You said Aunt Roberta."

"I did?" Shelby wrinkled her forehead. She looked at Roberta. "You're my aunt?"

Both women smiled. "No," Roberta said gently. "You might say that I'm Schatzi's aunt."

"Oh," Shelby laughed, "You do look a little young to be my aunt."

"Thanks for the compliment."

"Was that a compliment?"

"Yes. And I'll take one of those any day." She reached over and gave Schatzi a big hug and kiss. "Have to run, Burger Boy. Take care of your mom." She turned to Shelby. "You look fabulous."

Shelby smiled. "That's a compliment."

"No, it's the truth." Roberta was now crossing the patio. "See you in a few weeks."

Shelby fell back into the lounge chair. "I hope you two don't have any more surprises today," she sighed, bending down to give Schatzi a kiss, to which he immediately responded.

"Have we overdone it?"

"No," she said, seemingly captivated by the little schnauzer. "How can I not remember this wonderful life I had?" She looked at Ashley ruefully. "I have so many questions. She turned to Scott.

Ashley saw the same look. The longing in Shelby's eyes was as strong as the first time she'd seen him after regaining consciousness. She knew Shelby was in love with him.

"Could you and Ashley stay for a while?" Shelby asked.

Scott sat down next to her. "Of course we can."

Shelby smiled and cradled Schatzi in her arms. "Why did Roberta call Schatzi Burger Boy?"

"Because," Ashley said, "when he was a puppy you bought him a little rubber hamburger to chew on. He was playing with that the first time Roberta saw him. She flipped for Schatzi."

Shelby put Schatzi's tiny nose to hers. "He's so adorable."

Ashley and Scott smiled.

"Now," Ashley said. "Are you ready to learn more about Shelby Kincaid?"

"I think so."

Scott reached over with a reassuring hand.

She touched his hand. "So," she blurted, "when are you two getting married?"

Scott and Ashley broke out in laughter.

"Now that's my Shel," Ashley said. "Straight to the point."

Shelby turned a bright crimson red. "I'm sorry."

"Don't be. You were never one to beat around the bush. Honey, that's what made you so wonderful, exciting to know."

"I'm not so sure." Shelby began nuzzling Schatzi's ear.

Ashley reached over and ran her fingers through Shelby's short hair. "You're hair's really growing."

"Is it?" she said, touching it slightly. "What did it look like before they shaved it off?"

"Bouncy. You wore it kind of short but all one length."

She looked up at Ashley, her eyes serious. "How old am I?"

"Oh, about a year older than I am. You're forty one."

"You mean I've already turned forty . . . ?" Shelby moaned. "That's terrible news. When is my birthday?"

"October 18. And mine is October 20."

"I was hoping that I was younger," she laughed. "Why hasn't anyone mentioned my father?" The question seemed to come out of nowhere.

"Your father?" Ashley looked surprised. "Well honey, we really don't know a lot about your father. He died right after you were born."

"He did? How?"

"A car accident, I think."

"Don't I have pictures of him?"

"Pictures? I . . . I don't think so." Ashley couldn't remember ever seeing any pictures. In fact, no one had ever talked about her father. Not Shelby or her mother. "I've never seen any."

Shelby's face went somber. "You mean . . . no one knows anything about him?"

Ashley felt suddenly uncomfortable. She had never given Shelby's father a thought. "I'm sorry Shel, I don't know."

"You said my mother died when I was thirteen?"

"Yes. She was very sick."

Shelby fought back the tears. "Your family took me in after she died. Why?"

"We grew up together. We've been friends since we were born. Your mother and my parents were very close."

"Then wouldn't they know about my father?"

"I guess."

Shelby lifted Schatzi onto the ground. "I think I'll go lie down for a while."

Scott helped her from the lawn chair. "I know this is hard for you," he said, putting his arm around her shoulder. Shelby responded lovingly. "But if it's any consolation, Ashley and I love you very much." He kissed the top of her head.

"I love both of you very much," she said, smiling through the tears. "I'll be fine. Really, I just need to lie down for a while. And tomorrow—I'd like to go through those photo albums."

"That's my Shel," Ashley said giving her a hug.

Margaret was in the kitchen arranging a vase of her prize roses when they walked in. Margaret was a lover of flowers, forever doting over her patio garden. She had formed a garden club years back, and had been featured in several magazines.

Shelby put her arm around Margaret and commented on her roses.

Scott also complimented Margaret and asked if she and Victor were planning on attending the grand opening of Trudeau's. She said they wouldn't miss it and asked if he and Ashley would like to stay for dinner. Ashley quickly intervened, saying that they were having dinner at her apartment. They were tired after working day and night, preparing for the opening. They wanted a quiet evening at home. Margaret smiled and accepted her excuse as always.

Shelby walked Scott and Ashley to the front door with Schatzi close by her feet.

"Thanks for a wonderful afternoon," Shelby said. "This little guy was a real surprise." She smiled down at Schatzi who was now wooing and twitching his hind quarters.

"I'm glad," Ashley said, giving her a hug.

"Do me a favor," Shelby said. "Call Michael. Tell him I'll take a rain check on dinner. I'm really not up to going out."

"Of course," Ashley replied.

"Schatzi and I need some time together." Shelby reached up and hugged Scott. "You two have a romantic evening."

&

Maurice was parked outside the studio when Scott and Ashley arrived.

"Mademoiselle," he called, standing beside the old Jaguar Saloon. Ashley reached for Scott's arm.

"Maurice. What are you doing here?" She clutched Scott tighter.

"Monsieur DeLore needs to see you," he said politely.

"What?"

"Monsieur DeLore requests that you meet with him," Maurice was staring at Scott.

"Tonight?"

"Oui, Mademoiselle." He swung open the car door. "It's of the utmost urgency."

Ashley turned to Scott.

"Go ahead," he said. "I'll start dinner."

"No." She looked back at Maurice. "We'll follow you."

"Mademoiselle," he said with slight asperity. "Monsieur DeLore needs to see you alone. Please," and he motioned for her to get into the car.

Ashley could feel her heart racing. She turned to Scott. "This . . . this restoration is important. I've neglected it. I won't be long." She hurriedly

127

slid into the back seat of the sedan. As Maurice started to drive off Ashley lowered the window. "Call Michael and tell him Shelby's not up to having dinner tonight. His number is in the address book by the phone."

Scott nodded and waived.

"Come, Ashley." Tryn stood on the staircase clad in a black silk robe, his hand extended. The flames from the wall sconces cast a warm glow, catching the side of his face. "Come to me."

Ashley took each step slowly, determinedly. His eyes, as before, were captivating. She could feel his presence, almost taste his essence.

"Go into the bed chamber," he ordered.

As she passed him, that same overpowering presence began to take her. The hunger was enveloping.

As they entered the bed chamber, the walls seemed to move with an eerie dance. The roaring fire crackled, sending shadowy-like figures across the room. The bedside lamps glowed softly beneath their crimson shades. Tryn closed and locked the door. He reached out and pulled Ashley to him, pressing her firmly against his chest.

His sex was hard and swollen. He bent down, covering her mouth with his, feeding his appetite. He smothered her in his passion.

Again, that insatiable hunger swelled inside her. She dug her fingers deep into his thick black hair, as his mouth fed on hers. She tore at his robe, wanting to feel his nakedness, to devour his flesh, hold him in her hands and give him excruciating pleasure.

She fell to her knees and took him. She swam in the pleasure of his ecstasy.

Abruptly he lifted her—dragged her across the room and forced her onto the bed. He reached out and grabbed her blouse, ripping it open. Again he fed his hunger. She was consumed in it. She suddenly felt her nakedness as he stripped the last piece of clothing from her body, then pushed her face down onto the bed.

His robe fell from his body. His strong hands began spreading her legs. She became dizzy in the pleasure. Then he lifted her to her knees and thrust his sex deep inside. Violently he satiated his hunger.

When it was over, he put on his robe, then lifted her from the bed. He stared into her face as though studying a beautiful peace of art. His eyes were cold. "Go now," he said, turning and crossing the room toward the balcony. He pulled open the French doors and walked out into the night.

Maurice was waiting by the opened door as Ashley descended the stairs.

"Mademoiselle."

She stood next to him, studying his face. He quickly looked past her, lifting his chin slightly.

"Mademoiselle."

She lowered her gaze and walked past.

Five minutes later she was climbing the stairs to her apartment. She felt strange, as if awakening from an exhausting dream. Each step drew her closer to the door. To Scott. She reached out, then drew back, feeling sick. Her mind felt stagnant, her body spent. She felt her blouse. Oh God, the buttons. Two were missing. She fell against the hallway—frantic. She jumped at the phone's distant ring. Her hand flew to the door knob. She pushed it open and called to Scott. He appeared from the kitchen.

"I'll get it." She tore into the bedroom, stripped her blouse off and threw it across a chair. She jerked the phone from its cradle and fell back on the bed.

"Hi, honey," she heard Buzz say. "Sounds like you're in a rush."

"Buzz?" she whispered breathlessly, eyeing the doorway. "Why haven't I heard from you?"

"I apologize, honey. I had to go to Charleston. That restoration has become a nightmare. Too many chiefs and not enough Indians. That's not important though. We've finally heard on your birth certificates."

"We have?" she said, sickened by anxiety.

"You were right. The Bureau of Vital Statistics in Baton Rouge had no record of yours or Michael's birth."

Ashley suddenly felt like the air had been sucked out of her. "And Boston?"

"I heard from Boston today."

Momentary silence. "And?"

"You and Michael were born at St. Mary's Hospital in Boston, Massachusetts. Your home address was 40 Sea Road, Manchester,

Massachusetts. And Ashley," he hesitated. "Your mother's name on the birth certificate is Margaret Angelena Winthrop."

Silence.

"Honey."

"Oh. I was just thinking. I mean . . . Damn, I don't know what I mean."

"Precious, why don't you go to Victor and tell him everything. Your father loves you. Whatever he may have done, he did it to protect you and Michael. I'm sure of it."

"No. And I don't care what that birth certificate says. Margaret Winthrop is not my mother. And I'm going to find out what happened."

"How?"

"David Clarendon and Will Taylor."

"Good. That means I can keep an eye on you. Oh, by the way, I have a surprise when you get here."

"A surprise?" That's all she needed. More surprises. "What kind of surprise?"

"I'm not saying a word. You'll see when you get here."

"Buzz . . ."

"Is that Buzz?" Scott said, walking into the bedroom.

Ashley jerked around. "Huh, yes."

He handed her a glass of wine. "Tell Buzz hi," and he bent down and kissed her.

She flinched slightly, realizing that her mouth was sore. The inside of her lips had begun to swell.

"Scott says hello."

"Hello back," Buzz said. "How much longer is he going to be there?"

"I . . . huh. The opening's tomorrow night. Probably a few more days." Ashley looked up, noticing that Scott was staring at her.

"Call me before you leave," Buzz said.

"Okay." Ashley hung up the phone.

Scott was now staring across the room at the chair where her blouse lay crumpled. "How did your meeting go with DeLore?" he asked coldly.

"Oh, fine." Ashley breathed deeply, then pushed herself from the bed. "He was just upset with the workers. Thought they were snoopy. The man's eccentric. What can I say?" She laughed nervously and headed toward the dressing room. As she passed by the chair she reached down and grabbed her blouse. "I'm going to take a quick shower before dinner."

The rest of the evening was quiet. Scott had prepared poached salmon in a wine sauce. They both picked at their food. What conversation there was amounted to nothing more than polite, idle chit chat. After dinner, Scott announced that he had some last minute preparations before tomorrow's opening. Ashley knew better. It was obvious that he suspected more than a business meeting with Tryn. What was she going to do? She felt sick and dirty. Her guilt was making it difficult to even look at Scott.

Hours after Scott had left, she lay in bed looking out into the night toward the old mansion. Most of the houses stood dark. They seemed to be sleeping. Except for one. A faint glow was coming from the fourth floor attic. She turned away, struggling to wipe the memory from her mind. She looked back toward the light. It had vanished. She closed her eyes, feeding off the memory as she ran her hands over her breasts and down her body. She lifted her nightgown, almost feeling him exploring her. Finally she lapsed into sleep.

The night was clear, the moon shone brightly through the twisted limbs of the oak. The cold wind sang like a distant chorus.

Ashley found herself standing at the foot of an open grave. It was deep with darkness. The cold wind bit at her naked skin. Her body stiffened, then drew backward, as she realized in horror that she was standing in the middle of a small graveyard completely naked. The graves seemed to beckon her with their mouth-like openings, deep pits of blackness.

Suddenly, she felt something cold around her ankles. Paralyzed with fear, she cautiously lowered her head toward the ground. Her eyes caught its movement. A faint cry escaped her lips. The ground, she thought. It's moving. Somehow it had come alive. She screamed in terror, realizing that the ground was swimming with a mass of snakes, slithering in and out of each other. They began to coil their slimy, scaly skins up between her legs. She screamed out as she began to lose her balance. Her toes dug into the cold dirt. Her body swayed back and forth as she fought for stability, but she couldn't escape their grasp.

Then, as if in slow motion, she fell into the slime of coiling snakes. Their movement now seemed urgent and defiant. They coiled around her arms, pulling them taut over her head. They
glided down her breast, cinching her waist tighter and tighter. She tried desperately to scream.

The snakes tightened around her legs and spread them far apart. She struggled desperately to free herself, gasping with every breath. But the more she struggled, the tighter the snakes coiled around her and darted their fork-like tongues inside her. Again and again they toyed with her.

Violently they entered her, thrusting their bodies deep inside.

"No!" Ashley screamed, bolting from her pillow as Tryn's scent flooded her bedroom.

Chapter Ten

shley had been unable to reach Scott at the Casa Madrona. How, she pondered, was she going to make him believe that nothing had happened with Tryn? Why he suspected, she wasn't sure. She just knew he did.

She thought back, trying to remember the details of the previous night. Everything seemed hazy, dreamlike. She couldn't quite remember leaving DeLore House. She remembered Maurice though, standing in the doorway. How strange that seemed to her now. Had he known why Tryn sent for her?

But Scott was all that mattered now. She loved him. And she wanted to be with him forever, grow old with him. He was the one who made her feel safe and loved.

She couldn't bear the thought of losing him.

I have to take another shower, she thought. Tryn's scent still clung to her. She could even taste him. And if she allowed herself to think of him, that unbearable hunger would surface.

"Scott," she whispered, again and again, as the steaming water bathed her skin.

ಋ

It was eleven o'clock. The caterers were setting up tables and decorations in the courtyard. It was perfection: stone fountains, old brick floors, and heavy urns lush with plants. Wrought iron and stone garden benches were placed throughout. Scott had even hired a three–piece jazz combo. He wanted to give his guests the illusion of being in the French Quarter of old New Orleans.

When Ashley arrived, Scott was giving last minute instructions to the caterers. He had yet to notice Ashley.

"Ms. Winthrop," one of the florists said. Scott turned, hearing her name. "The renovation," the girl said. "It's beautiful." The girl looked to be no more than eighteen or nineteen, and seemed nervous in Ashley's presence.

"Thank you. I'm glad you like it." Ashley looked over at Scott. "May I see you in the office?"

Scott gave a few more instructions to the caterers, then followed Ashley to his office. He hurled some papers onto his desk. The tension was suffocating. She could see the hurt in his face, hiding behind the anger.

He glared at her, saying nothing.

God, it was breaking her heart to see him like this, A man who had given her her life's dream. She had fallen in love—now he was looking at her with such wounded eyes. Please Scott, she prayed, believe what I'm about to tell you.

"I want to know what's bothering you," she said matter-of-factly.

Scott held her gaze, then leaned back against the desk. "I don't know what happened last night between you and DeLore. And maybe it's none of my business. Except, I thought we meant something to each other. Did you really think I wouldn't notice? My God! His smell was all over you!"

Ashley responded instantly. "His smell was all over me because he WAS all over me."

"What?" Scott's face hardened into a frown.

"I never wanted you to know." Ashley tried to appear stern. "Why do you think I've let Michael and Stanley handle the restoration? Why do you think I wanted you to go last night? If I had wanted to go alone, I sure as hell wouldn't have asked you to go with me."

Scott straightened against the desk. "What are you saying?"

The question took Ashley momentarily off guard. "He wants more than a professional relationship," she blurted. Jesus, did that sound as ridiculous to Scott as it did to her.

"Then why did you go back there last night? You could have told that chauffeur of his 'no'."

"I thought I could handle it." Ashley lowered her head. "It looks like I didn't do a very good job. Did I?" Tears began to roll down her cheeks.

"You should have told me," Scott said pulling her to him. "Don't cry." He took her face in his hands. For a few short moments he just gazed into her eyes. Then he said. "I love you, you know."

Ashley stared through her tears and into Scott's face. She threw her arms around him. "And I love you."

ಬ

Ashley was on the phone talking to Victor and finding it dreadfully difficult. The guilt was eating her up. Why was she feeling these sexual desires? Fantasizing about her own father in this way?

"I'm glad you talked Shelby into going to Scott's opening," Ashley was saying. Trying to hide her guilt was distracting.

"So am I," Victor replied. "I've asked Blake Sheldon to come along. You remember Blake, don't you?"

"Your publisher. Yes."

"Blake's wife died of cancer a few years back. It really took a toll on him. I was glad when he accepted my invitation. I think he and Shelby will enjoy each other."

"Me too. That's a wonderful idea."

Ashley thought back to the time in the hospital when Scott had kissed Shelby's cheek. And there was no doubt in her mind; Shelby's hand had moved. Yes, Ashley thought, Blake Sheldon was a good idea.

"From what I remember," Ashley said, Blake's rather distinguished. Like you." As she said those words, that disturbing feeling of desire swept over her.

"Not that distinguished," he laughed, "Oh, by the way." Victor's voice sounded forcefully nonchalant. "How is that restoration up on Belvedere going?"

No response.

"Ashley?"

"I'm sorry. What?"

"The DeLore project. How is it?"

"It's coming along Dad, I've gotta run. See you tonight."

Ashley quickly hung up the phone. She couldn't bear talking to her father one minute longer.

Just as she started down the stairs to see Karen about a new shipment of antiques, the phone rang. She contemplated not answering it but decided that it could be important.

"My darling," Buzz said in his usual decorous manner. "Has David called you?"

135

"David? David Clarendon?"

"Yes."

"No. Why?"

"Well. It's the strangest thing. Will Taylor just called. He said he'd been trying to reach David for days. His answering service hasn't even heard from him. They said his calls have been piling up. Something's wrong."

"Why don't you go over there? Maybe he's sick."

"That's just what I'm about to do. When are you and Scott coming?"

"I don't know yet. Probably in a day or so."

"Honey," he said. "How are you? Any more nightmares or walking in your sleep?"

"Not really. I've had Shelby to take my mind off things. Scott too."

"I like the sound of that. And you can thank me for Scott when you get back to New Orleans."

"I'm indebted to you forever."

"You and Scott just be happy. Now tell me. How is our Shelby coming along? I haven't called her. Thought it might just upset her. Losing one's memory has to be traumatic."

"It is. But she's making progress. Her attitude is better. She's even coming to Scott's opening. Dad's fixed her up with his publisher, Blake Sheldon."

"Well. You don't say. Good for Victor. If only Les and I could be there. Too many deadlines hanging over our heads I'm afraid. Give him our best though."

"I'll be sure to," she said. "Oh, and let me know about Dr. Clarendon."

"I will."

ဆ

Buzz and Les drove through the iron gates of David Clarendon's house. Rosie, David's housekeeper, was standing by the front door.

"Why, Mr. Harper, Mr. Les, " she wailed, rearing back and clasping her hands. "My lordy, it sure is good to see ya. C'mon in."

"Good to see you too, Rosie," Buzz said, looking past her and down the hallway. "Is Dr. Clarendon home?"

"No sir, he's not. Guess he's still at Dr. Taylor's. Thoughts he'd be back before now though."

Buzz put his arm around Rosie. "Why don't we go into the parlor and sit down."

Rosie eased her small frame into one of the arm chairs. "What's wrong, Mr. Harper?"

"We hope nothing," he replied. "But Dr. Taylor called. Said he'd been trying to reach Dr. Clarendon for a week."

"Dr. Taylor? But I thoughts Dr. David was still with Dr. Taylor."

"No, Rosie, he left a week ago."

"Lordy Mr. Harper, I don't understand. If he had an accident wouldn't we know by now?"

"It's probably nothing," Les said, patting her shoulder. "Mr. Harper and I will make some phone calls."

"I'm scared, Mr. Les," Rosie said, studying the floor and shaking her head. This ain't like the Doctor."

"Try not to worry," Buzz said.

"Oh, Mr. Harper, but this ain't right. I can feel it," she said waving her hand. "Please excuse me, but I thinks I'll go to my room now. Thinks maybe I'll has me a conversation with the Lord," and she left the chair and walked down the hall.

"Poor Rosie," Les said.

"I know. David means a lot to her." Buzz looked at Les in dismay. "I think we'd better call the police."

ɞ

The night was unseasonably warm for November in Northern California. The heaters Scott had ordered for the patio were not needed. Other than a scattering of clouds, the sky was clear, and the night breeze almost nonexistent.

The crystal chandelier shone brilliantly through the beveled glass of the front doors, its prisms bursting with color. The perpetual motion of the waterfall beneath filled the room like a rain forest. Out in the courtyard were two large tables, each covered with an exquisitely designed presentation of the finest foods. There were prawns, smoked salmon, caviar, and cheeses from around the world. Chafing dishes were steaming with hot hors d'oeuvres, and two bars had been set up, one offering wine and champagne, the other mixed drinks.

Ashley arrived at six-thirty sharp, wearing a low cut, black beaded, floor length gown. Scott was out in the courtyard talking with the musicians.

"You've outdone yourself," Ashley said, walking up behind him.

He turned. His breath caught in his throat at the sight of her. Her long, black dress was accented by an antique, ruby necklace and matching earrings. Her hair was loosely pinned up in a twist. Scott just stood, gazing at her.

"You're breathtaking."

"You're not so bad yourself."

Stanley was the first guest to arrive. He came waltzing in, accompanied by a young man. He introduced Clayton to Scott and Ashley.

"May I present the divine Ashley Winthrop," he said, bowing and holding out his hand. Clayton was in his early thirties, about five foot eight, with short brown hair and a round babylike face.

"It's my pleasure," Clayton said. "Stanley speaks of you often."

Ashley looked at Stanley with an affectionate glare. "I have no doubt that he does." She turned to Clayton and smiled. "I'm glad you could come to the opening."

"Wouldn't have missed it," he assured her.

Stanley motioned to Scott. "And this is Scott Trudeau. The only man who has succeeded in taming my illusive partner here."

"Stanley," Ashley warned. "You're walking on egg shells."

Stanley laughed. "I live on egg shells," and proceeded to ignore her. Scott looked thoroughly amused.

Clayton complimented Scott and Ashley on the renovation and said he would like to be considered for one of the upstairs apartments.

The guests were now steadily pouring through the door. Trudeau's would no doubt be remembered as the most exquisite store ever to grace the little village of Sausalito.

"Hi darling," Ashley heard someone say, and looked up to see her father standing next to her.

"You look beautiful. Your grandmother's necklace does you justice."

Ashley caught her breath as again those strange feelings of desire came over her.

"Ashley," Victor said. "You remember Blake Sheldon."

"Why yes, yes I do." She managed to sound as gracious as possible. "It's good to see you again."

Blake smiled and shook Ashley's hand. "I had forgotten what a beautiful daughter you have, Victor."

Blake Sheldon was about six-two, in his early fifties. He had curly brown hair with a scattering of gray, dark eyes and a strong face. His voice was the first thing she noticed, unusually deep. He's perfect for Shelby, Ashley thought.

Shelby had now turned from talking to Margaret and walked up beside Blake. She was stunning. Her short black hair was swept back from her face, accentuating her large brown eyes. She wore a deep blue strapless evening gown. Her only accessory was a pair of pearl and diamond earrings. Her appearance was elegantly understated.

Margaret was dressed in a black lace two-piece dress. Her hair was done up much like Ashley's. In fact, except for Margaret's gray, their hair color was the same deep chestnut. Ashley ignored Margaret.

"Where is Michael?" Victor asked. "I haven't been able to reach him for days."

"I don't know," Ashley said not wanting to further the conversation. "I haven't seen him either."

It was now approaching eight o'clock. The store was buzzing with conversation. The persistent splash of the waterfall had faded into the clatter of voices. Ashley was by the bar talking to Clayton when she noticed a strange expression cross his face. As she turned to see what he was looking at, she felt someone touch her arm.

"If you will please excuse us," the man said, "I need to speak with Miss Winthrop." A hand tightened around her arm.

"Of course," Clayton said, still gazing into the man's face.

Ashley's first reaction was shock, then resistance. Tryn pulled her through the crowd to the far end of the courtyard.

Scott was talking to Blake and Shelby, and had not seen Michael arrive with Tryn. But minutes later when he went looking for Ashley, he saw them. Tryn and Ashley were sitting on one of the stone benches in the far corner of the courtyard. Scott stood by the courtyard entrance and watched as Tryn ran his fingers down the side of Ashley's face and onto her neck and shoulders. Tryn then pulled Ashley to him, kissing her violently.

"Scott," Shelby said, noticing that his face was flushed. "Are you all right?"

Abruptly, he turned. "Yes, of course," he stammered, forcing a smile. "Are you having a good time?"

Shelby reached up and touched his face. "What's wrong? You're as red as a beet."

Before Scott could answer, he saw Ashley and Tryn walking through the crowd toward the front door. Shelby glanced over at them. "Who's that?" she asked.

Scott didn't—couldn't—answer.

"Tryn," Michael said, turning and grabbing his arm. "I want you to meet my parents." Tryn jerked away, but failed to free himself from Michael's grasp.

"Mom, Dad," he said, prying them from the other guests.

"I'd like for you to meet Tryn DeLore. His . . ."

Tryn savagely tore his arm from Michael's grasp and plowed through the horde of people, pulling Ashley with him.

Michael stood with his mouth agape. He turned to Margaret and Victor not knowing what to say and noticed the look of horror in their eyes. Margaret turned to Victor, her body shaking. She clutched his arm. Victor said to Michael, "Your mother hasn't been feeling well. Give Scott our apologies," and they were out the door.

Maurice was waiting beside the old Jaguar Saloon. Tryn opened the back door, pushed Ashley in, then climbed in beside her. She sat silently as Maurice drove the car toward Belvedere. Her heart was no longer pounding, her pulse no longer racing; she was uncannily calm. She looked ahead as the old Jaguar sped up Highway 101. What is happening? she thought. The anxiety, the urgency that she had always felt with Tryn was absent. That powerful hunger was waning, ebbing slowly within her, seeping through her pores.

She looked over at Tryn. He was staring out the side window, his head turned slightly. She could see just a little more than his profile. He had, what seemed, a kind of defeat on his face. That omniscient countenance that he had once possessed was no longer present.

Maurice drove through the iron gates and past the newly-restored courtyard. The old cypress seemed to have lifted its branches in rebirth, though the house stood as before, smothered in ancient ivy.

As they crossed the terrace, she could see the parlor through the tall French windows and remembered that first night when Maurice had brought her to DeLore House. She felt none of that excitement now, noticing the faint light from inside. It occurred to her how lonely the room looked. Desolate. Void of life.

Maurice unlocked the door.

"Mademoiselle, Monsieur," he said, stepping aside.

Ashley entered the large hall.

"Thank you, Maurice," Tryn said. "I will need for you to wait," and he turned and led Ashley up the shadowy staircase.

As they walked through the large sitting room, Tryn stopped and stood by the small statue that Ashley had commented on the first time she had come to DeLore House. He reached out and caressed its cold, lifeless form. Ashley watched him curiously, thinking how sad he looked. Then he turned, crossing the sitting room and walking past her into the bedroom. She followed, not really knowing why, as he opened the French doors to the balcony. The moon cast a sheet of light across the stone floor. The cool night breeze was now moving in from the ocean. Tryn walked out by the balustrades. His hands wide apart, he placed them on the stone banister, staring into the night. Ashley came up beside him. She could hear the faint sound of the wind sweeping through the trees, and saw it ripple through his long dark hair.

She felt the urge to touch him, and for some reason, a need to comfort him, as one would comfort a very lonely person. She gently placed her hand over his. For a moment she wasn't sure if he had even noticed. Then slowly, he faced her. She could see him more clearly now. Somehow, she thought, he looked different, like someone who was dreadfully tired and troubled.

He gazed sadly into her face as though he were searching for something that lay beneath its surface.

"My beautiful Ashley," he whispered, touching her face with his fingertips, then cradling the ruby necklace in his hand. "My beautiful, beautiful Ashley." He gently pulled her to him, her head resting on his chest. "Forgive me," he said despairingly. He then took her face in his hands and kissed her forehead. "You can't know how much I love you."

The sound of those words stunned Ashley.

"You must go now," Tryn said. "Maurice is waiting."

Ashley reached up and touched his face. That same beautiful face that had captured her at first sight. But it no longer held its disturbing beauty. Somehow it had changed, had become sad and worn. Ashley started to speak.

"No," he whispered, and pressed his fingers against her lips. It's over. You must go."

She watched as Tryn slowly crossed the room and sat down in the arm chair in front of the fire.

Ashley stood on the balcony finding that she was unable to move. Nor was she able to think. She couldn't put her thoughts in order. There *was* no order. She felt completely and utterly alone. Abandoned. And then, as she stared into the room, she realized that Michael was standing in the doorway. It frightened her at first, seeing him there as if he had simply materialized. His eyes looked cold and threatening. He glanced toward Tryn. Ashley watched as he crossed the room. Tryn reached out to

Michael in a sort of gesture and uttered something. But she was too far away to hear. Michael nodded and went to her.

"Maurice is waiting for you downstairs," Michael said sternly.

Ashley opened her mouth to protest, but the words were lost. She gazed into Michael's face as though searching for an answer. To what, she didn't know. Why did he seem different? She then looked back toward Tryn. He sat still and solemn, staring into the fire.

Michael took her arm. "He needs for you to go."

She gazed into Michael's eyes, feeling strange. Empty.

"Go," he urged.

She nodded reluctantly and quietly left the room.

Maurice was waiting for her at the front door. She passed him in silence.

Chapter Eleven

Blake had brought Shelby home around eleven. It had been obvious to Shelby that Blake had been taken with Ashley. And Shelby's attention toward Scott had equally not gone unnoticed.

"Thank you for a lovely evening," Shelby said as Blake walked her to the door.

"It was my pleasure," and he bent down and kissed her cheek.

Shelby smiled and said good night, then went to find Victor and Margaret. They were in the library with the door closed. Shelby knocked gently.

"Margaret," she called. Victor opened the door.

"I just wanted to say good night," Shelby said. "And thank you for asking Blake. He's very nice."

"I knew getting out would do you good."

Shelby smiled and looked past Victor. Margaret was sitting in a chair holding a brandy snifter, looking dazed.

"Is Margaret all right?" she asked Victor.

"Just a headache. She'll be fine."

"Well, I think I'll go to bed. She looked toward Margaret again. "Good night Margaret."

Margaret looked up from her brandy. "Oh, Shelby," she said weakly. "Yes, good night."

The night breeze swept gently through the open window of the bedroom. Shelby lay awake thinking of Scott. Of how much she loved him and why Ashley had hurt him so terribly. Why had Ashley left with that man? Who was he? Scott had told her he had seen them together out in the courtyard, that the man had kissed Ashley.

As Shelby lay there mulling this over, she suddenly had the strangest sensation of light. She quickly sat up, thinking somehow that she wasn't alone. What's happening? she thought, frantically glancing around the room. It was as though everything around her had begun to unfold, somehow released from the darkness. The Victorian washstand across the room, the oak rocking chair she used to rock in when she was little.

"My God! she exclaimed. "She stared at the rocking chair. I remember the rocking chair." She frantically glanced around the room. Yes, she knew them all, down to the most insignificant piece. She turned and looked at the tall Victorian headboard, carved with precision detail.

At that moment the room slowly began to dim. It was as though the light was being sucked from the room. And then darkness.

ଚ

Had it always looked like that? she thought. Cold and distant?

Ashley wrapped the blanket tighter around her shoulders as she gazed out into the night. She did not know how long she had been sitting there.

Haphazardly, she fumbled for her wine glass. Lifting the empty glass to her mouth, she went through the motions of drinking from it. Then she held the glass out and let it fall from her hand.

Sleep, she thought. She needed to sleep. To close her eyes and lose herself in blessed sleep. But she hurt too much. All she could think about was Scott. How he must despise her. The memory of Tryn touching her, kissing her in front of all those people—in front of Scott. Oh God. She knew he had seen. He must have, at the very least, seen her leave with Tryn. NO, it sickened her to think about it. She had to escape. Drift far, far away into another place where there was no pain. Nothing.

She fell over onto the arm of the sofa, pulling the blanket tighter around her.

Soon, she fell into deep slumber. Deeper and deeper as if guided by an unknown hand, she found herself surrounded by a hodgepodge of places and people.

She found herself in a room. A most magnificent room. So large, so vast, that she could not see it, only feel it. Its love, its comfort, its almighty presence. She wanted to stay there forever. Then, as though a large hand had reached out and swept her away, she sensed that she was being pulled swiftly through a long, dark tunnel. Whatever it was that had her relinquished its grasp, and amazingly, she found that she was in a beautiful garden. Familiar music seemed to play all around her. She quickly turned to find its source. It was then that she saw her. This lovely woman—gliding toward her. As the woman approached, she reached out her hand.

"Come," she said. "Walk with me." Ashley took the woman's hand, not feeling its flesh, but the strength and assurance it possessed. They glided effortlessly through the maze of flowers and down a moss-encrusted pathway lined with lavender. Whisperlike, she said, "Follow me to the end." Then she slowly faded away.

"No!" Ashley cried, reaching out. "Please don't leave me. How can I follow you if you leave me?" and she fell onto the mossy bricks, sobbing.

In desperation, she looked up and saw that she was no longer in the garden, but in an old marble gazebo looking out across the garden. Its surface was aged and worn. In the distance, she thought she saw something. She grabbed the side of the banister, pulling herself to her feet. There, out across the lawn, were two Scottish Terriers running, as in slow motion, toward her. They leaped into her arms, sending her back against the banister. Tears streamed from her eyes as she kissed and hugged them, not getting enough of them.

"Jenny," she heard a voice say. She looked up. A man stood towering over her, his hand held out. "You must come in now." Ashley reached out and took his hand. "Oh Stefan," she whispered, drawing close to him, "I'm so happy." She followed beside him, her white dress gliding across the autumn leaves.

Then, quite suddenly, she found herself in a large room filled with paintings. They were lined against the walls in stacks. She saw the shadowy figure of a man standing behind the easel, a large canvas resting against it. As she moved closer, he spoke.

"Jenny," he said softly. "We must finish your portrait before you are too far along. Sophia has given me strict orders."

As Ashley moved closer, she turned and looked up at the canvas. She stood motionless as she gazed at the portrait. It was that woman. Jenny. Around her neck was a ruby necklace.

146

Ashley woke with a jolt. She found herself standing before her gold cheval mirror. Without thought, she reached out and took the scarf from the mirror, wrapping it loosely around her neck. She stared deep into the mirror, wanting to reenter the dream.

"Jenny," she whispered, touching the face of the mirror. "I don't remember your face."

Ashley stumbled across the floor, falling onto the bed. For moments she lay there, trying to will herself back into her dream. In the dream she had felt blessed happiness. Stefan, she thought, trying to bring his face into focus. But to no use. She couldn't see her dream now, only feel it.

In the distance Ashley could hear a faint ringing. Persistent. She shut her eyes, willing it to go away. But it grew louder. In defeat, she pushed herself up from the bed. Her breath caught in her throat. It was then that she realized the voice was hers.

Some semblance of reality began to sweep into her brain. The phone. She reached out, wondering where the voice was coming from. She heard someone calling her name.

"Ashley, it's Shelby."

The answering machine, she realized, grabbing the phone.

"Shelby?" Ashley said hastily.

"I need to see you," Shelby said.

Ashley fought to clear the cobwebs from her head. "Where are you?"

"I'm at Dad and Meno's."

Dad and Meno's? Shel? Shelby hadn't called them that since her attack.

"Yes," Shelby said as if reading her mind. "I remembered. "But there's more. I'll be there in half an hour."

More? Ashley thought, hanging up the phone. What did she mean by that? She pulled the lace scarf from her neck, placing it back over the mirror. "God, I feel awful," and she padded cautiously across the floor toward the bathroom, noticing her black evening gown, thrown over the back of the chair. She stopped and stared at it, remembering how beautiful Scott said she had looked. The tears rolled down her face, wondering how she would cope without him.

After mindlessly taking a shower and blow-drying her hair, Ashley trudged to the kitchen and started a pot of coffee. She glanced at the clock on the microwave. It was 9:15. She must call Buzz. Call him and tell him she was catching the first plane out of there. Yes, she would do that now, before Shel got there. She had to get out of Belvedere. The memories that lingered were smothering. And Tryn, she didn't understand, but the thought of Tryn saddened her. It was as though a part of her had died. And a part of her had died, knowing what she had done to Scott. Somehow though, this feeling toward Tryn was strangely different.

God. Why did Buzz have to live in New Orleans? Any place but New Orleans. She wondered if Scott had already gone back. The thought was like poison, eating at the pit of her stomach.

She poured a cup of coffee and walked out onto the balcony. The morning fog lay heavily over the bay. She could barely see the houses atop Belvedere.

"DeLore House", she whispered, as she stared through the fog. She felt helpless trying to understand what had happened there last night. There was no explanation. For last night or for the past three months. Except for Scott, it was like living in a distorted dream world.

"Ash," Shelby said, walking toward the balcony.

"Shel!" Ashley ran into the living room and threw her arms around Shelby.

"I remember everything," Shelby said.

Ashley studied Shelby's face as though confirming what she was seeing. "Everything?"

"Yes, last night." Shelby looked past Ashley. "It was the strangest thing. I was lying in bed when all of a sudden the room got bright. I began to feel this incredible sense of comfort. Oh . . . I don't know." Shelby shook her head and smiled. "All I know is that I started remembering. First the rocking chair and then the rest of the furniture. "

"Rocking chair?" Ashley laughed. "You've always loved that rocking chair. I couldn't get you out of it when we were kids."

"I know." Again Shelby looked past Ashley. "But then the room grew dark. The light . . . " Shelby smiled back at Ashley. "Now I remember."

148

Ashley shook her head in amazement.

"You think I'm crazy, don't you?"

"Crazy?" Ashley felt like laughing hysterically. "No, Shel, I don't think you're crazy."

Shelby gazed up at Ashley as if to reconfirm what she had said.

Ignoring this, Ashley said. "Shel, "Do you remember the man that attacked you?"

"Man? No." Shelby looked away. "I never saw him."

Ashley sighed in defeat. "I was hoping you had," she said, then turned and headed for the kitchen. "Want some coffee?"

"Yeah," Shelby answered, slouching into an arm chair.

Ashley poured a cup and handed it to Shelby, then studied her own cup of coffee. "Shel?" she finally said but didn't look up. "Did Scott see Tryn and me in the courtyard last night?"

"Scott? I . . . I don't know what you mean."

&

Will Taylor had roared down from Hattiesburg on Sunday, his Toyota Supra, as always, gobbling the highway, devouring Interstate 59. By the time he reached New Orleans, Buzz was in contact with the police. They had immediately filed a missing person's report, which until now, Sunday morning, had turned up nothing. The morgues and hospitals had been checked for John Does. When Will arrived late that afternoon, Buzz and Les were sitting out in the courtyard. Their faces bore the defeated look of hopelessness.

Les greeted Will at the door and showed him to the back courtyard where Buzz sat with a Scotch and water.

"Will," Buzz greeted somberly. "I do wish we had better news. But it looks like our dear friend has simply disappeared into thin air."

Will shook Buzz's hand and collapsed into a chair. "Bullshit. He's a dead puppy, and I want to know why."

Shaken, Les inquired if Will would like a drink.

"Damn right I would. Scotch, straight, on the rocks."

Buzz swirled his drink around inside his glass. "I haven't had a Scotch in years."

149

Les handed Will his drink. Will nodded. "The last time I had one was with David." He took a hefty gulp.

Les sat down across the black mesh table from Will.

"Is there anyone that David could have stopped by to see before coming home?" Les asked.

"Absolutely not," Will said, downing another gulp of Scotch. "He was anxious to get back. We were planning a trip to Massachusetts next week. He had a lot of rescheduling to do before we left. Besides, even if he had stopped somewhere, he would have told Rosie. Hell, he hasn't called his answering service since he left my house. "No! There's a goddamn skunk in this woodpile."

Just then the cordless phone rang. "Excuse me," Buzz said.

"Yes, Lieutenant, this is he."

Les and Will listened impatiently.

"Oh my, no," Buzz said. "Where?"

Will moved to the edge of his chair.

"Magazine Street!" Buzz exclaimed. "What? His suitcase was still in the car?"

Buzz then told the Lieutenant that he would be right down to claim David's suitcase. The police, however, wanted to hold his car for further inspection.

"They found his car?" Will asked.

"Yes, down on Magazine behind an abandoned building. The cops spotted some kids trying to break into it. David's suitcase was in the back seat."

"I need a cigarette," Will announced.

"Me too. Here, have one on me," Les offered.

"I've been trying my damnedest to quit these things."

"Well, I haven't," Les said. "It's one of my few vices."

Buzz studied Will. "Is it possible that David could have been involved in something . . .? Well, you know."

"Good Lord, no!" Will shrieked. "David was as pure as the driven snow. He had all the attributes of a saint. It has always amazed me how the two of us could be buddies." Will lowered his head in a cloud of smoke. "We were, though."

150

"You're right," Buzz agreed. "It's just that none of this is making sense."

"No, it's not." Will said as he drained the last of the Scotch from the glass. "But I'm not going to hang around and do nothing. I'm going to poke around Magazine where they found David's car. Call you later," and he was sailing across the courtyard. "I'll be staying at David's. Rosie's terribly upset."

Just as Will walked through the tall double doors and out onto Chartres Street, the phone rang.

"Buzz," Ashley said. "Shelby and I will be in New Orleans tomorrow. She has her memory back."

"That's the best news I've heard for days. Can she identify the man who did it?"

"I'm afraid not."

"And the police still haven't turned up anything?"

"Nothing."

"Is Scott with you?"

Hesitation. "No. I'll tell you about that when I see you."

&

Another hour and they would be landing in New Orleans.

Michael, she mused. Why had he been acting so strange lately? And why had he been at Tryn's that last night?

Ashley stared out the window of the airplane, remembering what Shelby had told her the night before.

"I know I lived somewhere else before New Orleans," Shelby had said. "I had no memory of it before. But Saturday night, after the party, when my memory started coming back, I remembered being in this big house, and there were other houses all around. Right next to each other, almost touching. And there were boxes, so many boxes stacked against the walls. People were going in and out of the house, taking furniture. Then I remember being on a train with my mother. It seemed like we were there for a long time. I thought we were going to live there. But we didn't. We moved in with you and Michael in New Orleans."

151

And that's when Ashley finally decided to tell Shelby the truth. In detail. The dreams, visions, the strange sensations of familiarity, the hypnosis. And Tryn DeLore. But revealing that she was certain her mother had been killed was the worst part of all. Shelby simply would not believe that Meno was not Ashley's and Michael's mother.

"Ash," Shelby said. "You asked me something last night. I didn't really answer you. But if you don't want to talk about it now, I'll understand."

Ashley managed a smile. "That doesn't sound like the old Shel."

"I don't feel like the old Shel."

"No, I guess you don't. Everything seems different. I feel like I'm in a fog."

"I know." Shelby began fidgeting with her nails. "You asked me if Scott saw you and Tryn in the courtyard the other night."

Ashley turned toward the window. She could now see the crescent shape of New Orleans, the winding Mississippi River, and the vast waters of Lake Pontchartrain down below. "You don't have to say it, Shel. I know he saw us."

Buzz was waiting at Baggage Claim when Ashley and Shelby arrived.

"My two precious darlings," he called, a smile as wide as his face, and he gathered them into his arms. "Mary Harper is going to sulk for days."

Shelby laughed. "How is Mary Harper? I haven't seen her in almost two years. Still spoiled and jealous?"

"To the nines she is. To the nines."

"Thanks for all the flowers you sent, Uncle Buzz," Shelby said. "It was kind of weird getting so many flowers from a stranger."

"Well, my sweets, Ashley tells me I'm no longer a stranger."

"I'm as good as new." Shelby said. "I even remembered Mary Harper."

Buzz laughed. "Come on my darlings, let's get your bags. I have a surprise waiting."

It was four o'clock, and the afternoon air bordered on chilly. January in New Orleans could offer up a nice chill.

Sadly, Buzz told Ashley and Shelby that David was missing, and that Will was staying at David's house. With this news, Ashley suddenly feared that her link with the past was threatened. She could always find another hypnotist, of course, but she felt comfortable and secure with David. She didn't want to start over again with some stranger.

"Are you ready for a surprise?" Buzz asked, as he turned off St. Charles onto Amelia Street.

Ashley turned to Buzz, forcing an enthusiastic smile. She felt sick, uneasy, being this close to Scott's house. Each car they passed, she feared might be his. Buzz still had not mentioned him. Thank God, she thought.

"What do you have up your sleeve?" Ashley said.

"Quite a lot, my darling. Now, tell me what you think," and he turned onto Camp Street and pulled up to the curb.

"Look at that house," Shelby said, peering out the car window. "It takes up the whole block!"

"Well?" Buzz asked. "Is it big enough?"

"Big enough for what?" Shelby teased.

"For us," Buzz said, stepping out of the car.

Ashley immediately left the car and walked toward the iron gates. She glanced back at Buzz. "You didn't! This is the old Fink Asylum, isn't it?"

"It is," Buzz said sheepishly.

"The what?" Shelby said.

Buzz walked up and put his arms over their shoulders. "Well, what do my girls think?"

"So that's why you were so evasive when I asked you about this house! How long have you been planning this?"

"A while," he said, opening the gate. "It came on the market about six months ago."

They walked up the long brick walkway that led to more than a dozen stairs. The house was an Italianate-style villa. Its main gallery was on the second floor, supported by six square columns. There were three

153

third-floor dormers across the front. The main structure of the house was brick that had been painted a soft mauve.

"Why do they call it an asylum?" Shelby asked.

"Well," Buss replied. "A man by the name of Rice built the house in the late 1860's. After that, a man named Fink left his fortune to the city for the care of Protestant widows and orphans. The city used that money to later purchase the house. That's why it was called the Fink Asylum."

"Are you all right, Ash?" Shelby said, noticing a distant gaze in her eyes.

"Precious," Buzz said. "What's wrong?"

"Nothing," she assured them. "I was just daydreaming. Old houses do that to me." She forced a smile. "Come on, I'm dying to go inside."

Ashley stood back, fighting the tears as Buzz unlocked the door. Coming to New Orleans was a horrible idea. All she could feel, could think about was Scott. Even her thoughts of Tryn had ebbed.

"It's a wonderful house," Shelby said, as they drove back to the French Quarter. "When you and Les finish with it, it'll be a showplace."

"Well, I'm just glad my two little darlings could be here. We'll have fun decorating."

Mary Harper was waiting when they arrived back on Chartres Street. She danced in circles, then fell to the floor doing her roll-over tricks. Buzz dropped to his knees with praises and kisses. She had not seen the two women. When she did, there was a sudden burst of growls and dancing about their feet.

"Mary Harper," Shelby scolded. "Your disposition has not changed."

Buzz laughed. "She doesn't like guests, especially Protestants. She's Catholic through and through."

"Why don't you take Shelby to the kitchen and show her where Mary Harper's treats are," Ashley prompted. "That'll give her an attitude adjustment. I'll take our bags to the bedroom."

"Come on, Mary Harper," Buzz ordered.

He handed Shelby the box of treats. "Go over there and sit down at the table. I'll open a bottle of wine."

"Here you go, Mary Harper," Shelby threw out a small treat. Mary Harper went scurrying after it.

Buzz handed Shelby her wine. "I'm so glad you and Ashley are here," he said, easing his tall frame into the delicate French dining chair. "How long can you stay?"

"As long as it takes. There are a lot of unanswered questions."

"Then Ashley has told you everything?"

"Yes, but there's more."

"More? What do you mean?"

"I mean that I remembered something that happened a long time ago."

"What is that?"

"It was before my mother and I moved to New Orleans. Before I met Michael and Ashley. I had never remembered anything before that time. But bits and pieces started to come. I remembered moving out of our house and taking a train here to New Orleans. And that's when I met Michael and Ashley. We moved in with them."

"Where did you move from?"

"I don't know," she said, throwing Mary Harper another treat. "But it wasn't New Orleans."

"Dear me," Buzz said, his usually bright face fading to grim.

Mary Harper turned in circles, begging Shelby for another treat. "No more treats, Miss Harper," and she reached down and picked her up. "That rotten disposition of yours has suddenly taken a turn."

"What's taking Ashley so long?" Buzz said.

"Maybe we should go check on her."

"No need for that," Ashley said, appearing in the doorway. "I felt like taking a shower. May I have a glass of that wine please?"

"Of course, my darling," Buzz took another glass from the cabinet.

"When is Les going to be here?" she asked.

"Any minute. He was stopping by the market on his way home."

Ashley sipped her wine in silence.

"My precious," Buzz said. "I see distress in those eyes. Is it Scott?"

Ashley fought back the tears. "It's more complicated than that. If we could wait for Les."

"Of course," Buzz assured her.

155

Les arrived moments later with an armful of groceries. "Shelby, darling," he greeted, placing the grocery bags on the counter. "You look marvelous," and he gave her a generous hug.

"You haven't change a bit," she said, studying his face. "As pretty and handsome as ever. Still have that dimple I see," and she pressed her finger into his chin.

Before Les had come to New Orleans he had worked in New York as a model. His full dark hair, sincere brown eyes and perfectly sculptured face had been seen in most of the high fashion magazines. Now, even in his late thirties, he had still not lost that baby-face masculinity that had once been captured by the camera.

"Oh stop," he teased, reaching over and kissing Ashley on the cheek.

"Get yourself an Old Charter and seven," Ashley said. "Then come over here and sit down."

"All right." Les glanced at Ashley curiously.

After pouring his drink, he sat down next to Shelby.

Ashley stared into her wine glass. "Scott and I," she began. A lump began working its way into her throat. She wrestled with it for a moment. "It's over," she said. "Scott and I are over. I know I've hurt him terribly." She looked up at Buzz as she fought back the tears. "And I don't understand any of it." She brought the wine glass to her mouth and took a long sip. "I believe—I think that a man by the name of Tryn DeLore is in some way mixed up in everything that's been happening to me lately."

"The man you were doing the restoration for?" Buzz asked.

"Oh stop it!" Les blasted, glaring at Buzz. "You know damn well who DeLore is. Stop pretending you don't." Les turned to Ashley, who now had a look of shock on her face. "Buzz and I know exactly who DeLore is. We've been buying antiques from him for at least nine or ten years. Those furnishings that were in the parlor before Buzz hid them away so you wouldn't have to deal with them were all bought from DeLore. The whole lot of them."

Ashley pushed her wine glass off to the side. Mary Harper was now snuggled down into Shelby's lap with one eye opened.

"You've known Tryn DeLore all along?" Ashley looked at Buzz as though wounded by this revelation. "Why! Why haven't you told me?"

Buzz gave Les a piercing stare. "I don't know," he said. "I truly don't." Buzz shook his head. "Les is right. I was wrong to keep this from you. I have no explanation for it. But why do you think DeLore is mixed up in this? He's a strange character, I'll admit. But what has he done?"

"He's turned my life inside out. Since the day he came into my studio I haven't been able to get him out of my mind."

"Well, I can understand that," Les said.

Ashley could see that Les was finding it difficult to hold back a smile, so Ashley offered hers. "It's not just that," she said. "His beauty was the least of it. I became obsessed with him. Not even falling in love with Scott . . . I couldn't get free of it."

Ashley described what had happened the night of the party, and the drive to DeLore House. Her strange feeling of sadness and Tryn's sudden change from his former domineering self and his words to her on the balcony. How Michael had suddenly appeared at DeLore House and how Tryn had told Michael that she had to leave.

"I don't know what to say," Buzz replied, his tall frame slumping against the kitchen chair. "How do you feel about DeLore now?"

"Saddened and empty. Ever since that last night."

"I'm so sorry about Scott," Buzz said. "Would it help if I talked to him?"

"You couldn't explain this to Scott. I can't even explain it. No. I couldn't bear to face Scott again."

"Well, my angel, time will heal. But I'm afraid time is not on my dear friend David's side. Will hasn't come up with the slightest clue. He's been combing every joint down on Magazine Street for the last two days now. Nothing. The police are baffled."

"Why would anybody want to harm Dr. Clarendon?" Ashley sighed, staring into her wine glass.

છ

Clayton walked into Belvedere Designs, greeted Karen, and marched straight to Stanley's office.

"He's not in a good mood," Karen warned him.

"Oh really," Clayton said, turning with a wink.

157

Stanley was half hidden behind a mound of very expensive fabric swatches. He hadn't noticed Clayton standing in the doorway, stroking his head and looking amused.

"You look like a one-armed paper hanger," Clayton laughed.

Stanley looked up momentarily, then back to his swatches.

"I could shoot Ashley Winthrop for hightailing it off to New Orleans and leaving me with this DeLore thing. I was counting on her to finish this project. I can't imagine what's gotten into her. She knows I don't like being in that house."

"My, my, aren't we in a mood," Clayton said, pulling out a cigarette and lighting it.

Stanley reared up from his desk. "Put that damn thing out," he ordered, walking toward a stack of Country Life magazines lined against the wall. "You know I can't stand smelling those things."

"Oh, lighten up, Stan. There's nothing worse than a reformed smoker," and he took another drag.

"Just because I came to my senses doesn't mean I have to endure your second-hand smoke. Now either put it out, or suck on it outside."

"He is in a rotten mood," Clayton said to Karen, as he opened the front door and extinguished his cigarette.

"I warned you," she replied, turning to answer the phone.

Clayton walked back into Stanley's office. "Why don't you like being in that house?" he asked, settling into Stanley's chair.

"I've already told you. It gives me the creeps. And so does DeLore."

"That DeLore guy is beautiful," Clayton said. "If I had been Scott the other night, I wouldn't have let Ashley within fifty feet of him. Where did she and DeLore go, anyway?"

"I don't know. Probably wanted an explanation for neglecting his project."

"I thought you were doing a great job. Wasn't he satisfied?"

"Who knows," Stanley grumbled, thumbing through another Country Life.

Clayton was mulling over the different fabric swatches. "Damn, these things are expensive."

"Stanley," Karen called. "Michael's on line one."

Muttering quietly, Stanley pushed himself up from the floor and picked up the phone. "Hi Michael," he said, forcing enthusiasm.

"Stanley, I want you to hold off on the DeLore restoration. Mr. DeLore's not feeling well."

"What's the matter with him?"

"I didn't ask what the matter was. Now let me talk to Ashley."

"Ashley?"

"Stanley," he intoned irritably.

"Michael," Stanley said, leaning against the side of his desk. "Ashley went to New Orleans yesterday."

"New Orleans? With Scott?"

"I guess. She left a note on my desk yesterday morning. Shelby went too."

"Shelby? Never mind, Stanley, I'll track her down," and he hung up.

Stanley put the phone back and looked at Clayton, who had his arms crossed and his feet propped up on the edge of the desk.

"Well, well," Stanley said, shifting his gaze out across the room. "Looks like I won't have to worry about the DeLore account after all. The creep has taken ill." A wry look crossed his face. "And I'm Charles De Gaulle come back from the dead."

Chapter Twelve

Michael walked out onto the balcony. Tryn was leaning against the balustrades, his head lifted.

"I can feel them now," Michael heard him say. "Almost within my reach. Their rhythm is taking me into their embrace. Their mystical voices call out to me. Oh, how I long for them."

"Tryn?" Michael said.

"It will soon be over," Tryn whispered. "The horror is finally coming to a blessed end." He breathed a sigh of relief. "The bondage is ebbing now. I can almost taste its release. If only I could stop the madness that is to follow." Tryn bowed his head. "But it is not within my power. Forgive me, Ashley," he cried softly. "Forgive me Shelby." Again he lifted his gaze upward into the night's fog as if pleading for heaven to embrace him. "The choice was made for you long ago. You have but one release." He steadied himself against the stone balustrade. "Thank GOD Victor was spared." He then lowered his head as if in defeat, and whispered. "Jenny."

"Tryn?" Michael called again.

Tryn slowly turned to Michael.

"Come with me," he said. "There is something . . ." He looked into Michael's face with great sadness. "Something I must do." He then took Michael's arm and led him from the balcony.

"Where are we going?" Michael was bewildered. "Tryn?"

Tryn did not answer.

As they approached the center room, Tryn lifted the brass lever, releasing the stone doorway. Retrieving the lamplighter, he lit the wick and went from sconce to sconce. The room slowly unfolded within the shadowy flames.

"Michael," Tryn said, walking toward a large desk. He lit the two candelabras that stood at each end. As though the sun had suddenly intruded into the shadowy room, the gold inlay of the desk seemed to ignite.

Michael was now standing within the glow of the flames, and remembering that night when Tryn had first seduced him. He had surrendered to him completely, and many nights afterwards. Why did it seem different now? That overwhelming passion had slowly waned. What he was feeling was rooted deeper than a sexual passion. Was it love? He looked at Tryn, who was now staring intently at him. Michael studied him for a moment, thinking that he somehow looked different. Had he noticed a change even before tonight? Yes, he concluded. That night when Tryn had insisted on Ashley leaving. Michael had seen a strange yet subtle difference to Tryn's face. And now as he gazed at it, he saw that Tryn's once beautiful face had become shallow, gaunt.

"It's time, Michael," Tryn said, leaving the desk and holding Michael in his gaze.

℞

Shelby turned out the bathroom light and climbed into the canopy bed. Ashley was still standing by the French window, staring out into the courtyard.

"Buzz said that Taylor guy was coming tomorrow. Are you sure you want some stranger digging around in our lives?"

Ashley took a deep breath.

"Ash?" Shelby quickly left the bed. She approached Ashley, gently touching the sides of her arms.

Ashley broke into tears.

"Oh Ash," Shelby said, resting her head on Ashley's back. "Go ahead and cry. Get it all out." Ashley turned and leaned against Shelby's petite little body. "I'm so tired," she sobbed. "I just want to close my eyes and sleep for a very long time."

The haunting melody of Lakmé seemed to penetrate every crack, every opening. It filled the house. Visions passed before her.

A smoke-filled room. A metal table spinning slowly. A pregnant girl stroking her belly, her face sad and worn. A small graveyard with ornate Gothic-style tombs. A young woman's portrait hanging over an enormous mantle. A delicate hand clutching a knife, blood dripping from its blade. The number nine seemed to mingle throughout, as the images

161

spun through her mind. She struggled to wake; then suddenly her eyes opened.

The scent of lavender filled the room along with the music of Lakmé. Jenny's fingers glided across the keys. Ashley found herself standing beside the piano bench. Slowly she reached out to touch her, but her efforts seemed imprisoned.

"Who are you?" she whispered to the ghost-like presence. It was like looking through a hazy fog. As she struggled to discern even the slightest curve of the woman's face or the color of her hair, she noticed it. Jenny was pregnant.

Suddenly Ashley found herself seated alone at the piano. Through the windows, the flickering gaslights sent shadows dancing across the room. The full moon's brilliance intruded into the shadows. Then, like a dark hand before a face, a cloud crossed the moon's path, eclipsing the light.

Why wasn't she afraid? she pondered, leaving the piano and walking toward the window. She thought back to the dream. It was like bits and pieces of life swimming past. She looked out across the courtyard. She could hear the wind rustling through the trees, their limbs bending and thrashing. The scattered leaves swirled like tiny tornadoes while a shutter that hung precariously from a house across the way banged against the brick wall. In the distance she could hear the faint roar of thunder. She looked up into the darkened sky. The rain will come soon, she mused, and left the window. She walked back up the stairs, thinking that she remembered nothing of leaving her bed. Why had this happened, when the furniture that had previously triggered her visions were no longer there?

As she lapsed into a deep sleep, she whispered, "Tryn."

Ashley woke the next morning to the sound of heavy rain beating against the windows. But the house was still. It had taken on a darkened dreariness.

For several minutes she remained within the soft covers of her bed, staring at the canopy. She looked over at Shelby, who was still lost in sleep. How could she sleep through this? she thought, rising from the bed. She peered out into the heavy rain, unable to see past it. "I need coffee," she muttered, and headed downstairs to the kitchen. The entire household lay silent. Not even Mary Harper was stirring. Was the storm really happening?

Starting the coffee, she then went to the parlor and stood in the doorway. "Take me," she said in defiance. "Show me what it is I can't remember." Then she crossed the room to the fireplace. With her eyes closed, she stood by the mantel and ran her fingers across the cold marble. Her mind was searching in the deepest, darkest corners of her memory. It was as though a piece of her had been locked away.

Without warning, the room suddenly and inexplicably drew cold. The rain was coming harder now, the shutters were banging against the house. She covered her ears, trying to close out the deafening sounds, when off in the distance she began to hear that same familiar melody. What had Buzz called it? Its notes felt dark and haunting. She could hear voices singing. They grew louder, raging through her like a violent symphony. She brought her hands over her ears, desperate for it to stop.

With fisted hands she pressed harder against her ears. Extraordinarily vivid, the collage of images that had invaded her sleep, began to flash before her. The images filled the room with their giant presence. Tryn's face appeared, intertwined through the images. She was surrounded.

Gradually, the permeating sounds began to lessen. The next thing she knew she was slouched on the sofa. She heard voices. Where were they coming from? Finally Buzz's face came into focus. Les was beside him. Shelby then appeared with a cold wash cloth.

"My angel," Buzz whispered, as Shelby bathed Ashley's face. "What happened?"

"I can't take it any more," she cried. "I've got to get out of here." She pushed Shelby's hand away and ran from the parlor.

∞

The sun glistened on the lingering raindrops. The flowers, ravished by the storm, seemed to shake their petals as they lengthened their stems toward the warmth of the sun. Even Mary Harper was exuberant as she pranced about the courtyard.

The air was cool and damp, but the sun was warming. Shelby and Ashley puttered around the courtyard, cleaning up after the storm. Ashley moved stiffly and robotlike, as she struggled with what felt like insanity.

Wiping the rainwater off one of the patio chairs, she slumped into its black metal mesh. "I'm calling Dr. Taylor," she said, noticing Mary Harper toying with a trapped lizard.

Shelby scooped another pile of debris into the garbage bag. "Why do we need Dr. Taylor?" She looked at Ashley with varying degrees of disgust.

"I'm going to lose my mind, that's why. I have to do something."

"We can do something without that guy Taylor," Shelby insisted. "And you're not going to lose your mind. You're too stubborn."

Ashley smiled. "You're sounding like the old Shel."

"Yeah," she replied and swooped another load of debris into the bag. "Now get back to work. We're moving to Camp Street today. The movers will be here in an hour. I told Buzz we'd meet Helen over at the new house and give her a hand."

An hour or so later the moving van arrived.

"Ashley," Les called, as she and Shelby were just leaving. "It's Michael." He handed her the cordless phone.

"Michael," she said, wanting to ask him about Tryn.

"Ashley" Michael said. "I'm sending you something. It's important. What is Buzz's new address?"

"Address? I don't know. Just a minute," and she called after Les.

Les wrote the address on a piece of paper.

"It's 3643 Camp Street 70115."

He repeated the address.

"What are you sending?"

"It's too involved," he said. "It'll come Federal Express. Priority."

"Michael," she persisted. "What is it?"

"Just look for it," and he hung up.

Ashley took the phone back to Les, who was giving the movers strict instructions on dismantling a large sideboard. That didn't sound like Michael, she thought.

As she turned to leave, Buzz approached. "Come on," he said, "I'll walk you back to the car. There's something I'd like for you to think about while you and Shelby slave over the new house," he laughed.

"I love slaving over old houses.".

"Good, then you can give this some thought."

"What's that?" she asked, reaching the bottom of the stairs.

"That this thing with DeLore is nothing more than a bizarre coincidence." He looked at Ashley for a reaction, but her expression was blank.

"Honey," Buzz explained. "Please don't misunderstand. I don't mean that I think you're over exaggerating. I'm just wondering if we are all reacting irrationally. My angel, the man's strange and no doubt can be very seductive. He's certainly not hard to look at. I can understand how he could have mesmerized you. Possibly that's all it was."

Ashley turned her blank stare into focus. "Uncle Buzz. It wasn't a simple act of seduction. It went beyond that. You would have had to experience it. I tried to explain it last night. I guess it just got lost in translation."

Buzz nodded complacently and opened the car door. Shelby was sitting behind the wheel, anxious to go. "So," he said, "what did Michael have to say?"

"He wanted to know your new address."

Shelby turned to Buzz. "Tell Les I'll take good care of his car. I have one just like it."

"Well, personally," Buzz said snobbishly, "I prefer a Rolls."

"Yes," she winked. "I know. See you at Camp Street."

"Shel," Ashley said, looking out the car window at the row of houses that lined St. Charles Avenue. "I was still a virgin when I met Tryn."

Silence.

"Shel," Ashley said, not turning from the window. "Did you hear me?"

"I heard you."

"Well, aren't you going to say anything?"

Shelby looked straight ahead, as if concentrating heavily on her driving. Ashley glanced over. "I thought I'd get a bigger reaction than that."

"What did you expect me to say? That I'm amazed?"

Ashley laughed. "No, I guess not. Too wrapped up in my relics," to quote Michael." She turned back to the window. "How many forty year old virgins do you think there are these days?"

"Two probably. You and me."

"What!" Ashley turned to Shelby with a glare of astonishment.

"You heard me."

"But I thought . . ."

"Exactly what I wanted you to think."

"I don't believe this."

"Believe it," Shelby said emphatically.

Ashley went back to staring out the side window. "Shel, don't you find it strange that neither one of us has ever had any serious romantic interest?"

"I've had a lot of romantic interest."

Ashley laughed. "Like who?"

"Like . . . well, like a lot of guys. I can't remember all the guys I've dated."

"I'm not talking about harmless dating. I'm talking about getting involved."

"Bob Chambers and I were involved."

"That's bull. The first mention of marriage and you started avoiding Bob like the plague."

"I did not," Shelby hissed.

"That's not exactly how I remember it."

"Shelby pursed her mouth and rolled her eyes."

"Shel," Ashley said. "Why didn't you ever tell me? You've always told me everything."

A long disgruntled sigh. "Because. I didn't want you to know. I thought there was something wrong with me. Why didn't you ever tell *me*?"

"Same reason."

"Well. You can thank Mr. DeLore for changing your life." Shelby remarked sarcastically. "I don't know who changed mine."

"What? What did you mean by that?" But Ashley knew full well what she meant. Shelby was in love with Scott and had been since she had regained consciousness.

"I mean . . . well, I just feel differently now for some reason. I can't explain it."

"I don't understand any of this," Ashley sighed.

Both women sat quietly. Then Ashley broke the silence.

"Shel. There's something else."

"There is?"

"Yes, there is."

"What?"

"It's about Dad and Michael."

Shelby seemed to lose control, plowing the car into the curve. It jumped the curve just as Shelby slammed on the brakes.

"My God!" Ashley cried. "What in the hell was that all about?"

"I don't know," she said slouched against the car door.

"You don't know!"

Shelby glared out the window. "What did you mean about Dad and Michael?"

Ashley took a breath. "I've been having strange feelings," she said. "When I'm around Dad. And once with Michael."

"Me too," Shelby blurted, then started the car, pulling out as another car swerved to miss being broadsided. It's blaring horn didn't seem to faze her.

Shelby pulled up to the Camp Street house driveway, pushed the remote and waited for the garage door to open. They could see Helen, Buzz's new housekeeper, at the kitchen window. She waved down to them.

"Shel," Ashley said. "What's happening to us?"

Shelby looked at Ashley with determined eyes. "I don't know. But I know where I'm gonna start looking."

"Where?"

"This Winthrop House you talked about under hypnosis." Shelby threw open the door. "Hell, the damn place must belong to your family. Why else would it be called Winthrop House?"

Ashley smiled in spite of the sickness that gnawed at her stomach.

"Miss Shelby, Miss Ashley," Helen called from the top of the side stairs.

"She's such a cute little thing," Shelby said, bouncing up the stairs as though nothing had happened. "She doesn't look more than a teenager. Hello, Helen, I'm Shelby, this is Ashley."

Helen's face radiated, as she hurried to greet them.

"Mr. Harper's told me all about you and Miss Ashley," she said, reaching out to retrieve their bags. "It's so good to have you here. Mr. Harper already has the downstairs rooms furnished. That's where you and Miss Ashley will stay."

"Looks like you have everything under control," Ashley said, trying to sound cheerful, as they followed Helen downstairs.

"Mr. Les got the place pretty much in order yesterday. You know how Mr. Harper is. Likes everything just so."

The downstairs had an ample living room, kitchen and bath. There were two large bedrooms off the wide hallway with private baths. The door to the outside opened out under the porch. Mary Harper's portraits had already been hung in the little sitting area just off the hall by the circular stairway. A miniature Queen Anne chair and footstool were appropriately arranged under the portraits.

The two women settled into their bedrooms, then went to find Helen.

"Ashley and I can start cleaning the third-floor bedrooms," she informed Helen.

"All right, Miss Shelby. If you're sure."

"I'm sure, Helen."

Helen left her vacuum and gathered a few dust rags and a can of Endust. "Are you sure . . ."Shelby cut her off in mid sentence and reached out for the dust rags.

"Give me those rags," she laughed.

"I don't know why I'm enjoying this so much. I hate to clean my house."

"It's not your house," Ashley said.

"These windows could use some cleaning," Shelby said, as she dug her rag into the corners of one of the windowsills. "It's dingy in here."

"Yeah, it is," Ashley agreed, reaching into one of the dormers and running her finger across a window pane. It was spotless. She tested another pane. Spotless. The window was clean. "This window's not dirty," she said, realizing that she felt strangely uncomfortable. "Shel?" She turned to find Shelby standing in the middle of the room, her arms clutched around her.

"Do you feel it, Ash?" she said, cautiously looking around the room.

"Yes." Ashley was clutching the dust rag with both hands.

They both turned in slow circular motions, as if searching for something invisible.

"What is it?" Shelby said.

"I don't know," Ashley said glaring into thin air.

Shelby released her arms. "It's gone."

"I know," Ashley whispered, "walking to the window and peering out toward the front gate. "Shel, I've felt that before. That last night at DeLore House."

"Tryn?"

"Yeah."

"Are you positive?"

"I'll never forget it."

"Then why did I feel it too?"

"I don't know," Ashley replied, shivering. "Let's get out of here. I don't like this room."

ᴤᴑ

By eight o'clock that night, except for the things that were packed away in various boxes, every piece of furniture had been arranged in the dining room and parlor. Helen and Les had the kitchen in running order and Les was preparing a make shift candle-lit dinner. Edward, one of Buzz and Les' assistants, had left the shop early and was pitching in full force. The parlor and dining room, which was one enormous room, had been put in impeccable order. Even the massive paintings and gilt framed mirrors were now gracing the walls.

"For God's sake," Shelby said. "I thought you wanted to get to the bottom of this. After what happened in that room this morning, I sure as hell do."

"Of course I do. But I don't want Buzz thinking we're afraid of his new house. He's already had to get rid of his furniture."

"Bull. Buzz has enough furniture to fill twenty houses. If you don't ask him, I will."

"Wine for the ladies," Les said, sailing into the parlor with a silver tray. Bowing slightly, he held out the tray. Miss Mary Harper jumped up beside Shelby and rested her chin on her lap.

Taking their wine, Ashley inquired, "Has Buzz found out any more about the history of this house?"

Les looked at her curiously. "Huh, maybe," he closed escrow today." Les turned and sailed back toward the kitchen.

Shelby's instincts rumbled. "Les," she called. "Come back here."

"Gotta check something on the stove," he said with a wave.

Shelby glared after Les. "Damn. If this secrecy shit doesn't stop, we'll never get to the bottom of this."

"I'll ask Buzz," Ashley said.

"You're damn right." Shelby tipped her glass and gulped a mouthful of wine. "What is it we expect to hear, anyway? That the DeLore family used to live here?"

"Lord, I don't know. No, of course not."

"Look at my two beautiful angels," Buzz crooned, entering the parlor.

"Les said you closed escrow today," Shelby blurted, eager to get to the point.

Buzz's expression went suddenly flat.

So, Shelby thought, I've struck a chord. And by the look on Buzz's face, a sour one at that. She squirmed in triumph. Ashley sat quietly, letting Shelby pursue what she had started, trying not to show her own eagerness.

"My, aren't we anxious," Buzz said coyly, forcing a smile, as he settled into a gold arm chair. Shelby returned the smile, thinking how dignified he looked with his silver hair and pearl-white teeth. His long, lean stature seemed to dwarf the little chair.

Buzz turned to Ashley. "Are you sure you're ready to talk about this?"

Ashley smiled nervously. "Talk about what?"

Buzz looked stilted and ungainly as he shifted from one side of his chair to the other. He stewed a bit more, then cleared his throat. Shelby looked on in amusement, thinking that she had never seen Buzz without perfect control and grace. He had certainly lost his grasp on this one.

"Angel," he began. "I talked to Will today. He wants to meet with you and Shelby tomorrow." Buzz turned to Shelby. "I told him about your recent memories of living somewhere else before New Orleans. He wants you to send off for your birth certificate."

Shelby laughed sarcastically. "Now wait a minute. I don't want some hot shot professor snooping into our lives."

"Shelby," Ashley said," David Clarendon recommended Dr. Taylor. I have a lot of faith . . . had." Ashley lowered her head, saddened by the thought of David Clarendon. "I think Dr. Taylor will be a big help. He's good at what he does." Ashley then turned to Buzz as though the subject were closed. "Tell us what you found out when you closed escrow."

Buzz looked down at the oriental rug, as if studying its pattern. "I found out who owned this house between 1949 and 1953," he said, not taking his eyes from the rug.

"And?" Ashley became anxious.

Shelby moved in closer.

"His name was Christopher Winthrop."

"Christopher Winthrop?" Ashley frowned.

"Who's Christopher Winthrop?" Shelby blurted.

"I don't know," Ashley said. "But the man I saw under hypnosis—the man with Jenny. His name was Christopher." She looked back at Buzz. "Did you find out anything about him?"

"No my love. Nothing more than that he sold the house to Judge Williams, the man I bought it from."

"Well," Shelby suggested. "Let's ask Judge Williams."

"I'm afraid that's impossible," he said. "Judge Williams is in a nursing home. He's not coherent. All of my dealings were through his lawyers."

"Then let's ask the lawyers," Shelby said.

"Maybe they could help us out," Buzz said. "I seem to remember some old timers still mulling around that firm."

"Jambalaya is served," Les announced, carrying a large tureen, steaming with the celebrated pièce de résistance of Cajun cuisine.

Buzz rose from his chair and cupped his arms. "Ladies," he said.

Ashley smiled and took his arm.

"I still don't see why we need this Will Taylor person," Shelby muttered, taking the other arm.

Chapter Thirteen

How deliciously alive he felt now, sealed off from the world, sitting by the blazing fire in this magnificent room with its mural walls and gilt-framed portraits. Michael looked past Tryn, who was sitting at the large writing table, and into the desolate forest painted on the wall beyond. It seemed to have captured the nuance of the storm that could only be heard as a distant roar through the heavy stone walls. He studied the mural of moon-streaked clouds above a dark and desolate forest. It was as though the storm was emanating from within the mural. Is this an omen of my doom? he mused.

He turned to contemplate the mural at the other end. Or am I to live in passion as this mural suggests? The provocative Sirens, with their haunting and seductive singing, seemed to be luring him into their web of pleasures.

Michael could feel his senses heighten. His loins ached with an overwhelming yearning. Immediately his thoughts went to Ashley, to Shelby. How would they react when they learned the truth? Horrified? Trapped? This excited Michael.

But he must not think of it now. There was so much rebirth to contend with. He could feel its power. The lustful passion was taking him. He could feel that glorious evil welling inside him.

He looked toward Tryn who still sat at the French writing table in the half shadow of the flickering candles, completely absorbed in his writings. Could Tryn possibly have the strength to complete the telling of this tale? To put his preposterous journey on paper seemed far too arduous an undertaking. But yes, he thought. Tryn would persevere. His passion now lay in this greater need.

Michael realized as he watched the shadows move about Tryn's tattered face that he no longer wanted to feel his body close to Tryn's, to bury himself in his sex. That need had ebbed, lost in the horror of what Michael now beheld within the shadows. He thought back to that first night when Tryn had taken him. How utterly beautiful Tryn had been. Michael still remembered Tryn's seductive power. As absurd an act as it had seemed to Michael that night, it had crept upon him like a sea of submission. Michael had thought the seduction sublime.

Again his mind went to Ashley and Shelby. He fantasized about them as he had never done before. Of how he would strip them naked, feed on them with his eyes, then take them violently. He would fill them with his lust.

Michael walked to his portrait that now hung among the many portraits in this secluded chamber. He stared deep into the canvas as though there were life beyond its surface. He turned to the mirror above the tall limestone mantel that framed the fireplace. Tryn's admonition resurfaced.

"Read these words with passion," he had said. "For if you lack the passion *The Gift* will not come to you."

Looking into that mirror and seeing the horror of his own decaying face had brought a terror beyond comprehension. He had never experienced such passion as he had felt at that moment. Those words that Tryn had told him to recite seemed to become a part of him as he repeated passionately. After the last word had been spoken, Michael once again looked into the mirror. The decaying face he had beheld only moments before, had now been transformed back into youthful beauty.

෨

"Blessed Mary mother of God!" Buzz screeched. "Les!" Buzz flung himself across the library floor with Mary Harper in tow, coughing and snorting. He bolted into the kitchen.

"Shit!" Les exclaimed. "What is it?"

"I think she's choking," Buzz stammered. "Sweet Mary, what do we do?"

"Give her to me." Les pulled Mary Harper from Buzz's fumbling hands. He sat down in the nearest chair, probed inside the tiny mouth, and retrieved a large molar. "She's losing her teeth. Hell, it was hanging by a thread." He laid the tooth on the kitchen table and returned Mary Harper to Buzz's trembling arms. Buzz let out a long sigh and smothered her with kisses.

"My precious angel," he crooned. "You gave Daddy a scare."

Les went back to pouring his cup of coffee. "Mary Harper," he said. When it's time for you to go to the great beyond, you better take Buzz Harper with you."

"Oh hush up," Buzz pouted, and opened the back door. "Come on angel, let's take our morning walk," and they were out the door.

"What was all the commotion?" Shelby asked, walking sleepy-eyed into the kitchen.

"Just Buzz in a frenzy over Mary Harper. She was choking on a tooth." Les turned and gave Shelby a morning kiss. "Coffee?"

"Please," she said. "A tooth?"

"Yeah. For Christ's sake though, don't say anything to Buzz. He's in denial. Refuses to believe she's getting old."

"How old is Mary Harper?"

"Who knows. Twelve, maybe fifteen." He handed Shelby her coffee. "Thanks."

"Good morning," Ashley said in greeting, unusually cheerful.

"Well," Shelby said. "You seem to be in a good mood this morning."

"Have a seat," Les offered, taking another cup and saucer from the cupboard.

"I'm looking forward to meeting Dr. Taylor," Ashley said.

"Dr. Taylor," Shelby grumbled.

"How did you sleep?" Les asked. "Any nightmares?"

"No, none."

"Good," Shelby said, getting up from the table. "What time is that guy Taylor getting here?"

"Nine," Ashley said. "And stop pouting. Dr. Taylor is an expert in solving mysteries."

"Sounds to me like he's and expert in snooping," Shelby growled.

"Didn't Buzz say yesterday that Will Taylor knew one of the old timers down at the law firm?" Les asked.

"Yes," Ashley said. "Some guy in his eighties and still going strong."

"That means he would have been in his early fifties when Christopher Winthrop lived here," Les said.

Ashley silently studied her coffee.

"Good morning, angels," Buzz crooned as he entered the kitchen with Mary Harper in tow. "Did you sleep well?"

"Wonderfully," Shelby replied. "Even Ashley."

"So your first night in my new house was peaceful. Good."

Les offered more coffee.

"Just a little more," Ashley said, turning to Buzz. "Are you and Les going with us today?"

"Buzz is," Les interjected. "I have two canopy frames to build and four pairs of drapes to design."

☙

Dr. Taylor stood by the front gate energetically ringing the buzzer. Helen was down the hall in seconds and pushed the button, releasing the gate. Will proceeded up the long brick walkway.

"You must be Helen," he said, climbing the many steps to the porch, huffing and puffing. His neatly groomed salt and pepper hair had now found its way onto his forehead. His equally salt and pepper mustache glistened with perspiration. But a childlike grin appeared on his face.

Helen smiled. "And you must be Dr. Taylor."

Will raised an eyebrow. "That's me," and he held out his hand. "That's a lot of stairs," he muttered, glancing backward.

"It's nice to meet you, Doctor," she said shaking his hand.

"Nice to meet you too, Helen."

Helen showed Will into the hallway. "Would you like a cup of coffee?"

"Sure would. Caffeine and nicotine are what keep me going in daylight, alcohol at night. And I hate those addicts."

Helen's face lit up with laughter. "Have a seat in the parlor, Dr. Taylor and I'll have your coffee in no time. Mr. Harper should be out in a minute." Helen hurried back down the hall.

"Are you trying to quit?" Shelby asked, standing in the doorway, watching Will maul a pack of cigarettes.

Will practically leapt from the sofa, throwing his pack of cigarettes on the French coffee table. Momentarily embarrassed, he said. "That obvious, huh?"

"Very."

"I'm Will Taylor," he said. "You must be . . . "

176

"So you're the infamous Dr. Taylor," Shelby said, sitting across from Will.

"Infamous?" he chuckled. "Some might say so. Does this mean you've read my books?"

"No." Shelby studied his face. "Ashley reads your books."

"I see."

"Good morning, Will," Buzz announced, walking through the dining room with Ashley at his side. "I see that you and Shelby have met."

Will stood up and straightened his trousers. "Shelby," he said. "Yes, I guess you could say that. I don't believe she's one of my most ardent admirers though."

"Shelby?" Ashley said with a look of warning.

Shelby just glared.

Buzz held out his hand in an introductory gesture. "Will, this is Ashley Winthrop. Ashley, Dr. Taylor."

"Finally I get to meet the famous Dr. Taylor. I'm an ardent admirer. Shelby, on the other hand needs an attitude adjustment."

"Call me Will, please," he said, taking her hand. "I don't mean to pry into your personal affairs." He looked toward Shelby. "But David thought I might be of some help."

Shelby only stared into Will's face, curiously unaffected by this comment.

"You've already been a big help. Dr. Clarendon is certainly a fan of yours," Ashley said, careful not to refer to David Clarendon in the past tense, though Will's detective work and New Orleans' finest had turned up nothing.

"David and I go back a long way," Will said. "But I'm not giving up hope that he'll be found. I'm a stubborn old goat. Right now, though, let us focus on this Winthrop mystery." Will turned to Shelby. "Ms. Kincaid," he said. "Buzz tells me you think you were born some place other than New Orleans."

Will's comment seemed to jolt Shelby. She had not taken her eyes from him. "Huh, yes, I guess you'd say that," she replied. "And Ms. Kincaid is not necessary."

Ashley frowned at Shelby as if to say, 'Stop pouting', then turned to Will. "I already know that my brother and I were born in Massachusetts.

40 Sea Road, Manchester, Mass." Ashley watched for a reaction. She knew that Will knew exactly where Winthrop House was.

"40 Sea Road." Will arched his eyebrow. "That's our Winthrop House," he said, then looked at Shelby. "I also think that since Shelby has been with your family for most of her life, it's quite possible that she too might have been born in Massachusetts."

Shelby offered no reaction, just a concentrated stare.

"What about your brother?" he said, turning to Ashley. "Michael, is it?"

"Yes," Ashley replied. But she knew Michael wasn't going to be much help. "I'm afraid Michael thinks I'm . . . well, let's just say this is entirely my and Shelby's quest."

"I see," Will said, considering Ashley. "And your parents? Am I to understand that they know nothing of what's been going on?"

"Nothing," Ashley said. "And I want to keep it that way."

"What if they are the only ones who can give us the truth? Have you thought about that?"

"I'll cross that bridge when I come to it."

"All right then. I guess our next move is to meet with old man Dabney and see what we can find out about this Christopher Winthrop."

❧

The law firm of Delachaise and Poydras was in one of the old mansions on Esplanade Avenue. Built during the early to middle eighteen hundreds, it had been restored in the mid thirties when George Delachaise and Antonine Poydras first set up practice. They had, through the years, built the most prestigious practice in the entire state of Louisiana. They had represented wealthy business men, celebrities, and politicians alike, in some of the most celebrated cases ever recorded. They were respected, and they were feared. Hewlett Dabney had joined the firm in 1938 at the age of 37. It was now the beginning of 1987.

Dabney stood about six feet, though he had once been taller. But he carried himself with pride and dignity. He still had a head of thick, wavy hair, that had been stark white since he was forty-five. He had a strong, lean face and bushy white eyebrows that he kept exceptionally well groomed. Fastidious in manner, and with an extraordinary gift for the art of law, he was respected by even the most arrogant young attorneys.

"Will, old boy," Hewlett greeted him, "It's been a long time."

"Too long," Will said shaking Hewlett's hand vigorously.

"Has there been any news about your old friend David?"

Will frowned. "Not a Goddamn thing."

Hewlett shook his head, looking distraught.

David and Hewlett had belonged to the same men's club for the past twenty years and had become friends. Hewlett had helped David out once when the husband of one of David's patients filed suit against him. It seemed that the woman, delusional that she was actually having an affair with David, confessed to her husband. The husband went berserk. Hewlett took the case and won.

Will made all the appropriate introductions and Hewlett escorted everyone into his office. Pictures of him with the many celebrities he had represented lined the walls and graced the bookshelves. Hewlett pulled up a couple of leather arm chairs from around the handsomely furnished room. He then settled into his swivel leather chair and looked across his desk. "So," he said to Buzz, "Will tells me that you bought Judge Williams' old place. That's a grand old house."

"Yes, it is," Buzz replied. "And it seems to have an interesting history."

"Oh yes," Hewlett agreed. "It housed some very unfortunate people in its day. But I'm afraid the city finally had to intervene. The widows just couldn't seem to maintain the health standards that were required. That's when Christopher Winthrop appeared on the scene and bought the place for a song. 1949 I believe it was. He separated the main house from the rear wing and sold the property to a group of developers. They're townhouses now."

"How was it that you were involved in the sale?" Will asked.

"Christopher Winthrop purchased the property from the city of New Orleans. We represented his interests in the transaction." Hewlett paused momentarily. "Winthrop was a strange bird. Strictly business, and very secretive. I handled the purchase for him. Didn't see him again until 1953. He wanted me to sell the house for him. Didn't want Realtors involved."

Hewlett shook his head despondently. "Soon after that, Lucy, my secretary, became involved with the man. I didn't learn this until four years later when he came back to tell me that he wanted to sell his house. I overheard Lucy and him arguing."

"Arguing?" Will asked, intrigued. "About what?"

Hewlett's face saddened. "I'm afraid Lucy was pregnant. As long as I live, I'll never forget that day. I could hear them from my office. Sometimes I think I can still hear that conversation."

"You will never speak of this again," Winthrop said in a cold, defiant tone. " *You will NOT give life to that thing inside of you. Is that understood!*

Lucy could barely speak. She was sobbing violently. *"Christopher. But this is our child. I carry it with love for you."*

"There IS no love with you!" Christopher roared. *"Do you hear me! I detest even the sound of the word. Just as I detest the sight of you."*

Hewlett bowed his head. "Winthrop stormed out of the office. I went to Lucy and comforted her as much as I could. I was simply astounded. I have never heard such hatred as was in Christopher Winthrop's words."

"Whatever happened to Lucy?" Shelby asked, unable to keep her silence.

"Well, it seems that Winthrop later sent her quite a sum of money. Possibly out of guilt. Lucy took the money, bought a small house on St. Charles Avenue, and started a bridal shop."

"A bridal shop!" Shelby exclaimed.

"Ironic, isn't it?" Hewlett said. "It was then that she began coming to me for advice. I've been advising her ever since. Not that she needed it. Lucy has sound business sense." Hewlett smiled. "And the most beautiful red hair."

"Where is she now?" Ashley asked.

"She now has four locations and lives in the top two floors of the new location on St. Charles. She bought that place about ten years ago. It's one of the largest homes on the street."

"Did she ever marry?" Shelby asked.

"No, she never did."

"Mr. Dabney," Ashley said.

"Oh no," Hewlett interrupted with an upheld hand. "Mr. Dabney makes me sound older than I aspire to be. Hewlett, please."

"Okay. Hewlett. Whatever happened to Lucy's child?"

A big grin spread across his face. "Have you ever heard of Sylina Vierhus?"

"Sylina Vierhus? The artist?"

"The artist," Hewlett said proudly. "Sylina is Lucy and Christopher Winthrop's daughter."

"I don't believe it," Ashley said. "I've worked with Sylina on some of my restorations. Her work is extraordinary. She travels all over the country."

"That she does," Hewlett agreed. "But I'm afraid she's married to her work."

"That sounds familiar," Shelby noted with a smirk.

Buzz had been sitting quietly taking in the conversation. "Hewlett?" he asked. "This Christopher Winthrop, can you tell us what he looked like?"

Hewlett grimaced. "I have tried to put that man out of my mind," he said. "But . . . well, as for his appearance, he was quite tall, a handsome man. The epicurean type, if you know what I mean."

"Where did Winthrop go after he sold the house?" Will asked.

"Have no idea," Hewlett replied. "Winthrop was a very secretive man. He guarded his privacy with a vengeance. I do wish I could be more help."

"You've been a big help," Will assured him. "Thanks for your time."

"Don't be silly," Hewlett replied. "Do you mind my asking though, the reason for your interest in this man?"

Ashley responded. "Dr. Taylor and I are tracing my genealogy. When Buzz found out that a Christopher Winthrop had once owned his house I became curious. Just thought I might have found a long lost relative."

Everyone said their good-byes. Hewlett assured Ashley that if he remembered anything else, he would call her. Buzz gave Hewlett his phone number.

Hewlett gently placed his hand on Ashley's shoulder. "To be honest," he said, "I think this relative of yours is best left undisturbed."

"You're probably right," she agreed. "Thanks for your time."

"Not at all," he said, reaching over to shake Buzz's hand. "I'd like to come by and see what you've done to the house. Judge Williams' failing health took a toll on the old place."

"You're welcome any time," Buzz said. "Just give me a call."

Will took Ashley's arm as they descended the porch. "Looks like our Christopher Winthrop was something of a bad hat."

"Doesn't say a lot for my family, does it?"

"I don't know about any of you," Shelby said as Buzz drove down Esplanade Avenue, "but I'm going to Winthrop House."

Will turned around and rested his arm over the front of the seat. "Do you mind if I come along?"

Shelby looked past him. "Suit yourself."

"Ignore Shelby," Ashley apologized. "She's taken leave of her manners. When do we go?"

"In a couple of days," Will said. "A friend of mine from San Francisco will be here tomorrow. In fact, you and Shelby know Blake. David said he was your father's publisher."

"Blake Sheldon?" Ashley said. "Yes, he is."

"Blake and David and I all went to the University of London. Blake's terribly upset about David's disappearance. He's going to stay with Rosie, David's housekeeper, while I'm gone." Will laughed. "If I know Blake he'll give the police a hefty piece of his mind if they don't start turning up some clues."

"Wish I could accompany you to Manchester," Buzz said. "I'm afraid Les and I have a grueling project coming up in Chicago."

Will laughed. "I'm not sure I can trust myself with two beautiful women."

Shelby made a face and turned her attention out the window.

Chapter Fourteen

"Ashley Winthrop," Stanley growled. "It's a bloody madhouse around here. "When in the hell are you coming back?"

Ashley lowered the phone with a sigh. "I don't know," she said, pressing it back to her ear. "Another week or so. I'm in the middle of helping Buzz with a project. I can't just walk out on it."

"You walked out on me."

"Stop it. You're making me feel guilty."

"Guilt is what's sustaining me," he said "Oh, I forgot. Your mother called."

Ashley cringed. "What did she want?"

"Wanted to know about the DeLore project. I told her it was on hold. That weirdo is sick again."

"Sick?"

"Yeah. Michael called the other day before he left for Europe, said the creep was sick and to hold off on the restoration. I couldn't have been happier."

"Europe? Why did Michael go to Europe?"

"I have no idea. Maybe to get as far away from that creep DeLore as possible."

"Look," Ashley sighed. "I'll be here at Buzz's if you need me."

"Not Scott?"

"No," she said, hoping Stanley wouldn't start with his incessant questioning. "I'm working with Buzz on his new house."

"Oh. So that's the important project. Well tell him that I need you here."

"Stop whining, Stanley."

Ashley sat at the writing table just inside the bedroom door, unaware that Shelby was standing in the doorway. Ashley carefully opened the velvet pouch that she held in her hand and took out a small box. She opened it and stared at the gold bracelet that Scott had given her for Christmas, just before his opening.

"Scott?" Shelby asked.

Ashley looked up. "Shel, I didn't see you standing there."

"It's beautiful," Shelby said, lifting the bracelet from the box. "Loving like this hurts too much?"

"Yes," Ashley said. "It does," looking at Shelby curiously.

"Why can't it be like it used to be?"

"Like it used to be?"

"Yes," and Shelby handed the box back to Ashley.

"Why, because you love Scott too?"

Shelby glared into Ashley's face.

"It's all right, Shel."

Shelby turned away. "I never wanted you to know that," she said. "I would never have . . . "

"I know. You're not to blame. I love him too."

Shelby laughed sarcastically. "Wouldn't you just know it, we finally fall in love and with the same goddamn man."

"And I went and screwed it up," Ashley said, closing the box and placing it back in the pouch. "Maybe you can do better."

Shelby started to laugh. Seconds later they were both laughing. Between laughs they cried. Mary Harper lurked outside the doorway and considered a growl.

"Ash," Shelby said. "I went to see Scott the other day."

"You did what?"

"Don't worry. He wasn't there. His housekeeper said he was on an extended trip to London."

"Why, Shel? Why did you do that?"

"I don't know," Shelby replied. "Guess I just couldn't stand seeing you so hurt. I thought I could make him understand."

"That was sweet. But please, my life is too complicated right now. It's better that Scott's not in it."

"Yeah," Shelby sighed.

"Why would Scott go to London?" Ashley said, thinking of her hypnosis and that place she had called Nine Thornton Square.

The vision of Winthrop House seemed to be forever embedded in Ashley's mind. She could see the tall Elizabethan chimneys, the intricate design of the mansion's facade, the marble balconies, the sweeping terraces encasing the tall, leaded French doors. And that window, feeling the dread of what lay behind it. The same dread she had felt at Dr. Clarendon's house when she had seen his attic window. It had reminded her of the window in her dream. Had Jenny been tortured behind that window? she wondered. Jenny's spirit seemed to be reaching out to her. Without a doubt, Ashley felt this to be true. But why now, after all these years? She didn't know the answer, only that it had all started when Tryn first arrived in Belvedere.

The thought of actually seeing Winthrop House frightened her. She didn't know if she had the courage to make the same ominous journey she had made in her dream. Would it be the same? Those menacing trees, their gnarled and sinuous branches that seemed to beckon her. The restless roar of the sea through that heavy fog. What would it be like to finally see such a thing?

Ashley pulled the covers close around her, glancing at the clock. It was just past midnight. She closed her eyes.

ॐ

The dining room table was draped in lace-scalloped linen. Two large, bronze urns overflowed with roses and lilies. Buzz always insisted on fresh flowers. A three-tiered candelabra stood on each side.

"Ashley," Les said. "Would you get the door? Prissy and I are up to our ears in the kitchen."

"Sure," Ashley smiled, thinking of Buzz and Les calling Helen Prissy. Glancing out the window, she released the gate and walked out onto the porch.

Ashley greeted Will Taylor, then turned to Blake. "It's good to see you again."

"Good to see you too," Blake said in his deep voice and kissed Ashley on her cheek. "I had no idea you and Will knew each other."

She looked at Will nervously.

"I told Blake that you were a fan of mine and that we were working on your genealogy."

"Yes," Ashley said, relieved. "My father introduced me to Will's work several years ago. I've been wanting to trace my family tree."

"I have too," Blake said. "Afraid the publishing world takes up most of my time though."

"Blake," Shelby sailed down the hallway and threw her arms around his neck.

"Good to see you, too." Blake said, trying to maintain his balance.

"Blake tells me you two had a date the other night," Will smiled at Shelby.

Shelby glared at Will, then looked up at Blake. "Yes, we did." She winked and took his arm. "Come on, I'll get a drink."

"I'm so sorry about your friend, Dr. Clarendon," she said, as they disappeared into the parlor.

"I don't think Shelby approves of me," Will said.

"It's not that," Ashley said. "Shelby's just strong headed. Thinks she can solve this mystery of ours without any outside interference. Don't pay any attention to her."

"That's not so easy to do," Will said, lifting an eyebrow. "She's adorable."

Ashley laughed and put her arm around him. "Come on, let's get a drink."

After dinner Blake asked Ashley to take a walk out in the courtyard.

"It's a beautiful night," he said, looking up at the full moon through the twisted branches of the oak tree. The cadence of the insects could be heard nearby.

"Yes, it is," Ashley replied as they walked toward the gazebo. "I love nighttime in the south. Nature seems to come alive." She looked at Blake and smiled.

Blake returned her smile and lit his pipe. Taking a long draw he said, "May I ask you something personal?"

"Personal?" She studied Blake's face. "Go ahead."

"You and Scott. Are you . . . "

"No," Ashley answered without hesitation. "We're not," and she turned away.

"When are you going back to California?" Blake asked.

"Oh, a couple of weeks, I guess. We're going to New England the day after tomorrow."

"Your family's from New England?"

"Yes," she said nervously. "Dad doesn't know I'm doing this. I want to surprise him. He's always been interested in genealogy. He has all of Will's books."

Blake chuckled. "Will's books make for good reading. And for successful publishing. I'm sure he'll do a superb job."

"I'm looking forward to it," Ashley said. "I think right now though, I'd better call it a night."

"Yes, I guess it is getting late. And I have an early meeting tomorrow with the police about David's case." Blake escorted Ashley up the front stairs. "I can't sit around here and do nothing. There has to be something they're overlooking."

"I know how you feel. It's the same with Shelby. The police haven't uncovered a shred of evidence. It's unnerving to think that psychopath is still out there."

"I know. Victor told me about Shelby. She's made a remarkable recovery."

"It's hard to keep Shelby down," Ashley laughed.

As they reached the front door Blake took Ashley's hand. "Would you like to join me for dinner tomorrow night? Antoine's is one of my and David's favorite restaurants."

"Antoine's," she replied, looking thoughtful. "It's been a long time since I've been there." She gazed into Blake's strong, wide face, finding that she liked his thick eyebrows. So different from the face she had fallen in love with. "Why don't we see if Shelby and Will would like to join us?"

"Shelby and Will?" Blake seemed thoroughly amused at this.

 જી

Before going to bed, Ashley opened the bureau drawer and lifted out a wooden box inlaid with mother of pearl. She took it to the writing table where the velvet pouch lay next to an alabaster lamp. She placed the pouch inside the box next to her grandmother's ruby necklace. Fleetingly, she thought of her grandmother, wishing that she could have known her. Kathleen Winthrop. What a beautiful name. Had Kathleen been as beautiful as her name? The only picture she had ever seen of her was so old and faded it could have been of anyone. How strange it felt thinking of her now. Ashley realized that she had never really thought about her grandmother. Kathleen Winthrop had died long before Ashley had been born. At least that's what she had been told. And her grandfather Winthrop had died when Ashley's father was very young. She wondered now what was fact, what may have been lies, and what the lies were designed to shield.

Why had she accepted a dinner invitation with Blake? The last thing she wanted was to get involved. Her life was a mess. She didn't need to bring Blake into it.

"For Christ's sake," she muttered. "It's only dinner," and she continued arranging a large vase of freshly cut flowers that had just arrived. Inspecting it one last time, she picked up the vase and placed it on the round table that stood center in the library. Ashley looked around the room thinking how much she loved the dark green walls.

"Your arrangement is beautiful, Miss Ashley," Helen said, as she sailed through the room.

"Oh Helen," Ashley called after her. "Do you know where Shelby is? We're suppose to be in the Quarter for lunch in thirty minutes."

"No, but I'll find her for you." Helen scurried back down the hallway.

I wonder why Shelby is so suspicious about Will? Ashley mused. Nothing she could say last night would convince Shelby to join them for dinner. One mention of Will and that was it. The answer was a flat no. Buzz and Les even talked to her this morning before leaving for Chicago, but without success. Ashley had never seen Shelby act this way about another human being.

"Miss Shelby?" Helen called, walking up the stairs to the third floor. "Are you up here?"

Helen poked her head into the various bedrooms calling Shelby's name. She couldn't image why Shelby would be on the third floor, but she had run out of places to search. All but two of the third floor bedrooms had been furnished. The front room was still empty. She stopped dead still when she saw Shelby standing in the middle of the empty bedroom, the sun streaming through the dormer window. Shelby seemed to be aglow as she stared into the sunlight, her head lifted upward.

"Miss Shelby?" Helen cautiously edged closer.

Still gazing into the sunlight, Shelby whispered. "Go to the shed. Lift the door." She quickly turned toward Helen, looking straight through her. "Please," she begged. Then her body went limp, and she collapsed to the floor.

"Miss Shelby!" Helen cradled Shelby in her arms. "Wake up!"

Helen looked around the room as if lost. Shelby lay heavy and still. Helen then tilted her head backward and screamed. "Miss Ashley! Miss Ashley!" She was still screaming when Ashley came bursting through the doorway.

"My God! What's happened?"

"Oh, Miss Ashley," she sobbed, looking to Ashley like a frightened child. "I don't know. She was standing here in the middle of the room, staring up at that window. The sun was so bright I could barely see her."

"The sun?" Ashley glanced toward the window, then quickly knelt down beside Shelby and felt her pulse. It was slow but steady. "Helen, go to the bathroom and get a cold wash cloth."

Helen fled into the bathroom, as a brilliant ray of light streamed through the window. Shelby opened her eyes. "Please," she muttered. "Hurry."

"Shel," Ashley said, shielding her eyes from the glare. "It's all right. You just fainted."

Shelby twisted her face into a frown. "No! You must go to the shed. Lift the trap door."

She stared at Ashley, then toward the window and into the light. Slowly but determinedly she lifted herself from Ashley's grasp. Ashley reached out ready to protest, but instead let her arms slide away as Shelby walked across the room, trancelike. Ashley looked back toward the window. It was dark and dreary.

Helen stopped in mid stride, clutching a dripping hand towel. Ashley motioned Helen quiet. They both followed as Shelby descended the circular stairs, walked down the long hallway, and out the front door. When she reached the brick walkway she turned toward the shed at the far end of the yard and ran to it. She lifted the door handle and sent the door slamming against the side of the shed. Ashley and Helen watched, Helen still clutching the dripping towel.

"Miss Ashley," Helen whispered, pressing closer. In the distance came a rumble of thunder. The sky seemed to grow darker. "What is Miss Shelby doing?" she asked. Helen clutched the towel tighter, water dripping down the front of her dress.

"I don't know," Ashley moved closer to the shed.

Shelby stood in the doorway, peering into the darkened shed. Muted streaks of daylight filtered through the cracks in the roof and around the foundation. The shed was a perfect ten by ten square with an old brick floor that had long since been smothered in heavy patches of moss. Picks and shovels and other lawn equipment hung on the walls. A riding lawnmower stood in one corner.

Shelby entered the shed and walked directly to the far right corner. Ashley and Helen followed cautiously. A stale, musty odor stifled them.

About that time Helen let out a yell as a daddy longlegs crawled up her arm. Helen's outburst sent Ashley reeling against the shed. A shovel and several garden tools came crashing onto the mossy bricks. Panicked, Helen ran across the soggy moss, frantically slapping and waving her arms. Ashley, securing her footing, crept back to the doorway to console her.

"Helen, go back to the house. Shelby and I will be fine."

"Lordy me, Miss Ashley, I'm so sorry." She peered cautiously over Ashley's shoulder. "Why, Miss Shelby."

Ashley turned to find Shelby standing behind her, looking tired and confused.

"What are we doing out here?" Shelby said, her hands and jeans wet and stained. She studied them for a moment, then looked at Ashley with a bewildered expression. "What happened?"

Ashley took Shelby's hands. "You don't remember?"

"Remember?" Shelby asked reflectively, as though a memory had suddenly formed in her mind. She turned and walked toward the far corner of the shed.

"Ash," she said, slapping her hand over her mouth. "He's down there." She fell to the floor, clawing at the moss-covered bricks.

Ashley dropped to her knees. Shelby was now clawing at the moss and pulling up bricks from the earth.

"David Clarendon. He's down there."

"What!"

Shelby pulled out another brick and threw it aside. She turned to Ashley. "There's a well under here." She went back, clearing the bricks from the shed's floor. Ashley joined in until they had uncovered a large area. It was then that they noticed that what lay beneath was not a dirt floor, but planks of wood.

Then they heard it. Faint at first. Almost imperceptible. Then a little stronger, like a moan. Shelby turned to Ashley. "Did you hear that?"

"Of course I heard it."

They glared at each other like two frightened school girls.

"I don't know if I can do this." Shelby said.

Ashley clutched her arms, trying to keep her hands from shaking.

Suddenly a loud crash erupted behind them.

Both women lurched forward, falling onto the wooden boards. Shelby caught the side of the bricks and held fast as Ashley hit the boards with tremendous force. The wood cracked, then gave way, plunging her downward.

Her first sensation was not of falling, but of cold, like a giant freezer had suddenly opened. Then came the clamminess and smell of thick musty earth. All in an instant as she fell into the blackness. Reaching frantically through the darkness, a sudden stabbing pain tore through her shoulder. She cried out, bringing her arm close to her body, realizing that she had fallen through the floor of the shed. Terror and fear took hold. And then she felt it, something mushy and cold beneath her. Her head was bent forward. And it hurt. God how it hurt. Her whole body hurt.

What was that! she thought. Again she heard it. Moaning, that incessant moaning. And the ever trickling sound of water. The sounds all seemed to merge, frightening, disharmonious. The moaning, the trickling water. The cold, the damp, the gooey mush. All of it. Oh God, the pain. She wanted to scream. Again she heard it. Or maybe it had not stopped. It sounded more human now. No, it sounded closer. Almost as though she could touch it.

"Ash," she heard Shelby call. "Goddammit Ash, answer me!"

"Shel," Ashley tried to call back, wrenching with pain as she whispered the words. "I can't move." She knew Shelby couldn't hear her.

"I'm calling 911," she heard Shelby yell. "Just hang in there."

Shelby tore from the shed, almost knocking Helen to the ground.

"Miss Shelby," she wailed, following in Shelby's wake. "What's happened?"

"Get a flashlight, Helen," she said, scaling the front stairs two steps at a time. "I'm calling 911."

Ashley was now feeling dizzy, and the pain—please, God, stop the pa . . ."

"Ohhhhhhhhh," came a sound. It brought Ashley back to consciousness. This time it was louder. Like the moan of someone sleeping next to you.

The darkness seemed to grow denser, more ominous. She took a breath then cried out as the pain split across her pelvis.

"Ohhhhhhhhh," the sound came again.

"David?" she whispered, barely able to form the word. "David." Calling his name felt calming. Someone else to bear this horror of being buried alive, and not knowing what crawling things might emerge from the earth.

"David," she whispered again. And then she felt it. Like an icy finger touching her cheek.

"Helllp me," the voice said.

She could now hear rapid breathing. Then, everything began to fade. Her thoughts—No control.

"Ashley," Shelby pointed the flashlight into the black hole. "The paramedics are on their way." Shelby scanned the beam of the flashlight across the floor of the pit. "Ash!" she screamed, almost losing her balance. From the waist down Ashley was lying in a pool of blood. A hand rested against her face.

Chapter Fifteen

"Ms. Winthrop?" Ashley heard the voice say.

She tried to focus her eyes through the blur, barely discerning the outline of a face.

"I'm Dr. Piazza," the voice said.

"Where am I?" Ashley closed her eyes in pain.

"You're in the hospital."

Why were the faces so blurry? And why did her head hurt? "Ohhh," she moaned, feeling a large bump on the back of her head.

"You've hit your head," Shelby said, taking Ashley's hand away. "Dr. Piazza's here with you."

The blurry faces began to take on form. She saw a row of shiny teeth framed by a salt and pepper beard and two smiling eyes looking down at her. Shelby's face was next to it. She saw that the man was wearing a long white coat. In fact, the whole room was draped in white. "Where am I?" she moaned.

"You're in the emergency room at Touro Hospital," Dr. Piazza said. "And you're one very lucky lady. That was a nasty fall you took."

"Fall?" Ashley looked around the cloth-draped room trying to put her thoughts in order. Then she remembered. The shed.

"Mr. Clarendon is in Intensive Care," Dr. Piazza said.

"Mr. Clarendon?"

"He was in that well," Shelby said.

Ashley frowned in disbelief. "Is he going to be all right?"

"It's touch and go. But we're hopeful." Dr. Piazza showed his pearly white teeth again. "So, how do you feel?"

"Feel?" Ashley closed her eyes and gently rubbed the back of her head. "Like somebody's hit me over the head with a sledgehammer."

Laughter. "Other than that, how do you feel?"

Ashley moved her arms and legs. "A little sore I guess."

"Ash," Shelby said, looking over at the doctor. "There's something we have to tell you."

"Tell me? Tell me what?"

"It's about the baby."

"The what?"

"Your baby," Dr. Piazza said gravely. "I'm afraid . . . well, you miscarried before the paramedics got to you."

Ashley glared at Dr. Piazza.

"I'm so very sorry," he said.

"I don't know what you're talking about."

Shelby looked at Ashley curiously. "You didn't know you were pregnant?"

"Pregnant?" She was pregnant? How could she not have known something like that? Again she said the word. "Pregnant?" like she wanted to hold onto the sound of it. "No." Ashley turned her face away.

"I'll leave the two of you alone," Dr. Piazza said. "The orderly will be down in a while to take her to her room. I'd like to keep her overnight just for observation."

"No!" Ashley pushed herself up on one elbow and began kicking the sheet off with her feet. "I'm not—whoo," she moaned, as Dr. Piazza steadied her.

"Young lady." His tone was stern yet gentle. "You're lucky to be alive. Now lie back down. You're going to stay the night. We're going to make sure you are as miraculously unhurt as you appear to be."

Ashley closed her eyes and laid back on the gurney. She didn't have the strength to protest.

"Ash," she heard Shelby say.

No, she didn't want to talk. She didn't even want to think. She turned over on her side amid several moans hoping that Shelby would just let her be.

"Blake wants to see you," Shelby said. "He's been so worried about you."

Blake? She didn't want to see Blake. No, that wasn't exactly true. She didn't want Blake to see her. "I'd rather not see anybody," she said.

The next day Ashley was released from the hospital. Dr. Piazza had gone over her x-rays again and again but found nothing to even hint that she had taken such a fall.

"Blake." Ashley turned from the mirror with surprise. "What are you doing here?"

"I came to take you home."

She turned back to the mirror and fastened her hair with a clip. "You didn't have to do that."

"I was here anyway. They've moved David to a private room."

David, she thought, still not able to accept his discovery. "They have? Will they let me see him?"

"I'm sure they will," Blake replied. "You were responsible for his rescue. And a beautiful face just might bring him around."

Ashley felt a slight tinge of embarrassment. "I'm afraid I can't take credit for David Clarendon's rescue. Shelby's the one . . . "

"Shelby?"

"Why yes," Ashley's mind raced for an explanation, not knowing what Shelby had told Blake. She wasn't even sure of what Shelby had remembered. "Shelby's the one who called for help. If it hadn't been for her, David Clarendon and I would still be down in that hole."

"That's a horrible thought."

"Actually," Ashley said. "He needs more time. I'll wait a day or so"

"Maybe you're right," Blake agreed.

Ashley looked at Blake, thinking how innocent he was of everything. And wondering what he would think if he knew how screwed up her life was. Well, he would never know. She would make certain of that. The fact that Buzz and Les and Will knew was bad enough. No, she couldn't go see David. Not with Blake, anyway. She didn't want Blake or anyone to know she had been hypnotized by David Clarendon. If she walked into his room he would be bound to show recognition. Then Blake would ask her questions. He would wonder why she hadn't mentioned that she knew him. Blake might even tell her father.

"To be honest," Ashley said as they waited for the wheelchair to come and take her downstairs, "I don't feel up to it."

"Of course. I don't know what I was thinking. Oh, by the way, I stopped by Buzz's house on the way over." He handed Ashley a coat. "You'll need this. It's cold outside."

"Thank you," she said slipping her arms into the coat.

"Buzz and Les are very upset about David being discovered on their property," Blake said. "The police questioned them. It had to have been someone who knew the property. Possibly worked for the previous owner."

"I know. Buzz called me from Chicago this morning. I told him it was a tragic coincidence and to put it out of his mind." Coincidence? she mused, still trying to convince herself. "Where is Shelby?" she asked nervously.

"She and Will are at Buzz's."

"Will?" Ashley eased into a vinyl armchair still feeling a little dizzy. She rubbed the side of her head. "Will and Shelby?"

Blake laughed and folded his arms over his wide chest. "Shelby is being civil to him. And Will has seized the opportunity. I think your accident did the trick. Shelby called him right after she phoned the paramedics. I was still at the police station."

"That's amazing." Ashley smiled up at Blake. She noticed that he seemed to be staring at her, the way one would stare at someone they weren't quite sure of, or maybe were trying to figure out. It was making her nervous.

"What did Shelby have against Will in the first place?"

"Oh . . . nothing really," Ashley replied, reaching for a plausible explanation. "Shelby can be a little possessive at times. She didn't feel we needed a high-priced snoop on this genealogy search."

Blake practically roared with laughter. "Well, something turned her around." He then took a different tone. "Shelby said you didn't want to call your parents. Are you sure?"

"Yes. Positive."

The orderly arrived with the wheelchair. Blake held out his hand to Ashley.

"Are you ready?"

She placed her hand in his. "I'll meet you by the front entrance," he said, guiding her into the wheelchair. As he turned to leave, she realized she was still clutching his hand. She quickly let go.

Blake smiled and left the room.

Ashley sat quietly as the orderly pushed the wheelchair through the corridors and toward the elevators. She couldn't get the thought of that old well out of her mind. Buzz had said he hadn't known it was there.

Whoever put David Clarendon there sure knew about it. But why there? And why David Clarendon?

※

The next day Helen had prepared a special lunch for Ashley.

"Miss Ashley," she whispered, gently setting the tray on the bed.

Ashley opened her eyes. "Oh, Helen, I must have dozed off." She sat up and looked around the room. "Where did Shelby go?"

"She and Dr. Taylor have gone to the hospital. Mr. Sheldon's been there all morning. So, how do you feel?"

"Better," she said, pushing herself further back into the pillows.

"You'll be as good as new before you know it."

Ashley smiled, focusing her eyes on the bed tray and noticing the Federal Express envelope. "What's this?"

"It came a few minutes ago," Helen replied.

Ashley stared at the return address as though it were surreal. It read, 440 Golden Gate Avenue, Belvedere, California.

"Miss Ashley," Helen said, perplexed. "What's the matter?"

Ashley gazed at Helen. "What?"

"Are you all right?"

"Oh, yes. I'm fine. Thanks for the lunch. It looks wonderful."

"Enjoy," Helen said. "And don't forget our afternoon walk. Doctor's orders. Oh, and Mr. Harper will be calling from Chicago this afternoon. He and Mr. Les are so worried about you."

Ashley smiled mindlessly. She looked back at the Fed Ex letter feeling strangely curious. It was addressed to both Shelby and her. Why Shelby? she wondered. Part of her wanted to tear into it. Another part wanted it to disappear. Then she remembered that Michael had said she would be receiving something by Federal Express. It had not occurred to her it would be from Tryn. Tryn, she mused. Had it been Tryn's baby she had lost and not Scott's?

Ashley looked despairingly at the beautiful presentation Helen had created. Hungry or not, she had to make the effort.

After several bites of crab salad and half a French roll, she put the tray aside. Her thoughts went back to the cardboard envelope that lay beside her. The bold letters printed across it. FEDERAL EXPRESS OVERNIGHT

Finally her curiosity took over.

As she lifted the linen stationery from the envelope, it instantly looked familiar. But the writing was like nothing she had ever seen. It was crude, barely legible.

What IS this?

02 January, 1987

My beloveds ≈

And so, alas we meet. This I had vowed could never be. My forbidden love has burned deep inside me. I am compelled now, in my sorrow, to give you my confession.

Evil is an inexorable force one dare not reckon with. But my strength is waning now, blessed peace is at hand. As I move toward the distant light—your heritage must be revealed. As cruel as this knowledge is, it would have been crueler still to leave you innocent of it. All those before you were too painfully aware of their fate. But, at the very least, they knew of its release. Without the understanding of what was happening to you, it would have most assuredly driven you to the depths of insanity.

Your lineage is a fusion of good and evil, and evil has won. You will soon come to understand this. My only hope is that you will somehow find your peace within the hopelessness that will descend upon you.

My confession begins on the Atlantic at Winthrop House. I now know that you have learned of its existence. But what you cannot know is that it is one of the most magnificent structures ever built. The size of it is not its grandeur, for there are larger dwellings throughout Europe. The architecture and workmanship are so grand that they are overwhelming. If you go there, you will understand my passion for it.

Winthrop House was built in the early 1600's. The reason for its existence, and the horrors that took place there for two centuries have, through the years, been chronicled and sent to Nine Thornton Square in London, England.

I begin my confession in the year 1855. It was then that Sophia Elizabeth Tanner and Louisa Colleen Tanner were born. They were identical twins, and

৪৩ ৯ ৫৩

DeLore's Confession

despised each other almost from birth. Their parents were poor, and the birth of their twin daughters brought bitter hardship. But they were the delight of their parents despite the hardships. Sophia and Louisa were beautiful children, and grew to be even more beautiful women. Their impoverished existence had always been an embarrassment for Sophia. She despised her parents for bringing her into such privation, and at the age of fourteen she fled into the dark half-world of Boston. The rage caused by her impoverished past had festered and would become her armament.

Sophia Tanner was not only a raving beauty, but a strong force against the adversities which she would face at this vulnerable age. By night she worked the seedy clubs of Boston, and by day she buried herself in literature and social learning. What she did not understand she sought to understand, and for that of which she did not have, she plotted. Sophia would someday, by her own determination, educate herself, and become a great lady.

Louisa, on the other hand, was as different from Sophia as she was alike in portrait. She had ever despised her sister's arrogance and ultimate betrayal of her family. As time passed, she saw the growing despair in the faces of her parents over the loss of their child. This only enraged Louisa further, and her vengeance grew stronger. But Louisa was a loving and gentle woman, and her vengeance waned with time, leaving only indifference.

Five years after Sophia's departure from her family, she met a young artist by the name of Tryn DeLore. Tryn was a remarkably talented painter, but had yet to achieve distinction. He was young, handsome, and seemingly very poor. In no time, he captured the heart of Sophia. But Sophia, determined not to marry a starving artist, continued her search for wealth, all the while hopelessly in love with Tryn. But what Sophia did not know was that Tryn had no intention of loving her. He saw her only as someone to satisfy his own lustful, sexual obsessiveness. Tryn had found a most perfect scenario. A selfish and driven woman with a deep-seated obsession for personal gain. Her love would never pose a threat to him. She was too consumed with her own self gratification.

So the affair began, satisfying each of their needs to fulfillment. Then one day Sophia escaped the slavery of dark night clubs and smoke-filled rooms, finding a respectable position at the library. It was there—where she had spent those long days in search of learning—that she met Andrew Winthrop. Sophia was not yet aware that he was an exceedingly wealthy man. Andrew was taken by Sophia's beauty and enticed by her air of independence. Andrew, like Tryn, was alarmingly handsome. But Sophia's heart had been lost to Tryn. She rejected Andrew's advances until she learned of his great wealth, and that he lived in the magnificent Winthrop House in the small village of Manchester, Massachusetts, commonly known as Manchester by the Sea.

One month later, Andrew Winthrop married Sophia Tanner. It was not a publicized event, for Andrew Winthrop was not a public person. Few knew him personally. But he was respected for his philanthropic causes. He reigned kinglike, but was left to his eccentric existence. Although word did leak out of Andrew and Sophia's marriage, it was only discreetly whispered. Andrew Winthrop was feared as well as loved.

Ashley started, suddenly realizing that Helen was standing beside the bed, calling her name.

"I'm sorry, Miss Ashley," she heard Helen say. "I didn't mean to scare you. It's time for your walk."

Ashley let out a long sigh, wishing she had not been interrupted and slipped the papers back into the envelope. "All right, Helen."

While Ashley and Helen walked the grounds, Miss Mary Harper was off in the thicket pursuing lizards. Winded, but victorious, she plopped down on her stomach along side Ashley who was sitting in the mesh lawn chair inside the mirrored gazebo.

"Helen," Ashley called "Would you please bring me the Fed Ex Envelope that's on my bed? I think I'll sit out here for a while."

"Won't be a minute," Helen called back to Ashley as she scurried off across the courtyard with Mary Harper at her feet.

Ashley looked up into the crisp, blue sky, thinking how perfect New Orleans could be in January, and wondering if it would be colder tomorrow.

"Oh, Helen," she called out.

"Yes, Miss Ashley?" Helen replied breathlessly, stopping beside a giant urn.

"Would you also bring my lace scarf? It's in the drawer of my bedside table."

"Yes ma'am," she answered, and turned, disappearing around the corner.

Ashley smiled sentimentally, thinking how Helen's exuberance reminded her of Shelby and how glad she was that Shelby and Will were getting along. She couldn't wait to show them this letter. Or "confession" as Tryn put it. Her thoughts went to Tryn, remembering his words. A fusion of good and evil, and evil has won. Ashley clutched her arms as a cold dread passed through her.

"Miss Ashley," Helen said, standing beside her, holding out her scarf.

"What?" Ashley replied, looking up at Helen with no apparent recognition.

"Oh. Thank you," she answered, taking her scarf and noticing the Fed Ex envelope that Helen had placed in front of her.

"Would you like something to drink?" Helen asked. "Maybe some hot tea?"

"You're too good to me," Ashley said, forcing a smile. "Hot tea would be nice."

"You're nice to be good to," Helen smiled timidly. "I'll be right back."

Ashley watched Helen disappear up the back stairs. She looked down at the envelope. The words reverberated through her head.

Evil has won.

What did he mean? Evil? Could this have been the reason her parents had lied to her and Michael? Had this so called evil forced them from Winthrop House?

But who was this Tryn DeLore of the late 1800's? Tryn had said the man was a poor struggling artist? Surely that Tryn DeLore wasn't related to the DeLores who had built that incredible house on Belvedere in the late 1700's and early 1800's. Had they lost their fortune, leaving their heirs penniless and struggling to make their own fortune?

Ashley gazed at the envelope. Her thoughts went back to the night of Meno's birthday dinner. Both her father and Meno had acted strangely when Tryn DeLore's name was mentioned. She and Shelby had both noticed it. But why? Had there been some kind of family tragedy that involved the DeLore family? Something so horrible that her father had been forced to deceive them? And where did Shelby fit in?

Ashley fell back into the lawn chair and took out the pages again.

Andrew Winthrop guarded his anonymity with a vengeance. His and Sophia's wedding was attended only by the Winthrop family, most of whom came from across the Atlantic. Unlike the States, England flourishes with the Winthrop heritage.

Only weeks after Sophia and Andrew's marriage, Sophia went to him with the news that she was pregnant. She was radiant in her telling, knowing that she was carrying Tryn's child and not Andrew's.

"Andrew, my love." Sophia brushed her face against Andrew's, feeling its soft contours yet lost in her passionate desire for her beloved Tryn. "I will soon give you a child," she said.

Andrew pulled her close. "And a beautiful child it will be," he said, turning Sophia's face to his. He stared deep into her eyes with a most intriguing smirk. "You will give me many beautiful children," and he kissed her violently.

Andrew was consumed, knowing that he would now produce another heir to the Winthrop Legacy. Male or female, it would carry the Winthrop name as well as The Gift. It would be a beautiful creature. This time, however, Andrew had not married from within the family as he had in the past. He married an outsider. He had been overwhelmed by Sophia's beauty, and was obsessed by her.

In 1875, Christopher was born. As expected, Christopher was a beautiful child, and through the years he grew to be a beautiful man, as did his younger brother Stefan. Andrew had now grown complacent in his marriage. He had married beauty, and produced beauty. This had been his ultimate goal, and he had succeeded. Sophia had fulfilled his needs, and was no longer an important part of his life. He had even lost the lustful attraction he had once enjoyed.

Sophia was aware of the waning of his desires. He had even moved from the East wing to a separate bedchamber. This was of no concern to Sophia, as long as she could steal away and have her trysts with her beloved Tryn.

In the year 1899 Christopher's brother, Stefan, returned from England with his bride-to-be. Her name was Jenny Erskine. Christopher would later discover that Erskine was not her real name. Christopher, as was everyone at Winthrop House, was taken with Jenny. It was as though heaven had suddenly opened up and presented Winthrop House with its loveliest angel. Everyone seemed to change. Sophia, who had always been a strong and domineering force, now grew gentle and loving.

In Jenny's innocence, she failed to see what was happening. Sophia had fallen in love with Jenny. Andrew saw it, as did Christopher and Stefan. But what Stefan did not see was that Andrew, too, had fallen victim. Jenny had, in a matter of only days, captured the inhabitants of Winthrop House. Christopher, however, kept his emotions hidden. Later, when Stefan's jealousy over his mother's affection caused him to ravish Jenny relentlessly, accusing her of unnatural acts with his mother, Christopher let his love for Jenny be known to her. It was during Jenny's pregnancy that Stefan's jealous rage began, forcing Jenny into the arms of Christopher. They fell desperately in love, spending stolen moments in the cottage down by the sea.

When Jenny would go to the double parlor and play her beautiful music, Christopher would play his cello.

"My beloved Christopher," Jenny pleaded. "Why is it not God's plan for us to profess our love?"

Christopher stopped his playing. "Our love **is** professed," he replied. "To each other and to God. Dearest Jenny, we must be patient. Soon we will be free of this wretched prison." Christopher cautiously placed his hand on Jenny's, searching the room in fear of discovery. "You are the very soul of my life. I could not love another as I am loving you at this moment and for all time."

Christopher's heart was breaking for his beloved Jenny. Her radiant brown eyes were now burdened with sadness. Christopher left his cello and drew closer to Jenny. He lifted his hand and gently stroked her long dark hair. She reached for his hand and brought it to her lips, caressing it with her kisses.

"I would wait an eternity my love," she whispered, "if you were to ask it of me."

"Not an eternity," Christopher replied. "Only until your baby is born. Then we will leave Winthrop House and take the midnight sail across the Atlantic. Europe will be our home. The three of us. Your child will be my child. And we shall raise him in our love."

It was Christopher who gave Jenny the strength and hope to endure Stefan's rantings. Christopher fought with the anger inside him, wanting to take the very life from his brother Stefan for the mental anguish he was causing Jenny. But Jenny begged him not to confront Stefan for fear it would only give

Stefan cause to suspect. So they continued their plan of escape. How little Christopher knew of his own impending fate! A fate that would steal him from his beloved Jenny and twist his life.

Jenny's love for Stefan had long since died, destroyed by his jealousy over what he called his mother's unnatural desires for his wife and his delusion that Jenny returned these desires. But to this day, no one ever knew of the love and devotion Jenny and Christopher carried for each other.

Before the deterioration of Stefan and Jenny's marriage and before the tragedy that took their lives, Sophia arranged for Jenny's portrait to be painted. Tryn had now become quite celebrated. Even before Tryn had made a name for himself, he was indeed a very wealthy man and had painted many of the portraits that hung inside Winthrop House. Upon first meeting Tryn, Sophia assumed him to be both penniless and unknown. There would be many things that Sophia Winthrop would come to learn while residing within those opulent walls.

Just before the birth of Jenny's baby, Tryn summoned Christopher to his home, which overlooked the Atlantic just north of Manchester. Christopher and Tryn had met only a few times. The day Christopher turned eighteen, he was sent to have his portrait painted. It was then that he noticed Tryn's uncanny resemblance to himself, but he never mentioned it to anyone. After several sittings his portrait was completed and he never saw Tryn again until this day. The day whose events I will now reveal to you.

Tryn showed Christopher into his studio and told him there were important things that must be told. Tryn walked to a desk and took a picture from the center drawer. He handed it to Christopher. It was a picture of a woman cradling a baby in her arms. Upon looking at the picture, Christopher thought it to be of his mother, Sophia, holding either himself or Stefan.

"Her name is Louisa," Tryn said. "She is your mother's twin sister."

Christopher looked at Tryn in shock. "But how do you know this?" he said incredulously.

"Because I fell in love with her years ago. Your mother's sister was not only beautiful to look at, she was the epitome of beauty." He looked toward the ceiling, his face distraught and weary. "She was the most angelic creature I have ever known.

He went to the studio window. As he began to speak, his words became whispered and labored. Christopher drew closer.

"You said you fell in love with her?" Christopher said.

A cynical look suddenly crossed Tryn's face. A face that had, in only a matter of minutes, become worn and tired. It was apparent to Tryn that Christopher had noticed this, and he reached out.

As Tryn touched his shoulder, an overpowering sensation stirred inside Christopher. He remembered having that same disturbing sensation years before when he had sat those long hours while Tryn painted his portrait. They were strange feelings, unlike anything he had ever experienced. He had thought that if his portrait had taken even one more day, he would have begged Tryn to let him stay. He had too often during those sittings fantasized about Tryn touching him. His body would stir with desire. And now, eight years later, those desires were surfacing again as Tryn drew closer and caressed Christopher's face.

"My beautiful Christopher," Tryn whispered." My young Adonis," and he kissed him passionately. Christopher responded like a weak child succumbing to a sublime pleasure.

"Make love to me," Christopher begged.

Tryn ran his fingers across Christopher's lips. "Ssssssh," he sighed, then lowered his hand. "I can feel your hardness through your trousers. Your desire pleases me. But our time has passed, my young and beautiful child."

"What do you mean?" Christopher demanded, as Tryn withdrew his embrace.

"Please," Tryn said. "I know it is difficult. But there is so much I have to tell you. Let us go now and sit by the water."

Tryn took another picture from the desk drawer and put it in his pocket. He left the studio and Christopher reluctantly followed. There were stairs leading to the water's edge. Tryn led the way down the stone stairway.

"I come here often," he said, and walked over to a stone bench and sat down. Christopher sat down beside him. He could see a sort of desperation in his eyes, and there were deep lines running down his face that were not there before. His skin had become pale, and his dark hair was nearly snow white. What was happening? he pondered. Was he losing his mind, somehow imagining these things?

Tryn reached out and clutched Christopher's hand. Christopher pulled back slightly, as he noticed the brown spots across the back of Tryn's hand. He could see the veins as though the skin had simply vanished, leaving only those grotesque spots and web-like veins to cover the skeleton hand.

"Please," Tryn said. "Let me begin."

So Christopher listened intently, as Tryn told him what had come to pass, and what would ultimately become his destiny.

"The first time I saw Louisa," he began, "was at a showing I had at one of the small colleges in Boston. I thought the stars had fallen from the heavens and had aligned themselves into this perfect creature.

"Her beauty enticed me. Not only was she beautiful to look at, but she possessed virtue and innocence, and kindness. These purest qualities were as strong and powerful as her physical beauty. And that should have been my warning. These qualities were my nemesis. But her beauty was so alluring that I ignored what I knew would ultimately be my demise. So I ventured into this ecstasy of danger."

Christopher could see the strength draining from Tryn. "Tryn," he said. "Shouldn't you go back inside and lie down?"

"No, my son," Tryn said softly. "I must continue. I am compelled to offer you The Gift."

Christopher looked puzzled by this.

"I can still, even now, feel her next to me. Her sweetness, her innocence, her precious love," Tryn continued. "Oh, Christopher. I am feeling that overwhelming love even now."

Christopher could see the tears pool in Tryn's eyes.

"I knew though, that this purest love would destroy me. But as I fought it, thinking only of my sexual obsessions, and forsaking all else, I found that I was beginning to weaken. So I fled. I could not; I would not let this woman's love destroy me."

It was now becoming more difficult for Christopher to make out Tryn's words, so he moved closer, feeling a sudden rush of sympathetic love.

"As though it were only yesterday," Tryn continued, "I can see Louisa standing there by the water's edge; the sea breeze sweeping her long, dark hair across her lovely face. She stood there, looking out across those waters."

'Tryn,' Louisa said, a gentleness in her voice. 'I am carrying your child. Tomorrow I leave for England and will be married.' She then turned to Tryn, 'I will never love again the way I have loved with you,' and she reached up gently touching Tryn's face. 'My dearest love,' she whispered.

206

"Her touch was so slight that I could barely feel it," Tryn said to Christopher, "yet at this moment I feel it. She then looked into my eyes. God, I can still see her sadness. And she turned and walked away. I never saw her again."

Tryn was gasping with sorrow. Again Christopher urged him to go and lie down, but he was adamant that he must finish.

"The picture that I showed you," Tryn said. "Louisa is holding my child." Then he reached in his pocket and handed Christopher a picture of what looked to be Louisa and a young woman. Christopher looked stunned. "Jenny!"

"I know. I was just as shocked when I first realized who she was."

"I don't believe this," Christopher said. "Does Jenny know?"

"No," Tryn answered. "Louisa never told her."

Tryn took a long, slow breath. "I befriended Jenny while she sat for her portrait. I told her that her mother and I had been dear friends. I even showed her these pictures. She soon grew to trust me and told me about her family. No one other than Stefan knows the kind of life Jenny was forced to live at Nine Thornton Square. And Louisa and I are the only ones that know that Jenny is my child."

Tryn then told Christopher that Jenny's name was Arden, not Erskine. That her family had been servants, and that Jenny had become pregnant by one of the sons of their employer. Before the baby was born Louisa and her husband were killed as they returned home from the village. Shortly after the baby was born it was taken from Jenny. She was then sent to Nine Thornton Square where she eventually met Stefan.

Tryn explained briefly about Nine Thornton Square.

"My son," he began. "I am much too weak to reveal all of what presides over that evil dwelling. You will have much time to learn of this later. But it is the core of the Winthrop Heritage, and a vile and immoral place where Jenny was abused. They thought they could conquer her; could not be tainted by her love and purity. That same purity that her mother Louisa possessed. But as it was with me and Louisa, so it was with Jenny and Nine Thornton Square. Her virtue was great. They were only too anxious to allow Stefan to take her to Winthrop House. It was either that or dispose of her. I am sure they found it intriguing to release this eternal threat to Winthrop House. It would have been an enticing scenario for them to see if the men at Winthrop House could conquer her."

207

"Tryn," Christopher said. "Who are these people at Nine Thornton Square? And what is this evil you speak of?"

Tryn sighed as though he dreaded what he must say.

"Christopher," he whispered, looking up. Christopher almost gasped at the sight of him. His face seemed almost to be withering before his eyes. Tryn continued, barely able to utter his words.

"Would you want to keep your youth forever?" he asked.

"Ashley," Blake called as he walked up the long brick pathway.

Ashley hurridly shoved the papers back into the envelope. "Blake," She forced enthusiasm, while the words of Tryn's confession clouded her mind. "It's good to see you."

Blake sat in the black mesh lawn chair studying Ashley. "The outdoors must agree with you." He held her gaze and took tiny puffs from his pipe.

"I feel remarkably well," she said and looked away. He was making her nervous.

"Good, because David's been asking for you."

She glanced back. "Asking for me?"

"David wants to meet the beautiful lady who shared that black hole with him."

"He remembers?"

"Only vaguely. I told him most of it."

Ashley grew anxious. Told him? Told him what? That she had a miscarriage? Did Blake know? Did Will? She hadn't thought to ask Shelby.

"If you hadn't been in that shed looking for flower pots we might never have found David," Blake said.

Flower pots? So that's what Shelby told him. "Which reminds me." Ashley tucked the envelope beneath her arm. "I never did find those pots," and she rose from her chair. "On second thought I think I'll go lie down."

"Too much beautiful weather for one day?"

"I think so," Ashley replied. Blake offered his arm. She took it, feeling the strength beneath her hand. She suddenly had the urge to pull him close to her. She tightened her grasp around the Fed Ex envelope instead. "Thank you," she said entering the downstairs doorway. "I

apologize for my lack of hospitality. Afraid I'm a little off kilter." She
smiled, making contact with his eyes, then quickly looked away. She
didn't trust herself to look at him. Her emotions were too fragile.

"You need to rest as much as possible," Blake said. "I hope you're
not planning on that trip to Boston any time soon."

"Boston?" Ashley replied, as though it had not even entered her
mind. But it had. She had been thinking of it while reading Tryn's
confession. Just the thought of being in Manchester and seeing Winthrop
House gave her an eerie feeling. She wasn't certain if she could *ever* go
there. "I don't know. Maybe I'll just let Will and Shelby go. They really
don't need me. Besides, Shelby's the one who loves this genealogy stuff."

"Shelby? I thought you were Snoop Taylor's avid fan."

Ashley laughed in spite of having to explain her way out of this and
realized how good laughter actually felt. But keeping this secret of hers
from Blake was draining. "I *am* a fan," Ashley said. "But it looks like
Will has finally won Shelby over." That was a vague response, she
thought.

Blake took several concentrated puffs from his pipe. "What would
you like for me to tell David," he asked as Ashley opened the door to her
bedroom.

She turned to him. The sweet aroma of his pipe seemed to draw her
in. She found herself wanting him to force her into his arms. Lose herself,
helplessly, in that delicious passion. That burning passion that Tryn had
released in her. She needed to feel it again.

The next thing she knew, felt, was Blake's lips caressing hers. Soft
and gentle at first, as though familiarizing himself with her. She felt his
hands on her face, strong and firm as if guiding her, tilting her face from
side to side as each kiss became more and more passionate.

"No Blake. Please." She pushed away. "I'm sorry. It's just . . . it's
too soon." She stared at the envelope, pressing it closer to her chest and
feeling horribly foolish. Even guilty, as if she had been cheating on Scott.
Blake had done exactly what she had wanted him to do. It was probably
written all over her face. Like the first time with Tryn. He had said she
seemed to have wanted to be kissed. Had she seemed that way now with
Blake? Yet with Blake she remembered his kiss. Why had she not
remembered Tryn's?

"I need to lie down," she said turning away.

Ashley entered the bedroom and closed the door. How could she have allowed herself to fantasize about Blake like that? She hadn't even begun to deal with the loss of Scott. Would Blake have kissed her if he had known that only a day before she had been pregnant, and not knowing if the baby was Scott's or Tryn's? She was reasonably certain he didn't know about her miscarriage. Wondering how she was going to deal with Blake, she remembered what she still clutched in her arms. She sat down at the writing table thinking of those last words, as she slid the papers from the envelope.

"Would you want to keep your youth forever?"

"My youth?" Christopher replied, almost wretching at his grotesque sight. And before Christopher could think, he blurted, "Yes, Forever."

Tryn lowered his head as though in defeat. "Go then to the closet where I keep my supplies. You will find a long narrow box. Take it back to Winthrop House and seek out Andrew. I have told him the truth about you. He does not know about Louisa and Jenny, only that I have allowed myself to fall in love.

"I knew that I had lost my battle a few years back. It was only when I learned from Jenny of Louisa's death that I knew why I had suddenly lost the battle. It was just after her death, although I did not know of it at that time, that I began to age. Her dying began my release. It was in her dying that her love conquered, reaching out and breaking through this evil."

Tryn touched the side of Christopher's leg with his frail hand. "Two things you must know. You are my son, Christopher; mine and Sophia's. Andrew Winthrop is your grandfather; I am Andrew's son. My name is Nicholas Winthrop. I took the name Tryn DeLore over a century ago from another family of evils. There was bitterness between our families. But you will learn more of this if you go to London.

"You see, my son, I was absorbed in my vision of becoming a great artist. I was also absorbed in making my mark without the influence or interference of the Winthrop fortune. So after I received The Gift I broke away, changed my name and was determined to make my own fortune." Tryn smiled. "I was a stubborn man, for it took me a lifetime. Of which for me was an eternity. So it mattered not how long it took. As you know, many of the portraits that hang on those evil walls of Winthrop House were painted by me. However, I did not accept payment, nor did I receive recognition for them. Very few outsiders have ever seen them. But I did eventually attain recognition for my outside work and have become substantially well off. My fortune is yours now, to do with as you see fit. But now you must go to Winthrop House and to Andrew, your grandfather. He will tell you what I am no longer able to tell. Please, my son, go now. Leave me to my dying."

Christopher rose from the small stone bench, weak with shock. He wanted to reach out and cradle Tryn in his arms, comfort him in his dying. But the sight of him was revolting, so he slowly turned his back and began to walk the two dozen steps back to the house. Half way up, he turned and looked toward the bench. There was no one there, just a pair of shoes. In the distance he saw Tryn's black velvet coat tumbling across the jagged rocks. Before Christopher looked away, he saw a wave reach out and carry the coat into its ebb. Nicholas Winthrop, he thought.

As Christopher approached the studio of stucco walls and high arched windows, he motioned to his driver who had been sitting patiently in the hansom, that he would be returning. He soon returned with a narrow box tucked beneath his arm.

On the way back to Winthrop House, Christopher stared at the Jaguar ring and the walking stick. They were identical to Andrew's.

As soon as the horse pulled the hansom up the drive, coming to rest at the fountain, Andrew appeared from the front door. He stood there with his walking stick in his left hand.

"Come with me, Christopher." Andrew turned, crossing the entrance hall and climbed the staircase.

The third floor of Winthrop House is nearly identical to the third floor of DeLore House. Only Andrew and Nicholas knew of the secret room. Christopher, who had explored the catacombs and hidden passageways in his youth, was shocked as they entered this magnificent room. Except for the portraits, and a few pieces of furniture, the room looks identical to the room at DeLore House. But, of course, Christopher knew nothing of DeLore House or this room.

"So," Andrew said. His tone was arrogant and pompous. "My son Nicholas has told you the truth." Andrew reached out his hand. "Give me the box,," he said, and placed it on the French writing table. He opened the box and took out the walking stick and gold ring, handing them to Christopher. "Put the ring on the little finger of your left hand." Christopher took the ring and slid it onto his finger. "Take the walking stick in your left hand and go to the middle of the room. Stand on the Winthrop Crest and face the mirror that hangs over the fireplace." Christopher obeyed, walked to the center of the room and faced the mirror. Though the mirror was a good twenty-five feet away, he could see his reflection as though he were only inches away.

Andrew took something from the writing table, then stood directly in front of Christopher. "Look at me," he said. "Do you see my youth? My dark hair? The smooth taut skin of my face? Look at my hand, Christopher," and he raised his left hand. The ruby eyes of the Jaguar seemed to pierce his own eyes as he felt their heat. The room ignited with a crimson hue. He could feel his body stir, like rhythmic waves undulating all around and through him. Then it began to fade, slowly ebbing until all he noticed was Andrew's youthful hand.

"Look into the mirror, Christopher," Andrew demanded.

Christopher raised his eyes toward the mirror. His stomach turned in horror as he saw his face begin to deteriorate. Bit by bit it grew lined and leathery. His eyes seemed to shrink into his skull, his mouth withered, causing his teeth to protrude slightly. He stood paralyzed within the revulsion of this thing.

"Read," Andrew said, and held a scroll in front of him. He slowly unrolled the parchment. "Read it with your very soul. For if you lack the passion, The Gift will not come into you."

Christopher read those words with more passion than he had ever dreamed possible.

My beautiful, my desirable, my eternal countenance
I humbly offer myself to you, open myself to your passions
Take from me goodness and righteousness
Spare me the antipathy of its destiny
Bind my soul with your iniquity
I stand before you in absolute submission
I implore you
Come into me!
Come into me!
Come into me!

Andrew lowered the scroll and told Christopher to again look into the mirror. Christopher raised his eyes, terrified of what he might see. But there, reflected in the mirror, he watched as his face began to grow younger and younger, until what reflected before him was a beautiful man. Andrew turned Christopher to face him.

"Give not your heart and soul in love, my young Adonis, for it will take your youth into its grasp. At this very moment, you are becoming desensitized to the destructive forces of love. This is not to say that you will not be vulnerable. Evil is not without its weaknesses. Righteousness is a powerful force, and once you let it penetrate, it will destroy you."

He turned Christopher toward the far wall. "Do you see those Sirens? They are calling for you, to give you deep pleasures. Don't allow love to intervene and strip you of these heightened pleasures. Look now toward the other wall. That's a reminder of your doom if you dare succumb to love's goodness. Those black trees, entangled within their agony; their life sucked from their limbs, just as the life was sucked from your father, Nicholas. Remember what you saw today as the life drained from your father, a once beautiful and youthful man. He was a fool to have allowed this." Andrew turned from Christopher and walked back to the writing table. "You have now lost the only thing you were allowed to love. Your father," and he held his hand out to Christopher. "Come, my beautiful grandson. Let me give you pleasures beyond what your mortal soul has ever dared. Come to me Christopher, satiate that lustful passion that now burns deep in your loins."

Christopher went to Andrew, drawn to him by a hunger so powerful that he found himself tearing at Andrew, his mouth sucking at his body and feeding the powerful lust that now welled inside him. He had never dreamed of such passion.

After it was done, Andrew said to Christopher.

"I received The Gift when I turned twenty-six. The same age as my father and his father before him. They too were fools, and allowed love to destroy them. I offered it to my son, Nicholas, when he turned twenty-six, and now he has offered it to you. You were not allowed to receive it before your twenty-sixth birthday, though anytime thereafter. I will offer it to Stefan next year. I have many sons who still reside at Nine Thornton Square."

He opened a panel and lifted out a large portrait.

"Come. It is time. We must hang your portrait." He turned the gilt-framed canvas toward Christopher. "Your father painted this only weeks ago. He knew that he was compelled to offer you The Gift and that you would accept it. No one has ever refused."

Christopher gazed at the canvas. As with all the other portraits hanging in this magnificent room, he too would take his rightful place, sitting tall within the painted canvas, his legs crossed and his left hand resting on the gold handle of the walking stick. The ruby eyes of the Jaguar piercing into the viewer's eyes.

After the portrait was hung, Andrew turned to leave the room.

"You will need time for your body to desensitize itself to the forces of righteousness."

It was on that night, October 18, 1900, that Jenny's baby had been born. Christopher could hear her cries echoing through the corridors. He fled Winthrop House for Europe. Jenny now posed an even deadlier threat. Not only through the love that Christopher carried for her but because of the powerful and obsessive lust he now possessed. Jenny Winthrop was his sister. Incest was a most sublime passion. It also made for a stronger lineage.

Several months had passed. Christopher was becoming stronger. His obsession and lust for the follies of pleasure were strengthening. His vanity deepening. He returned to Winthrop House. Upon his arrival he learned that his brother Stefan had been killed, and that Jenny had died in a tragic fire that had destroyed the cottage down by the cliff. The same cottage where he and Jenny had spent precious moments together. The news of Jenny's death came as a threat to Christopher. He could feel the sorrow building inside him. So he immediately took to the sealed chamber room to strengthen his powers. With his powers strengthened and the threat of Jenny at bay, he could now remain at his beloved Winthrop House.

But Andrew's death. That was puzzling. Had it been Jenny's influence? Christopher had thought Andrew far too strong an evil to have allowed this.

Later that night, after returning to Winthrop House, Sophia summoned Christopher to her bedchamber. Within moments, she began screaming obscenities at him.

"Goddamn your soul! Christopher," she ranted as though she had suddenly taken leave of her sanity.

Christopher was horrified at his mother's outrage. She had never spoken to him in anger.

"You have bargained your soul to the devil!" She snatched the walking stick from his hand. Christopher saw the piercing stare of her eyes as she beheld the gold Jaguar ring. Her beauty was spellbinding.

She withdrew. "This morning upon your arrival, when I saw this, I knew he had offered you *The Gift.* And you have accepted it."

Christopher was shocked, but held her gaze as he replied, "I have."

It was then that Christopher thought he saw, behind the anger and rage—sadness. She clutched the gold handled walking stick and turned away. Christopher watched in disbelief as she crossed the room and stood by the window that looked out across the gardens. He remembered thinking how remarkably youthful she still was at forty-five. Her long, dark hair showed no hint of gray. The lace dressing gown revealed her soft smooth shoulders. For the first time, he was seeing the resemblance. It was subtle, but Jenny was caught up in there somewhere. Had Sophia seen it? Had she known about Tryn's affair with her sister Louisa? Why had she never mentioned her sister?

"Tryn . . . I suppose I should say Nicholas. He fought for years not to love Louisa," Sophia said, as though she had read Christopher's thoughts. "He fed his lust for sex with me, because I looked like her, while he fought against his love for her. He never knew how much I truly loved him. But my love for wealth and status was my obsessive passion. We have both paid dearly. His obsession for youth, mine for wealth. You, my dear sweet Christopher, will now have to live with your passions, your obsessions. Give yourself to love and you will, as your father did, decay and be swept away.

"Oh yes," she said and faced Christopher. "Tryn revealed it all to me as he began to age. He told me of his affair with Louisa, how much he loved her. And I told him how much I had hated her sweet gentleness, her pathetic submission to poverty. I despised her almost from birth. How dare she have my beauty and be so simple minded."

Sophia then told Christopher how she had escaped her impoverished home in search for wealth.

"I wanted so to stop this curse from coming to you. The only possible way I could have accomplished this was to take you from Winthrop House. But it was my obsession, my greed, that kept me here. Stefan has escaped the curse." Her gaze fell from Christopher. "I have seen to that."

Sophia told Christopher that she had murdered Stefan. She had thrust a knife into his heart.

"I did not do this hideous deed to save Stefan from the curse of youth. I killed him to save my beloved Jenny. I have learned unspeakable things. I will not, however, torture myself by speaking of them. Do not ask me further about it. If only he could have been spared those years of torment I inflicted upon him. I am to blame for his undoing; his jealously; his madness. I've never loved him. It was you I loved. You——my and Tryn's child. I watched you grow into manhood. I saw in you my beloved Tryn in the purest form: free to give your love, to share your dreams and hopes and desires, to live with compassion."

Tears were now falling down Sophia's cheeks. "Your soul has given you a choice. You have chosen HELL. She handed Christopher the walking stick. "Andrew's love for Jenny," she said, "brought not only his demise but redemption. He has left me his fortune. I will never allow Winthrop House or its fortune to pass again into the hands of evil."

Sophia turned from Christopher. Just as she reached the far window, she stopped, but she did not turn to him.

"My love for Jenny caused her great pain. Andrew's love for her caused his death. Walk with caution, my son." And with that she ordered Christopher from the room.

Christopher had now realized his disinheritance.

Sophia did say that she would allow Christopher to reside at Winthrop House indefinitely, but he would never have access to the Winthrop fortune.

What Sophia did not know, and Christopher learned later, was that the women, born of a parent with The Gift, would simply, by birthright, never age beyond their twenty-sixth year. This will be explained in detail as I further my confession.

If a Winthrop male chooses not to marry within the lineage and marries an outsider, the wife will only be allowed to remain within the family while her beauty and youth survive. These women are then killed by a slow and agonizing strangulation. They are placed in a glass top coffin and stored in a subterranean cavern beneath Winthrop House. They are viewed often by those Winthrops who need reminding that aging is a wretched sight. The corpse's face not only shows the deterioration of their once youthful skin, but the terror of their strangulation. Sophia, however, escaped this horror, though she had no knowledge of it. She had yet to lose her youthful beauty. And now Andrew was dead, and she the sole heir to the Winthrop fortune. She did not, however, have rights to the European fortune. But it wasn't the fortune that Christopher yearned for. Nicholas had left him an enormous amount of money.

Christopher wanted the magnificent Winthrop House.

It was an obsession, much like his obsession for power and sexual pleasure.

The next night Sophia was found in her bedchamber. She was dead. There was no apparent reason for her death. Possibly though, Sophia too had succumbed to righteousness. And in her sorrow, the loss of her beloved Tryn. Of Jenny. The tragedy of her son Stefan. But above all, her beloved Christopher. Lured into the depths of hell.

Christopher suddenly found himself alone. Andrew, Stefan, Sophia, and Jenny. Only the servants remained. And he had been disinherited. But to whom, he often wondered, could Sophia have left the Winthrop fortune?

He went immediately to Fredricks and Rothchild, the law firm in Boston that handled his family's legal matters. They were polite but not forthcoming with even the most trivial piece of information. At this point though, it was of little concern to Christopher. He still resided at Winthrop House, and that was of great importance to him. Again, he left for Europe.

Ashley put the papers aside and walked into the bathroom. For several moments she just stared into the mirror. Then moved closer, touching the skin around her eyes, her mouth. Turning her head from side to side, she inspecting her neck. Her skin was perfectly smooth, taut, unlined. No trace of age. Not one sag or wrinkle. Why had she never wondered about this? People had always complimented her on her beauty, her youthful appearance. How she looked half her age. That's what Scott had said. Again, she studied her face searching for a hint of her forty years. But this is ridiculous, she thought. Why would she remain ageless when the rest of her family . . . "Stop!" she said, suddenly aware of the absurdity.

"Stop what?" Shelby laughed.

The sound of Shelby's voice sent Ashley reeling. She reached for the towel rack to brace herself, sending the neatly placed towels into a heap on the floor.

"Ash!" Shelby cried, going to her rescue. "Jesus. I didn't mean to scare you."

Ashley glared at her. "What in the hell were you doing sneaking into my room like that?"

"I didn't sneak into the room," Shelby retorted. "What's the matter with you?"

Ashley stormed past Shelby. "Nothing's the matter with me. Other than you scaring the shit out of me." Quickly, Ashley gathered Tryn's confession and stuffed it back into the envelope.

"Why are you so angry?" Shelby looked bewildered.

Ashley stood at the writing table and stared down at the Fed Ex envelope. "I'm not angry," she replied, carefully opening the center drawer and sliding the envelope inside. She turned to Shelby with a smile. "I'm just on edge. My head hurts. That's all."

"Dr. Piazza said it would. That's what your medicine's for."

"I know," Ashley sighed, falling onto the bed. "Could you get it for me?"

"Sure."

"Shel," Ashley called. "I'd like for you and Will to go on to Manchester without me. I really don't feel up to it."

"Me and Will?" Shelby said, handing Ashley a capsule and a glass of water.

Ashley took the medicine and drank it down. "Why not?"

"Because. I want to wait for you."

Ashley looked thoughtful. "I don't know, Shel. I'm not sure I want to go."

"What!"

"It's true. I don't think I want to know about this Winthrop House or what happened there. Maybe it's better left in the past."

"Well I'm not going to leave it in the past," Shelby said emphatically.

"No. I didn't think you would."

Chapter Sixteen

"How much are you charging for this detective work of yours?" Shelby asked Will.

The taxi turned onto the old cobblestone street that led through the main part of Manchester. The Willow Inn, one of the oldest structures in the village, lay just ahead, resembling an old European style country inn.

Will arched an eyebrow and looked serious. "I don't come cheap," he said, glancing at Shelby out of the corner of his eye.

Shelby held her response and continued gazing out at the lighted shops along the street. Finally she turned to Will with a glare. "What does that mean? 'I don't come cheap' ".

Will pretended to be serious. "I think you were the one who referred to me as infamous. And infamous people command high prices."

"I was right about you all along." Shelby shifted in her seat. "You're nothing more than a high price snoop. As far as I'm concerned you can turn around and go back to where ever it is you come from."

The driver pulled up in front of the inn and turned off the engine. "This is the Willow Inn," he said, and got out of the car, letting in a burst of cold air. Will shivered and followed him, leaving Shelby to stew a bit longer. Shelby muttered a few obscenities and stepped out of the cab.

Will paid the driver, thanked him, and took the bags.

"I can carry my own bag, thank you," she snarled and grabbed the handle. Will held fast and kept on walking with Shelby trailing a step behind.

"Let go of my bag!"

Will stopped abruptly and faced Shelby. "Stop acting like a spoiled child," he ordered.

Speechless and completely taken off guard by Will's assertiveness, Shelby released the bag.

"After you," he said firmly and motioned her ahead.

Shelby found herself obeying. Will smiled triumphantly and followed Shelby into the small lobby decorated in Early American style. They walked across the large hooked rug to the reception desk.

"I'm Dr. Taylor," Will told the desk clerk.

"Yes, Dr. Taylor," the young man replied. "We were expecting you. It's a pleasure to have you staying with us." The clerk pulled out two cards. "I've put you and Ms. Kincaid across from each other. Room 14 and room 15. They're two of our best."

Will thanked the clerk and asked that their bags be taken to the rooms. He then asked for a telephone.

"Over there," the clerk said, pointing to a small sitting area.

Will took Shelby's arm and escorted her across the room. "We've got work to do."

Shelby followed, offering little resistance, and sat down beside him. Will pulled out a Boston phone book and handed it to Shelby.

Shelby stared at it. "What's this for?"

"See if there are any Winthrop's listed. I'll call information." Will began dialing.

Shelby looked through the book.

Moments later Will hung up the phone. "Nothing," he said "There are no Winthrop's listed in Manchester."

Shelby closed the phone book. "None here either."

"What?" Will began searching diligently through the W's. Shelby crossed her arms and looked bored. "You're right," Will finally admitted. "Nothing." Then started thumbing through the pages again.

"What are you looking for now?" Shelby looked irritated.

"Kincaid," he said. "What was your father's first name?"

Shelby frowned. "My father?" The question struck her as odd. She couldn't remember ever being asked that. "Huh, Thomas, I think."

"Thomas," Will repeated, scanning through the T's. "No Thomas, but here's a T. R. Kincaid." He looked at Shelby. "Should I give him a call?"

"Call?" The thought made her anxious. "And say what?"

"That I'm looking for the relatives of Thomas and Natalie Kincaid."

Shelby wrestled with the idea. "Go ahead," she said.

After several rings a woman answered.

"Mrs. Kincaid?"

"Yes," the woman replied.

"Mrs. Kincaid. My name is Dr. Will Taylor. I'm a genealogist. I'm tracing the family of a Thomas and Natalie Kincaid. Would you happen to know them?"

"Thomas?" the woman said.

"Yes. Are you a relative?"

Pause. "Oh no," the woman said. "We weren't related. But I knew of them. I could be wrong, but I think his wife left Boston soon after his death."

"When was that?"

"I'm not exactly sure," the woman replied. "Some time around 1948, 49."

"How did her husband die?"

"Die?" the woman asked, as if puzzled by Will's question. "Why . . . he—was murdered."

"Murdered?" Will glanced over at Shelby who sat anxiously on the edge of the sofa. "How did it happen?"

"A real tragedy," the woman said. "It was in all the papers. He and another woman were found dead in the woman's apartment. They never found the killer. And very little was ever written about it. A real mystery. Especially when it came out that his wife and child had been left penniless. Thomas Kincaid was thought to be quite wealthy. As I said, we weren't related, but having the same last name and all, well, I've never forgotten. There's probably more that I'm not remembering. It happened so long ago and—well, my memory's not what it use to be."

"Mine either," Will chuckled. "Thanks for the information."

Shelby looked at Will nervously. "What did she say about his being murdered?"

"She said that Thomas Kincaid didn't die in an auto accident, that he was murdered. It was in all the papers." Will paused. "All it takes is a trip to the library."

"Who was that woman?" Shelby asked.

"Just someone with the last name of Kincaid. No relation."

Shelby's eyes grew suddenly determined. "Let's go to the library."

"We'll go into Boston tomorrow before we go searching for Winthrop House." He glanced down at his watch. "Seven-thirty. Come on, let's find a restaurant. I need a drink. Oh, by the way. I'm taking this case pro bono."

Shelby glared at Will. "Then why didn't you say so in the first place?"

"Because, you're cute when you're ruffled."

ಐ

The next morning Will and Shelby rented a car and drove into Boston. For two hours they scanned through the microfilm searching for any mention of the murder of Thomas Kincaid, Finally they saw it: Front page, August 12, 1949.

Corporate Executive Found Murdered

Thomas Kincaid, CEO of Bangor Corporation, was found today, along with an unidentified woman, brutally stabbed to death. It is alleged that the apartment building where the double murders took place was owned by Bangor Corporation. Kincaid was survived by his wife, Natalie Kincaid, and a daughter, Shelby Kincaid, age 3. Details are sketchy.

Shelby stared into the screen, seeing her name glaring back at her.

"I wasn't prepared for this," she said. "No wonder my mother never talked about my father."

"But what I don't understand is why he left you and your mother without a dime."

"How do you know that?"

"The woman on the phone. She said your father was supposedly wealthy. But he left you and your mother penniless. I'd like to know why."

"How did she know that?" Shelby asked. "It doesn't say anything about that here."

222

"Maybe there's more." Will began scanning through the newspaper pages of the next several days looking for any mention of Thomas Kincaid. But nothing had been mentioned about the murder until two weeks later. And though it made the front page, the article was short and to the point.

Kincaid Double Murder
Wife of slain executive, Thomas Kincaid, left penniless. Natalie Kincaid and young daughter forced from their lavish uptown brownstone. Her husband's murderer still at large. Police have few leads in the case.

"I wonder how much Ashley's parents know about this?" Will said.

"Enough," Shelby replied. "They must have been close to my mother. Why else would they have taken us in like they did?"

"Yeah," Will said reflectively.

"What are you thinking?"

"That I want to see your birth certificate."

"My birth certificate? Why? It's pretty obvious isn't it?"

"I don't have any doubts that you were born here," Will said. "I'd like to know where you lived. The birth certificate will give your mother's address."

"I remembered a house."

"I know. Buzz told me. I'll call the Bureau of Vital Statistics tomorrow. Right now, I want to find Winthrop House."

"What if this old man Louis won't talk to us?"

"I can be very persuasive."

"You're telling me?"

Shelby and Will drove their rental car up the long, winding cobblestone road toward Winthrop House. Autumn had begun to give way to winter, leaving only a hint of color still clinging to the trees.

"Unbelievable," Shelby marveled, peering out the car window. "Are you sure these directions are right?"

"Positive."

The road twisted through a long tunnel formed by the impinging branches; the absence of foliage made little difference in the tomblike effect. The gnarled and sinuous limbs intertwined, forming a coil of darkness.

"Where did this fog come from?" Will remarked.

Shelby gazed out the window, as though mesmerized, while Will downshifted expertly as the road became steeper. The car promptly obeyed, taking hold and speeding onward with an added surge of power.

Shelby cracked the window slightly. The bitter cold rushed in, sucking the warmth from inside the car, but neither Shelby nor Will noticed. The sound of the waves was almost deafening.

Then, as they rounded another bend, far off in the distance, ominously, Winthrop House emerged. A massive structure of stone and mortar. Will slowed the car as he and Shelby gaped through the tall, intricate iron palisade.

The road lay straight ahead now, a long sweep of cobblestones like an ancient avenue leading to a twenty foot tall, double-hung gate. Through the fog, they could see streaks of sunlight reflecting off the gold tips of the iron gates. As they drew closer, the gates came into focus. On the front of each gate the letter W was scripted in gold. Will pulled the car up to the stone post that stood several feet from the gates. He rolled down the window and reached out, pushing a button below a small speaker. Shelby sat anxiously. Will pulled his arm back into the car, numbed by the damp, bitter cold.

"Yes." The voice sounded gruff and unfriendly.

He glanced over at Shelby as if to say, 'What do I do now?' Then he turned and reached his head out of the window. "My name is Dr. Will Taylor," he said in his most dignified manner. "I am a friend of Ashley and Michael Winthrop's. Ashley and I are researching her family history. She has asked that I contact a man named Louis who lived here at Winthrop House when she was a child. Could you be of help to us?"

There was momentary silence. "You may leave your phone number. If Mr. Carter wishes to speak with you, he'll call."

"I am staying at the Willow Inn down in the village. Room 14. My name is Dr. Will Taylor. Please tell Mr. Carter that it's important."

There was a click, then silence.

224

"I think that was a sign for us to leave," Will snickered.

"Well, I'm not exactly thrilled to be here," Shelby said, looking through the creeping mist. "It's spooky as hell. Can you believe that house?"

"Ashley told me you liked spooky old houses."

"Oh she did?" Shelby glanced at Will and noticed a mischievous gleam in his eye. She remembered seeing that same look right after Ashley was brought home from the hospital. Ashley's accident had somehow drawn Shelby to him. No. That wasn't exactly true. She had been drawn to Will the first moment she laid eyes on him, watching him sitting there in Buzz's parlor mauling that pack of cigarettes. The feeling had frightened her. Only once had she felt like that. But with Scott she had felt safe, she couldn't act on those feelings. He had belonged to Ashley.

"Don't look at me like that," Shelby said, shifting in her seat. God he was making her nervous. She looked out the side window and took a breath. "Come on, let's get out of here."

Will turned the car around and started down the long drive, another grin working its way across his face.

∞

"Blake," Buzz was saying. "Helen called me today. I'm terribly concerned about Ashley. Helen says she refuses to leave her room and has hardly eaten. I don't understand what brought this on. I thought she was anxious to go with Will and Shelby to Manchester."

"I don't understand it either. How much longer are you going to be in Chicago?"

"Another month at least. But if need be I'm on the next plane. What about David? Do you think he's well enough to help?"

"He's stronger. But he's had a hell of a concussion to say the least. The pneumonia is gone. I'll speak to him, though. I'm tempted to call Victor."

"Let's give Ashley a couple of days. In fact, tell her you're going to call Victor. See how she reacts." Buzz paused. "I still can't believe David was found on my property."

Chapter Seventeen

Will and Shelby decided to browse through the numerous antique shops that lined the village streets of Manchester. They hoped to have a message from Louis Carter by the time they returned to the inn.

Walking along the old cobblestone sidewalk, they crossed the street toward several more shops. They passed a few small boutiques, a coffee shop and a locksmith, then came to an alleyway. It was lined with more quaint shops and cafes. There was one shop in particular that caught their attention. Hanging from two brass chains was a dark green oval sign which read: The Cobweb, Rare and Antique Books.

Shelby tugged at Will's coat, then drew back. She had not meant to do that. "Come on," she said, "let's go in."

"I thought you'd never ask," Will replied, and they were off at a gallop. Panting from the half sprint down the uneven cobblestones, Will reached out and turned the brass knob. The tiny bell above the door announced their entrance.

"May I help you?" a gentle voice called out from the back.

"Yes ma'am." Will peered over the rows of bookcases. Finally a petite lady emerged. Her silver hair was swept back from her face in a tidy bun. She wore a beautifully ruffled high neck blouse and a long, wine-colored woolen shirt. As she approached, Will smiled and nodded. "My name is Dr. Will Taylor, and this is Shelby Kincaid. I research family history. Your shop caught my eye."

The lady offered her frail hand. "*The* Dr. Will Taylor?"

Will looked embarrassed. "I guess so."

"Oh my," the lady replied. "This is an honor." She looked toward Shelby.

Shelby smiled and offered her hand.

"Shelby?" The lady said this as though bemused. She studied Shelby's face. "I'm, Aggie Carter. What may I do for you?" She turned to Will. "Are you researching your next book?"

"Not a book." Will glanced around the cluttered shop. "I'm researching a friend's genealogy."

"I see. And what is your friend's name?"

"Winthrop," he said.

"What!" The word gushed from her tiny mouth. "Why . . . do you want to know about them?" She quickly turned to Shelby with a suspicious look. "Who are you?"

Shelby gazed into the woman's face, bewildered.

Aggie quickly looked away and studied Will. Her expression began to calm. "Please," she said, "I need to sit down."

"Of course," Will said, gently touching her arm and escorting her to the back of the shop where there was a large roll-top desk and several antique wing chairs. Will looked back at Shelby and discreetly arched an eyebrow. Shelby knew exactly what he was thinking. This lady knew something. She also wondered if Will had caught the lady's last name. Carter.

Aggie Carter settled into the chair. "Why would you want to research the Winthrop family?" she asked nervously.

Will thought for a moment, wondering if he should simply tell the truth. He was certain that this fragile little woman knew something. He looked at Shelby as if contemplating his next step then turned back to Aggie. "Shelby's stepfamily used to live here in Manchester. At least we think they did."

"Stepfamily?"

"Victor and Margaret Winthrop took Shelby in when she was about four years old. They had a daughter, Ashley, and a son, Michael. Have you ever heard of them?"

Aggie looked thoughtful. "I'm afraid not. It's been far too many years." She lowered her gaze as though saddened. "I once lived at Winthrop House. But I have not allowed myself to think of those years."

"You lived at Winthrop House?" Will stirred in his seat.

"Yes. I was born there. My family were servants there."

"For whom did your family work?" Will asked.

Aggie sighed. "Andrew Winthrop and his wife Sophia. They had two sons: Christopher and Stefan."

Will and Shelby exchanged glances at hearing the names.

"When were you there?" Will asked.

Aggie smiled. "Too many years ago. I am 95."

"That's impossible," Shelby muttered, studying Aggie's face.

"You're very kind." Aggie patted Shelby's hand. "And so lovely. You remind me . . . " Aggie reached up and gently touched Shelby's cheek. "You have such a lovely, gentle face. And the most beautiful eyes."

Shelby smiled with embarrassment. "Thank you."

"Who lives at Winthrop House now?" Will inquired anxiously.

Aggie's face withdrew into sadness. "I don't know. I left there many years ago. My mother and I moved to a farm outside of Manchester. I only recently opened this little book shop." She lowered her head. "Dr. Taylor," she said softly. "I think Winthrop House is better left in the past."

"Please. Call me Will. But why do you say that?"

"Because. Winthrop House is evil. It is Satan's house. You must not go there."

"I am told," Will said, "that a man by the name of Louis Carter is living there."

"Who?"

"A Louis Carter. Do you know him?"

"No," Aggie replied reflectively.

"I'm afraid I'm not going to be able to leave Winthrop House in the past," Will said, rising from his chair. "My friends have hired me to research their family. Thank you for your time anyway."

Aggie looked up at Shelby, who was now standing next to Will. "You say the Winthrops adopted you?"

Shelby smiled. "More or less."

"I see."

Will decided to inquire further. "Aggie. Why do you say that Winthrop House is evil?"

Aggie's face turned cold. "I saw unspeakable horrors in that house." She lifted a delicate hand to her face.

Shelby gently touched Aggie's shoulder. "We didn't mean to dredge up unhappy memories. It's just that my stepsister . . . well, let's just say she needs to find out about her past. She's been having some bad dreams."

Aggie considered Shelby. "She would be better off not knowing."

Will and Shelby left Aggie's shop and drove back to the Willow Inn. Whatever it was that Aggie knew, she didn't want to talk about it. Their only hope now was that a message would be waiting from Louis Carter. And sure enough, there were two: one from Blake, the other from Louis Carter. Mr. Carter had asked that they be at Winthrop house at four o'clock. It seemed that he was anxious to meet with them.

"Now we're getting somewhere." Will looked excited.

"After what Aggie said, I'm not sure I want to go."

"Really? Then I'll go without you."

"You're not going anywhere without me," she retorted, following after Will down the hall. He stopped in front of his room while Shelby began fidgeting for her key.

"Where are you going?" A sly grin began working across his face. "I thought you weren't going anywhere without me?"

Shelby appeared to ignore this, unlocked her door, trying to remain composed. Will was making her terribly nervous. "You know what I mean," she said, hoping she didn't sound as awkward as she felt.

The next thing she knew, Will's arms were around her. She felt his chest pressing into her back. A slight gasp escaped her throat. Then the dizziness came. Will pulled her closer, wrapping his arms tighter around her.

"Why don't you come in my room while I call Blake. Then we'll drive up to Winthrop House together." He turned her around to face him. "I don't want to go without you."

Shelby tried to speak, but the dizziness only got worse.

Will took Shelby's hand and led her across the hall into his room. "Have a seat." He motioned to the wicker chair.

Will sat on the bed and called Blake who was at the hospital with David.

"Blake, it's Will. How's our friend David?"

"Ornery as ever. They have him sitting up now. He says he wants you to know that his belly has shrunk."

"Well, You can tell David that I haven't had a cigarette in over twenty-four hours." Will smiled at Shelby who was sitting on the edge of the chair fumbling with her nails.

"I'll let you tell him yourself," Blake said. "But David's not exactly why I called."

"What do you mean?"

"It's Ashley. She's been acting strange. Been locked up in her room since you and Shelby left. Helen was about the only person she'd talk to. She wouldn't even talk to Buzz. He has called her four or five times from Chicago. Now she's left. Helen went down to see about her late this morning. She was gone, bags and all."

"Ashley's gone?"

Shelby took a sudden turn and leapt from her chair. "Gone where?" she said grabbing the phone.

"I don't know," Blake said. "Maybe she changed her mind and decided to go to Manchester."

"And not tell anybody?"

"I'm worried about her. I've just about decided to call Victor."

"No. Ashley would kill us if we did that. If she's decided to leave without telling us then that's her business."

"If you say so," Blake said reluctantly.

But Shelby wasn't surprised to hear that Ashley had picked up and left. It was obvious that something more than nightmares and falling into wells had been bothering Ashley. But exactly what, she wasn't sure.

Again, the restless fog swirled about the grounds of Winthrop House. Will clutched the steering wheel, as he waited for the tall iron gates to open. Shelby shifted slightly and crossed her legs, then uncrossed them. They heard a loud clicking sound. The gates had begun to open.

Shelby anxiously glanced around at the giant evergreens and stately oaks. How strangely familiar it seemed, as she remembered Ashley describing her dream. She looked toward Winthrop House. They were almost upon it. Her eyes went to the round stone-encased window high above.

"Look," Will said anxiously. "There's someone standing by the front entrance."

Shelby took her eyes from the dark window. "I wonder if it's Louis."

"I doubt it. It's probably the butler. The downstairs butler."

"Yeah," Shelby agreed nervously.

Will brought the car to a halt next to a massive stone fountain flanked by tall Griffins. A wide terraced walkway led to the marble and stone lancet archway. Set deep into the arch stood what looked like a twelve to fifteen foot door. Though the man was very tall, he seemed dwarfed by it all as he proceeded down the stone walkway.

Will and Shelby left the car, both feeling overwhelmed.

"Dr. Taylor," the man announced with an outstretched hand. "I can't tell you how honored I am to meet you."

Will and Shelby saw that the left side of the man's face was blemished with a hideous discoloration.

Will shook the man's hand. "It was good of you to have us." This man was not the butler—upstairs or down.

"I'm Louis Carter," he said warmly, and turned to Shelby.

Shelby smiled and offered her hand. "My name is Shelby Kincaid. Ashley Winthrop and I have known each other since we were children."

"It's so nice to meet you, Miss Kincaid." Louis bowed his head as though saddened. "I had lost all hope of ever seeing Ashley again. She and Michael were so dear to me. The whole family was." Louis turned to Will. "Why don't we go to my cottage and have some tea."

Will looked at Shelby with a gleam of excitement as Louis ushered them across the cobblestone driveway. "I find it much too lonely living in the main house. As you can see, it's quite large. My little cottage serves me well. In the winter time when the house is closed, its almost like a tomb. Shut off from nature's lullabies."

"It's beautiful here," Shelby said, looking out through the mist toward the cliff's edge. "Like a piece of heaven."

"That it is," Louis replied.

Completely entranced by this phenomenal house and the vast grounds, they almost didn't notice it. But there it was, just as Ashley had described it.

"This is the family cemetery," Louis said, as they approached a small wrought iron fence.

Shelby looked up at the tall, hovering oak tree, remembering Ashley's description from her dream when she had heard a voice telling her to go back. Ashley had had that dream only moments before Shelby had regained consciousness.

"Some of these graves date back as far as the sixteen hundreds."

"That's interesting," Will remarked.

"Most died at an early age though. All males. And except for a handful, all of the females lived to be uncommonly old." Louis chuckled. "I think I'm old at 86 until I remind myself that some of those women lived to be over a hundred."

Shelby shivered and pulled her collar closer under her chin.

"Come along," Louis coaxed. "You can look through the cemetery another time."

He turned to Shelby. "The gardens are magnificent during the spring and summer months."

"Ashley said she used to help you with your flowers." Shelby studied Louis, awaiting his reaction, hoping that Ashley's recollection while under hypnosis was accurate.

"My little Ashley remembers that? Goodness, but she was so young."

Louis ushered Will and Shelby into his cozy guest house that was no more than a small living room and kitchen, a bedroom, and an ample room that now served as a modern bathroom. Although the house lacked space, it was, as was the main house, a magnificent piece of architecture. The wide stone stairway led to a leaded glass frontage. All of the windows rose high, almost to the slate roof line. From the west side the jagged cliffs along the twisting Atlantic coastline could be seen for miles, giving way to an endless stretch of ocean.

"Ashley and I were great buddies." Louis laughed. "She was always at my heals." He motioned toward a round oak table. Please, have a seat. Except for the staff that keeps up this enormous estate, I am all alone here. Clancy, my faithful Golden Retriever, died a few months back. I miss her terribly."

"I'm a dog lover too," Shelby remarked.

"A lot easier than children," Will chuckled. "I have two chocolate labs."

"Never did trust people who didn't love animals." Louis took the iron poker from its stand and began stoking the fire. "How does a cup of tea sound?" he asked as the fire took on added life, sending a glowing warmth throughout the cottage. "I always keep a kettle simmering."

"I'd love a cup of tea," Shelby said, taking off her coat and draping it over the back of her chair.

Will sat down, turning his attention to the family cemetery. "There must be quite a history to this old place," he said.

Louis poured the tea and then joined them at the table. "Is Winthrop House going to be your next project?"

"A project of sorts. Ashley is interested in her genealogy. She's hired me to trace it for her."

"I see," Louis replied. "Have you had much success?"

"I have had NO success," Will responded with disgust. "I was hoping you could help me out."

"That's quite amusing," Louis said. "And it was I who hoped that you could help me out."

"Help you?" Will looked baffled. "I don't understand."

"Dr. Taylor," Louis said. "I have read every book you have ever written. It has been my hope for many years that you would one day look into the history of the Winthrop family."

Shelby suddenly realized, as she listened to Louis, that the dark crimson mark that had so startled her at first had become less noticeable. The inner man now seemed to overshadow the deformity. In fact, Louis Carter was actually a handsome man. Even at his advanced age he still had strong contours to his face, a healthy crop of silver hair, and a tall and stately stature. His voice was that of someone who had grown wiser through the years.

"What do you mean?" Will asked.

Louis sipped his tea. "How fortuitous it is that you have come here. Many times I have considered contacting you. Not a year ago I wrote to you. I don't know what it was that kept me from sending the letter."

"Why is it that you want to know about the Winthrops," Will asked curiously. "Are you related to them?"

"Oh no," Louis replied. "I mean . . . I don't know who I'm related to."

Will glanced at Shelby. "I don't understand."

"Neither do I," Louis sighed.

"Were you there the day that Ashley and her family left Winthrop House?" Shelby asked anxious to hear Louis' reply.

"Yes, and by far the saddest day of my life. The Winthrops were like family. I had not been blessed with a family. Mine were killed when I was very young." Louis lowered his head, smiling timidly. "I was nothing more than an employee, I oversaw the staff and the grounds." He looked back at Will and Shelby. "But they treated me like family. And I loved them like family."

"I know what you mean," Shelby said.

Will started to speak, then hesitated.

"What is it?" Louis asked.

"Why did the Winthrop's leave?"

"I have never known why."

"They just walked away and left you in charge?" Shelby asked. "Without an explanation?"

Louis smiled sadly. "Yes, it was rather like that. You see, Victor Winthrop was heir to neither Winthrop House nor the Winthrop fortune."

"He wasn't?" Will said curiously.

"No. And that's why I've hoped for so long that you would write about the family. Uncover the mystery."

"Mystery?" Will stroked his mustache.

Louis sipped his tea. "I have never told a living soul this. No, that isn't exactly true. I did tell someone once." Louis' face grew cold.

Will and Shelby were now seized with curiosity.

"As far as I know," Louis continued, "only the law firm that represents the Winthrop family knows the truth. Not even when I was contacted and given this incredible news would they divulge the source or the reason behind it."

"What news?" Will pressed.

"That I am the sole heir to Winthrop House and its fortune."

"You!" Will was noticeably astonished.

Louis smiled. "My precise reaction."

"But why?"

Louis shook his head. "That's what I have yearned to find out for more years than you know."

"Do you mean that Victor and Margaret don't even know?" Shelby asked.

"I never told them."

234

"But Victor must have known that the estate didn't belong to him," Shelby said.

"I would certainly think so. And that may be one reason why he left. But something tells me not."

"Why do you say that?" Will asked.

"Because, his decision to leave was sudden. One day he and Margaret announced that they were moving. The next day they were gone. They just packed up and left within two days. The only furniture they took was Ashley's bedroom suite. Mrs. Winthrop asked that I ship it to them. It seemed little Ashley couldn't part with it. I had it sent a few days later after Margaret called and gave me an address."

"Where was that?" Shelby wanted to know.

"An address in New Orleans. On Jackson Street. I sent them Christmas cards and birthday cards every year, but they never responded. I stopped when the cards started coming back." Louis looked out toward the foggy cliffs. "Whatever drove them from Winthrop House also drove them from me." He looked back to Will and Shelby. They have never spoken about this house, have they?"

"No, Louis," Shelby replied, "they haven't. That's why we're here. Ashley and Michael were never told that they had lived at Winthrop House."

"I am not surprised," he said. "They were so young, and I'm sure Victor and Margaret felt they needed to shield them from whatever it was that happened here. If only I knew, though, what it was that sent them away."

"Maybe you will, Louis," Will said with optimism. "Do you know a woman by the name of Aggie Carter?"

"No. I don't believe so."

"She has an antique book shop down in the village. Shelby and I spoke to her yesterday. Seems she and her family were servants here back in the late eighteen hundreds. Worked for Andrew and Sophia Winthrop, I think their names were."

"Yes," Louis said. "There's an Andrew and Sophia Winthrop buried out in the family cemetery."

"Have you ever heard of Stefan or Christopher Winthrop?" Shelby asked.

Louis' eyes again grew cold. "Christopher Winthrop?"

"Yes. Did you know him?"

"I knew who he was. He was Victor Winthrop's father."

"Father!" Shelby and Will said in unison.

"He didn't deserve the title," Louis sneered. "Christopher Winthrop was a selfish man. And certainly unworthy of the love his wife Kathleen had for him. He lived in Europe, not at Winthrop House with his family." Louis's face turned somber. "After Kathleen was given the news of Christopher's death she disappeared. Left all of her belongings and simply vanished. He had broken her heart and no one will convince me otherwise. I think she had resigned herself through the years to somehow accept her husband's absence. But the day when the news came that her husband had been lost at sea, well, I saw the defeat and despair in her eyes. I think she simply gave up.

"What Christopher Winthrop did to his family was unforgivable. My family was tragically taken from me, but the fault did not lie with them."

"Victor must have despised his father," Shelby said.

"There isn't a word strong enough to express Victor's anguish and hatred toward his father. As far as Victor was concerned he never had a father. I know he blamed him for Kathleen's disappearance."

Will and Shelby stirred in their chairs.

"I only met Christopher Winthrop once," Louis continued. "You see, after finding out about my inheritance, I didn't go to live in Winthrop House right way. For me to go there and announce that the entire Winthrop fortune had been turned over to me, an orphan, a deformed man with no family, was not possible."

"What did you do?" Shelby inquired restlessly.

Louis smiled. "I did what I loved best. I became a landscape architect. And did quite well if I say so myself. Eight years later, in 1925 I was twenty-six then, I applied for a job at Winthrop House. I had made a name for myself, which helped a great deal. Kathleen Winthrop was not a stranger to my work and seemed very impressed. She hired me on the spot. I had already decided that I would never reveal my position as proprietor of the estate until I learned the truth."

"If you had had control of the estate for the previous years," Will asked, "where was the money coming from to maintain this enormous piece of property?"

"There was a separate account set aside just for that purpose. I left that as it was, in the hands of the law firm. They had the authority to disburse what monies were needed to keep up the property."

"So what you're saying is that Christopher Winthrop and his wife, Kathleen, did not have access to the Winthrop money?"

"From what I was told, the entire fortune was given to me to do with as I saw fit."

"That's incredible," Will sighed.

"Mystery doomed to remain just that," Louis said in defeat. "I'm no longer a spring chicken." He smiled at Shelby. "Not much time left."

"That's hogwash," Shelby blurted. "You have many years. You're still handsome too."

"Oh my dear," Louis' face ignited. "What a delightful thing to say. But it's not necessary. I know I am not handsome." He smiled at Shelby. "It's all right, sweet child, I've lived with this birthmark far too many years. I've learned to accept it."

"I don't say things I don't mean. You are handsome."

Louis turned to Will. "I think I'll refrain from argument."

"With Shelby, it's best."

Louis offered more tea as Will continued his questioning.

"When was it that you were contacted by the Winthrop lawyers and told about your fortune?"

"My eighteenth birthday," Louis replied. "They sent word to the orphanage in Boston that I had come into a great deal of money. Naturally, I thought it was money left to me by my parents, or maybe even relatives that I didn't know I had. Both of my parents were orphans, so I was left with no one to care for me after their death. When I heard about this it gave me renewed hope. But I found my life to be an even bigger mystery than I had imagined."

"Because of the money?" Shelby asked.

"No. there was that, of course. But they informed me that my name was not Carter but Tanner."

"Tanner?" Shelby shook her head then looked at Will.

"That's all the lawyers would tell you?" he said. "Nothing more?"

"Nothing," Louis sighed. "They handed me the legal documents and a gold box."

"A gold box?"

"Yes. But there was nothing but an old lace scarf inside." Louis smiled. "It was a beautiful scarf. I gave it to little Ashley."

"You gave her that scarf?" Shelby said.

"Why, yes." Louis smiled proudly. "She loved it so, would wear it around her neck from sunup to sundown. I could never have taken it from her. Ashley was a precocious child," he said proudly. "She seemed so focused for such a young thing." Louis studied Shelby momentarily. "Ashley still has the scarf?"

"Oh yes."

"Louis?" Will asked. "Did Victor ever see his father?"

"I don't think so. Keep in mind though, I did not come to Winthrop House until Victor was grown and away at Harvard. But from what I could gather from Victor and Kathleen's conversations, he didn't. Except, of course, for Christopher's portrait that hangs in the west wing of the house."

"Portrait?"

"Yes, the house is full of them. I think almost everyone who has ever lived at Winthrop House has a portrait hanging on those walls. Other than myself, of course."

Shelby glanced at Will, then back at Louis. She had been anxiously awaiting the next question. "Have you ever heard of a woman named Jenny Winthrop?"

"Jenny?" Louis said thoughtfully. "Why yes, there is a gravestone out in the cemetery. Stefan and Jenny Winthrop. It's their child's grave. It died at birth. You are welcome to take a look."

"Yes, I'd like to do that." Will stood.

"Are Michael and Ashley coming to Manchester, I hope?" Louis said to Shelby.

"Michael's off in Europe somewhere," Shelby replied. "He's an architect and goes there about once a year to study the buildings."

"An architect," Louis beamed. "That's a grand profession. I bet he's a real lady's man, too."

"Can't argue with that."

"What about Ashley? What has she done with her life?"

"She's a very famous designer and restorer of vintage homes."

Louis smiled as if amused. "Little Ashley loved Winthrop House and all its marvelous furnishings. Even at such a young age she was intrigued by this grand old place."

"She hasn't changed," Shelby assured him.

"I can't tell you what it has meant to me to have you come here. I haven't looked forward to much these past years."

As they walked by the little cemetery Louis turned to Will, "You are welcome to go in and look at the gravestones." He went to the gate and lifted the latch. "I'll even go with you. It's been years since I've ventured inside here."

Will and Shelby went from stone to stone. Hazy streaks of late afternoon light filtered through the mist and the oak's branches. Each gravestone was more ornately carved than the next. Louis moved through the grassy corridors not really looking at the stones, but more like someone who had something weighing heavily on his mind.

"Will." Shelby motioned for him to come and see. Will wound his way through the grave sites, and over to where Shelby knelt down beside a small headstone.

The stone read:

Baby Winthrop
Born to Stefan and Jenny Winthrop
Died at Birth

"There's no date," he noticed.

Shelby looked thoughtful. "Do you really believe that it's Jenny Winthrop's spirit that Ashley is seeing? That Jenny's the reason for everything that's been happening to her?"

"Do you have another explanation?"

"No, but I thought you might."

"I think I have an explanation for the dream Ashley's been having since childhood. I don't know what exactly happened then, but I think it was real and she's suppressed it all these years. As for everything else, I guess we'll just have to keep an open mind."

They continued browsing through the cemetery, stopping to read the inscriptions, when Shelby noticed a small marker unlike all the others. There were no intricately carved designs, In fact, nothing but, "Winthrop Child" had been inscribed.

Will and Shelby then said their good-byes to Louis. Shelby was feeling slightly nervous at the thought of going inside the main house, so Will declined Louis' invitation for later in the week.

"That's the dearest man I think I have ever met," Shelby remarked as Will drove out the gates. "Did you notice he didn't ask why Ashley hadn't come with us?"

"Yes," Will replied. "I also noticed that he didn't have a lot to say about living at Winthrop House all these years."

"What do you mean?"

"I mean, I think Louis Carter, or Tanner, whatever his last name is, knows a lot more than he's telling."

"Maybe. But hey, the man just met us. I wouldn't expect him to unload."

"He certainly came forward with the news of who Winthrop House belongs to."

"Where is all this fog coming from?" Shelby remarked, as they worked their way down the narrow, winding road. Winthrop House had faded from sight.

Chapter Eighteen

"Dr. Taylor," the desk clerk announced as Will and Shelby passed by. "There's a lady over there waiting to see you. She's been here for over an hour."

Will looked across the room and saw Aggie sitting on the sofa still bundled in her coat and gloves.

"Aggie," Shelby called. "What on earth are you doing here?" She sat down next to Aggie while Will pulled up a chair.

Aggie raised an unsteady hand. "Don't ask me to explain. I couldn't even if I tried." She turned to Will. "I will tell you about Winthrop House. If you are certain that you want to hear it."

"I'm certain, Aggie. It's very important to Ashley Winthrop and to Shelby."

"All right then," she said. "Could we go someplace else? I think I would like a glass of sherry. Maybe over to Ruby's Chowder House. It's just across the alleyway from my shop." Aggie smiled. "Ruby has the best chowder in town. And she keeps a bottle of sherry on hand."

"Of course." Will said, helping Aggie up from the sofa.

Ruby's was a small dimly lit restaurant with tables draped in rose-colored cloths. In the center of each table was a tiny oil lamp casting eerie shadows. The room buzzed with muted conversation. The wide, planked floor creaked beneath each footstep as they walked toward a table in the far corner of the room. Will helped Aggie with her coat, feeling a renewed hope to unraveling the mystery of Winthrop House.

Will and Shelby each ordered a glass of wine and a bowl of Ruby's chowder. Aggie asked for her usual glass of sherry.

"When I was about seven," Aggie said, "I started to keep a journal. I only wrote in it once after leaving Winthrop House. There were few memories I held dear while I was there. But those few blessed memories have carried me through."

Ruby arrived with their drinks and three steaming bowls of her prize chowder. Aggie took a long sip then settled comfortably in her chair.

"I'll never forget," she began, her eyes taking on a reflective gaze. "It was June 12, 1899, and the beginning of my happiest days at Winthrop House. I was seven and had lived in the servants' quarters of this magnificent house since birth. My mother and father oversaw the cleaning staff and administrative duties. My father died when I was five. His death affected me greatly, and I soon withdrew into myself. My schooling was done privately at Winthrop House. My whole world revolved around the great mansion. So I came to know well my prison of opulence and propriety."

Aggie paused and sipped her sherry.

"By the time I was seven, I knew every secret passage, every nook and cranny, rooms that seemed to have no purpose. I withdrew from reality and into my own world of fantasy."

Will leaned back in his chair. With eyes glued to Aggie, he leisurely swirled his spoon through the steaming chowder. Shelby seemed to ignore the chowder completely, with elbows propped firmly on the table.

"But that day in 1899 changed my life. I can still remember how warm and bright it was. The sun seemed to cast its rays like crystals across her lovely face, as the horses pulled their coach up the winding road. Mr. Stefan was bringing his fiancé home from England. Her name was Jenny. When I saw her I felt that an angel had fallen from the sky. I later felt that God had sent her to me. It troubles me to say it, but I never loved my mother as I loved Jenny.

"Jenny had also won the heart of my dear mother. In fact, as I later became aware, she had also won the heart of Sophia Winthrop. And this became her torment.

"Stefan was a strong and handsome man. Strong in every way, except with his mother, Sophia. He was somehow imprisoned by her. I've never known why. I do know that she was Stefan's undoing. Andrew Winthrop, Sophia's husband, was not controlled or manipulated by his wife. He was a strong-willed man and, like his sons, incredibly handsome.

"On August 25, 1899, Stefan and Jenny were to be married. I remember how exciting that was for me. Jenny had asked that I be her flower girl. Sophia objected. I was merely a servant's daughter. But Jenny persevered and I was presented with the most beautiful dress I had ever seen."

"It must have been a grand affair," Will said.

"Oh my no," Aggie replied. "Just a small intimate wedding. The Winthrops were dreadfully private and only invited special friends, most of whom were from England. It was a beautiful ceremony though, held in the old marble gazebo just at sunset. Afterwards, Mr. Stefan presented Jenny with a wedding present. George, one of the servants, came walking across the grounds with a big basket tied with beautiful yellow ribbon. He placed it on the long, linen-draped table. Mr. Stefan told Jenny to open it. I remember my elation when I saw them. Two adorable black Scottie puppies. Jenny was overjoyed. After she hugged Mr. Stefan, she gathered up those furry little things and smothered them with kisses.

"Later that evening Sophia gave Jenny an exquisite ruby necklace with matching earrings. Mr. Christopher, Stefan's brother, gave her a beautiful lace scarf."

Will and Shelby exchanged glances.

"Jenny and Mr. Stefan soon left for their honeymoon by private rail car to San Francisco. The Sutro family, who had also attended the wedding, had prepared as a wedding present, one of their private suites in the magnificent Victorian Cliff House overlooking the Pacific Ocean.

"If it had not been for the Scotties, Doogie and Winston, I think the weeks would have been unbearable. I had promised Jenny that I would take good care of them. Two long months later, Stefan and Jenny returned. I begged her never to leave me again."

Aggie's eyes took on a longing gaze. She seemed to project herself backward, into the moment.

"As the months passed, Jenny would sit for hours, playing the piano in the grand ballroom. Sometimes I would see the birds fill the trees, as though they had come from far away just to hear her sweet music. Mr. Christopher would bring in his cello and accompany her. Sometimes even Sophia would come into the room and read while Jenny played. Somehow Sophia's hard, callous exterior that had always been so evident seemed to crumble away. She now puttered around the magnificent gardens and would sit with Jenny, engrossed in needlepoint and conversation. Sophia's husband, Andrew, also seemed entranced by Jenny. I had never seen him quite so taken with anyone."

"Jenny must have been very special," Shelby remarked.

Aggie turned to Shelby and smiled sweetly. "My yes."

"Please." Shelby gently touched Aggie's arm. "I didn't mean to interrupt."

Aggie's expression quickly fell back into that distant gaze.

"Christmas had come. This was a time that I will keep as a sweet remembrance. We had never celebrated Christmas at Winthrop House. The Winthrops were not a religious family and had always kept the Christmas spirit at bay. But this Christmas, erected in the grand entrance was the biggest Christmas tree I had ever seen. Sophia had sent the servants out for the finest decorations. That night, Christmas Eve, everyone, servants and all, helped to dress this magnificent tree. Jenny sat at the piano and played Christmas songs, while everyone sang. This was a Christmas I would keep in my heart always.

"One evening in April of the next year, Jenny and Mr. Stefan called everyone into the library. Never had there been a meeting called of the staff unless there was a problem or an important function, and the only event Winthrop House had seen for a long time was Mr. Stefan and Jenny's wedding. After everyone had gathered around, Mr. Stefan made the announcement.

"Jenny was expecting.

"A few months later, Sophia arranged for Jenny's portrait to be painted."

"There's a portrait?" Will asked.

"Oh my yes. Jenny went to the studio every day for her sitting. After a while, she persuaded Sophia to let me go with her. An artist by the name of Tryn DeLore was a friend of Andrew Winthrop's and a marvelous painter. He had painted most of the portraits that hung on the walls of Winthrop House. He lived in a very beautiful house on the coast, just north of Manchester, where he had a studio. I liked him and have since wondered what became of him. He too seemed to be taken by Jenny."

Shelby fell back into her chair. "What name did you say?"

"DeLore," Aggie replied. "Tryn DeLore."

"Oh." Shelby let it drop.

"A few weeks later, Doogie and Winston and I had been exploring. We were coming down the secret stairs and through the hidden corridor when I heard shouting. I knew I was close to Jenny and Mr. Stefan's bedroom. I had known all the hidden corridors and secret doors from the time I was five. I often wondered if Sophia knew that her house was a maze of secret passageways.

"Doogie and Winston followed behind me. I can still see those flickering candles casting shadows along the narrow corridor. We finally reached the back of the bedroom and I huddled beside the panel that was concealed next to the fireplace. Mr. Stefan was shouting at Jenny. He was accusing her of loving his mother more than him. He said that he had overheard his mother telling Jenny that she loved her more than she had ever loved Stefan. He became furious, yelling awful things; words I had never heard. Jenny pleaded with him that it wasn't true. I will never forget how my heart broke listening to Jenny's sobs. The rage in Mr. Stefan's voice terrified me. Then Doogie started to whine. I was afraid Mr. Stefan would hear us, so I quietly sneaked back to the servants' quarters. Later that night Jenny came to get Doogie and Winston and to tuck me in. Her eyes were so sad and swollen from crying.

"The arguments were getting worse. It had now become my ritual to smuggle myself into the hidden corridors with my candle, and crouch by the secret door to Jenny's room, listening to Mr. Stefan torment her. Once I almost pushed open the door, wanting desperately to make him stop. He was yelling, threatening to tell Sophia where Jenny had come from. I have never known what he meant by that.

"His jealously of his mother had become an obsession. I had always sensed his hatred for her, and wondered why such a strong, handsome man would permit her domination over him. I learned later from my mother that Sophia had never loved Stefan as she had Christopher. I have never known why.

"I would now sit huddled in the darkness, knowing that I was helpless to save Jenny from this tormented man. Once I came close to telling my mother, but I didn't. I was afraid she might scold me for eavesdropping. Besides, I would have to tell her about the secret passageways. So, I continued my nightly tryst with the catacombs of Winthrop House, ensconced behind a secret panel, while I wept in silence.

"Then finally October came. Winter had settled in early that year. I can still remember how barren and disconsolate the trees looked. Jenny would sit at the piano and play her beautiful music. But it no longer flowed with serenity and beauty, only sadness. Even Mr. Christopher, who would sit by her side playing his cello, seemed saddened. I often think back to those sad times, even though I vowed never to remember, and it becomes so clear to me now how much Mr. Christopher had grown to love Jenny. I think through her anguish over Stefan, she had fallen in love with him. But Mr. Stefan never noticed, he was too obsessed with his belief that Jenny loved Sophia. Shortly after the birth of her baby, Christopher left Winthrop House.

"I can still remember gazing out through the tall, leaded windows, feeling as though I had suddenly been abandoned, that nothing was left but the naked trees, cold and angry like Mr. Stefan, a man I had once loved but no longer knew. I never understood how someone could change so drastically. There was such bitterness and rage.

"Anyway, one night it was getting late, and I knew I must leave my secret place before my mother came looking for me. Mr. Stefan was in Jenny's room again. He had not slept in the same bed with her since that night when he accused her of loving his mother. He was reviling her with his filthy accusations.

"Late at night, I used to sneak back to my hiding place just to see if Jenny was all right. Most of the time she would be sobbing in her bed. But that night when her room was silent, I found the courage to open the secret panel. I peered through the small opening and saw her sitting in her rocker. She was staring out into the night. I can still remember how her long white gown had caught the glow of the moon. She just sat there, rocking back and forth, her dark hair cascading over her shoulders. Oh how my heart bled for her.

"But that night, October 18, 1900, would take the very soul from her. The days and months that followed were a horror."

Will and Shelby glared at each other with morbid curiosity.

Aggie's face suddenly grew ridged, while her eyes glistened with tears.

Shelby wanted to reach out and comfort her, but feared it would only make it worse. She forced herself still.

"Just as I started to leave my secret place, Jenny suddenly screamed. I froze with fear. What had Mr. Stefan done I wondered, determined to crack open the panel. I pushed it open and saw Jenny doubled over in

246

pain, screaming. 'The baby! The baby!' Mr. Stefan quickly carried her to the bed and ran out, calling for Sophia. As soon as he was gone, I ran to Jenny's side. She was in so much pain I don't think she even knew I was there. And there was nothing I could do to take the pain away. It was so great that it seemed to reach out to me, like it had devoured Jenny's body and needed more to feed on. And then I heard footsteps. I quickly ran across the room and ducked back into my secret passage, leaving a small crack in the panel.

"The pain I watched her endure was unbearable. I honestly thought it would kill her. Her screams were screams of childbirth, which I knew so little about. The doctor had been summoned but did not arrive in time. Jenny's baby was born, with the help of Sophia and my mother, who ran back and forth with tubs of hot water. I sat numb as I saw the baby being born. In only minutes I saw Sophia wrap Jenny's baby in a blanket and leave the room. I can still remember how sad she looked.

"I remained crouched in the darkness, thinking that Jenny was dead. And then, to my amazement, she moved. She opened her eyes, seeming not to know where she was. Sophia was now at her side while Mr. Stefan stood motionless, glaring at her. My mother was straightening the bed and removing the tubs and towels when I heard Sophia tell Jenny that her baby was dead.

"The sorrow that Jenny was now forced to bear was beyond belief. She begged and pleaded with Sophia to let her hold her baby. To touch its tiny face and hands, press it close to her and to say how much she loved it. But Sophia would not allow it. She insisted that it would only cause her further torment.

"So Jenny never saw her baby. Two days later they had a small ceremony at the family cemetery out by the big oak tree beside Winthrop House. A tiny coffin was lowered into the ground with a small sculptured headstone that read:

Baby Winthrop
Born to Stefan and Jenny Winthrop
Died at Birth

"Until the day Jenny died she lived with this torment. That tragedy caused a darkness within her, but a darkness that later enabled her to endure what I am about to tell you. Not even from the grave, should Stefan Winthrop be protected from the atrocities he inflicted upon my dear sweet Jenny. Atrocities that an eight year-old child watched in horror within the secret hideaways of Winthrop House.

"It was early one morning, around the beginning of December, and Mr. Andrew had still not come down for breakfast. This was extremely unusual. Mr. Andrew always had a big breakfast of sausage and hot cakes. But this morning it was late and he still had not arrived at the dining table. I remember being fearful that he might be sick. He had appeared very tired, which was not at all like Mr. Andrew. I had never known him to be sick, and I had not seen him for several weeks. Moments later, Sophia came to the kitchen to tell us that Mr. Andrew had passed away in his sleep.

"I can not describe the grief and sorrow that lurked within Winthrop House the months that followed. Jenny's baby was gone and now Mr. Andrew. Jenny would sit endlessly at the piano playing her Lakmé. The lovely concertos that had once filled those massive rooms with joyous beauty were now replaced by haunting melodies. Even Sophia had lost her new-found zest for life and had regressed into her former cold self. Sometimes at night I would find her sitting in the library just staring at Jenny's portrait.

"After a while, Jenny began spending her days and nights in the little stone cottage down by the cliffs. Nothing Sophia could say would bring her back to the house. After I finished my school work, I would run down to the cottage and stay with her. She would read books to me, and sometimes I would read to her. But I could tell she didn't hear my words. She would just gaze out the window toward the little cemetery. I knew she was thinking of her baby. But I would read on as though she were listening. A few days later, Sophia brought a piano to the little cottage. She knew how much Jenny loved her music. If the truth is to be told, it is that Sophia Winthrop loved with her very being my dear, sweet Jenny.

"Then one day Mr. Stefan, who had been off in England, returned, bringing two of his friends with him. I didn't like them because Jenny seemed to be terrified when they would come around. I don't think Sophia liked them much either, and I wondered why she didn't make them leave. Maybe it was because they were important men. They had these titles like Baron and Lord.

"Sometimes I wish I had never seen what I'm about to reveal.

"Late one night, I was having trouble sleeping. I wanted so to go to the cottage and crawl in bed beside Jenny. I stood by my window looking out toward where the cottage stood, nestled down by the water's edge, wishing I could be with her, when I saw figures moving through the night. I could faintly hear Doogie and Winston barking. As they came closer to the house I realized in horror what I was seeing. It was those two men that Stefan had brought from England. They had Jenny between them. She had on her long, white bed gown and nothing else, except for the thing they had over her eyes and mouth. She was struggling desperately, as they forced her along the stone pathway and into the house.

"I was in shock. But as quickly and quietly as possible, so as not to wake my mother, I left my bedroom, entering the main house through my secret passageway. I cautiously lit my candle, which I kept on one of the hidden shelves just inside the corridor, and began my journey through the maze. If I had not searched and lived those catacombs, I would never have known the horror that befell my Jenny. In the beginning, I wished that I had not seen those horrors, but later my knowing saved her.

"The sounds of Winthrop House travel and are magnified within the catacombs, and after a short exploration, desperate to locate where those awful men had taken her, I heard voices. They were in one of the small rooms in the attic. It had been one of my favorite rooms, small and far away from the reality of the world. The large, round window would give just enough light so I could play and read my books without the candle. But why, I wondered, would they take Jenny there? I knew she didn't want to go with them. Then I remembered the thing around her eyes and mouth. Suddenly I became deathly frightened.

"I climbed the stairs two at a time, desperate to get to her. Yet I knew I was helpless to do anything but witness what I feared was the unthinkable. I was certain they were going to kill her.

"Their voices became clearer as I approached the secret panel. I lowered my candle to the floor, noticing that I had left the panel partially open. I prayed that I had not been heard, and moved closer to the opening. It was then I thought my heart would stop.

"Jenny's body lay naked and strapped to a large metal table. The thing around her eyes was gone, but her mouth was still covered."

"My God!" Shelby distorted her face in disgust.

Will bowed his head and messaged his temples.

"I could hear her deep, crying moans," Aggie bravely continued. "The eight candles on the metal table were the only light: four on one side and four on the other. They were short candles, but you could see Jenny clearly; the rest of the room was lost in shadow. One of the men was standing at the foot of the table and one at the head. They would run their filthy hands over her, then put their mouths all over her. Then they took turns putting their hands between her legs. Behind the thing that was over her mouth, I could hear her muffled screams. And I could see her eyes wide with pain. I watched in terror and with agonizing helplessness.

"Somehow, though, I had to find a way to stop them. Just as I started to leave and run from that horror chamber, I saw a tall, dark form emerge from the corner of the room. The man reached out and lit the candle that he held, then brought it below his face. I choked back a cry. It was Mr. Stefan. He was draped in this long black robe, his face partially covered by a large hood. He stepped back from the table and motioned to one of the men.

"The man stood at the end of the table and undid the front of his trousers and climbed on the table between Jenny's legs. He pushed at her over and over as hard as he could, then fell on top of her. I heard her cries while these men hurt her. After the last man got down from the table, Mr. Stefan walked over to her. I don't remember what his words were exactly. I think it was because I didn't know what they meant. But it was something about his mother not being able to do what they had just done.

"All the next day I just stayed in my room feeling sick. I thought Stefan and those men had killed Jenny. But the next morning when I woke, I tore out across the lawn and down to the cottage. Jenny was at the piano, playing her beautiful Lakmé. I remember looking into her face and thinking how sad she looked. And somehow, it seemed she wasn't my sweet lovely Jenny.

"What I did next took every ounce of courage I had. I sat down next to her, but she seemed not to notice. Carefully I chose my words.

"'Jenny,' I said. 'I saw something very bad the other night.' She continued to play, but I could tell by her eyes that she had heard me. 'I wanted to help you.' I said, 'but I didn't know how,' Suddenly, her hands were still. I thought she was going to speak, but she didn't. She only began to play again like I had not spoken. Like I was not even there. Tears flooded my eyes. I couldn't bear to see her like this. The tragedy of losing her baby had taken the life from her. Now, that horrible Mr. Stefan and his filthy friends were destroying her. I was filled with anger, and I jumped up from the piano bench and shouted, 'I saw them! I saw what they did!'

"My body shook with anger. And I was terrified that I should not have spoken those words. Jenny stopped playing. I was standing, gazing wide-eyed into my face. It seemed as though she couldn't speak, and the terror in her face almost assured me that she couldn't. Then, in an anguished whisper, she called my name.

"'Aggie,' she said to me, 'what are you saying?' I drew closer, my eyes firmly planted on hers.

"'I won't let you go back there,' I said. 'I won't let them hurt you.'

"Then she took me by the shoulders. 'How do you know this?' she asked. Her eyes were wild and confused. She pulled me over to the sofa. 'Aggie, what! What did you see?'

"For a moment, I became frightened, seeing the rage in her eyes. But I fought it. 'Jenny,' I said. 'I have to tell you,' and I began to cry. 'I didn't mean to snoop, but I saw those men take you in the house. I was afraid they were going to hurt you. Oh Jenny, I was so afraid. So I got my candle and walked through the secret corridors until I found you. And then when I found you . . . Oh, Jenny, why were those awful men doing those horrible things to you? I wanted to kill them, burn them up with my candle.' Jenny pulled me to her.

"'Aggie,' she said. 'I would give my soul if you had not seen.' She held my face in her hands and told me that I must not say anything. She said if I did, Mr. Stefan would see to it that she would never see her child again. I was shocked at her words; I had no idea what she meant; her child?

251

"Jenny was tormented, knowing that I had to carry this burden. Somehow she was convinced that, because of her silence, and the pleasures her husband gained from her torture, somehow she would be reunited with her child. I'm afraid I thought that Stefan was playing some kind of horrible joke on Jenny, making her think her baby was alive. But she never spoke of this again. I almost asked her once, but thought better of it. If she wanted to speak of it, she would.

"So, I lived with this agony for what seemed like an eternity. I even visited that chamber of horrors, crouched behind the secret panel. I think I felt that if my poor sweet Jenny had to suffer this torment, I should have to bear the suffering as well. So, I would go night after night, enduring my own agony while Jenny endured hers. But Jenny was stronger willed than I. After weeks of watching this torture, I found it impossible to keep silent. The first person I told was my mother. It frightened her so at first, that I'm not sure she wanted to admit that what I was saying was anything more than outrageous imagination. But she had to concede to its truth when I all but dragged her through the corridors that night and she saw with her own eyes.

"After seeing this abomination, my mother went straight to Sophia. A few nights later, Jenny was again taken to the room in the attic. Mr. Stefan would always wait until early morning to send the two men to get Jenny. And you could always hear the faint barking of Doogie and Winston in the distance. Sophia and my mother followed quietly as I led them through the secret corridors of Winthrop House. Sophia had not known they existed. I don't think I've ever seen rage contained with such determination as she watched her son in his tormenting pleasures. When we finally left the secret corridors, Sophia bent down and hugged me. 'You are a brave child, Aggie,' she said, then looked at my mother. 'You should be proud.' It was at that moment that I thought I saw a tear fall down Sophia's cheek. Then she smiled a sad but determined smile. 'I must take care of this matter,' she said, and she walked down the hallway, through the grand entrance hall, and up the wide marble staircase.

"Three nights later just after early morning, Jenny came running into our quarters. Her white dressing gown was covered with blood. In her left hand was a large kitchen knife. Her eyes were wild, and she was unable to speak. My mother and I didn't know what to think. All we did know was that we had to protect her. If it hadn't been for the fire down at the cottage, I'm not sure how we would have managed it. No one even knew there had been a fire until later that morning. Jenny was still in shock and unable to tell us anything. Sophia had gone down to the cottage that morning to discover a charred stone shell. Nothing was left but the stone walls and slate roof. Stefan was in the main house, lying face down on that horrible metal table in the attic room. The hood covered his head and his black cape was draped over the side of the table. He had been stabbed once in the heart and once in the back.

"It was assumed by all that Jenny and the two men visiting from London had fallen victim to the fire. Stefan's murder was a mystery, and remains a mystery to all except myself, my mother, and Jenny. Although Jenny regained little memory of that night till the day she died, she knew she had killed Stefan. With what my mother and I saw—Jenny's bloodstained dress and the knife she held in her hand—we also knew.

"Jenny was thought to have perished in the fire. Only my mother and a few servants knew that she was safely hidden away in our quarters. It was much later that she revealed to us what had happened. She had set the cottage and those men on fire. She was never the same after that day.

"Weeks had now passed, and Sophia receded within herself. Her family was gone. Sophia had lost her will to live. This strong, beautiful woman had became a beaten and distraught figure. Even the long, dark hair that I had always admired seemed to loose its radiance.

"Sophia now spent her days and most of her nights in the library. She would sit in the old rocker by the fireplace, staring at Jenny's portrait. She never knew that Jenny still remained at Winthrop House. No one knew, except for us and a few of the servants. Days later, my mother went into the library, hoping she could persuade Sophia to come to the dining room for dinner. Before the tragedy, Sophia had always insisted on having her meals served elegantly in the main dinning room. But she was not in the library, and neither was Jenny's portrait. My mother rushed upstairs, fearing the worst. And there, in her bedroom, sitting by the window that looked out over the gardens, was Sophia.

"She was dead.

"And to this day, we do not know what happened to Jenny's portrait or her personal belongings. Her bedroom had been stripped. Only the furnishings were left. I still think that Sophia was more familiar with the hidden corridors of Winthrop House than she let on. And if I could bear to return there, I would search for my Jenny's portrait. But the thought of returning to a place that was so ravished with sadness and horror is inconceivable.

"Sophia Winthrop left my mother and me an extravagant sum of money, which we used to buy our farm. I will never understand this act of generosity. Sophia was not a generous woman. Maybe it was her way to repay me for exposing Stefan and his torturous deeds. That money was greatly appreciated. We took George, one of the other servants, with us to help with the care of the farm. Jenny loved the farm. So did Doogie and Winston. They lived to be very old and sired several large families, of whom I have a great-grandson and great-granddaughter. Their names are Jocque and Spencer.

"As you know, I no longer live on the farm. Jenny and I bought this little book shop just last year. I turned the farm over to George's grandchildren. I still think of George from time to time, remembering Jenny's wedding day and George walking across the lawn with that big basket tied with the yellow bow. George's grandchildren have done a beautiful job redecorating the farm, and have made a wonderful home for the Scotties."

Aggie looked out across the room distantly.

"I once prayed that I would never lose my Jenny, after she barely escaped that horrible tragedy at Winthrop House. And I suppose my prayer was answered. I may not have had the happy, alive Jenny that I knew in those early days, but I had what was left of her to give."

Aggie turned to Will and Shelby.

"We never spoke of Winthrop House again after Sophia's death. It was a nightmare we could no longer face.

"We buried Jenny this past October, in the little village cemetery overlooking the Atlantic. I often wonder, though, if she had not yearned to be buried beside her baby at Winthrop House."

Aggie smiled warmly. "But I don't think of Jenny and her baby lying beneath the earth, but at long last united in love wherever the sweet and loving and gentle people go when they leave us. I was not prepared to give her up, and I still find it difficult to believe she is no longer beside me. But she is and always will be in the deepest part of me."

Shelby sniffed and wiped her eyes. "Jenny Winthrop died this past October?"

"Yes," Aggie replied. "She was 103, and as beautiful as the day I first saw her."

Chapter Nineteen

The night was bitter cold. Will and Shelby escorted Aggie back across Willow Alley to her book shop where she had an upstairs apartment.

"I do hope that I have helped you in some way," Aggie remarked as they crossed the cobblestone alleyway.

"You have helped a great deal," Will assured her. "I regret though, having dredged up unpleasant memories."

Aggie unlocked the door, then turned to Will. She smiled sweetly. "My memories aren't all unpleasant. I hold dear those few precious moments that Jenny brought to Winthrop House." Aggie reached over and touched Shelby's face. "You remind me so of my Jenny. She had those same smiling brown eyes." Aggie then said good night, closing the door behind her.

"If I did not believe in the spirit world before," Shelby said as she and Will drove back to the Willow Inn, "I do now."

"Glad to hear it."

"Really? Why?"

"Because. I've seen some strange phenomena in my years of research."

"Then if Jenny has been making visitations to Ashley, what is Jenny trying to tell her?"

"For starters," Will said, "both of Jenny's children were taken. We are reasonably sure the first one was given away, possibly put up for adoption. The second child died. I think Jenny wants Ashley to know what happened to her first child."

Shelby didn't respond.

"Well, do you have another explanation?"

"What? Oh, no. I wasn't thinking about that."

"What then?"

"I was thinking about what Aggie said about Jenny's portrait. The artist. She said his name was Tryn DeLore."

"So?"

Shelby looked over at Will. "Buzz didn't tell you about that?"

"About what?"

"I'm not sure. But there's this man. He moved into an old family mansion on Belvedere. He hired Ashley to restore it. That's when all this started. The man's name is Tryn DeLore."

"I see."

Shelby followed Will down the hallway toward their rooms. He unlocked his door and pushed it open, then turned to Shelby. He took her arm, gently pulling her to him.

"You do have smiling brown eyes," he said, cradling her face in his hands.

Shelby closed her eyes, finding it difficult to breath. "Oh my God," she whispered, as she felt Will's lips touching hers. His body pressed her firm against the wall, his mouth gently caressing hers. She lifted her arms and brought her hands to his face, touching him gently then eagerly, as she relinquished herself, then buried her fingers into his hair. The next thing she knew he was carrying her across the room and lowering her onto the bed. Slowly he undressed her. She suddenly felt the desire rush through her body. She had never dreamed of such ecstasy. "Will . . ." His name fell from her lips, as the cool air invaded her nakedness.

He was exploring her now, working her breast with his mouth while he quickly undressed. Shelby reached down to feel the soft swirl of hair on Will's stomach and followed its trail to the wiry patch that framed his hard erect penis. "I want you," she sighed, suddenly feeling an overwhelming passion. She opened her legs slowly, pulling him into her.

Lifting her buttocks, Will gently entered her. But Shelby thrust her hips upward, again and again, pressing him deeper. Moments later they had reached that perfect rhythm. She had become lost in their passion. And then it happened. As her body reached its orgasm, it took her so forcefully that she practically lost consciousness. She had never experienced orgasm. Had never dreamed of such a feeling. It was the most extraordinary thing she could have ever imagined. Deeper, deeper she pressed Will's penis inside her. She couldn't get enough of him. So Will fed her hunger with every ounce of strength and passion he had, until they both collapsed, exhausted into each others arms.

"I'm impressed," Will said, holding Shelby in his arms.

Shelby looked up. "Are you making fun of me?"

"Fun? I should say not." He reached down and kissed the tip of her nose. "You are a passionate woman. And that, Ms. Kincaid, is impressive."

Shelby smiled and cuddled in closer. "You bring out my passion."

"Good."

Both fell silent, savoring the moment. Shelby closed her eyes, thinking how utterly complete she felt.

Will broke the silence. "You know. I think I've wanted to hold you in my arms from the very first moment I saw you standing in Buzz's parlor."

"I wasn't very nice to you was I?"

"You weren't very nice to me for days."

"I'm sorry," she said, lowering her head. "I thought you were just a high priced snoop. And then—then you started to scare me."

"Scare you?" Will lifted Shelby's chin. "What is that supposed to mean?"

Shelby lowered her eyes.

He made her look at him again. "What did you mean by that?"

"It's going to sound crazy."

"I'll be the judge of that."

Shelby then explained Ashley's strange relationship with Tryn DeLore, and that Ashley had been a virgin, without romantic interest, until her encounter with Tryn. And, that she too had been a virgin, pretending to be interested in sex. But after the attack everything had changed. She explained about Ashley and Scott and her own feelings for Scott.

"You're the first man who has ever made love to me," Shelby said. "It scared me when I first met you and started having sexual desires." She looked back at Will. "I told you it would sound crazy."

He looked thoughtful. "No, not crazy, just interesting."

"Will."

"Yeah."

"I think Ashley has gone back to Belvedere to see Tryn."

ℭ

The next morning before Will and Shelby left for the village cemetery to find Jenny's grave, Louis called. He invited them to Winthrop House for lunch. They both anxiously accepted.

Even in winter, the cemetery remained beautifully kept, with its large oaks and stately evergreens. As they entered through the iron gates they felt a gentle yet bitter wind sweep up, causing a faint rustling sound through the trees.

They walked from headstone to headstone, finding Jenny moments later in the furthest corner of the cemetery. The beautifully carved stone was etched with tiny rosebuds. Will and Shelby stood in reverence as they read the inscription.

Jenny Winthrop
Born 1883 - Died 1986
An angel lost has found her way

"I would love to have known her," Shelby said.

Will pulled her close. "Yeah, me too."

They walked from the cemetery in silence

"Hey," Will said breaking the silence. "We have about three hours before our luncheon date with Louis. Do you feel up to driving into Boston?"

"Boston?"

"Your birth certificate. I was going to have it mailed, but why do that when we can just go and look it up?"

Shelby took a deep breath. "Is this ever going to end? It's wearing me down."

Will gave Shelby a stern glance. "It's going to take a hell of a lot more than this to get you down."

"That's right," Will said to the clerk behind the tall counter. "Shelby Kincaid. Her parents were Thomas and Natalie Kincaid. The year was 1945."

The clerk walked over to a computer, punched in the information and stared at the screen. He punched in more information and stared some more.

The clerk walked back to the counter. "Sorry sir. Can't find any record. I even looked a couple of years before 1945 and after."

Will seemed bemused. "Do you mind looking up one more?" He gave the clerk Ashley and Michael's information. Within seconds the clerk returned.

"Yes sir," the clerk confirmed. "We have those records."

"I see," Will said. "Thank you for your trouble."

"Don't look so depressed," Will said as they left the building. "All that means is that you weren't born here. You're parents probably moved here later."

"I'm sick of all this mystery. Victor and Margaret know what happened. I know it."

"Do you think they'd tell you?"

"I don't know. Anyway, I couldn't ask. They'd wonder why. Besides, if Ashley's right and Margaret really isn't her mother—oh hell, this whole thing is driving me insane."

The drive to Winthrop House was no less spellbinding than the first time. That same ominous fog blanketed the journey. There were reports that a snow storm was headed their way.

"These New England winters are treacherous," Will said. "You Californians don't have the stamina for them."

"And you Southerners do?"

"I have the stamina of an ox." Will twitched his mustache and kept his eyes sternly on the winding road.

Shelby glanced at Will, thinking how adorable he was. She was reminded that she no longer thought of Scott.

"Dr. Taylor, Ms. Kincaid," Louis greeted from the terraced walkway. "I am honored. Since meeting the two of you, I have become a new man. Afraid I have lived a rather reclusive life."

Shelby and Will smiled at seeing this dear man so invigorated.

"Please," Shelby said. "Call us Will and Shelby."

Louis nodded. "Will and Shelby it is."

Will took a long lingering breath, thinking of seeing inside Winthrop House. As they started toward the doors, Shelby clutched Will's arm.

"What's wrong?" He whispered.

"Nothing." She forced a smile.

Will and Shelby stood in the middle of the entrance hall completely awed. Hanging from the center of the twenty-foot ceiling was an enormous crystal chandelier. The arms of the chandelier appeared to be real gold. Straight ahead was a wide, marble staircase that terraced upward, then split left and right to the second floor. To the left of the entrance was a double-tiered stone and marble archway flanked by four large pillars.

Through the archway were two rooms, separated by more arches and marble pillars. Each room held an ornately mantled fireplace on the north walls and both had been set with a blazing fire. At the east and south walls were fifteen-foot leaded and beveled windows draped in heavy silk damask, and tied with huge gold tasseled cords. Weighty tapestries hung from the stone walls, while murals adorned the ceilings and bordered the walls.

Shelby gazed into the massive double rooms, reminded of Ashley's memories under hypnosis. The furnishings that Buzz had purchased from Tryn DeLore must have long since been replaced with these seemingly priceless antiques. A piano stood just past the center archway. It faced northeast, allowing the pianist a view of the sea.

Louis watched his guests with amusement.

"I thought we would have our lunch in the library," he said, turning the gold knobs and pushing open the double doors. Will and Shelby followed as he went around the room lighting the two massive gold chandeliers. "The light in this mansion is still provided by gas lines and candles. Other than that you have all the modern conveniences."

Louis finished lighting the last arm of the chandelier and retracted it upward as the flickering lights danced in large ominous circles on the molded ceiling. The library, walled in heavy cherry wood, grew vibrant within a rich glow. The tall leaded windows were draped in a dark emerald green velvet with large gold tasseled rope tiebacks. One wall of the forty by thirty-foot room was shelved with ancient books, concealed behind ruby-red stained and leaded glass. It reflected subtly the dance of the light.

"This room is magnificent," Shelby exclaimed, turning and looking straight into the mammoth fireplace. Cradling a roaring fire were two large ornamental brass andirons.

"Look at that mantel," Will said, referring to the stone carvings of mythical maidens that flanked each side of the fireplace. He walked over to inspect it. "Interesting carvings," he remarked, stroking the maiden.

Shelby reached over and slapped his hand. "Will!"

He laughed and withdrew.

"Nice of you to go to all this trouble," Will said to Louis. The table was set elegantly, draped in white linen with two small candelabras at each end.

"No trouble at all. Russell was very pleased when I told him about our luncheon guests. Please, have a seat. As I have said, I do very little entertaining. Only Father Meyers from the orphanage where I lived the early part of my life, and sometimes a few of the nuns." He turned to Shelby. "Would you like tea? Or, I have coffee and soft drinks if you'd like."

"Tea is fine."

Louis poured from the silver tea service. "How about you, Will?"

"Don't mind if I do."

"Of course," Louis continued, as he filled Will's cup. "Father Meyers was not at the orphanage when I was there. The orphanage has been my only family for eighteen years."

"Where did you go after you left?" Shelby asked.

"I moved to a small apartment in Boston and worked for a wholesale florist. At night I studied landscape architecture. It had always been my dream. I was very lucky. My work was appreciated." Louis smiled. "Kathleen Winthrop appreciated it."

Shelby noticed Will squirming in his seat and knew he was anxious to probe into Louis' early years at Winthrop House. However, he engaged in idle chit chat until after lunch.

Russell soon arrived carrying a large silver tray. With impeccable elegance, he presented a first course of hot asparagus soup. Russell appeared to be middle aged, had a neatly trimmed beard and was decked out in a waiter's uniform. After they had finished the soup and he had removed the china soup bowls, Russell served them a small salad, followed by poached salmon and sautéed vegetables.

"Russell has been with me since just before Victor and Margaret left. He was an orphan at Merrick's Orphanage. I noticed him right away. I remember the day he first arrived. I happened to be there talking with Father Meyers about adding another dormitory wing. Russell was a quiet child. He reminded me a little of myself when I was his age. I convinced Victor to let me bring him to Winthrop House." Louis beamed. "He takes such care of this old place."

"And you too," Will said. "The man wasn't about to let us in to see you."

Louis laughed. "He's a bit overprotective."

After lunch Russell cleared the table, and humbly accepted lavish praise from Will and Shelby for an expertly prepared lunch. Shelby noticed that Louis seemed to have settled into the moment, as if to savor it. How lonely a man he must be, she thought, seeing the happiness in his eyes, as she and Will made idle conversation with Russell.

"Louis," Will finally said. "Remember Aggie Carter? The lady who lived here with her family years ago?"

"Yes," Louis replied. "You said they were servants."

"That's right. I was thinking you might enjoy meeting her."

"Why yes. I think I would. What a lovely thought."

"Then may I tell her you'll stop by her shop?"

"Yes, you said she owned a book shop in the village? Of course, please do."

"Good. She has a bookstore called The Cobweb."

"I am a lover of books." Louis said, looking over at Shelby who was staring at the bare wall above the fireplace."

"What is it, Shelby," Louis asked.

"What?" She turned Louis.

"Preoccupied?" he asked

"Oh." She looked back to the empty space above the mantel. "Aggie said Jenny Winthrop's portrait used to hang over this fireplace. It disappeared after Sophia Winthrop's death." She turned back to Louis. "Aggie thinks it's hidden somewhere behind these walls."

"How interesting." Louis glanced toward the mantel. "I've often wondered why there wasn't a portrait hanging there. Funny." Louis frowned. "That wall hasn't held a portrait since I've been in this house."

"Louis," Will interjected. "Did you know there were secret passageways inside this house?"

"Oh yes. The servants filled me in. They rarely go behind those walls, though." Louis smiled slyly. "And neither have I."

"Aggie knows about them too," Shelby said. "She played in them as a child."

"I'm afraid I don't share her sense of adventure." Louis looked thoughtful. "All these years, and this woman has been right here in our little village. But," he sighed, "I rarely go into the village. The people stare and whisper. I think they are afraid of me. Winthrop House has become my opulent prison. I have my beautiful gardens though. And the servants, well, they take care of my needs. I visit Boston from time to time; see a play or go to the museums. And visit the orphanage."

"Strange you should call it your opulent prison," Shelby remarked. "That's exactly how Aggie referred to it. Her prison of opulence."

"Well. Looks like your Aggie and I have a great deal in common."

"Yes. I think you do."

"What did you say the name of her shop was?"

"The Cobweb," Shelby answered. "It's in Willow Alley."

"Louis, my man." Will rose from the table. "Your hospitality has been exemplary."

"And you and Shelby have been a ray of sunshine. I can't tell you what it's meant to me. I just hope that Michael and little Ashley will be coming soon. As far as I'm concerned, this house belongs to Victor and Margaret and their children. It's a lonely old house. It needs the sound of laughter and the love of a family again. I hope that will be possible."

Shelby went to Louis and kissed his cheek. "I'm sure of it. We all know how much Ashley loves old houses."

Louis beamed.

"Oh," he said. "Where are my manners? You must want to see the rest of the house."

"We'd love to."

Will and Shelby looked on in amazement as Louis climbed the massive staircase as though he were taking no more than a leisurely walk. "You're in hellava good shape, Louis." Will panted, then stopped to catch his breath. "Damn those cigarettes."

"I climb these stairs everyday. Good for the old ticker."

Will just shook his head.

The west wing corridor was dimly lit. Ornate floor candelabras with fat candles emanated a soft, shadowy glow. Portraits lined the walls.

"I told Russell you might want to see the portraits, so he lit the candles for us." Louis reached out and took one from its perch. "I wish I could tell you who all these people are, but I'm afraid I can't. Margaret was the one who showed me Christopher's. Quite honestly, I'm surprised Victor ever mentioned his father to her." Louis walked to the end of the corridor. "As I said, I only met Christopher Winthrop once." He raised the candle.

The portrait seemed to come to life as the flame illuminated its surface. The man in the portrait was standing. He had on a ruffled shirt with billowing sleeves, tight leggings and a heavy leather belt with a large gold buckle around his waist. His hair was dark, and though full, it was cut short. His beautiful face showed gentleness and kindness.

"This man doesn't look menacing," Will said.

"No he doesn't," Louis agreed. "That's the one distinct difference. When I met Christopher Winthrop that first and only time, I had not yet seen this portrait. It was years later that I learned from Margaret whose portrait it was. I, too, felt as you." Louis held the candle closer to the face. "The Christopher Winthrop I met resembled this portrait. The difference is—there is no evil in the face of this man."

Shelby stood glaring at the portrait.

Two hours later Will and Shelby had completed their tour of Winthrop House. It was now getting close to dark. They said their good-byes while Louis faithfully promised to call Aggie.

"Eighty-six years," Louis remarked, "and now this. I have two dear friends, and tomorrow," Louis grinned. "I'm calling on a lady."

Chapter Twenty

Except for the distant lights of the city and the floor lamp that stood next to the armchair, the room lay dark. Ashley sat curled up in the soft cushions reading Tryn's confession.

Winthrop House
1919 to 1938

It was the year, 1919, and Winthrop House still remained out of reach. Christopher could feel it slipping from his grasp. Yet, no one had come forward to claim the house or the Winthrop fortune. So he played the role of master of the grand mansion and decided to marry. Christopher's eternal youth and extraordinary good looks had not failed him. There was only one woman he felt worthy to become his wife. The beautiful and provocative Kathleen. Her beauty could capture the coldest of hearts. But a heart turned to stone by its pact with vanity had no fears. Kathleen's spell of seduction stirred only an obsessive yearning to have her. Love was the ultimate passion he dare not fall victim to.

Christopher had met Kathleen while in Europe. She worked at one of the museums in Paris and had become devoted to him. Her mother had recently died, and her father was in a nursing home.

The wedding was held at Winthrop House. The guest list consisted entirely of the Winthrops from England. Christopher demanded extreme privacy, as had Andrew before him.

Kathleen was the most exquisite creature Christopher had ever seen, with the exception of Jenny. While Jenny was small and delicate in her beauty, Kathleen was tall and elegant, like his mother Sophia. He had made the perfect choice for mistress of Winthrop House.

In 1921 Kathleen gave birth to a son. They called him Victor. By this time Christopher was becoming restless. He was not one to stay close to home, and feared he would lose control and begin to feel love for his son. He was bewildered by this. Andrew had not mentioned that this might occur. It was a desperate time for Christopher. He struggled to hold on to his vanity, his life, his youth. Why, he could not fathom, was he feeling this strong sense of love for his son? He could not allow this child to destroy him. So he would conjure up that grotesque image of Nicholas, his father, decaying before him, as well as the vision of himself that day in the mirror when his grandfather, Andrew, ordered him to peer into its surface. He would never be free of that hideous sight, the decay of his own flesh.

But not even these horrid images nor his retreats to the chamber room were enough to sustain him, and he withdrew from his family, fleeing to England and Nine Thornton Square. He, however, did see to their well being, and showered them with material things.

Kathleen begged Christopher to not stay away.

My dearest Christopher, she would write. I can not bear this loneliness, these endless days without you close to me. If you must sail to Europe for such a long stay, then why must your son and I remain here? We would gladly endure the journey and make our home there. For it is only with you, my dearest love, that I am at home. Winthrop House, as beautiful and magnificent as it is, lies cold and desolate without you.

Little Victor needs the love of his father. I can only give to him a mother's love. He will need the guidance as he grows that only a father can give. If not for me, my love, then for your son must you cling to us. My heart breaks to think that you would not want us near you. I cry with such sorrow as I lie in our bed without you next to me. Please come to me soon.

My love,

Kathleen

But Christopher would not hear of Kathleen leaving Winthrop House. And the lengthy voyage across the Atlantic was his excuse not to return with any frequency. It was some time later that Kathleen began voicing her desire for another child. Christopher rebelled at the thought. How could she want another child when he wasn't a father to the one he had?

But Kathleen needed to fill the void that Christopher had left. His dear sweet Kathleen, his faithful wife, who even in his absence, remained true, and raised their son Victor with strength and love. Kathleen's last letter to Christopher was one of pleading.

My dearest Christopher,

My love for you has become despair. My hopes and dreams of our life together, lost. What has forced you from me, I do not know. I know only that I have loved you with all my being. If you must deprive me of your love, your presence, the feel of you next to me, then I beg you, give me another child. At the very least I will again have a part of you.

My love,

Kathleen

Christopher did not return to Winthrop House. Victor, of course, had grown to detest even the sound of his father's name, and could not bear to lay eyes on him. How could a child love a father that would not allow himself to be loved? But this was Christopher's curse, his price for immortality.

Christopher did return to Winthrop House in 1938. He knew Victor would be away at Harvard. Christopher had prepared himself for a startled reaction from Kathleen, as he, of course, had not changed other than in hairstyle and dress. He hoped these changes would convey a certain maturity that he knew she would expect. But Kathleen's reaction was not one of amazement at his still youthful presence, but a strange defiance. These emotions sent a surge of desire through Christopher. Kathleen's beauty had yet to fail her, and her resentment fueled his obsessive lust for her.

As Christopher followed Kathleen into the library, she inquired if he would like a glass of wine. It was then that a man came walking into the library, his arms heavy with logs. The October winds had begun their journey inland.

"Louis," Kathleen said with dignity. "This is my husband, Christopher Winthrop." Her introduction lacked affection.

Louis stopped momentarily and turned to Christopher. "It is a pleasure," he said.

"Louis is our caretaker," she informed Christopher, praising Louis for his gardening talents.

Christopher noticed what looked like a birthmark on the man's face. The entire left side was crimson colored. As he watched the man, he began to think that he looked strangely familiar.

"How long will you be staying," Kathleen inquired.

Christopher replied that he had not made a decision as to his departure. Then, as soon as Louis was gone from the room, Christopher swept Kathleen into his arms. He took her that night as he had never done before. The next day he was gone.

Ashley turned the page as if programmed. She stared down at the name.

Margaret

The war was raging in Europe and Christopher was becoming anxious. He could not see himself a prisoner in a Nazi concentration camp nor stand by and watch his country ravished. So he discretely booked passage back to the States, knowing he could not return to Winthrop House. You see, two years earlier word had been sent to Kathleen that he had been lost at sea during a violent storm. At last he had finally severed all ties. But upon his arrival into Boston Harbor, he learned that Kathleen was no longer at Winthrop House. It seemed that she had simply vanished. Not even Victor knew of her whereabouts. This news came as a shock to Christopher as well as a blessing. It sickened him to think of seeing Kathleen aging. Christopher also learned that his son Victor had married and that the bride's name was Margaret.

But with Victor there, Winthrop House was still out of reach for Christopher. He could not bear the thought of seeing Victor. So Christopher returned to his father Nicholas' house by the sea. The same house where his portrait had been painted, where he had learned of his eternal youth.

It was now January, 1942, just a month after the attack on Pearl Harbor. Christopher learned that Victor was to leave for California, and would soon be shipped overseas. So, no one at Winthrop House would know who Christopher was. He felt safe returning to his beloved Winthrop House. How could Christopher have known the pleasures that would follow and the vengeance those pleasures would ultimately take.

Christopher was in awe at seeing Margaret. Her sensual presence was disturbing. It stirred that obsessive passion that forever raged inside him. But he knew that he must plan his course with patience—play into her loneliness by filling the void that Victor had left.

So he told Margaret his name was Tryn DeLore, grandson and namesake of the artist who had painted many of the portraits at Winthrop House. He said that he had lived in Europe most of his life and had always wanted to see the magnificent Winthrop House where his grandfather's paintings hung. Margaret was delighted and graciously showed him through the house. With exception of Christopher, she was unable to identify the subjects of the portraits. It amazed Christopher that Victor had so much as acknowledged him. She, of course, had no way of knowing that this was actually his own portrait. She told him that Christopher had been lost at sea many years back. Nothing more was said, but

Christopher knew she had noticed the resemblance between that painted canvas and himself. He had seen it in her eyes. But she never spoke of it.

Time passed. Christopher saw more and more of Margaret, yet he was careful not to become overzealous in his growing need for her. He played his role brilliantly, becoming her friend and confidant during those lonely times. They would go into Boston to the theatre, and have late-night dinners. Everything was going as Christopher had so meticulously planned, knowing it was only a matter of time before she would give herself to him. But the struggle to contain his passion was unbearable.

You must understand that when love has become a forbidden emotion, your passion, your carnal desires become obsessive, consuming. And Christopher had never bridled his emotions. He had always yielded to them. He was growing impatient. He was also growing leery of Louis.

Yes, Louis still resided at Winthrop House as grounds keeper, and Christopher was sensing a certain apprehension in Louis. Maybe Louis did not approve of this man, Tryn DeLore, and Margaret's relationship. Maybe he had noticed the resemblance to the portrait of Christopher Winthrop. Or possibly he remembered that brief encounter years back when Victor's father had returned home. Was Louis suspecting his true identity? Possibly yet improbably since Victor's father would have been, looked, much older.

One year had passed. Christopher now felt Margaret slowly falling into his grasp. Word had come that Victor was missing in action. Margaret was losing hope. Christopher, on the other hand, did not allow himself to think of his son. His only thoughts were of Margaret. Just as he had hungered for Kathleen, he now hungered for Margaret.

And so it came to be. Margaret had finally surrendered to Christopher's impatient arms, seeking comfort for the loss of her husband. Three months later Christopher moved into Winthrop House and back into his chambers on the third floor. At last he had everything: youth, wealth, a passionate woman, and his beloved Winthrop House.

It had been over two years since they learned of Victor's fate. Then, In April of 1946, Margaret went to Christopher with the news that she was carrying their child. Outraged by this news, Christopher vehemently forbade Margaret to have the child. He knew his weakness. A weakness that would force him to flee Winthrop House. So he insisted that he wanted nothing and no one to come between them. Margaret was devastated.

"Tryn," she cried. "You are the love of my life, the father of my child. How could you want to destroy what we have created? Our child will only strengthen our love."

But Christopher held his ground, and told Margaret that under no circumstances did he want a child, and turned away from her.

Margaret now had to endure the pain of Christopher's rejection. Her torment was becoming unbearable for him. She would spend hours sobbing in her bedroom. So Christopher left her and began wandering through the back alleys and half-world of Boston. The same world his mother Sophia had fled to in her youth.

Margaret's pleas kept ringing in his ears. He struggled to wipe her desperation from his mind. He must not fall victim to the goodness of her soul. Somehow, he had to remove himself from her. His beloved Winthrop House was, alas, within his grasp. No one was left now but himself and Margaret. Unfortunately, Margaret had become a threat. He could not let her have the child. So after much conversation with her, an idea came to him.

He agreed to the birth, knowing that his plan would work flawlessly. It was then that he contracted Dr. Mullholland, whom he knew was not beyond reproach or deceit. Christopher's offering of $75,000.00 insured Dr. Mullholland's eagerness that Christopher's plan would be carried out.

On October 18, 1946, Margaret went into labor. Dr. Mullholland was summoned to Winthrop House and delivered a baby girl. He told Margaret there were respiratory problems and had to rush the baby to the hospital. He later called with the news that the baby had died. It was then that Christopher did to Margaret exactly what Sophia had done to Jenny. He refused to let her hold or see her dead baby, proclaiming that it would be too difficult for her. He simply forbade it.

Christopher did, however, see to it that the child was given to a prominent family. And he was adamant that he know who this family was. They, however, were not revealed the child's parents.

Margaret was devastated over the loss of her baby. But three months later she discovered that she was again pregnant. Christopher went into a violent rage. He blamed Margaret for not protecting herself. She had sworn that this would never happen again.

Then the news came. Victor had been rescued and was being flown back to the States. He would be sent to a veteran's hospital in Hawaii, then flown to Boston. He would arrive home in about a week.

Christopher found himself in turmoil. He knew that Victor was not the heir to Winthrop House, but who, he still could not fathom, had his mother left it to? Christopher hoped that Victor would eventually want to acquire his own property and leave Winthrop House. And Christopher had all the time in the world to wait it out. Victor did not.

Now that Victor had returned, Margaret insisted that Christopher leave. She told Christopher that she was planning to tell Victor of her pregnancy after he had been home a few weeks. He would never know that the baby was not his. How familiar this sounded to Christopher, as he thought of his mother, Sophia, using the same deception with Andrew. It had come full circle. How ironic, he mused, that his own son, Victor, would be the one deceived.

However, abandoning Winthrop House was not in Christopher's scheme of things. Though being near Victor was dangerous, Christopher felt that his vanity had strengthened enough to endure it. He suggested to Margaret that she find a plausible explanation for his presence. Otherwise, Victor would have to know the truth.

Margaret was convincing with her story, telling Victor the same lie Christopher had used. She told Victor she had insisted that Tryn stay on as their guest for as long as his business kept him in Boston. Margaret believed that he was contracting for the shipment of rare stones and artifacts for museums and selected galleries in the New York and Boston areas. It was an impressive facade.

Victor never mentioned this man Tryn's resemblance to his father's portrait. He never spoke of his father at all. It seemed that he had been erased from Victor's memory. And Christopher's obsession to regain Winthrop House was giving him the power to resist that destructive force of love he feared with being near his son.

Months passed and finally the announcement came that Margaret and Victor were going to have a child. Christopher gave his congratulations and inquired whether they were planning on remaining at Winthrop House. After all, it seemed such a large house to have to maintain. Victor's answer was disturbing. He informed Christopher that his family would always reside at

Winthrop House. That he had been born there and could not imagine living elsewhere. That his mother, Kathleen, had loved the house.

Christopher fought for composure after hearing those words. But he held fast, as again, he felt a surge of passion for Margaret. It was now a more forbidden hunger than before and one that Christopher relished. So again, Margaret retreated into their world of sexual pleasure. As he took her, he fantasized that he was raping her—killing the life that grew inside her. The one thing he knew might destroy him. He tore at Margaret in violent passion. A passion that spawned Margaret's desire. She could not be satiated. She had become as much a part of his obsession as he had.

But Christopher did become satiated with Margaret and again turned to Winthrop House, his insatiable passion. He bade farewell to his hosts on the pretense that his business was taking him across the seas to New Zealand. Acrimony burned in Margaret's eyes, as she tried to veil the wound Christopher had inflicted by this news.

Christopher thanked Victor for his and Margaret's hospitality. He then offered his good wishes on the upcoming birth of their baby and took his leave. He had no intention of traveling the waters of the South Pacific. Christopher Winthrop was going to reclaim his beloved Winthrop House.

Patiently he waited and plotted the haunting of Winthrop House. How utterly delicious that felt to him, his triumph eminent.

Not certain whether Victor had explored the secret catacombs of Winthrop House as he himself had as a child, he remained cautious. For these hidden corridors would be his refuge. He would walk the vast halls, showing himself in half shadow, then disappearing into the walls. He would have his victims fleeing Winthrop House to save their sanity. It would then be, as it should have always been, HIS. No one had come to claim their inheritance. Christopher had decided that no one would.

Late at night, he entered the caverns leading to the subterranean rooms under Winthrop House, the crashing waves warned him of the forthcoming tide. So he quickly made his way through the caverns with his lantern. For someone not familiar as he was with the ever-changing terrain of the caverns, it would have been treacherous to attempt such a thing. But he had spent hours exploring these passageways, and not even his long absence during his marriage to Kathleen had impaired his memory. So with his lantern, he moved quickly.

On his visits to Nine Thornton Square, the family had told him about The Tomb, located in one of the subterranean rooms behind the stone door. This was where the outsiders were kept. The aged, mortal women who were strangled to death and placed in a glass-top coffin for viewing. This would be a grotesque scene, he knew, for he had participated in these viewings at Nine Thornton Square. He also knew that it would strengthen his vanity, and his resolve.

Lifting his lantern, Christopher crept through the maze of tunnels that webbed the earth beneath Winthrop House. He remembered seeing that stone panel years earlier when he and Stefan explored the caverns. It had fascinated them. They would spend hours trying to figure out the secret to opening it. Stefan had even asked Andrew about it once. Andrew went into a rage and ordered them to never go into the caverns again. He had provided them with no explanation.

But now he had the explanation. He knew exactly how to open that ominous-looking door. As he approached it, the memories flooded back. He and Stefan standing there in frustration, their quest a failure. The frame of the door projected out about eight inches with a wide rope-like border. Christopher raised the lantern so that he could see just below the top of the border. As a child he would never have been able to reach this distance. Slowly he ran his fingers up the border, feeling for the slight separation in the stone. He could feel dampness, the rough, time-worn surface as he searched. Then he felt it, slight but definite. He then remembered what the family at Nine Thornton Square had said.

'Take that section of stone, push it straight in, then to the right. That will release the door. As you enter the Tomb, there will be torches that run along each wall. The coffins too, are lined against the walls. You will find a large drum of kerosene just inside the opening. As you light each torch and proceed further into this Tomb, the contents of each coffin will be revealed. This will be a revolting sight. But a sight you must force yourself to endure. Let these corpses be not lost on you, but a reminder that righteousness is quite capable of destroying you. We warn you too, that arrogance can be deceiving. It can give you false security and cause you to venture into forbidden pleasures. Pure love and virtue are powerful forces, as powerful as evil. Let these corpses show you that mortality lingers patiently.'

Christopher did as the family had told him and released the stone door. He could feel a surge of cold as though an icy hand had reached out to pull him into this tomb of death. Even the stir and subtle roar of the sea had grown distant.

Christopher stood at the mouth of the tomb as he fought with the raging fear that was slowly consuming him. He forced himself to light the first torch. He lifted his lantern and felt a mass of cobwebs as he pushed through. As far as he could see, there was an endless stretch of coffins lining the walls. But he had not advanced far enough into the tomb to see the corpses that lay inside. Christopher reached out and lifted the first torch from its iron bracket. He then turned to find the drum of kerosene, just as they had said. Carefully he dipped the torch into the liquid. After lighting the torch, he proceeding deeper into the cold chamber. Cautiously, he approached the first coffin and lowered the flame close to the dust-laden glass. A large spider seemed to shriek in horror as the fiery torch moved closer. It scurried in a frenzied path across the dusty glass and disappeared down the far side. Christopher felt suddenly amused, thinking that he too would like to flee.

The glass was so covered with dust and debris that it was impossible to see through it. Reluctantly he reached out and began clearing a small area. Slowly and meticulously he brushed the face of the coffin, revealing its ghastly contents.

Christopher wrenched at the sight. It looked more monstrous than human—hideous, distorted in horrid agony, its yellowed white hair stringing down from its rotted head, Its bony hands covered with patches of flesh, reminding him that it had once been a living, breathing human being. Christopher also knew that it had once been a beautiful being. An outsider chosen to propagate for the family, who they could torture to death after the aging had set in. A supreme reminder for the family to view. A moment of wretched horror certain to strengthen their vanity.

Christopher turned in disgust from this hideous thing and fled from the tomb. But as it had at Nine Thornton Square, this hideous sight had recharged him, giving him that surge of vainglory and self-conceit that was his life's blood. Nothing would stop him now. He would conquer Winthrop House and banish his children from it forever.

Christopher walked back through the caverns and climbed the crude stairs to the double doors that opened into the cellar above. He had, before bidding farewell to Margaret and Victor, taken the lock from the door. He then returned the lock and made his way through the secret panel and into the hidden corridors. He entered his quarters on the third floor and locked the door from the inside. This was where he would reside. The locks he had installed before his departure would insure privacy. It was of no concern to him that they might wonder how the door had been locked, it would only add to the haunting.

That night, he caused a great commotion.

After laboriously removing his portrait and concealing it in a compartment behind one of the corridor walls, he crept behind the fireplace of Margaret and Victor's room and peered through the sliding panel. It was now past three o'clock in the morning. He saw that Victor was heavy with sleep. Margaret was not at his side. She had just left the bed and was walking toward the bath chamber. Perfection, he thought, stealing his way back through the passageway and stopping by the wall in the East wing hallway where his picture had hung. He had already placed a lantern on the floor just under the vacant space. Lying beside the lantern was a piece of clothing he had torn from his ruffled shirt like the one in the portrait. He also cut a small gash into his arm and soiled the torn cloth with his blood. He let out a tormenting scream. Moments later, he saw their shadows. From the side hall, he stepped out into the darkness and raised his lantern.

"Victor, my son," he called in distress.

Victor turned abruptly, Margaret clinging to his side. They seemed frozen in horror.

Christopher had groomed himself down to the finest detail. It was as though he had simply stepped out of the portrait, with the exception of the ruffled sleeve on his left arm being torn away, and his entire arm covered in blood. He lowered his lantern, discretely snuffed the flame, and disappeared into the wall. His haunting of Winthrop House had begun. He had never seen such terror as he saw in Victor and Margaret's faces that night.

Two weeks passed before Christopher resumed his haunting. But during those weeks he watched their every move, heard their every word. Victor finally told Margaret about his father. How he had left them though continuing to lavish them with outrageous gifts. Had left them in this magnificent house, a house most would sell their souls to have. But that his father had completely and utterly rejected him, yet he never knew why. And that his mother had lived in a fairy tale world of endless excuses for her husband's behavior. He had early on grown to loathe his father.

As Christopher listened to Victor give this account, a twinge of guilt came upon him. This feeling seized him, and he quickly withdrew into the concealed chamber on the third floor. He rejected the sensation again and again until it subsided. He was not there to fall victim to the love for his son, he was there to banish him from Winthrop House.

Margaret was now eight months pregnant and Christopher's little tricks were taking their toll. Not only did he appear as Christopher Winthrop, fading slowly into the dark walls and letting out ghastly screams, but he would find his way into various rooms of the house, rearranging this or that. And stealing food. The haunting of Winthrop House had become exciting for him, and he found himself becoming more brazen in his efforts. He had almost succeeded in his attempts to regain Winthrop House when Margaret went into labor. Victor rushed her to the hospital.

He found out two weeks later, to his horror, that Margaret had given birth to twins. At that moment he felt as he imagined a vampire would feel, knowing that the sun would soon rise and devour him. So late one night he gathered his satchel and lanterns and descended back into the depths of the caverns and out to the sea. He fled to New York where he lost himself to women and hard drink. His money was plentiful, and for three years he fed his passion for sex and vanity. He had everything except Winthrop House, his one obsession that was ebbing from his reach. This obsession was growing stronger. Yet, he had to discipline himself. He would not let his children destroy him. And so he returned.

He saw his children at play once, but only from a distance. Ashley, you were out in the gardens with Louis, planting spring flowers. Michael was swinging on an old tire swing that hung from the giant oak by the gazebo. Christopher did not allow himself but a moment of this, for he felt his senses giving way. They would surely have failed him if he had allowed them to. So he turned away from the window in his quarters. He would, as he had for the last several nights, steal through the secret corridors in his haunting. He knew that Margaret and Victor were just about at their wits' end. He had already heard talk of their leaving. He would hasten their decision. Oh, how delicious it was for him!

He went to the attic room to make preparations. The old metal table still remained. The straps that he knew Stefan had used to tie Jenny those many years ago were still there. Although his mother had not told him about Jenny's torture, what little she had revealed was enough for Christopher to surmise the truth. Seeing that table, and those leather straps, confirmed what he had expected. He and Stefan had discovered the attic room when they were boys.

It was only too clear now, what Stefan had done to Jenny. Christopher had fantasized about using that table. He would now carry out those fantasies. And he knew he would need the straps to restrain Margaret.

It intrigued him, wondering when she would recognize him as her lover, and not the ghost of Christopher Winthrop. He became painfully aroused, thinking about what he wanted to do to her.

The next morning, Victor left for the University where he was studying for his Master's degree in law. Michael and Ashley were outside with Louis. Margaret had just finished her morning bath when Christopher appeared at her sitting room door. He stood there, in the doorway, dressed as always in his torn ruffled shirt and leggings, the lantern swinging slightly from his hand.

Margaret turned, reaching for her robe as she took the towel from her body, and saw him standing there. She gasped, stumbling backward. As Christopher began to walk toward her, she suddenly collapsed to the floor. Christopher gathered her in his arms. Her nakedness was torturing his senses, so he covered her breast with his mouth as he pulled her closer to him. He entered the secret passage from the sitting room and turned to insure that the panel was closing properly. It was then that Christopher saw Ashley standing just inside the sitting room door. After the heavy paneled door closed, he immediately put this sight from his mind and continued on through the hidden passageways. Ashley's cries followed him, then faded, as he entered the attic room.

His desire for Margaret was burning wildly, his loins aching. She was so vulnerable now, and he would have her on the table and strapped down before she could resist.

Margaret suddenly began to stir. He quickly laid her naked body on the table and secured the strap around her neck. She was his now, helpless and delicious in her torment. He grabbed her arms and pulled them tight over her head, crossing her wrists and strapping them down. He saw the overwhelming fear in her eyes, but she failed to utter a sound. It would have been futile, for no one would have heard her screams. He was certain that no one knew of this room. It had been locked from the inside after Stefan's body had been removed. He felt safe from discovery as he caressed the beautiful nakedness of

Margaret's body, following its contours to the delicate secret between her legs. He spread her legs and strapped her ankles. She did not resist, simply lay there, her eyes distant.

Seeing Margaret like that was bringing back visions of Jenny. Through the years, it had tormented Christopher to visualize the horror of what Stefan must have done to her. He had fought it, but it had stayed with him. Even his dreams were filled with her agony. This had been the only woman he had ever loved. A love that would be forced from him if he accepted *The Gift*. And he had accepted it, before he realized what it would mean for him.

And so, my dearest ones, may God forgive me, I had my way with Margaret. I will not detail the pleasures I took with her, only to say that they were ecstasy for me. When I had finished, I released her from the table, unlatched the door and told her to go. My body was drained, My loins spent. I closed the door, latched it and returned to my quarters through the hidden passages, and fell into my bed.

I did not concern myself with how Margaret managed the distance from the attic room to her chambers that day in her nakedness. And I have never known if Ashley understood what she had seen. I did know, however, that I was triumphant.

One week later they were gone. And then, soon after, the mystery of the disposition of Sophia's estate was partially solved.

I was sitting in the library, feeling pleased with myself. Louis had not commented on my return, simply going about his duties as usual. But this night, as I sat by the fire sipping wine, waiting for the servants to prepare my dinner, Louis appeared. He was dressed in dark brown trousers, a tan shirt with a paisley ascot of burgundy, tan and dark green. His coat was a dark tan corduroy. At first I was taken off guard by Louis' gentrified presence. Not even the crimson splotch that ran down the side of Louis' face could hide his beauty. As I gazed on him, I suddenly felt a restlessness. Inexplicably, I wanted to draw close to Louis and yet—a rising fear began to well inside me.

I rose from my chair, not certain what was happening to me. The omniscience that I had possessed, that gave me power, was waning. Who was this man, this mere servant? Louis placed a folder on the library table.

"What is it you want?" I demanded. My hands had begun to shake. I glared at Louis as I struggled with an overwhelming desire to embrace him. Fear now engulfed me.

Louis opened the folder and took out several papers. He turned to me and said, without apparent emotion. "Mr. DeLore, if you would be so kind as to look over these documents, you will see that I, Louis Tanner, am the sole owner of Winthrop House and of all its holdings."

I looked on in horror as I heard Louis' words.

Louis Tanner! Had I heard him correctly? Tanner was my mother's maiden name. Hadn't Kathleen told me Louis' last name was Carter? Of course she had. And Margaret, she had called him Louis Carter.

Who WAS this man?

I couldn't speak. What hold this man had over me seemed to have sapped the life from me.

"I never divulged my inheritance to Victor Winthrop," Louis said. "As long as he and his family chose to remain at Winthrop House, I felt no need to offer this information. I would not have known how to explain such a thing. I have no explanation for it now. Victor and his family have, for reasons unknown to me, chosen to leave Winthrop House. It distresses me. However, it does not distress me to inform you, Mr. DeLore, that you are no longer welcome here. You are not a member of the Winthrop family, merely a grandson of the artist who painted their portraits. You are nothing more than a vile seducer, Mr. DeLore." Louis then drew near to me. My body grew rigid.

"I trust," Louis said, his face only inches from mine, "that you will be gone within the hour?"

Louis then turned from me. As he approached the doorway he looked back. "Your torment at Winthrop House is finished." He left the room.

I staggered back to my chair, Louis' words still ringing in my ears. I knew I must leave Winthrop House.

Returning to my father Nicholas' house, I gathered my belongings and fled. I had learned that England had been badly damaged during the war, so I decided to take up temporary residency in the French-influenced city of New Orleans. Several weeks after arriving there, I purchased a large home in the uptown area. I resided there for several years before returning to England. Before leaving New Orleans, I learned that I had again, fathered a child. This, though, was part of my destiny.

Before I finish my confession, there is something of great importance that you must know. I am sure you have wondered about the influence this wretched Gift has over you. And this I promise to reveal. But for now, I must rest.

୨୦

As Ashley proceeded up the walkway, DeLore House seemed to be fading deep into the fog.

Her hands trembled at the terraced entrance. She reached for the door knocker. Struggling to find her courage, she rapped against the door. Her heart was pounding, worse than the first time she had found herself standing in front of this ominous door. She waited anxiously, knowing it would take Maurice some time to answer. Again she knocked and waited.

Suddenly the door opened. She saw Maurice standing in the shadowy entrance, an unusually welcome smile gracing his face.

"Come. Monsieur DeLore is expecting you."

Expecting me? she thought.

There was a moment when Ashley felt she could not enter. Then finally she lifted her foot and stepped through the doorway.

"If you will follow me," Maurice said, as he closed the door behind her.

The oil lights were flickering dimly. The house felt chilled in the deafening silence. The only sound was an occasional creak of the stairs as she followed Maurice to the second floor.

"Mademoiselle Winthrop," Maurice announced, as they reached the top of the stairs. "Monsieur DeLore is very ill," he said as he turned and walked through the sitting area toward the bedroom. Ashley noticed that the statue she had commented on that first day was no longer there.

Maurice opened the bedroom door and motioned for Ashley to enter. "Please, Monsieur DeLore is waiting."

Ashley took a breath and entered the room.

The fireplace was ablaze, causing a rich shadowy glow. The only other light came from the oil lamps on either side of the bed. Maurice walked to the foot of the bed and held out his hand. "Please," he said, gesturing for her.

Ashley felt as if her legs would betray her. And then she heard it. Weak. Strange.

281

"Ashley," the voice called. Maurice took her arm and guided her to the side of the bed. The heavy damask fabric that draped the bed was closed. Maurice pushed one of the panels aside, tying it back with the tasseled cord. Ashley looked down, her eyes adjusting to the darkness. As Maurice lifted the other panel, the muted glow of the lamplight fell across the bed. Ashley flinched. Her hand flew to her mouth in a muffled gasp. She stared down at the pathetic form that lay beneath the counterpane. As though her body had been flooded, an overwhelming sorrow seized her.

"No!" She reached out, groping toward the grotesque form. She fell to the bed and embraced it, sobbing as though her heart was breaking.

"Beloved Ashley," Tryn whispered. "My precious child. It pains me so to hear your sorrow." After a long while, she lifted her head and stared into Tryn's face. A face ragged and lined and horribly aged. "Beautiful Ashley," he whispered. "There is so little time left, and yet so much I must reveal to you. My confession is not finished.

"I am free now." He gently caressed her face with a trembling hand. "Free of this evil that the Winthrops are cursed with. Poor Stefan was spared, only to endure another evil, our mother's obsessiveness. An obsessiveness that turned her against him. Victor was the fortunate one. My weakness saved him."

Tears fell from Ashley's face. Her heart seemed to be crumbling inside her.

"Beloved child," Tryn said. "I must not waste these precious moments. You and Shelby must know what awaits you."

"Shelby?" Ashley glared into Tryn's eyes.

"Yes my love. Shelby, your sister. My and Margaret's first child. I think I knew this the moment I first saw her standing there, the very image of Jenny. It was Michael who told me that her mother was Natalie Kincaid. That was the woman she had been given to." Tryn closed his eyes. Ashley saw the tears roll down the sides of his tattered face. "I was Shelby's attacker. It was Shelby's likeness to Jenny that threatened me, so I lashed out at her. I could feel Jenny reaching for me through her. Little did I know that it was through you that Jenny sought to destroy my vanity." Tryn took a shallow breath, his hands trembling, and looked away. "I had also become threatened by David Clarendon and your hypnosis. Michael informed me of this. I feared discovery. It is by my

282

hand that David Clarendon was beaten and thrown into that well on Camp Street. The house where I once lived. And it was Jenny who saved him and guided Shelby to his rescue. It was also Jenny who caused your miscarriage. Our son would have been born into this evil out of incest. He would have been a pure evil. Your miscarriage was a blessing from God. Now Jenny has come to me. Her love is with me. Obsession no longer haunts me. I now find peaceful happiness in my dying. Soon I will be released from this wretched body. I will go into the divine light. It will give me new life."

Ashley sensed a peacefulness in Tryn's sunken eyes. Eyes that had once taken her into a passionate ecstasy. His thick dark hair now thin and yellowed. The once beautiful face, the soft, taut skin was marred with deep webbed lines. Gentleness and compassion had taken the place of a once vile, obsessive and youthful man.

"I have always loved you," he said. "Loved you so dearly that I was forced not to accept it but to lock it away in the deepest part of my heart. It was my precious Jenny who released me from this torture and saved my soul from eternal damnation. Through you, she destroyed me. I have now found blessed peace in loving." He stared hard into Ashley's face. "There are desperate times awaiting you. You must know this truth, come to an understanding of it before you pledge your love. I must also tell you. Unless you mate with a true Winthrop, your children will all be females. Only a male Winthrop is capable of fathering a son. Unlike the males, the females will have inherited *The Gift* from birth. They will never age past their twenty-sixth year."

Tryn closed his eyes as though in terrible pain.

"This wretched body," he sighed. "Soon I will be free of it. There is still much you must know of this evil. I was compelled to offer Michael this eternal damnation. If only I had stayed away from him as I did Victor. But it is too late. Michael has now become what I once was. He will become obsessed with lust for you and Shelby. And, my daughter, you and Shelby both will be helplessly drawn to him."

"No! Shelby can't know about this. "I will not rob her of a normal life."

"My child," Tryn sighed wearily. "There will come a time when she will have to be told. Her youth will be her betrayer."

"No. Please no."

"You and Shelby must not bear children," Tryn warned. "It would only serve to continue this evil."

Ashley buried her face into the counterpane. "This is a nightmare."

"My precious child," Tryn sighed. "If only I could have held you and watched you grow. Nurtured you as a father should. If only we had not been robbed of those precious moments. You of loving, me of watching you grow. This wretched evil," he sighed. "You are now free to love. I released that in you and Shelby when I took your virginity. "If only this evil could be destroyed."

"What is it!" Ashley cried. "Where did it come from?"

"That, my child, is a long and laborious tale. One I am now incapable of telling. Though Michael knows, I warn you, stay as far away from him as possible. He will be driven with lust for you, to propagate with you and continue the evil."

Tryn turned away. "I am in dreadful pain," he whispered. "But there is one last warning I must give to you. This man, Tryn DeLore. Many, many centuries ago, far too many for you to comprehend, amid betrayal, greed and incest, he and his mother and father became bitter enemies. It's a long and complicated story. But my warning is this. There may be true DeLores, offspring's of this man that have survived the centuries. We have never been certain of this. But if this is so, they will have been lying in wait for us. They will have become so powerful, so enraged, that they will seek their revenge on the Winthrop family."

"Why?" Ashley said. "Why would they be vengeful?"

"I have not the strength left to reveal the reason. Only that you should be warned of its possible existence. Our Father, Leopold Winthrop, who still reigns at Nine Thornton Square, has warned that the DeLore vengeance would strengthen, and possibly culminate, becoming the ultimate evil. I assure you, such an evil will destroy, will take your youth as surely as love has taken mine. Michael, however, in his arrogance, will be at great risk. I have warned him of this. He appears not to listen."

"Where is Michael?"

"Michael, I fear, has gone to New Orleans to seek out my daughter, your sister, Sylina, a child I fathered with a woman years ago." Tryn then turned back to Ashley, his face little more than a skeleton. "My heart breaks with love for you, my precious child. Walk with caution. If you find that you cannot bear to live with this wretched curse, you have but one release. The gold handle of the walking stick that Michael now carries: turn it counter clockwise and lift it from its shaft. You will see that attached to it is a small diamond blade. This is your only weapon against an eternity of damnation. Thrust it into your heart and be released. Though you will find murder abominable, this diamond blade is also your weapon against Michael and all other Winthrops who have *The Gift*. Unlike the male Winthrops, you are doomed to love now that your virginity has been taken. I cannot warn you enough. You will have overwhelming love and passion for Michael. He of course, will only wallow in his lust for you.

"Find your happiness, my dearest one, away from these Winthrops. My true happiness came from those few stolen moments at Winthrop House with my beloved Jenny."

Tryn then closed his eyes and placed his hands across his body. At that moment, a brilliant light embraced him. The brilliance then took its leave. All that was left was Tryn's bed clothing.

Ashley stared at the empty bed. The sorrow and pain she felt seemed to break away. The sorrow and pain of losing her father after a lifetime without him. She reached out and placed her hand where Christopher's body had been. She thought of Victor, the man she so dearly loved. And then it came to her. Victor, Christopher's son, was her half-brother. Thank God, she thought, he had escaped this madness. And she would see to it that Victor would never learn the truth. Never.

Ashley pushed herself from the bed and slowly crossed the room. She stopped momentarily, remembering the first time she had stepped foot in this room. How innocent she had been of the horrors that awaited her. Horrors she would now have to face.

"Mademoiselle."

Ashley turned to see Maurice standing in the doorway.

"Monsieur DeLore has asked that I give you this." He handed her a package. "You must go now," he said, and led her down the stairway to the front door. "Michael is now in my care." He lowered his eyes. "I will be his servant just as I was Monsieur DeLore's."

Ashley left DeLore House and drove back to her studio. It was past six o'clock, Stanley and Karen had already gone. She climbed the stairs to her apartment, poured a glass of wine and sat down on the sofa. She felt drained and numb. She stared at the package. It was wrapped in a beautiful Victorian paper and tied with a gold ribbon. She opened it and saw a note lying on top of the tissue.

This statue was sculpted by Nicholas Winthrop, my father. Sophia had him do this sculpture of Jenny after he painted her portrait. I took it from my mother's room on the day of her death. It was dangerous of me to keep it, but my arrogance afforded me that luxury.

Early that morning, when I went to my mother's room only to find her dead, I knew that I could not remain at Winthrop House while my beloved Jenny's portrait still hung in the library, the sight of divine countenance would surely have destroyed me. So I hid the portrait behind the mantel wall. You need only to turn the head of one of the maidens to reveal it. I also hid Jenny's personal belongings. Though many of her personal things were destroyed in the cottage fire, there were still some beautiful pieces of her clothing in the third floor bedroom. I hid them in a secret room behind one of the east wing bedrooms. If you decide to venture behind those walls, I would like Shelby to have Jenny's clothes.

As for my fortune, it is beyond comprehension. You and my other children will come to realize this. I have divided my estate among all of you; Victor, Shelby, you and Michael and Sylina, I have made these arrangements through Bank of the West's main office in San Francisco, Ask for Henrietta Moretti.

I have left my home in France to you and Shelby and Sylina. My father Nicholas' home, just up the coast from Winthrop House, I have left to Michael. As for my vast art collection and antiques, I have left those to you and Buzz Harper.

May God in his mercy find forgiveness and leave you blameless of this wretched curse. Be strong, my child, and in that strength find eternal happiness.

Your father,

Christopher Winthrop

Ashley unwrapped the statue of Jenny and stared at the delicately molded features and thought of what Christopher had said. She smiled, thinking that she did see a resemblance to Shelby.

Ashley had gone over it a thousand times in her mind. She knew exactly what she would say, how she would approach her mother. Not Meno, not this woman she had kept at bay since childhood, that horrifying moment at Winthrop House, but her mother. A woman who had fallen under the spell of Christopher Winthrop over forty years ago.

Ashley stood on the front porch of Margaret and Victor's old Victorian, ringing the door bell. She had never stood on the porch and rung the door bell. Moments later the door opened.

"Ashley?" Margaret said. "Why . . . "

"Mom." Ashley smiled into Margaret's eyes.

Margaret stared.

"May I come in?"

"Come in?"

"Or maybe I should come back another time."

"Come back?" Margaret gazed at Ashley.

"Mom," Ashley smiled and walked passed her. "I need to talk to you."

Margaret closed the door and followed Ashley down the hallway to the breakfast room. Ashley sat down and motioned to Margaret to do the same.

Margaret eased down in the chair. "You haven't called me Mom in years."

"I know. That's why I'm here. There's something I have to tell you. It's about Tryn DeLore."

Margaret stirred in her seat. "Who?" she asked, as if she had never heard the name.

287

Ashley continued. "After I took the DeLore restoration," she said, "I was in his library one day making notes. On the desk I saw a beautiful leather-bound book with gold cording. Scripted across the front was the name Winthrop. So I opened it. I realized after leafing through it that it was a journal. I couldn't imagine why Tryn DeLore would have a journal with our name on it, so I decided to read it."

Margaret began fidgeting with her hair.

"Mom. I know everything. You don't have to live this lie any longer."

Margaret glared. "What do you mean, lie?"

"Mom. I know about Tryn DeLore, about what happened when Dad was thought to be lost in the war. I know Shelby's my sister. I know about Winthrop House."

"No!" Margaret bolted from her chair. The tears flowed from her eyes.

"Don't, Mom." Ashley went to her. She took Margaret into her arms. "I remember Tryn DeLore carrying you behind the wall of your bedroom. I was there, standing in the doorway."

Margaret collapsed back into the chair. "Oh. My poor baby."

"All these years I kept dreaming about it. It was distorted, but I kept seeing this beautiful house and this faceless man carrying a woman in his arms. Mom, I thought you were dead. I was never able to perceive you any other way. And you had taken my mother's place. That explains why I've treated you the way I have. Please forgive me?"

"Forgive you?" Margaret sobbed. "Oh no. I'm the one who needs forgiveness." She looked at Ashley with saddened eyes. "I betrayed your father. I let that horrible man into my life."

"So did I."

"What?"

"I was just as seduced by this Tryn DeLore as you were by that one. I have even lost Scott because of him."

"Oh no. But . . . who is he? I—Margaret squeezed her eyes shut. "That night at Scott's opening—when Michael introduced your father and me to this man. It was as if I were seeing Tryn DeLore all over again. As young and beautiful as he was the first day he came to Winthrop House. The resemblance was astonishing."

Who is this man? Ashley thought. Even if I told you, you wouldn't believe it. "I don't know, Mom. He doesn't talk much about who he is or where he comes from."

"Oh, Ashley. My poor baby. Can you ever forgive me?"

"There's nothing to forgive," Ashley assured her. "Now tell me. How much does Dad know?"

Margaret wiped her eyes. "Up until the night of Scott's opening, he knew only about Shelby. That night, I told him everything. After coming face to face with that man DeLore—I just found myself confessing. Before, I couldn't bear to tell him that you and Michael were not his children. But I didn't tell him that I continued to be with Tryn after he came back from the war. I could never hurt him that way."

"He never has to know that," Ashley said. "But we have to tell Shelby that you are her mother. She's already suspecting something. After she regained her memory she started having other memories. Of moving out of a house and taking a train to go and live with us."

"My God. Shelby actually remembered that?"

"Yes. But, how did you find out that Shelby hadn't died?"

"I received a letter from Natalie Kincaid," she said. "Natalie wrote that she had something urgent to talk to me about. I couldn't imagine what it was. We were only acquaintances."

"But how did she know who her child's real mother was?"

"Dr. Mulholland finally told her."

"Dr. Mulholland? Why? Tryn had paid him a half a million dollars to stay quiet."

"Because, he was dying. Besides, Natalie was desperate and I'm sure convincing."

"Desperate?"

"Yes," Margaret said. "She had lost everything. Her husband was a wealthy man and they were a respected Boston family until he was found out."

"Found out?"

"It was horrible," Margaret said. "Natalie's husband and another woman were having an affair. They were both found murdered in the woman's apartment. The woman was married to a business associate of Natalie's husband. Natalie soon learned that nothing they had belonged to them. Not their house, not even the furnishings. Everything was in the name of some New York corporation. And the shipping company she thought her husband owned was really owned by this corporation. She was left with nothing. That's when she went to Dr. Mullholland. She wanted to find a good home for Shelby. He told Natalie what he had done. She was horrified. That's when she came to me. She knew that Victor didn't know about Shelby, so she wrote to me saying that it was urgent, that she had to see me."

"Had you heard about the murders?"

"Yes. I had also heard what had happened to her. So when I received the note, I called her. They had given Natalie two weeks to vacate her home. She had little money and nowhere to go. Her husband had no family, and Natalie's family was of no help. Her mother was dead and her father had more or less disowned her when she married. All of Natalie's friends were business related. They would have nothing to do with her after the murders. It was a tragedy."

"How did she tell you about Shelby?"

"It wasn't easy." Margaret thought momentarily. "It was early in the afternoon, two days before we left for New Orleans." Margaret looked up at Ashley. "Did that journal tell you why we left Winthrop House?"

"Yes. Tryn terrified you and Dad."

"Margaret shook her head. "He actually had us believing that the house was haunted. I guess then . . . you know about the attic room?"

"Yes."

"That's when I knew that Tryn was responsible. Tryn certainly looked enough like Christopher Winthrop to have us believing in ghosts. But—that day he came into my bedroom—" Margaret looked away.

"That's in the past," Ashley said. "Don't even think about it. Now go on, tell me about Shelby."

"Well," Margaret said thoughtfully. "I answered Natalie's letter, and asked her to come to Winthrop House. Victor was at the University. When she arrived, she had Shelby with her. I remember thinking how vibrant and beautiful she was. She was four years old and the entire time she was there, ran from one end of the parlor to the other."

"Sounds familiar," Ashley laughed.

Margaret smiled. "Natalie then told me about her desperate situation. And about going to Dr. Mullholland, that he had confessed what Tryn had done."

Margaret paused and looked out the window.

"I can't describe what I felt when I heard her telling me that this beautiful little girl was my child. I had been grieving for her in silence for the last four years. I had not been allowed to hold her, to say good-bye to her; nothing. Tryn had just ripped her from me, then told me she was dead. And that's what I believed. He even pretended to bury her out in the old cemetery at Winthrop House. He wouldn't even allow me to give her a name. Her little headstone just says Winthrop Child."

"Was Natalie asking you to take Shelby?"

"Yes. She was destitute. But I knew that I couldn't tell Victor about Shelby. So that night I told Victor that Natalie had come to me for help. I explained her situation. It was Victor who refused to separate them. He insisted that they move with us to New Orleans. After we arrived, Victor sent her through business school, then got her a secretarial job in a law firm. When we moved to San Francisco she started working for Victor, editing and proof reading his manuscripts. And you know the rest. It was horrible to watch her suffer. She fought that cancer for so long. It was after Natalie's death that I told Victor the truth." Margaret paused. "What happened to Tryn? Did the journal say?"

"He was thrown out of Winthrop House."

"Thrown out? By whom?"

"The heir to the Winthrop fortune."

Margaret's mouth dropped. "The heir? Who? Victor tried for years to find out who actually owned the estate."

"Louis Carter."

"Louis! But you can't be serious. He was our caretaker."

"I know. Not even Louis understood his strange bequest."

"Louis," Margaret said again. "I simply can't believe it." She smiled as though the thought of Louis had taken her back. "You and Louis were inseparable." She looked at Ashley. "You don't remember him, do you?"

"I didn't. Not until I started seeing a hypnotist friend of Buzz's."

She then told Margaret about her hypnosis, about Will Taylor, and the fact that Will and Shelby had gone to Manchester to see Winthrop House. And about Shelby's recent memories.

"May I tell Will and Shelby about the journal?" Ashley asked.

Margaret stared into Ashley face. "I feel so dirty."

"No. Don't say that. Tryn DeLore took advantage. No one will ever blame you."

Margaret sighed. "All right."

"I think you should be the one to tell Shelby who her mother is."

"I've wanted to tell her for so long." Margaret paused. "I wonder if I could get Victor to go back to Winthrop House."

"I was hoping you'd say that. I want to go too. But not without you and Dad."

Margaret leaned back in her chair. The tears were starting to come again. She reached out and brought Ashley's hand to her lips. "I can't believe it. I love you so much."

"I love you too, Mom."

"Hi, Mom," Ashley heard Michael say.

Michael and Sylina came walking down the hallway, Michael tapping his walking stick along the hardwood floor. Ashley stood up and moved closer to Margaret as if shielding her. Michael seemed to notice this with amusement.

"Michael," Margaret said, looking at him with a curious frown. "Your hair. I don't think I've ever seen you wear it that long."

"It's my new image," he said, smiling. "You approve?"

Ashley glared at Michael. He caught this out of the corner of his eye. "Oh. Where are my manners. Ashley, you know Sylina." Ashley breathed a sigh.

"It's good to see you again."

"Mother, this is Sylina Win . . . ", and he gave a half smile. "I mean Vierhus."

"It's nice to meet you," Sylina said to Margaret and held out her hand.

"What a beautiful name. I'm happy to meet you too."

Ashley was getting restless, not sure what Michael had come here for.

"Sylina's name is not all that's beautiful," Michael said, turning to look at her. Sylina had long curly red hair she wore pulled behind her left ear and cascading over the right side of her face. Her eyes were a vibrant green framed by thick dark lashes. She was tall, at least two inches taller than Ashley.

"Michael." Sylina lowered her head as if embarrassed by his compliment.

"Would anyone like a cup of coffee," Margaret offered. "Or some tea. I think I have a box of English Breakfast in the cupboard."

"I'd love a cup," Sylina said.

"Have a seat, Sylina," Margaret said. "I won't be a minute. "Are you having tea?" she asked Ashley."

"I'll help you," Ashley said.

"No," Margaret said. "I'll get it."

Ashley looked at Michael with a warning stare and sat down. Michael ignored her.

"I'll just have coffee," he said and started toward the kitchen. Margaret stopped in her tracks as she watched Michael cross the breakfast room floor. She had not noticed the walking stick when Michael first arrived. Ashley realized what Margaret had seen. The walking stick, Ashley thought. Tryn/Christopher must have carried the same one when first meeting Margaret. She then thought of the Jaguar ring, now certain that Michael was wearing it.

"Mom." Ashley quickly left her chair. "Sit down. You and Sylina talk about New Orleans. That's where she's from. Sylina's a wonderful artist." Ashley looked over at Sylina and smiled, wondering what Michael had told her, if anything. "Sylina and I have worked together on several of my restorations."

"You're from New Orleans?" Ashley heard Margaret say, as she hurriedly left to confront Michael.

"Damn you!" She seethed at him. "What in the hell do you think you're doing? Goddamn you!" She reached out and grabbed the walking stick. It was then that she felt it. That overwhelming desire, to feel him touching her, giving her insatiable pleasure. She drew back and released the walking stick. As Michael reached out for it, Ashley saw the Jaguar ring. Michael took a step toward her. Then he drew even closer. Ashley took a breath and glared at him. "Stay away from me," she warned. Michael smiled. Then his smile turned into a smirk.

"Stay away?" He laughed. "Gladly, I don't need you anyway. I have Sylina. And soon, I'll have Shelby."

"NO! You touch Shelby and I'll kill you."

Michael threw his head back in quiet laughter. "Maybe I'll leave Shelby alone," he said. "If you're willing to make a pact with the devil."

"What are you talking about?"

"I'm talking about you, my beautiful and desirable sister. Your resistance excites me. Taking you is even more enticing now. I can feel you squirming in my arms." He began to scan Ashley's body. "Yes. Just thinking of spreading those beautiful legs feels delicious." He reached out and grabbed her hand. "Touch it." He firmly pressed her hand against his erection and forced her to him. "God, you feel good," he said, as he ran his hand under her dress and between Ashley's legs. "Spread your legs," her ordered, forcing them apart.

"No, nooo." Ashley fell against Michael.

"Yes," Michael said, and slid his hand into her panties. "You're wet from wanting me." He jerked her face to meet his. "You are mine," he said glaring. "And don't you ever forget it. You give yourself to me, when I want it and as long as I want it." He released her and smiled. "Then your sweet Shelby will be safe from me." Michael laughed sarcastically. "You have told her, haven't you?"

"No." Ashley jerked away. "Not until I have to."

"Oh that's amusing."

"What have you told Sylina?"

"I didn't have to tell her anything. She was overcome just by my presence. And I rather like it that way." Michael tapped his walking stick on the tile floor. "Maybe we'll tell Shelby and Sylina together about their little *Gift*." "When they're eighty and still look twenty-six."

Ashley tried to ignore Michael's sinister wit and started preparing the tea. He walked over and poured himself a cup of black coffee, returning to the breakfast room where Margaret and Sylina sat in animated conversation.

Michael sat down next to Margaret and placed his walking stick against the wall. That was when Margaret saw his ring.

Michael noticed this and moved his hand closer. Margaret flinched. "I bought this from Mr. DeLore," Michael said. "And the walking stick," He laid it on the table. "Mr. DeLore has wonderful taste, don't you think? I paid a price for these pieces." He looked at Margaret and sipped his coffee.

"Sylina," Margaret said wearily. "If you will please excuse me, I'm not feeling very well." Margaret rose from her chair and left the breakfast room.

Ashley had been standing in the doorway watching this. She excused herself and went after her mother.

"Well, Sylina," Michael said. "Looks like I'll have to serve your tea."

"I'd rather go back to your house." She smiled seductively and took his hand. "It's boring here."

Ashley heard the door closing from the upstairs bedroom. "They're gone," she informed Margaret.

"I'm sorry, but seeing that ring and that walking stick . . ." She looked up at Ashley from the side of the bed. "Michael. He—he looked—he acted so strange."

"I know. I think he's a little overwhelmed by Tryn. Influenced by his wealth and good taste in art and such. It'll pass." She smiled and took Margaret into her arms, hoping that explanation would suffice "When is Dad going to be home?"

"Oh. Around six I guess."

"Will you be all right if I go back to the studio? There are some last minute things I need to get done if Dad agrees to go to Winthrop House. Besides, you two need to be alone when you tell him."

Margaret looked up at Ashley. "Of course I'll be all right. You have made it all right."

Chapter Twenty-One

Michael.

Ashley closed her eyes. God! She could still feel him. Oh how she wanted him.

At the blare of a horn Ashley opened her eyes and saw the green light. She quickly turned left onto Marina Blvd., passed the St. Francis Yacht Club, and headed toward the Golden Gate.

Her mind was like a labyrinth of cobwebs. She had to get all her lies in order, make them sound plausible. No. Make then sound factual. Tomorrow she would go into the city to Bank of the West and meet with—what was her name? Henrietta something. Then it actually dawned on her. She was a wealthy woman. So were Shelby and Sylina. And Michael. She wondered if Michael knew. What had Christopher told him? But that didn't matter. She would give Michael his rightful share. As for Victor, she had carefully planned her story to explain his sudden wealth. The same story she would tell to Shelby and Buzz and Les.

That Tryn DeLore's grandfather, her and Michael's and Shelby's father, had left them an enormous sum of money. That only after discovering the journal was she aware of this. It was also after reading the journal that Margaret's indiscretion was revealed. Tryn, of course, had no intention of revealing the contents of the journal until she confronted him with it. She then had her lawyer contact Tryn. Tryn then sold the house to Michael and left for Europe.

Yes. That lie should work. She wondered, though. Would Victor refuse to take the money? Money that in truth had been left to him by his own father, Christopher Winthrop.

God. The lies. Always and forever—lies. Lies to conceal who and what she really was. A woman damned for eternity. The thought was horrifying. But the thought of taking her own life was equally as horrifying. Would it be so after years of existing in this eternal damnation? Would she finally weaken, no longer able to endure it? And Michael. Even with the incredible desire that had consumed her, the desperate hunger for him, she loathed what he had become. Christopher had said that she would begin to feel love for Michael. How soon, she wondered, would her lustful desire turn into love? She would never find the strength to destroy him if she loved him. Could she now? Amid the hunger and the hatred, take his life? The thought sickened her.

"Ashley," Karen greeted, as Ashley walked through the studio door. "You were up and out of here bright and early this morning. There's a Mr. Sheldon waiting in your office. He's been there for over an hour. I told him I didn't know when you'd be back."

"Blake?" Ashley looked toward her office.

"Yes. He was insistent that he wait."

"Where's Stanley?"

"He had an appointment in the city. He should be back in about an hour or so."

She started toward her office.

"Ashley." Blake stood and dropped the magazine back in his chair. "Thank God you're all right."

"What?" She briefly glanced at Blake and walked behind her desk. "Why wouldn't I be?"

"You haven't exactly been acting yourself."

"I'm fine," she said, not looking up, as she shuffled through several folders.

Blake closed the door and walked around the desk. He took Ashley's arm. "Look at me," he ordered in that deep voice Ashley still couldn't get out of her mind. Blake jerked her arm and forced her to face him. Ashley felt the air rush into her lungs.

"Blake, please," she begged.

Blake took her by the shoulders. "Look at me."

Ashley reluctantly looked into Blake's eyes. "Why are you doing this," she sighed, wishing he would just leave. She could not allow herself to fall in love with Blake. He deserved better, a normal person. But touching her like this was making her weak.

"I want to know what's wrong," he said sternly. "Why you wouldn't talk to Buzz and why you just picked up and left. I happen to care about you, Ashley Winthrop." He took her face in his hands. "I don't think that comes as a complete shock."

Before Ashley could respond, she felt Blake's mouth on hers. That delicate, sweet smell of pipe tobacco filled her nostrils.

"No," Ashley whispered.

Blake took her in his arms, kissing her again and again.

"No, Blake", she insisted. "I can't." She pushed against his chest.

Blake held fast, clutching her chin in his hand. He stared deep into her eyes. "Why don't I believe you?" And he kissed her again.

Ashley suddenly felt the passion overtaking her. She wanted him, every inch of him. It was the same sweet passion she had felt with Scott. She cupped her hands around his strong face and pressed her mouth hard against his.

℞

"There it is," Louis said, "Willow Alley." Russell turned the Lincoln Town Car to the left and stopped beneath the sign that read: The Cobweb Rare and Antique Books.

Louis stood momentarily in front of the shop. "Who are you really, Aggie Carter?" he said, then reached out and opened the door. The tiny bell announced his arrival. Louis looked across the rows of bookshelves and saw a lady coming down the far stairway. She had obviously not heard the bell because she had not looked up nor acknowledged him.

Louis gently closed the door. Again the bell sounded.

"May I help you?" he heard the woman say. Aggie walked toward Louis with a strained expression.

"Miss Carter," he said, knowing that his deformity was the cause of her apparent uneasiness. "My name is Louis. I called you earlier."

"Oh, my yes," she said. "Please, do forgive me." Aggie approached Louis and held out her hand. "It's so nice to meet you."

"It's nice of you to have me," Louis said, taking her hand. "Seems we have something in common."

"My yes. It seems that we have. Please, would you like to join me for a glass of sherry," and she gestured for him to follow her up the stairs.

"I would be honored," he said, sounding quite formal.

"I always have my sherry around 4 o'clock. It gives me a generous appetite for dinner."

Aggie showed Louis up the stairs and into her modest apartment. She offered him a chair next to a side table draped in antique lace. A small Tiffany lamp and two porcelain figurines sat on the table. Louis looked around the eclectic little room, slightly tense.

"Miss Carter," he said, hesitating.

"Please," Aggie motioned. "I would much prefer Aggie," She smiled, handing him a small crystal glass of sherry. Louis took it.

"Thank you, Aggie," he said, studying the design of the glass. "You know, I think I have a set of these same glasses."

Aggie poured her sherry and sat down across from him. "Sophia Winthrop gave a set of these to my mother many years ago." Aggie sipped her sherry.

"Yes," Louis said. "There are still many of these glasses in the china cupboard."

"How and when did you come to live at Winthrop House?" she asked.

"Around 1926. I was employed as gardener and caretaker."

Aggie smiled knowingly, as if she had just been given confirmation of her thoughts. "If I recall, you came highly recommended."

"Recommended?"

Aggie smiled. "You did some beautiful work at my farm many years ago."

"Your farm?"

"Why yes, the old Jackson Farm."

"The Jackson Farm," Louis said, bemused. "Of course. That was my last project before going to Winthrop House. I remember quite clearly now." Louis thought for a moment. "Azaleas, wasn't it? I seem to remember showing you and another lady the proper way to plant and care for them. Yes," he said, as if the memory had crystallized. "Your friend loved her gardens very much. That impressed me."

"You have a remarkable memory," Aggie said. "And yes, Jenny did love her gardens. She spent hours there."

"Jenny?"

"Yes, Jenny was my dearest friend. More like family really. I lost her only this past October."

"I'm sorry."

"Louis," Aggie said. "Will Taylor has asked that I show you my childhood diary. I kept it while I lived at Winthrop House. He seems to think you should read it."

"Yes," Louis said. "He believes it might help me find some long awaited answers."

"Answers?"

"Yes, I'm afraid so. You see . . . " Louis seemed hesitant to continue. "You see, Aggie, I learned many years ago that I was the heir to Winthrop House. To the entire estate." Louis saw Aggie's curious frown. "I have never learned who left this incredible fortune to me or why."

"I see." Aggie held Louis' gaze. "Then by all means, you are welcome to read it."

Aggie removed the journal from a desk drawer and handed it to him. "I hope you will find your answers. I must warn you, though, Winthrop House saw terrible tragedies."

&

Ashley sat between Victor and Margaret as the limousine wound its way through the little village of Manchester. She held their hands tightly. That strange sensation she had felt toward Victor had not lessened. She could still feel the sexual desire, but it had long ago turned into love. Now that she knew the source of that love and the reason for the sexual desire, she was somehow able to cope with it. And Victor was coping with the knowledge that he was not her real father. If only she could tell him who she really was. Who Michael and Shelby were. That they were all bound together by the same man. Christopher Winthrop.

"I don't think I really appreciated how beautiful this little village was when we all lived here," Margaret said, peering out the window. "It's hardly changed."

"Look," Victor said, pointing out the window. "That's the same movie theatre I used to go to in the thirties. It looks the same."

Ashley laughed. "They have sound now."

"They had sound then too," Victor retorted, smiling and nudging Ashley's side.

"I'm so nervous," Margaret said. "I never thought I'd come back here." She looked over at Ashley. "It's going to be good to see Louis again though."

"I think we're all a little nervous," Ashley said. "But Will and Shelby will be there. And Dad will finally meet the great Dr. Will Taylor."

"Oh," Victor said. "I forgot. Blake called this morning. Seems that Dr. Taylor called and invited him to see Winthrop House."

Ashley stiffened. "Why would he do that?"

Victor eyed Ashley. "I thought you'd be pleased."

"Why would you say that?"

"Oh, just thought you might enjoy his company."

Ashley didn't respond, but leaned back and rested her head against the seat, remembering the past two nights. Why had she let it happen? Blake had stayed. Had made love to her practically all night. It made her dizzy just to think of it. She couldn't let it happen again. She wouldn't do this to Blake. Somehow she had to find the strength to let go. She should have left him a note, something, telling him she couldn't see him again. Not just leave without a word.

Ashley thought of Stanley and the lie she had conveniently made up for him. A long lost relative on her father's side had died and left her and Michael a sizable inheritance and a mansion in Manchester, Massachusetts. How absurd that all sounded to her now. But Stanley had taken it all in without question. He even believed her when she told him that Tryn DeLore had gone back to France and that Michael would probably buy DeLore House. More lies.

"Michael's not taking this very well, is he," Victor said to Ashley. "He adamantly refused to come with us."

"I don't think it's that. He's just wrapped up in that old DeLore mansion. In fact, just before I left, he said that Tryn had gone back to France. I think Michael's thinking about buying the mansion."

"I don't understand what's come over Michael," Margaret said. "He's acting so strange."

"It'll pass." She squeezed Margaret's hand. "Oh—my—God," Ashley glared out the window as the limousine approached the narrow road to Winthrop House.

As though caught in some strange time warp, Ashley saw this vision as it passed before her. Moment by moment, as if reliving her childhood dream. The cliff road, narrow and winding. The sheltering oaks, looming ominously. She reached across Margaret, slowly opening the window. Victor and Margaret, too, seemed mesmerized as the window gradually lowered. The biting cold seized them as though their breath had been sucked out. Ashley closed her eyes, clutching their hands, while the sea pounded in their ears.

"Sweetheart," Victor said. "Are you all right?"

She did not answer. Again, she was back in her dream, traveling up the dark road to Winthrop House. Her mother and father were not beside her. She was alone, the pound and stir of the waves echoing through her head. She heard her screams, but there was no sound, only the memory. She slouched back into the soft leather seat as Winthrop House suddenly appeared, looming tall and vast.

The limousine pulled up by the large fountain and stopped. Ashley sat spellbound.

"I'm not sure I can do this," Margaret said, as Victor opened the door and stepped out.

Ashley suddenly came back to reality. "Of course you can," she said. "We both can." She scooted across the seat, pulling Margaret with her.

They followed Victor out onto the cobblestone driveway. Victor put his arm around Margaret. "There it is," he said, staring up at the giant structure.

"It's the most beautiful thing I've ever seen," Ashley said.

"My mother loved this house," Victor said. "She never wanted me to leave it."

"Ash!" Shelby said, bursting out the door and down the walkway. Will Taylor and Louis stood in the doorway.

"So what do you think?" she said, smiling up at them. "It's something isn't it."

"Oh yes," Victor said smiling into Shelby's eyes.

"Where's Michael?" Shelby asked. "Isn't he coming?"

"No," Ashley said. "He's too busy buying DeLore House."

"DeLore House? You've got to be kidding." Shelby seemed to mull this over for a moment, then with her usual animated smile looked up at Victor. "Louis is dying to see all of you."

Louis stood by the doorway with Will next to him, both with smiles stretched across their faces.

"Thank you, Will Taylor," Louis said. "You've brought my family back to Winthrop House."

"It was nothing," Will teased.

"Louis Carter," Victor said, holding out his hand. "God, it's good to see you."

"And you," Louis replied, shaking Victor's hand vigorously. "It's been too many years."

"Yes, it has."

"Far too many," Margaret said and put her arms around Louis.

Louis hugged her gently.

Ashley stood and watched this momentous reunion, wishing she could remember the moments with Louis that she had seen under hypnosis and that her mother had told her about.

"And this is Ashley," Victor said. "A bit bigger than the last time you saw her."

Louis gazed into Ashley's smiling face. "My little Ashley. She's all grown up. And so beautiful."

Ashley reached up and gave Louis a big hug. "Thanks for having us. Winthrop House is . . . well, extraordinary."

Louis smiled warmly. "I have longed so for this moment."

"Dad," Shelby said, "This is Will Taylor. Will, Victor Winthrop."

"It's a pleasure," Will said, shaking Victor's hand.

"The pleasure is all mine. I've been a fan of yours since reading your first book." He chuckled. "Ironic, isn't it. You being responsible for this little reunion."

"Afraid I can't take all the credit. This was a joint effort."

"Well, I appreciate what you've done. Oh, and by the way. I hear you've invited our publisher, Blake Sheldon."

"Yes," Will said, looking over at Shelby. "That was Shelby's idea."

Ashley turned to Shelby with a stern look.

Shelby quickly took Ashley's arm and pulled her past Louis and up the stairs. "You're not going to believe the inside of this house."

"You're not going to believe what I'm going to do to you. Why in the hell did you have Will call Blake?"

"Never mind," Shelby said and opened the door. "He's not coming. And I don't blame him after the way you just took off without a word."

Ashley let out a sigh of relief. Yet deep down wishing he were there.

"Disappointed?"

Ashley's heart almost stopped as she saw the entrance hall come into view. "And I thought DeLore House was spectacular. How could I not have remembered this?" She walked into the vast hall looking in all directions. "The parlor," she said and walked through the double archway. "That's where I saw Jenny. She was sitting over there playing the piano." Ashley pointed past the second archway. And Christopher, she thought. He sat there next to the piano with his cello." She proceeded through the archway and stood by the fireplace. "This is the room where I saw Buzz's furniture. It all looks so different now."

"You want to go upstairs and see your mother and father's bedroom?" Shelby asked. "Or maybe you'd rather wait."

Ashley turned to Shelby. "No. I need to see it. Get it over with."

Everyone else went into the library while Ashley and Shelby climbed the stairs to the second floor.

"There are portraits hanging all over this hallway," Shelby said. "Louis has no idea who they are except for one, Christopher Winthrop."

"Christopher?" Ashley stopped at the top of the staircase. "I'm not ready to see that. Just show me where the bedroom is."

"You don't know?"

"What?" Ashley turned and looked down the long hallway. There, at the end, was the double doorway. She stood motionless. Finally she proceeded, past the tall candelabras and gilt-framed portraits. She saw nothing but what was in front of her. Shelby followed close behind.

As she reached the end, Ashley took hold of the double door knobs and pushed the doors open. In front of her was a tall sheer-draped window that looked out over the sea. To the left was a large bed, to the right a chaise lounge, behind the chaise lounge a paneled wall. Ashley went to the wall. "This is where I saw that man holding my mother," she said and touched one of the panels.

Shelby sat down on the chaise lounge. "I can't believe Dad's taking this so well."

"I don't know that he is," Ashley replied, looking around the room. "He wouldn't let on to us anyway."

"Ash," Shelby said. "I found out what happened to my father."

"What?" Ashley turned toward Shelby. "What did you say?" She sat down on the chaise.

"Will and I went to the library. I saw it in black and white. He was murdered. That's why no one ever talked about him." Shelby looked up at Ashley with saddened eyes.

"No," Ashley said. "That's not true."

"Ashley's right." Shelby looked up to see Margaret standing in the doorway.

"What?"

Margaret went to Shelby. "Sweetheart," she said taking her hand. "Please forgive me. I only wanted to spare you. My life was a mess. Not even Victor knew the whole truth until a few months ago."

"What are you talking about?"

"I'm talking about my first child," Margaret replied. "Ashley said she told you. About the journal. Tryn had me believing that my baby had died. But you didn't die." Margaret's eyes now filled with tears. "He gave you to Natalie and Thomas Kincaid."

Shelby stared at Margaret in stunned disbelief.

"I don't blame you if you hate me," Margaret said. "For lying to you all these years. But I just couldn't bring myself to do it. You loved Natalie so."

Shelby stood up and began fidgeting with her ring.

Margaret and Ashley waited anxiously.

"You?" Shelby twisted her ring in circles. "You are my mother?" She then turned to Margaret. "You and Victor are my parents?"

Margaret lowered her head.

"No, Shel," Ashley said. "Not Victor. Tryn DeLore is our father. Remember?"

Shelby's face went blank. "Oh," she said as if struggling to put the pieces together. "Then—that means you are my real sister. And Michael, he's my brother." She raised her head and stared into space. "Then I do have a family." Her eyes were now flooded with tears.

"Can you forgive me?" Margaret said.

"What?" Shelby sniffed and turned to Margaret. "Forgive you? I love you. I always have." Shelby fell to her knees and embraced Margaret.

Ashley sat back with a smile and wiped her own tears. Whatever she had to do, she would not let Michael near Shelby. He would not take this happiness from her.

The fireplace in the library was ablaze. Will and Shelby were rummaging through the massive bookcases, mesmerized by the endless volumes, some of which were handwritten, dating as far back as the twelfth century. Victor and Margaret seemed lost in their memories.

As Ashley questioned Louis about her early childhood, thinking that she had not remembered his discolored face during the hypnosis, she also noticed Will and Shelby, seemingly wrapped up in an intimate conversation. How amusing it was, seeing them like this, when only a week before Shelby would have nothing to do with him.

"Why are you smiling?" Louis asked.

"Oh, I was just noticing our two love birds over there."

Louis smiled. "They've been a joy to me these past few days."

"Shelby's been a joy to me all my life," Ashley said.

"Yes. And now you've discovered that she's your sister. I was thrilled when Will told me that you had confided in him. How did Shelby take the news just now?"

"Deliriously happy."

"I do hope Margaret knows how I feel about all of this. She went through so much pain during those years that Victor was missing."

"I'm sure she does. It would be nice, though, if you told her yourself."

"And I will. I want her to know that I understand. Tryn DeLore took unfair advantage of her grief. And now, to find out that he abandoned his own children, and even had Margaret believing that Shelby had died. The man was incorrigible. I loathed him." Louis frowned. "My greatest moment was throwing him out of Winthrop House. I honestly believe I would have killed the man if he had refused. What amazes me, though, is that he actually kept a journal. And to leave all of you his wealth. That seems so out of character for the man."

"Maybe he had a conscience after all," Ashley smiled. "But if I hadn't run across that journal while I was restoring DeLore House, I would never have known about the inheritance. His grandson would certainly not have revealed it to me."

How easily she had said those words. The lies were getting easier. She was even beginning to believe them herself. If only the lies were truth and the truth nothing more than a distorted nightmare.

Russell appeared at the library door and announced that dinner was served. As Louis escorted Ashley to the dining room, she looked up at the blank wall over the fireplace where Christopher said Jenny's portrait had hung. She then looked down at one of the mythical maidens, remembering Christopher's words. 'You need only to turn the heads of one of the maidens to reveal it.' But how would she explain to everyone how she knew about Jenny's portrait? Then it dawned on her. She could have easily been revealed this in one of her visions.

After dinner, which Russell had prepared with great care and elegance, Will asked that everyone go back to the library. There was something he wanted Victor and Margaret and Ashley to read.

"Shelby and I and Louis have come to know a woman by the name of Aggie Carter," he began. "She lived here at Winthrop House back at the turn of the century. She knew the woman, Jenny Winthrop." Will looked over at Ashley. "We all now know the dreams that Ashley has been dealing with. Under hypnosis she revealed this woman, Jenny Winthrop. Aggie Carter kept a childhood diary during those years she and Jenny lived here at Winthrop House. With Aggie's permission I made copies of her diary for all of you to read."

"Ashley," Will said. "Jenny Winthrop lived to be 103. She died only this past October."

Ashley looked at Will in disbelief. What had he said? She stared down at the diary. Slowly and silently she began to read.

As Ashley read Aggie's last words she still could not grasp it all. Jenny had not died in the fire? But of course not. She had eternal youth. Had Christopher never thought to question this? Maybe not. He knew her righteousness, her shear goodness. Somehow, she had escaped the evil. The divinity of her soul had conquered, finally releasing her into death. But what about Aggie? Jenny would have remained youthful. Had Jenny confided in Aggie, told her about . . . but no, Jenny never knew about *The Gift*. My God, Ashley thought. Jenny Winthrop lived her entire 103 years as young and beautiful as ever. What could she have thought? How could she have coped with it? But Ashley would have to put this out of her mind. She was the only one who knew about *The Gift*. And until she was forced to tell Shelby, she was going to keep it that way.

Ashley suddenly thought back to what Will and Shelby had told her the other day over the telephone. That Louis' real name was Tanner. Sophia, she mused. That had been Louisa's and Sophia's maiden name. Ashley was probably the only one who knew that. Had it been Sophia who had left Louis the Winthrop fortune? Given him the name Louis after her sister Louisa? Could he possibly be Sophia's child? Her child by someone other than Andrew Winthrop? Had Andrew known, and forced her to give her child away? Could that be the reason he was given the name Carter, not Tanner or Winthrop? Give him the last name of a servant to keep suspicion away? A thought seized her. Could Louis be Sophia and Nicholas' child, and Christopher's brother? Had he been sent away because of his deformity and escaped acceptance of this evil *Gift*?

Chapter Twenty-Two

Will and Louis drove down into the village hoping to persuade Aggie to join them and the Winthrop family for dinner. With gentle coaxing, Aggie finally agreed.

"Are you going to be all right?" Louis asked her, as they approached Winthrop House. "Maybe this wasn't such a good idea after all."

"Louis," Aggie replied bravely, sitting between the two men and looking toward Winthrop House. "Somehow I feel that my Jenny wants me there." She turned to Louis and smiled sweetly. "I can feel that Winthrop House is once again filled with love." She looked back up at the mansion as they drew closer. "It's a beautiful place. When there's love."

Russell had prepared the dining table with fresh flowers, candelabras, and the finest Royal Bavarian china. The delicately etched crystal sparkled beneath the enormous Venetian chandelier.

Russell called everyone in for dinner, announcing that the menu for the evening was Chicken A La Russell; boneless chicken breast stuffed with spinach, mushrooms and cream cheese, and served with a sherry prawn sauce. Several staff members assisted Russell, serving the meal and assuring that wine glasses were refilled.

"No thank you," Aggie replied after her second glass of wine. "I'm afraid two is my limit."

Will said that he had not yet decided on his limit and gracefully accepted a refill.

Louis sat at the head of the table looking pleased. Everyone had gravitated to Aggie, especially Ashley. Aggie appeared, as did Louis, lost in bliss.

After a dessert of lightly frozen grapes, topped with whipped cream and a pinch of nutmeg, everyone retired to the double parlor. Aggie had learned earlier in the evening that Louis was not only a master gardener, but quite the pianist. So with slight coaxing, Louis was ushered to the piano. Aggie sat in a small French chair close by.

"This is where Christopher would sit," Aggie said reminiscently, "when he would accompany Jenny on his cello." She smiled and closed her eyes.

When Louis finished playing, everyone sat quietly as though savoring the moment.

Will gazed at Louis as if studying him. "Louis," he said. "There's something I'd like your permission to do."

Everyone looked at Will curiously.

"Of course, Will, what is it?"

"Well—I'd like to exhume the coffin marked Baby Winthrop."

"What?" Louis rose from the piano.

"Will!" Shelby exclaimed. "What on earth?"

Will turned to Shelby. "I don't believe Jenny's baby died at birth."

Aggie frowned. "Why would you believe such a thing?"

Will turned to her. "Didn't you say that you were watching from your secret hiding place during the birth?"

"Yes."

"Think back. What happened when the baby was born? You said Sophia took the baby immediately from the room. Did she hold the baby up and spank it? They did that in those days, to start the babies breathing. Did anyone do that?"

"Oh no. Sophia just wrapped the little thing in a blanket and ran from the room."

"Yes, that's exactly what you told us. And a child would have remembered if someone had held the baby up and spanked it. That's not something a child is likely to forget, is it?"

"No, I guess not," Aggie agreed.

"And I think I know why they didn't do it."

"You do?"

"Yes. But I'll need to open the coffin."

Aggie turned to Louis as if to help permission for Will.

Louis nodded. "All right, Will. I'll leave it in your hands."

Will's face brightened. "Thanks, Louis. Do you have a shovel and some lanterns?"

Shelby glared at him. "Tonight!"

"Yes, tonight." Will arched an eyebrow.

"Then I'm going with you."

"Are the lanterns still in the garden house?" Victor asked.

"Yes," Louis said. "I'll help you."

"Mom and I will stay with Aggie," Ashley said.

She turned to Aggie after the others had trooped out. "Would you show me the room where Jenny had her baby?"

"Why of course, my dear. Follow me, we'll go up the back stairway. It has more landings, easier on an old woman's legs."

Ashley took her mother's arm as they ascended the back stairs. "You'll never look like an old woman, Aggie Carter."

As they reached the second floor Aggie turned down the west-wing corridor where many portraits lined the walls. Aggie pointed out Sophia's portrait.

"Sophia Winthrop was a bitter woman," she said, looking up at the large gilt-framed canvas. "Her beauty always frightened me. It seemed strange that such beauty could be so callous. She changed though, for a while, after Jenny arrived."

"Sophia was Victor's grandmother," Margaret said.

Ashley stood in front of the large canvas, noticing the signature at the bottom left corner.

Tryn Delore.

Nicholas Winthrop, she thought, looking up at the portrait of Sophia, who was standing by a French table, her hand resting gently on its surface. She wore a floor length gown of emerald green velvet with long sleeves and a deep, revealing neckline. Her hair was dark, and hung in ringlets over her left shoulder. An expression of superiority was revealed in her exquisite face. Ashley looked deeper into the dark eyes. Was she imagining it, or could she actually see the demons lodged inside the very soul of this woman? A woman whose life had been driven by an obsessive passion for self-fulfillment, greed, and power. A woman who, in the end, fell into the love of another, freeing her from herself. Sophia had loved Jenny as obsessively as she had loved Tryn, Nicholas Winthrop, Jenny's father.

Ashley smiled wryly, wondering what Sophia would have thought if she had known that Louisa and Nicholas were Jenny's parents. As she mused about this her eyes went to the necklace around Sophia's neck. She stared at it. Aggie and Margaret both noticed.

"Why Ashley, my child, what is it?" Aggie said.

"That necklace."

"Yes," Aggie said with admiration. "It's exquisite isn't it? Sophia gave that necklace to Jenny on her wedding day. She wore it when her portrait was painted. Oh, if only you could have seen her portrait. It was the loveliest thing Mr. Tryn ever did. As you will see, he painted all of the portraits here at Winthrop House."

Ashley turned to Margaret. "That's my necklace," she said and looked back to the portrait thoughtfully. "Where is Kathleen Winthrop's portrait?"

"There isn't one," Margaret replied.

"I wonder why? And why didn't Dad tell Michael and me that his mother disappeared. He told us she died of tuberculosis."

"I don't know," Margaret said sadly. "Victor loved his mother dearly. I don't think he ever accepted the way he lost her."

"How terribly sad," Aggie said. "But this means that Christopher Winthrop was your grandfather."

"Yes," Ashley said. "I guess it does."

How strange it felt to Ashley to say that. But Christopher was not her grandfather. He was her father. And Victor was not her father but her brother. Ashley abruptly turned to Aggie, "Would you show me Christopher's portrait?"

"Of course." Aggie continued down the dim corridor. "Christopher was such a dear sweet man."

Margaret refrained comment.

The candles and gas lamps burned dimly along the stone walls as they passed each portrait. Aggie pointed out Andrew Winthrop.

"So this is Victor's grandfather," Margaret said, staring into Andrew's beautiful face. "Victor never knew for certain who his grandfather was. I'm not sure that Kathleen Winthrop knew."

"Christopher looked very much like his father," Aggie said. "As you can see, The Winthrops were a handsome lot. As is your father. And your brother, I would imagine. Will did say you had a brother?"

Ashley didn't answer. Her mind seemed to be swallowed up, as she gazed at Andrew's portrait. She envisioned Christopher in that secret room as Andrew presented him with *The Gift*. Gift, she thought. How obscene the name.

"Yes," she finally said, turning to Aggie. "Michael."

"Here," Aggie announced with pride. "This is Christopher Winthrop. The man my Jenny so dearly loved. I never will understand why he left after the birth of Jenny's baby. But when he did return, it was too late. We had to keep Jenny a secret, for fear they would charge her with Stefan's murder. Maybe my mother was wrong, though. Christopher did love her so. I'm sure he would have protected her."

Ashley looked into Christopher's face. "I'm sure your mother made the right decision," she said, thinking how beautiful Christopher was. Nicholas had captured his son's essence, even down to those vivid blue eyes. She thought, momentarily, that he would step from the portrait, embracing her as he had that night in Belvedere. She quickly pushed the thought from her mind.

"The stairway to the third floor is just down this corridor," Aggie said. "Jenny moved to this bedroom after Stefan became so outraged about his mother."

As they advanced down the corridor, Ashley thought of the secret room that stood sequestered, center, on the third floor. She thought of Aggie exploring all the secret corridors and rooms behind those walls and wondered. Could it have been possible that she found a secret passage into that room? She knew Christopher had not, he had said that the room had eluded him all those years. But Aggie. Winthrop House was, as she had said, her opulent prison. She had withdrawn into a fantasy world behind those walls, spending full days at a time searching out their secrets.

"Aggie," Ashley said. "Do you know about the large room on the third floor, the one in the center with no windows?"

Aggie stopped at the foot of the stairs. "You know about that room?"

"Yes," Ashley replied. "That journal I told you I found at DeLore House mentioned that room. There's one just like it there."

"What room are you talking about?" Margaret asked.

Ashley explained about the chamber room at DeLore House and that there was suppose to be one identical at Winthrop House.

"I never knew," Margaret said in amazement.

"Come," Aggie said, as though she wanted no further discussion. "Let's go to Jenny's bedroom."

As Ashley reached out toward the banister, she froze.

"What is it?" Aggie said.

"It's nothing. Just the banister. There's one just like it in New Orleans. It was in my hypnotist's home."

"It is rather scary looking," Aggie said. "Looks like a snake. I remember being a little afraid of it when I lived here."

"Me too," Margaret said, running her fingers around the post.

They all laughed and climbed the stairs to the third floor.

"Here we are," Aggie announced, opening the door. She took a long-stem match from a brass holder on the corridor wall. "If I remember," she said, "there's a light just inside the door." She reached up and turned the knob. The gas quickly ignited, sending shadows dancing about the ceiling and on the floral wall covering.

"The room is empty," Aggie said.

"That wallpaper!" Ashley exclaimed. "It's just like the pattern in my bedroom." Slowly, she walked in circles, looking from wall to wall. "So that's why it seemed so familiar. I had seen it before. This must have been my bedroom." She turned to Aggie. "The furniture. Do you remember what it looked like?"

"Honey," Margaret interrupted. "This *was* your bedroom. We had Louis ship the furniture to New Orleans when we moved. It's the same furniture you have now."

Ashley grew thoughtful. "No wonder. Aggie, do you remember a lace scarf? It was very old. Even back then, it would have been old. Did Jenny ever have one?"

"Oh my yes. Christopher gave it to her as a wedding present. She wore it always. I don't know whatever became of it, though."

"I have it. Louis said he gave it to me when my family and I left here."

"You have my Jenny's beautiful lace scarf?"

"Yes." Ashley watched Aggie's anxious face."

"I would so love to see it again."

"Of course. I brought it with me."

Aggie clasped her hands with delight.

"We'll stop by the room where I'm staying tonight," Ashley promised.

"Looks like they're on their way back," Margaret said, peering out toward the cemetery. She could see their shadowy figures moving back toward the house, their lanterns swinging to the rhythm of their walk.

"You said that Jenny's baby was born in this room?"

"Yes," Aggie replied. "Over there." She pointed to where the old Victorian bed had once stood.

A soft smile rose on Ashley's lips. "I've slept in that bed almost all of my life."

"We'd better get back," Margaret said hurriedly. "They'll be waiting for us."

On their way, Ashley stopped by her room and got the scarf. Aggie held it tightly as they walked down the stairway to the library.

Will gathered everyone around the large fireplace, flanked by the mythical maidens. The same fireplace where Louis had announced to Tryn that he, Louis, was the heir to the Winthrop fortune and that Tryn was no longer welcome at Winthrop House.

Will and Victor placed the little marble coffin at their feet. Will looked at Aggie, who was sitting at the far end of the fireplace, still clutching the scarf.

"Aggie," he began. "I have already opened the coffin. My suspicions have been confirmed."

Aggie stared at Will.

"However, I was not expecting to find this." He lifted the lid from the coffin. Inside was a small piece of parchment, rolled and tied with what looked to be a dark blue ribbon, old and faded.

Except for the crackle and gentle roar of the fire, there was silence. Everyone anticipated the revelation of a long kept secret. Will untied the ribbon and opened the parchment. It read:

December, 1901 -This is my confession of conscience:
What I did on the day, October 18, 1900, is known only by my son Stefan, and Dr. Ronald Mullholland. I have paid dearly for his silence.

315

I am a self serving, cold-hearted woman, driven by the evils of the unbearable need for social status and self-gratification. Born into the depths of poverty, I spared no pains in my escape, carrying with me outrageous stories of a wealthy childhood of a family lost to me in tragedy, but in truth forsaking my illegitimate daughter, by giving her to be adopted. I lived, through the years, with fear that she would search me out, exposing me for what I am. I also lived with guilt for what I had done. So in my way, I eased that guilt.

Years later, after learning that my daughter had married and that she and her husband were looking for work as domestics, I persuaded Andrew, my husband, to hire them at Winthrop House. I knew that she did not know who I was. She had been adopted only weeks after she was born and never knew of me. I, however, knew what had become of her.

I was only a child myself when I became pregnant. Her father was an older boy that I fell fancy to. Upon learning of my pregnancy, he left, never to be seen by me or my family again. It was a terrible time for me. I had barely turned thirteen, and my love for this man, though I truly did not know the word, inspired me to want my child. This emotion lasted only a few months. As I grew larger, my figure distorting, my energy waning, I became bitter, resentful. I also had a twin sister whom I have never acknowledged. She was unbearably good and sweet and disgusted me, willing to live with the poverty our parents had borne us into. I despised her every time I looked at her beautiful body as I watched mine grow uglier. I soon wanted nothing to do with my child, and freely gave her up.

But there was guilt. Not only did I think of my daughter every day of my life, I kept a distant but watchful eye, for I had found out quite by accident where she had gone. No one knew this. So when I learned that she and her husband were seeking work, I brought her into my life and into Winthrop House.

How is it then, that I can love her as I do, and forsake her still, as I have? I have gone to my grave never telling her this. I watched my grandchild being born, and still, I rejected her. Sweet innocent little Aggie. How many times I wanted to put my arms around her, and hold her close. Tell her that I loved her in my way. But something deeper and more vile twisted up inside me. It tortures the mind, and sweeps the soul.

And now Jenny's unfortunate child, whom I shudder to behold, whom I cannot bear to give the Winthrop name, will never know the truth. I will give to him the name, Carter, my daughter's married name. Only upon my death will I give him my maiden name, Tanner. In the place of his inherent name, I have bequeathed to him its fortunes.

I have now spoken my conscience on this parchment. Somehow, I feel that confessing these unspeakable deeds, if only to myself, will ease the pain.

Forgive me, my beautiful Jenny. If only I could cradle you in my arms as a lover would. As I so yearned to do. My undying and forbidden love for you is tarnished only by my love for self. I destroyed the very soul of my son, Stefan, by the obsessiveness that burned inside me. I was helpless to fight my way clear of its grasp. I also took his life as I thrust a knife deep into his heart.

From this innocent little deformed child, whom I have named Louis Carter, and whom I cannot bear to reveal to the world, I do not ask forgiveness. Not even a saint could forgive this selfish, tragic deed. May you find the love you deserve sweet Louis. And may the Winthrop fortune pave your path with unforeseen opportunities.

My son Christopher has chosen an evil and destructive path. I shall not speak of him further, but will go now to the cemetery where the little coffin is buried beneath the ground. That is where my confession will lie.

I sign my name to these revelations of conscience. Even in my dying, for I no longer have the will to live, this wretched guilt is still with me.

Sophia Tanner Winthrop

Will stared at the parchment. Everyone else stared at Will. The silence was deafening.

"Well," Will said, half joking. "It looks like I am the only outsider here."

He turned to Louis. "Louis Winthrop," he announced. "Stefan and Jenny's son. The rightful heir to Winthrop House."

"Welcome to the family," Victor said, leaving his chair. He held out his hand to Louis.

Louis took it, gazing into Victor's face in a state of shock. "That divine lady was my mother?" A tear found its way down his cheek.

Aggie clutched the lace scarf, her face wet with tears. Both Ashley and Shelby were kneeling beside her.

"Sophia," Aggie seemed elated. "It was Sophia who killed Stefan. Not my precious Jenny." She looked into the blazing fire. Her eyes now saddened. "Jenny went to her grave thinking she had killed her husband."

Louis went to Aggie and took her tiny hand. She looked up into his eyes. He gently pulled her to him and gathered her fragile body into his arms. They held each other, crying softly.

"Jenny's scarf," Ashley said, stroking Aggie's shoulder.

Aggie looked down at the scarf, then handed it to Ashley.

"No. It belongs to Louis. That's why Sophia wanted him to have it. It belonged to Jenny, his mother."

"Why don't we let Aggie keep it." Louis smiled and draped the scarf around her neck.

Aggie reached up and pulled Louis' face to hers. She kissed him firmly on his birthmark. "My Jenny's beautiful child. If only she could have known you."

"But she did," Louis said. "I helped her plant her azaleas."

"You surely did, sweet Louis. You surely did."

Louis turned to Victor and Margaret. "I don't know what to say."

"You don't have to say anything," Margaret said, giving him a generous hug.

"I would like to call it a night." Aggie said. "Do you mind terribly?"

"Of course not," Shelby said. "I think we all need a good night's sleep."

"I'd like to look for Jenny's portrait and belongings tomorrow if everyone is in agreement." Aggie said. "I would so like for Louis to have them."

Will responded with great pleasure. "I was going to suggest that myself."

Ashley thought of revealing to Aggie that Jenny's portrait was hanging behind the fireplace. But she could see that Aggie was very tired. It was better left until tomorrow.

Louis escorted Aggie down the back hallway to one of the guest rooms that Russell had prepared especially for her.

"Sophia was a wonderful person," Aggie said, as though trying to convince herself as well as Louis. "She was always good to us. Maybe not loving, but she cared for our well-being. She left us quite a sum of money. Now I know why."

Louis smiled, thinking of the fortune she had left him. "I guess Sophia just did the best she could. I'm sure she loved us both, in her way."

Aggie smiled. "Your father was also a good man. I loved him very much until . . . " she hung her head with disdain. "Stefan was so tortured by Sophia." She looked back at Louis. "You must remember him as he was before the jealousy turned him into that monster. He adored my Jenny. Just maybe too much."

"I will always think of him that way," Louis said.

Chapter Twenty-Three

"There are many rooms hidden behind these walls," Aggie said, following the lighted path of the oil lamp she carried. "I have always thought Sophia concealed Jenny's things in one of them. But I never ventured here after Stefan's death. I stayed close to Jenny."

"This is unbelievable," Will said, closely following Aggie. "I could spend days behind these walls."

"Some other time," Shelby ordered, creeping behind him.

"I'll be glad just to find what we're looking for and get out of here," Ashley groaned. "Why don't we try the west wing first? Don't you think Sophia would have used one of the rooms closest to her bedroom?" She remembered that Christopher had said he stored Jenny's clothing there.

"You're probably right," Aggie said. "And don't you worry, we'll find what we're looking for, then Will can sneak around these walls all he wants."

Louis reached over and patted Will on the shoulder while ducking a seasoned cobweb. "I'll be happy to set you up in one of these secret rooms," he chuckled. "You can write your next book in the privacy of the old Winthrop catacombs. By the way, what's your next book going to be about?"

"Winthrop House," Will replied, as a small mouse sent Aggie screeching, and her oil lamp swaying.

"Hang on there, Aggie," Will said, steadying his own lamp.

"I never was fond of those little creatures."

"Winthrop House, huh," Louis muttered.

Aggie was now inching her way up a narrow winding stairway.

"This place goes on forever," Will said.

"Oh yes," Aggie replied, finally reaching a coved corridor. "I spent hours exploring these corridors when I was a child. It kept me thoroughly entertained."

As they approached a turn, Aggie lowered her lamp. "See, over there." She pointed to a large panel. "That panel slides all the way back.

You can get a large piece of furniture through there. But over here," she reached down and opened a small panel. "See, it's just large enough to peer through."

"Whose room is it?" Ashley inquired, kneeling next to Aggie.

"It was Sophia's."

"Will," Ashley said. "You and Shelby are staying in Sophia's bedroom."

"Let me see," Shelby nudged Ashley aside. "Well, so we are. I hope the old bat doesn't mind."

"What's that?" Ashley exclaimed.

"What's what?" Everyone looked in Ashley's direction. A cold breeze suddenly rushed through the corridor.

Aggie seemed not to notice. She was now approaching a large panel at the end of the corridor. "Somewhere behind this wall is a secret room lined with wardrobes." She looked back at Louis and smiled. "I don't remember exactly where the secret panel is," she said, running her hand along the moldings, gently pushing.

"I found it!" Will exclaimed, as the center panel jolted open.

As everyone peered inside, they saw a large but narrow room flanked with wardrobes. The musty smells that had encroached the dark corridors were no longer present. The sweet smell of lavender flooded the room.

"My Jenny," Aggie whispered, as she entered.

"My mother's things are here?" Louis asked.

"Oh yes. They're here all right." She went to one of the wardrobes and opened it. Inside was a row of beautiful antique gowns. Aggie reached up and took one from its hanger. "This was her wedding gown," she said. "And the gown she wore when she sat for her portrait. Look at the intricate handwork. There must be hundreds of pearls sewn into the lace."

Aggie turned around and held the gown up in front of Shelby. "How beautiful she looked in this gown." She smiled into Shelby's eyes. "You are so the image of her."

Shelby smiled and lowered her head.

Louis gently took the white lace fabric and brought it to his cheek. His tears fell silently onto the lace.

Ashley went to him. "I think I have something very special to show you when we get back."

Before leaving the room, they searched all the wardrobes. Each contained clothes and articles that had belonged to Jenny Winthrop. Elegant gowns and exquisite lingerie, all hand made by the finest seamstresses.

Louis turned to Aggie. "Her portrait's not here," he said sadly.

"I know." Ashley touched his shoulder. "But I think I know where it is."

Everyone was silent, all eyes fixed above the fireplace. Ashley placed her hand on the head of one of the mythical maidens, remembering Christopher's words.

'You need only to turn the head of the maidens to reveal it.'

Ashley tightened both hands around the stone head and turned. A loud clunk sounded. The panel above the mantel moved, rotated outward and then slowly turned as Jenny's portrait appeared. Jenny was standing, as though suspended in time, draped in a flowing white lace gown, dripping with pearls. The low neckline revealed the ruby necklace.

Shelby was entranced upon seeing Jenny's face. Her resemblance to Jenny was staggering. Louis just stood, gazing up at the portrait. Suddenly the room seemed filled with the scent of lavender. As though it had formed from within the molecules of the scent itself, an indiscernible mist flowed down from the portrait and surrounded Louis. A soft smile grazed his lips. He lifted his hand and touched his face where the crimson birthmark had once been. That hideous disfigurement that had caused Sophia Winthrop to take him from his mother those many years ago.

The room suddenly became still. No one spoke or hardly breathed. What they had just witnessed was beyond explanation. Yet, somehow, they found they had accepted it without question.

Chapter Twenty-Four

Russell had not seemed to notice the absence of Louis' birthmark. Possibly he had surreptitiously witnessed the miracle, possibly not. Whatever the case, he was now thoroughly preoccupied with preparing for Shelby and Will's engagement party. Louis' gardens were now in Spring bloom. Louis had instructed Russell and Aggie how to arrange the floral design for the marble gazebo

"Ashley Winthrop!" Stanley wailed, marching into the library, and glancing from side to side. "This place is spectacular!"

"Thought you'd like it."

"Like it!" Stanley gazed at the fireplace. "Oh, by the way, I hear Scott's history. Didn't think that would last. Have you gone back to your relics?"

Ashley closed her eyes and wished herself to disappear, or better yet, that Stanley would. "That comment was unnecessary."

"I was only teasing. So. Where is this Blake Sheldon Shelby was telling me about?"

"What?" Ashley looked irritated.

"Aren't you seeing some guy named Blake?" Stanley was inspecting one of the mythical maidens. "The guy who took Shelby to Scott's opening."

"Stanley. Blake Sheldon is my father's publisher. I've known him for years. Can we divert this conversation somewhere else?"

Stanley looked at Ashley suspiciously.

She responded with a bored expression.

"Where's this Buzz Harper I've been hearing about for the last five years?" he asked, taking his attention back to the maiden.

"I don't know. Probably outside talking to Louis and Aggie."

"That's who was talking to Louis? Mmmm," He turned back to Ashley. "This is going to be some party. I've never seen anything like this place. Except maybe that creepy DeLore House. I can't believe Michael's buying that place. So, where's Shelby's new honey? I want to meet him."

"Where's *your* new honey?" Shelby said, strolling into the library with Will.

"Shelby darling," he cried, striding across the library floor and giving her a hug. "Congratulations."

"Why thank you Stanley," she said, and turned to Will. "This is the infamous Stanley I've warned you about."

"None of it's true," Stanley insisted, shaking his hand.

"Where is Clayton?" Shelby asked.

"He's married to his restaurant, not to me."

Will snickered slightly. "Nice to meet you Stanley. How about a drink?"

"Thought you'd never ask. Vodka and tonic please."

Will and Stanley headed to the bar. "One vodka and tonic coming up."

Shelby turned to Ashley, a serious look on her face. "Ash, I have to talk to you."

"What's wrong?"

Shelby pulled Ashley down the back hallway. "It's Michael."

"Michael? What about Michael?"

"I don't know." Shelby began rubbing her forehead. "He called Will this morning."

"He did what? He doesn't even know Will." Goddamnit, she thought.

"He was acting like the overprotective brother. Asking Will all kinds of dumb questions." Shelby lowered her head and turned away.

"Shel. What is it?" She could see that Shelby was forcing back tears.

"Ash," she said, taking a deep breath. "I love Will more than anything in this world."

"Then why are you so upset? He loves you too."

"I know," Shelby whimpered. "I couldn't believe it when he asked me to marry him."

"Then why are you crying?"

Shelby looked down at the floor and began fidgeting with her hands. "Because, I can't quit thinking about Michael. I think about him all the time." She looked back at Ashley. "You told me you were having weird feelings like that. You told me that when we were in the car that day."

"I know," Ashley said. "But it passed. It was nothing. Just my emotions being all mixed up with these dreams. That's all. You don't still feel that way about Dad, do you?"

Shelby hesitated. "Not really. It's Michael. Ash, what's wrong with me? Why am I suddenly feeling like this. I've known Michael practically all my life. I've never felt like this before." Shelby pressed her fists to her face.

Ashley put her arms around Shelby. "Where was Michael when he called?"

"Will didn't say. He just said that Michael was asking all sorts of questions. Saying things about Will taking good care of me and all. I don't know. What's gotten into Michael anyway? He's never cared who I dated."

"I don't know, Shel," Ashley consoled with a hug. "Michael's been acting weird ever since he and Tryn met. I'm glad Tryn's gone back to France. Maybe Michael will get back to normal." Ashley held Shelby at arm's length. "I want you to stop thinking about Michael. Do you hear me? Stop. These feelings probably have something to do with your memory loss. Who knows? Put it out of your mind. You love Will and that's all that matters."

"I do love Will," Shelby said, drying her eyes. "I never imagined how good love could feel."

Ashley smiled, hiding her misery. If only she could allow herself to feel that same kind of love. She had felt it once. That precious love she had had with Scott. She hungered for it just as strongly has she had hungered for Tryn. Just as she hungered for Michael at this very moment. The thought sickened her.

"Now pull yourself together. You don't want Will seeing you like this."

Shelby hurried upstairs to freshen her makeup while Ashley went to find Buzz. She located him in the kitchen where he was discussing an extensive redecoration of Winthrop House with Russell. Ashley had asked Buzz to send for the original furniture that he had stored on the second floor of his antique shop.

Buzz gave Ashley a big hug. "Les is green with envy that he had to stay in Chicago. He's dying to see this place."

"He can see Winthrop House when he's finished."

"So. How does it feel to have this mystery of yours solved?"

"Wonderful," she lied.

"By the way. I talked to your mother. I think I eased her mind about the journal. She understands why you told me. You and I did go through a lot." He kissed Ashley on the forehead. "I only wish you could find the happiness I see in Shelby's eyes."

"Why do you say that? I *am* happy."

Buzz smiled sadly. "I was hoping you and Blake would find each other. He cares a great deal for you. You do know that."

"I know," Ashley sighed. "It's just that . . . well, it's too soon with all that's happened. I need time."

"Of course you do."

"Miss Ashley," Russell announced. "There's a phone call for you."

"Oh, that's probably Mrs. Vance," Ashley said to Buzz. "She's one of my best customers. I invited her to see Winthrop House. She was going to call and let me know when she arrived."

"Thank you Russell," she said, taking the phone.

"Ashley," the voice said. "I've just arrived in Manchester. I'm staying at the Willow Inn."

"Michael?"

"Yes. Michael. I thought Sylina and I would join the party. We'll be there shortly. I'd advise you not to try and keep me out. You'll regret it." He hung up.

"Michael? Buzz said, overhearing.

Ashley stood frozen to the counter, the phone still in her hand.

Ashley waited nervously by the iron gate. Why was he coming here?

A few minutes later, she saw a car driving up the road.

Michael guided the car through the open gates. "Get in," he ordered.

Ashley opened the back door and slid in.

Michael drove the car up the cobblestones to Winthrop House. "This house is impressive," he said, gazing up at the stone structure. "Very impressive."

Ashley left the car. Michael and Sylina followed her up the walkway and into the entrance hall. Everyone had left the library and had gone into the gardens. Michael caught Ashley's arm.

"Show us to the Chamber," he said.

Ashley looked at Michael with an incredulous stare. "What?"

"Do it, Ashley. Now!"

Ashley felt Michael's power taking her. The desire started to swell. The dizziness. She turned and led them to the sequestered room on the third floor.

Reaching the secret panel, Michael pushed Ashley aside. He opened the panel and pulled the lever. The side of the wall released with a grinding sound. He forced Ashley into the darkness. He and Sylina followed as he closed the wall. He then reached for the lamplighter and began lighting the sconces. The room seemed to ignite.

Ashley stood huddled against the wall, terrified of what Michael was going to do. He walked toward her with a sarcastic smile, as he brought the lamplighter close to her face. She could feel its heat. Forcefully, he seized her.

She cowered against the wall. "Please," she begged. "Don't do this."

Michael extinguished the lamplight, letting it drop to the floor.

"No," she whispered, as he lowered her onto the marble floor.

She could see Sylina in the distance, a sinister grin spread across her face.

&

Victor had called everyone into the parlor. Even David Clarendon had made it to the event. His doctors warned that he was not up to making the trip but he ignored them, threatening Blake that he would make the trip alone if Blake would not accompany him. So Blake flew back to New Orleans and escorted his good friend to the infamous Winthrop House where his other good friend, Will Taylor, would be announcing his engagement. Even Mrs. Vance, who had still not recovered from seeing Winthrop House, was present. Aunt Roberta and her husband Dick, who was a pilot for TWA, had flown in late the night before and was staying at the Willow Inn.

Will and Shelby stood in front of the fireplace for the announcement.

"As some of you know," Will began, smiling down at Shelby. "I have been fortunate or unfortunate, depending on how you look at it, to have been married twice." Will looked over at David Clarendon and saw a grin working at the corners of his mouth. Will raised an eyebrow and looked away. "Frankly, I had vowed never to fall into the clutches of matrimony again. That is, until I met this lovely lady. One week ago, I decided to take my chances and ask Shelby to be my wife." Will turned to Shelby who was gazing up at him. "She said yes."

Everyone cheered as Will took Shelby's face in his hands and kissed her. Michael and Sylina were standing just inside the entrance hall and had not been noticed. Michael had a smirk spread across his face.

Ashley looked over at Blake, who was standing by David Clarendon. Their eyes met. At that moment she wanted to run to him.

"Before we go back to the drinks and hors d'oeuvre," Victor announced, "there is something I'd like to give my daughter, Shelby. He held up a small velvet box.

"Some years ago," he said to Shelby, "I gave Ashley my mother's ruby necklace. But this was also very special to my mother. I wanted you to have it on your wedding day." He took out a small gold locket. "I always thought the picture looked very much like you." He opened the face of the locket and handed it to Shelby.

Shelby stared down at the picture. Ashley was standing next to Victor and noticed the locket's design. "I know that locket," she said, taking it from Shelby.

"You do?" Shelby said, giving over the locket.

Ashley studied its gold face and pearl inlay, then looked at the picture. "This locket belonged to Jenny." she whispered. "This was the locket she gave to her baby daughter just before they took her away. I remember seeing it while I was under hypnosis."

Ashley turned to Victor. "This was Kathleen's?"

"Yes. The day she disappeared, I put it in the safe along with her ruby necklace."

"Did she know who the woman was in the picture?"

"I don't know. She said that her parents had given the locket to her as a child. You think it belonged to Jenny Winthrop?"

"I know it did. Look at this picture. There's no doubt about it. You saw the portrait in the library."

Victor studied the picture. "It didn't occur to me."

Ashley looked at Victor in amazement. "That means that Jenny Winthrop was your grandmother."

"My grandmother?"

"Yes," Ashley smiled. "Your grandmother."

Victor seemed lost for words.

"I couldn't have asked for a more wonderful wedding present," Shelby said, kissing Victor on the cheek.

"Well now," Will whispered to Ashley. "Looks like Jenny Winthrop has succeeded in making her children known."

Ashley smiled confidently.

Then it dawned on her. If Kathleen Winthrop was Jenny's daughter, then Kathleen would have been born with *The Gift*. And she would not have aged. Was it possible? Could she still be alive and look no older than she did when she disappeared? The thought of this sent chills up Ashley's spine.

"Congratulations," Michael said, walking up to Will.

Will turned to see Michael towering over him.

"I'm Michael Winthrop," he said. Michael looked at Will with an arrogant smile while placing his hand at the side of Shelby's face. Shelby looked up at Michael like a frightened child. He bent down and kissed her, clutching the back of her neck and pressing her mouth hard against his.

"So my big sister is finally settling down," he said releasing her. Shelby seemed paralyzed. Michael whispered to Will. "Remember. You had better keep her happy." And with that he turned and strode back across the parlor, tapping his walking stick.

"I apologize for our brother," Ashley said to Will. "He can be an arrogant son of a bitch."

Will forced a smile. "Think nothing of it."

Shelby put her arms around Will. "I love you," she said squeezing him tightly.

"I didn't know Michael was here," Victor said to Ashley.

ℰℴ

The gazebo was draped with garlands of baby orchids. A harpist had been hired and Louis had been coaxed to accompany at the piano.

Russell had prepared an exquisite table in the entrance hall. The servants were in full dress, the men in tuxes and the women in long white service gowns. Everyone was milling around, drinking champagne and sampling an elaborate array of hors d'oeuvre.

"I can't bear to give up Burger Boy," Roberta was saying to Shelby. "I'll never get to see him now that you're going off to live in . . . what was the name of that town?"

"Hattiesburg," Shelby said and turned to Will. "Darby and Molly aren't too excited about Shatzie coming to live with them."

Will arched his eyebrow. "My puppies are insanely jealous."

Shelby turned to Roberta. "Where's Dick?"

"Getting me a drink," Roberta replied.

"Well," Shelby informed Roberta. "I've decided to let Shatzie go and live with his Aunt Roberta and Uncle Dick."

Berta's eyes grew huge. "You don't mean it!"

"Of course I do."

"Dick." Roberta announced. "We don't have to give Shatzie back."

"I know," Dick said nonchalantly, handing Roberta her drink. He winked at Shelby.

Berta threw her arms around Dick who looked like a young Jimmy Stewart.

As the evening progressed, a few of the guests were making their farewells with elaborate praises for Winthrop House. Mrs. Vance still had not regained her composure after seeing it. She had also fallen head-over-heels for Louis.

Earlier, Louis had called Shelby into the parlor.

"Shelby," he said. "I would like to give you a small token of my love." He reached down and lifted a box from the French writing table. It was tied with a big yellow bow. "You are only too deserving to have this," he said, handing her the box.

Shelby carefully untied the bow and opened the box, lifting the statue. She turned to Louis. "Oh Louis," she sighed. "It's . . . Jenny. Isn't it?"

"Yes, Ashley gave it to me. But I would love for you to have it. I would also like for you to have some of her clothes. They would fit you perfectly."

"Thank you," and she reached up kissing his cheek. "I'll always treasure them."

"Where's David?" Ashley asked Buzz.

"I think he's in the billiard room with Blake. Come on, I'll go with you."

"That had to be the most frightening experience," Margaret was saying to David. "How long were you in that horrible place?"

"They tell me about two or three days. I'm afraid I lost all sense of time. But thanks to Shelby and Ashley I survived. Thank God Ashley wasn't seriously hurt."

Ashley smiled at David, then briefly looked toward Blake. "You look wonderful," she said to David.

"So do you," he replied.

"Ashley tells me you hypnotized her," Margaret said.

"Why, yes," he said, looking up at Ashley. "She was having trouble sleeping. Bad dreams mostly." He smiled at Margaret. "It only took a couple of sessions. She's as good as new."

Ashley smiled nervously, then looked over at Blake who was standing at the far end of the couch. She could tell by the look on his face that he was wondering why she hadn't told him about knowing David.

"Your Winthrop House is spectacular," David commented to Ashley.

"Mmm?" Ashley said, not taking her eyes from Blake. "I'm sorry," she said, "What did you say?"

David smiled. "I said that your Winthrop House was spectacular."

"Oh. Yes. It is, isn't it. But it's Louis', not mine."

"That's not what Louis tells me," Buzz intervened.

Ashley didn't respond, but instead walked over to Blake. "Can we talk?" she asked, touching his arm.

Blake looked hard into Ashley's face. "I don't think so. There's really nothing left to say. Besides, it's getting late. I should take David back to the Inn. We have an early flight in the morning." Blake then placed his hand gently on the side of Ashley's face. He looked at her as if studying her every feature. Ashley reached up and cupped her hand around his. Blake pulled his hand away and went to David.

Ashley felt as though she would crumble into a million pieces. She had been so certain. Positive that Blake loved her. Had she pushed him too far? Was he now out of reach?

David and Blake were saying their good-byes. David went to Ashley, thanking her for asking him and making her promise to visit him when she was in New Orleans. She watched as the two men left the room.

"What's the matter, precious?" she heard Buzz say.

"The matter? Nothing." She smiled, looking over at Buzz.

"I don't believe you."

Ashley reached up and patted Buzz's broad chest. "I'll be fine. You don't have to worry about me any longer." She kissed him on the cheek. "Why don't you go and find Stanley. He's dying to talk shop with you. I need to talk to Michael."

"What's gotten into Michael anyway? He's acting like a son-of-a-bitch."

Ashley just shook her head. "Who knows."

"Who knows?" Buzz said and turned Ashley to face him. His eyes narrowed. "Are you certain DeLore has gone back to France?"

Ashley looked Buzz square in the eyes. "He's gone." And with that she turned and left the room.

Michael and Sylina were standing outside on the walkway, talking to Victor. Sylina had her arm around Michael, her expression: superiority and arrogance.

How could Sylina have turned into this monster? Ashley thought. Worse yet, how could Ashley have allowed herself to weaken as she had, falling into their lust? The thought of it repulsed her as well as excited her.

"Did Ashley tell you?" she heard Michael say to Victor. "I've bought DeLore house."

Victor was studying Michael. "Yes. And it looks like that's not all you bought from the man." Ashley could see Victor staring at the gold-handled walking stick. Then Victor lifted Michael's left hand and commented on the ring. "I've never known you to like rings." he said, releasing his hand.

"This is not just any ring," Michael replied with arrogance. "It's very old." A cryptic smirk then crossed his face. "I'd say it's priceless."

Ashley walked up beside Victor.

"Ashley," Michael said, tapping his stick on the walkway. "You'll never guess who I ran into while in London last week." He looked at Ashley as if waiting for a response and gave a sardonic laugh. "None other than Scott Trudeau. Seems he's getting married. And you won't believe it. Her name is Dolores Winthrop. Can you beat that?"

The moonlight gives the reassurance
of familiar landmarks
until a line cloud from the southwest,
black as a cape, occults the moon
and darkness crosses the road,
the lid of a sarcophagus sliding shut.

john p. freeman, "Night Vision" from
Standing on My Father's Grave (Singular Speech
Press, 1995).

Epilogue

1992

A shley drove up the winding roads of Belvedere, the memory of that first journey embedded deep in her mind. She could almost see Maurice, his black chauffeur's cap perched squarely on his head, with his proper yet aloof manner. She still remembered their words.

"Have you been with Mr. DeLore a long time?"

"Yes," he had answered.

How long? she had often wondered.

Michael had grown increasingly twisted and vile these past five years, as had Sylina. Michael's powerful influence had consumed her. She had become as evil and narcissistic as he had.

Ashley's thoughts went to Christina, her precious daughter. Her and Michael's daughter. She closed her eyes in anger. The thought of Michael putting his hands on Christina enraged her. Michael had tortured Ashley from the moment Christina was born. He had relished his miserable game, describing in detail how he would take Christina's virginity as soon as she was ripe for the taking.

"Mademoiselle," Maurice said, opening the front door. She saw Michael standing at the foot of the staircase.

"How pathetic you look," he said as she approached. "Wipe that distraught look off your beautiful face. Too bad Sylina is in London, she so loves to participate in our sessions."

Ashley ignored this. She forced herself to concentrate on why she was there, not let Michael distract her with his arrogance. She knew Sylina was in London and Michael would be alone.

Ashley kept her eyes on the walking stick as she followed Michael up the winding staircase, remembering Christopher's words. *The gold handle of the walking stick that Michael now carries, turn it counter clockwise and lift it from its shaft. You will see that attached to it is a small diamond blade. This is your only weapon.*

"So tell me, how is our Shelby these days? Still playing wife to that pathetic mortal?" he laughed. "At least you had the good sense not to marry Blake Sheldon, just fuck him."

Ashley squeezed her hands into fists and continued walking.

"We will be a while," Michael called back to Maurice. "And by no means do I want to be disturbed."

Maurice nodded. Ashley thought she saw a smile rise on his lips.

The sconces were lit, casting those eerie shadows Ashley had never forgotten when she and Tryn had first climbed those stairs. Tryn had been just as arrogant, just as beautiful, and just as alluring as Michael was now.

Each step she took drew her closer to unthinkable horror. But it was a horror Michael was forcing her to commit. As they passed through the sitting area, Ashley reached out and touched the empty space where Jenny's statue had once stood.

"Stop your sentiments," Michael scoffed, noticing this. "Maybe you need to make a little visit to the fourth floor. Take a look at those pathetic mortal women lying in their coffins. It's a strengthening experience."

Ashley cringed at the thought.

Michael saw her revulsion. "You are almost as pathetic as *they* are." He opened the bedroom door, dramatically flinging it aside.

"My beautiful Ashley. Consider yourself fortunate." He reached out to her. "Come here," he demanded, forcing her to him, their faces only inches apart. Michael smiled as if reveling in the pleasure of lusting after his own sister. Incest was the ultimate obsession. It strengthened one's passion and made for a stronger lineage.

"Is that baby still growing inside Shelby's belly?" Michael smirked.

Ashley struggled to keep her mind focused.

"You pathetic little fool," he laughed. "Did you really think I'd leave Shelby to that weakling of a husband?"

Michael's words came at her with such force that a stunned look of horror shadowed her face.

"I will wager," he boasted, "that the child inside her is a true Winthrop. Strong and beautiful in its evil." Michael smiled deep into Ashley's eyes. "Shelby's sexual appetite is delicious. She surrendered to me completely."

Violently Michael pressed his mouth on Ashley's.

"Monsieur," Maurice called.

Michael looked up with a start. He glared at Maurice. "What is it!"

"You have a visitor, sir."

"I TOLD you! I do not want to be disturbed!" Michael raged.

It was then that she appeared, as though she had simply materialized. Michael released Ashley with a gasp. His face grew suddenly pale. Ashley turned, frightened at what she might see.

The figure seemed to glide across the floor. Her appearance was so startling that neither Michael nor Ashley could speak. As the figure drew closer, Ashley realized that it was a woman. She was incredibly tall, several inches taller than Michael. Her hair, the color of liquid gold, glistened within the movement of the lamplight. Her beauty was surreal. She moved toward Michael without so much as a glance toward Ashley. Her eyes were focused intently on him. As she passed, Ashley felt a surge of bitter cold. *And then the evil.* Slowly it churned, like a heavy muck, swirling around her.

"Michael Winthrop," the woman intoned. Her voice sounded as though the words had long since been spoken. Stopping within inches of him, the woman lifted her hand to Michael's face. Slowly she grazed his cheek with her fingertips. Ashley cautiously moved away, noticing the floor length dress the woman was wearing. It was a deep crimson velvet with heavy embroidery. The neckline was cut deep, revealing the woman's full breasts and porcelain-smooth skin. Ashley suddenly felt that she had stepped back a dozen centuries as she gazed at the woman, marveling at her beauty. Her face appeared to be in perfect symmetry, like an expertly cut diamond.

Michael flinched at the woman's touch as he looked into her deep aqua eyes. They seemed to harbor dark secrets and a wealth of knowledge. She appeared to be looking not at him, or through him—rather inside him.

"Who . . . who are you!" he cried.

The woman smiled slowly.

"I am *Tryn DeLore*," she replied, as Michael pressed his hands to his face. He staggered, then fell against the doorway. Struggling, he turned, half running, half stumbling into the bedroom. He grew deathly silent as he raised his eyes toward the large beveled mirror that hung over the fireplace. Trembling, he stared into the mirror, horrified. And there, staring back at him, he saw his once-beautiful face decay, line by line, into a sunken portrait of himself. His full lips withered around his teeth. His cerulean eyes darkened and receded deep into his skull, now draped in long strands of yellowish-white hair. He glared into the mirror as if unable to conceive its horror. Michael then lurched forward and fell to his knees. Slowly, his body trembling, he reached out toward the woman. She smiled as one would when comforting a helpless child. But she did not go to him at once. She turned to Ashley, who stood paralyzed, remembering Christopher's warning. The DeLore's vengeance will have become stronger, and possibly culminated into a superior evil. I assure you, such an evil will destroy your youth, as surely as I am now destroyed.

"Go now," the woman said in that distant voice. "Go, leave DeLore House." She turned and entered the bedroom, closing the door behind her.

"How pathetic," Ashley heard the woman say to Michael as she broke into a rage of laughter.

Maurice escorted a shaken Ashley through the sitting room. They descended the winding staircase.

As Ashley drove back down the driveway and through the iron gates, she looked back to DeLore House. It seemed to shrink, then fade into the fog.

She could feel her heart pounding, her hands clammy. She couldn't think. All she could see was that incredible woman.

Tryn DeLore?

Her presence was still blinding Ashley's thoughts. The sight of Michael's face was embedded in her memory.

Tryn DeLore. She ran the name through her mind again. Where had the woman come from? Then she remembered the smile on Maurice's face. He had announced this woman seemingly without fear. Had she been in the house when Ashley first arrived? Had Maurice known all along that she would be there? Did he know her?

But then, what did that matter now? Tryn DeLore or whoever the woman was had succeeded in destroying Michael. It was done. And Michael's destruction would not be on Ashley's hands. She must now go to Shelby. The thought of Shelby carrying Michael's child sickened her. What a fool she had been to believe that Michael would keep their bargain. She had kept their filthy bargain, had succumbed to him at his beck and call. And he had promised to leave Shelby alone. But bargaining with Michael was like bargaining with the devil himself. There *were* no bargains. She could not allow Shelby to carry this child to term. She had to find a way to stop the evil.

London, she thought. She would go to London. To Nine Thornton Square. She had to learn more about this evil. Where, in God's name had it come from? She had to understand more fully its weaknesses, its strengths. Only then would she have any hope of destroying it.

Suddenly a thought seized her. Christopher had used the name Tryn DeLore as deception to gain reentry into Winthrop House. But why had Nicholas Winthrop chose to use the name? Why had Leopold, the man who obviously ruled the Winthrop family allowed this? Weren't the Winthrops and DeLores supposed to be bitter enemies? Had Leopold not warned they may have culminated into a superior evil? And why had this woman, Tryn DeLore, allowed her to leave DeLore House without harm?

Who *was* this person? This Tryn DeLore?

CR

~And Now~

Allow yourself a glimpse into the Winthrop's

Evil Legacy

CR

Prologue

"Get them out of my sight!" Leopold stormed, flinging his gold handle walking stick toward the door. Take them to the dungeon and cast them into the furnace."

The spindly man trembled as he stood in the massive doorway, perspiration inching down his face. The blood from his hands dripped silently, as he struggled to hide his fear.

"Yes, my lord," he answered, bowing, and lifting his bloody hands. "Your wishes are mine." He looked briefly toward Leopold who was a good twelve inches taller.

"You obsequious little fool," Leopold sneered. "Be silent. I am not interested in your ingratiating mutterings." He then glared deep into the man's nervous eyes. "And be warned. Carlotta is never to give birth again. Do what you must, but do it well." Leopold reached out and gathered the trembling man by the shirt. "If you dare to disobey me, I will send YOU into the furnace."

"Yes my lord," the man answered with great trepidation as he looked up into Leopold's beautiful face. Not even the distortion of anger and rage could mar the perfect symmetry of this extraordinary face.

Leopold suddenly released his hold, sending the man almost crashing to the floor.

"Carlotta will pay a price for her deception," he seethed, looking toward the half-conscious girl who lay near lifeless upon the blood-soaked bed, her dark hair fanned around her. Leopold looked back down at his servant with a maniacal glare. "Cut out her reproductive organs and close up her sex. She is never to bear children nor satiate her passion again. And be quick about it," he ordered slamming the heavy door behind him.

The man stood motionless for several moments. Then he turned. "Tie her to the bed," he ordered to the two women servants who stood horrified. "Are you deaf!" he screamed. "You heard what the master said."

"But Bernie," one of the women protested.

Bernie looked anxiously into the woman's distraught face. "We must carry this out." He looked briefly toward the other woman, then lowered his gaze. "We have no choice." He then gathered his satchel. "Molly," he ordered. "You and Sadie tie her wrists and ankles. I will do this as quickly as I am capable."

Leopold stood by the stone arches, looking out into the fog-draped night. Off in the distance a faint glow emerged. Another merchant ship, he mused, eager for wine and olive oil. He listened intently. Within moments Carlotta's screams echoed into the night.

A smile graced Leopold's lips. He lifted his head and breathed deeply.

"It is not finished."

reface

Zeus, god of gods, stood in his palace, which lay at the center of the universe and beheld a moral deterioration. His divine creation had toppled into the depths of sin and destruction.

"I offer you divine love," he had said, as he first molded man and woman from the elements of the universe. "I also offer great knowledge. As your home, I give to you a vast and abundant land. Upon this land I have placed mighty oceans, flowing rivers and fertile soil ready for cultivating. Go, my children, be fruitful and multiply. Fill your land from the fruits of your loins, and live in righteousness."

And so was the genesis of mortal man. Molded by God and blessed with his love.

But as time progressed, corruption, greed and deception wove into the very depths of their souls. Mortals had now proven incapable of righteousness. Divine love had crumbled and diminished.

Zeus pondered this dilemma with great sadness. He had not considered that the seeds of evil would be so powerful as to corrupt the divinity of his creation.

Should he banish his children from the face of the earth?

This dilemma was a tremendous burden, so he gathered the other gods and goddesses around him and debated the issue. After much discussion a decision was forthcoming.

Mortals would not be destroyed. They would be left to their own destruction.

But Zeus had grown weary in his failure to create a divine race. He deliberated this failure and reached a final judgment. Since the elements of the universe were too infiltrated with the powers of evil, Zeus decided to send a god and goddess to live upon the earth and propagate.

Poseidon, lord of the sea and god of earthquakes, and Aphrodite, the goddess of love and beauty, were chosen and received a magnificent island which lay west of the Pillars of Hercules in the Atlantic Ocean. It was larger than Asia Minor and Libya combined. It was an island the size of a continent.

It was *Atlantis*.

Aphrodite and Poseidon soon had their first child. They called him Trynathian. But then a strange occurrence took place. Aphrodite found that she was no longer able to conceive. It had been eight or more years and had become painfully evident that there would be no more children.

Word soon reached Zeus that the marriage between God and Goddess was producing only one child. Zeus again pondered failure. He agonized over this as he continued to watch mortal man and woman fall deeper and deeper into sin. But it was not until his divine children betrayed him that he was forced to bear the ultimate pain of despair.

In order to continue their family, Poseidon and Aphrodite took mortals as their mates. Aphrodite had traveled to Greece where she fell in love and remained there, never to return to Atlantis again. Poseidon went to Portugal where he met a woman named Cleito. She was of great wealth and possessed royal blood. In a matter of weeks they fell in love. Poseidon whisked her away to his paradise of Atlantis where he built her a magnificent gold palace high upon a mountain top in the center of the island.

To insure protection of his beloved wife, he surrounded the palace with five concentric rings of water and land. Two were of land, and three of sea water. He carved these rings with the effortless ease of a god, thus creating an inner island for their palace. Poseidon commanded warm and cold springs to bubble from the earth, for he vowed that his descendants would never lack for water.

Poseidon's son, Trynathian, was given a large piece of land to the east where he would rule as King. He too fell in love with a mortal woman.

Atlantis, through the years, grew in population, and the remaining land was eventually divided between families. The royal family of Atlantis had, at long last, emerged.

Generations after generations Atlantis flourished in peace and prosperity. It was inexplicably a divine kingdom. Its mines and forests, its vast pasture lands and streams were abundant. Wild animals roamed plentifully, and freely in deep forests. Anything that was not provided by the fruitful earth was imported.

Atlantis had now grown in wealth and influence, its rule extended to many other islands until it reached as far as Italy and Egypt. However, the polluted seeds of mortal man had now seeped into the righteous souls of the Atlantians. Poseidon and Trynathian's marriages to mortal woman had spawned a lineage of impurity. But the ultimate travesty was the unforeseen influence this impurity had upon God's divine children.

Through time, Poseidon and Trynathian had been influenced by these impurities and had become ambitious and greedy. Aphrodite, too, had suffered the same deterioration and was now engulfed in self love. She had reigned over all of Greece for many centuries as their goddess of love and beauty. Adored and worshipped and feared. She possessed, not only seductive love and extraordinary beauty, but eternal youth.

Poseidon and Trynathian too, possessed youth eternal and beauty beyond expression. And these extraordinary traits were all that stood between them and mortal man. For they had fallen into the clutches of sin and corruption.

Soon a great war was launched by the people of Atlantis. Their armies were to attack cities in Europe and Asia. Their goal: to conquer the Mediterranean world. The land now called Italy was gravely threatened. Libya fell before them and became captive. Greece and Egypt braced themselves for invasion. However, it was the ancient Athenians, ruled by their narcissus Goddess Aphrodite who had taken the brunt of the invasion. But with valiant courage and military skill, they led an alliance of Greeks, overpowering the Atlantians and saving themselves as well as the Egyptians from slavery.

It was not until days later that the reason behind the Athenians counter attack and ultimate betrayal was learned. After what looked like a triumph for the Atlantians that day, they became passive and overconfident of their conquest. Trynathian, out of incestuous love for his mother, Aphrodite, and his overpowering greed for power, betrayed his father. Poseidon and his men were caught in a surprise attack forcing defeat.

Zeus's sorrow had now reached insurmountable heights. He stood in the very center of his palace, lifted his mighty arms and cried out in agony. His tears flowed like melting glaciers then rushed with an overwhelming force. His mighty roar shook the universe.

The earthquakes and floods were so devastating that most Athenians were swept to their death. Then, almost within seconds, the island of Atlantis was also struck by a violent earthquake. Within a span of one day and one night, so devastating were the floods that Atlantis was swallowed up by the sea and vanished. Not a trace of this once magnificent island remained.

An Evil Legacy
Book 1
Prequel to DeLore's Confession

On that fateful day, 9,000 years b.c., all of Atlantis was lost, and most of Athínai. Among the survivors were Poseidon, Aphrodite, and Trynathian. The three found themselves next to a jagged cliff, the sea still angry and pounding violently. Suddenly, the earth around them seemed to dry, becoming parched and cracked. The wind swirled with great force, sucking the dust from the hot earth. A tremendous flash lit up the sky and pierced through the black clouds, driving a pointed bolt into the earth. Within seconds it had vanished. Left in its wake and lying within the dust were two crudely assembled leather books, two gold rings with heads of a Jaguar cat and piercing ruby eyes. Along side the gold rings were two gold handled walking canes. They too with heads of the Jaguar cat.

Poseidon reached down with trembling hands and lifted one of the books from the parched earth.

It read:

My sorrow is beyond your capability to understand. It is everlasting. I weep even now as you read my words. Your punishment is also everlasting. Only in death is there hope of release.

My children, you have forsaken me beyond forgiveness. You have allowed obsessive ambition, greed, betrayal and lust disease your souls. Souls that had once been pure and clean. You have allowed yourselves to fall into the depths of sin. And sin is where you shall remain. Righteousness is now your nemesis. Love your enemy. As the sunlight destroys the undead, so shall love destroy you.

Poseidon, I have placed bitter hatred in your heart toward your son, Trynathian. You will never again feel the slightest emotion of love for him. Obsession and lust will serve you now. Lust for sexual pleasures will torture you as will your obsession for beauty and youth. And be warned, you fall victim to pure love and you will wither and decay in a most agonizing death.

Trynathian, you will forever endure an overwhelming love for your father and become tortured by his rejection. Likewise, you will become increasingly plagued by the incestuous love you hold for your mother. Again I warn you, as it is with your father, give into love and face death. It is only the love for your father that is not forbidden.

Aphrodite, your destiny will be an eternal love for Poseidon as well as Trynathian. A love you will never experience in return. For Trynathian could not survive if he weakened and fled into your arms. Poseidon will detest the very mention of the word, only be bound to you by an overwhelming lust. His obsession for you will only strengthen his vanity. You will burn with obsession for this eternal youth and beauty, and the insatiable need to be loved and adored. It will never leave you. Never. As for the children that you bear with Poseidon, they will be both male and female. If you chose to bear children with mortal man, they will all be females and too possess this evil Gift. The females will not be drawn to other males until their virginity is taken by another with this evil. Only then will they be free to love.

Now, my children, I will offer you a choice: This Gift of evil, of eternal youth and beauty, or death, and in death, forgiveness.

Sickened by the horror of it, Aphrodite cried out, "I will NEVER choose death."

"I fear not this evil *Gift*." Trynathian roared. "Never will I chose death over eternal youth."

Poseidon was the last to answer. He looked up into the heavens, his face stern. "Life!" he cried. "Never death!" and he lowered his eyes back to the parchment and continued to read

My sons, if you have made your final decision to accept this evil Gift, then you must follow these instructions. Go and look deep into your reflection. And with great passion utter these words. For if you lack the passion the Gift will not pass to you, and you will age and die.

My beautiful, my desirable, my eternal countenance

Take from me goodness and righteousness
Spare me the antipathy of its destiny
Bind my soul with your iniquity
I stand before you in absolute submission
I implore you
Come into me!
Come into me!
Come into me!

You must look into your reflection and recite these words often
Aphrodite, your passion will flow into your female children for
eternity. They will, as you, have no need to recite these words. THE
GIFT will be theirs, never to age past the year twenty-six. But it will
be different for the males. Upon their twenty-sixth year their father's
or another male of the same evil will be bound to reveal and offer
them THE GIFT. They will be helpless to resist.

The fiery eyes of the Jaguar ring will stoke the fires of evil,
while the walking stick guides you along its treacherous path. The
Jaguar cat is a cunning predator. You will become that predator.
Jealousy and greed will forever lurk within your souls and the
souls of your offspring's. This will always pose a threat within your
family. Though mortal man can not harm you, your own are quite
capable.

My children, I now bid you farewell.
You have been the ultimate betrayal.

It was a laborious journey back through the ruins of Athinai. The earth had shaken so violently that it utterly lay in ruins. Except for the palace where Aphrodite had reigned for many centuries. It stood untouched. The lavish waterfalls flowed undisturbed into the fountain as though the city had not been ravished by the hands of God.

As they entered the palace Aphrodite turned to Trynathian. "I will not send you away empty handed," she said with longing in her eyes. "And it will be impossible for you to stay." She then turned to Poseidon. "I am giving our son half of my wealth. The rest will be ours," and she walked into the palace. Poseidon did not respond. When Aphrodite returned, carrying a large satchel filled with priceless jewels, she found Poseidon kneeling by the fountain. She rushed to him in protest saying that Trynathian would be the first to read the words, imploring *The Gift*

Poseidon knew that there would be a great confrontation if he tried to keep his son from taking *The Gift* first and closed his book. Trynathian then took his book and knelt by the fountain. Within minutes, he was repeating the words with an overwhelming passion, for his reflection was that of a decaying being. But as he recited the words, it began to revive, becoming once again, youthful and extraordinarily beautiful. It was then he heard his mother speak.

"Do not turn to me," she said. "I have placed your cane and the gold ring next to you. Take them, along with the satchel, and leave the palace. Remember always God's warning. You must never come to me or your father again."

Trynathian was suddenly stricken by the powerful love he was feeling for his mother and father, but withdrew in horror, remembering the decay he had, only moments before, seen upon his face. Trynathian fled from the palace.

Poseidon then knelt and beheld the same horror as his reflection appeared in the water. He too spoke the words with an overwhelming passion, then rose from the fountain as though he had been given new life. The sensation swelled inside him. He felt a strength so powerful that it took a moment to fully comprehend it. The clouds above him looked ominous and dark. In the distance silent flashes of light appeared then disappeared while the heavens rumbled with thunder. Poseidon lifted his face and roared with laughter, then turned to Aphrodite. He reached out and took her by the arm, forcing her into his embrace.

Poseidon and Aphrodite reigned over all of Greece for many centuries. Their wealth was so vast that it was no longer comprehensible. They owned a palace in Sintra, Portugal and a grand mansion in London, England. In the early fifteen hundreds they left Greece for their palace in Portugal, leaving their home in Greece to what family was left. A family forever ravished with greed and jealously and threatened by the powers of love. Less than a century later their children had all fallen to destruction. Only memories were left of this once royal family, and through time became legend then myth. The mighty God and Goddess, along with their family had faded deep into mythical history.

Poseidon and Aphrodite had since shared their time between Sintra and London. Upon their arrival in Sintra they had changed their names to Madeline and Leopold Winthrop, living quietly and discreetly in their lavish palace overlooking the Atlantic where their magnificent island of

Atlantis had once stood. They were now possessed with the obsession of creating a strong and eternal lineage, determined that the forces of greed, jealously and love would not be their children's destruction as it had in the past. Leopold would guard his family vengefully from these influences. His insatiable desire for Madeline aligned with her deep love for him produced many children. Leopold rained with an iron fist. Several of his children were brutally slain by his own hand when their plans to flee the clutches of their family were discovered. The others, however, found abundant pleasure through incest and self love accompanied by their great wealth, and had become indifferent toward mortals. Mortal man was their servant, fulfilling whatever purpose they desired. They lived within their opulent palace indulging in narcissism, incest, and the love for power.

Leopold and Madeline had, at long last, succeeded. They had molded their children into their own creation. Strong and powerful and eternal. But Leopold would soon learn what he had often feared. His son, Trynathian, who too, had gathered great wealth, had arrived in Sintra and was building a magnificent palace just to the north. At first Leopold did not know it was Trynathian. He too had changed his name. He called himself Tryn DeLore.

Leopold discovered that after Trynathian had left them that final day and journeyed north, he had come upon his daughter, Melana. She had, years before, left Atlantis to be with the man she professed to love. Trynathian had forbidden this, but she fled the island late one night with the help of two of the servants. Trynathian had not laid eyes on her again until then. The very sight of her threw him into a rage of lust and anger. The incestuous passion he was experiencing was consuming, and he forced her with him. For thirty years he held Melana prisoner to bear his children. But as the years passed, so did her youth. At the age of forty-eight, Tryn DeLore took the life of his daughter. He placed her in a glass-top coffin and hid it away in the dungeon of his palace in France. He frequently visited the coffin to view her decayed body. This was a constant reminder of the consequences he would ultimately face if he weakened and fell into the destructive forces of love.

Through the centuries, Tryn had remained knowledgeable of his mother's and father's whereabouts. The deep love he carried for his father had not waned, and the forbidden love for his mother, though still with him, was kept at bay out of fear.

Tryn also had been forced to live a discreet and secretive life for fear of discovery. He, like his father, did not want to be feared as one might fear or detest a freak, or be looked upon and whispered about as though he were suspected of evil doings. They both demanded respect and admiration. And they had managed this, though there was and would continue to be a display of uncertainty and caution among the mortals. But suspicion and rumors would rear then fall along with mortal man. And as the world's population grew, the Winthrops and DeLores receded further into obscurity.

But Tryn had not been successful in creating a strong lineage as had his father, Leopold. Tryn's offspring's had been born of mortal woman. Tryn's daughter, Melana, had not possessed *The Gift*. Their children were dangerously vulnerable to the outside influences of mortal man. All of Tryn's sons had fallen into love's destructive force. And his daughters had taken their own lives, incapable of living with the centuries of grief and sorrow as their mortal loves grew older, succumbing to death.

Tryn was now left with loneliness, despair, and a voracious love for his mother and father. He knew that if he acted on the love for his mother it would destroy him. But the insatiable hunger he felt for his father was not forbidden and had to be fed. So he plotted, if not to win his father's love, to satiate himself with his flesh. He left his mansion in France and journeyed to Portugal. His plan of seduction would begin.

Tryn slowly pulled his father into his web of lust and passion. Leopold's hatred toward his son lay in shadow as the evil force of sexual greed consumed them. Leopold would go to Tryn's palace often. It was there one night when Tryn showed his father the decayed remains of his daughter, Melana, who he had transported from his mansion in France. Tryn explained how the grotesque sight strengthened his vanity. Leopold felt the same surge of strength as he too beheld this, but berated Tryn, calling him a fool to believe that he could have produced a strong lineage with a mortal woman.

Many centuries had now passed. Tryn could see the pleasure in his father's face, knowing that his son would never succeed at creating a strong lineage. Leopold had pure evil within his own family. Tryn knew it would never be offered to him. His only hope was his mother. He knew, though, that he would be at great risk. The incestuous love for his mother was still with him. But his arrogance and obsession for immortality had strengthened. He would have to rely on that strength.

One night while Leopold was away, Tryn went to Madeline. It was torturous for them to behold each other, but their plan was set. Madeline chose her daughter, Carlotta, to bear Tryn's children. Madeline warned

Carlotta that if she ever divulged her mother's betrayal to Leopold she would have her killed. If and when Leopold realized that Carlotta was with Tryn and not simply missing, she must profess her love for Tryn. *She* was to carry the deceit, not her mother. And so it was. Carlotta went with Tryn. Within only weeks she had fallen deeply in love while Tryn fell into a lustful passion of desire. His obsessive passion for Carlotta saved him from loving her. But two weeks before she was to give birth, she was betrayed.

Rosalyne, one of Carlotta's many sister's, who had been banished into servility because of her inexplicable lack of beauty, harbored insane jealously for her beautiful sisters. Carlotta, unaware of this jealously, had confided to the obsequious Rosalyne that she was in love with Tryn and was fleeing the palace to be with him. She could not reveal to Rosalyne that it was, in truth, her mother who was forcing her to go. So Rosalyne, to gain favor with Leopold, waited until a few weeks before the birth, then told him of Carlotta's betrayal.

Discovering this, Leopold ordered Carlotta's reproductive organs cut from her body and her sex closed. She would never again bear children nor indulge in sexual pleasures. Rosalyne, fearful that Carlotta suspected her betrayal, fled Winthrop Palace late one night. Leopold was outraged at learning that he had lost a family servant. You see, for the past five centuries, disturbingly aware that a muted gene lay in wait, rearing its head indiscriminately and producing inferior offspring's, Leopold had banished these mutants to a life of subserviency and ignorance of their true heritage. They knew nothing more than that they had been orphaned at birth and had been taken in by the great Leopold Winthrop, saving them from a life of poverty. Leopold now had a sufficient number of these mutants to serve the needs of his superior though sequestered family.

As soon as Carlotta was physically able, she too fled Winthrop Palace. Leopold searched endlessly but with no success. His failure to find his Judas daughter forever raged inside him.

That night when Leopold had learned of Carlotta's pregnancy and had taken her from Tryn's palace, he found that Tryn was away and would not be returning until the next night. Leopold lay in wait for Tryn. As Tryn entered the palace gates, Leopold thrust the diamond blade of his walking stick deep into his son's chest. Tryn's last words to Leopold were: "Father, forgive me." Leopold was stunned momentarily by this. He then gathered Tryn in his arms as he felt a glimmer of remorse rush through him. It was then that the bitter hatred withdrew and Leopold was overcome with an insatiable love accompanied by unbearable sorrow. He could feel God's words speaking to him.

'Your hatred now turns to eternal sorrow. The hell of despair will forever torture your soul.'

Leopold carried Tryn to the bedchamber. A trail of blood marked their journey. He laid Tryn on the massive bed, stripped him of his clothes and washed him, then dressed him in fresh clothing. Afterward he went to the servants and told them that their master had suffered heart failure. The next day Leopold returned with a glass top coffin, laying his son to rest in the chamber that stood center inside Winthrop Palace. This chamber was where his male descendants went to receive *The Gift*. It was lavishly groomed with mural walls and heavy fabrics. The chamber stood in a vacuum free of time's deterioration. Leopold placed his son's coffin in front of the enormous fireplace which stood just under a large gilt-framed mirror. Trynathian would remain there throughout eternity. His youthful beauty radiating behind the glass. Leopold fell to his knees amid sobs, his arms embracing the coffin.

Madeline too was tortured by the loss of her son, knowing that it was her betrayal that had brought about the tragedy. She should have never agreed to see Trynathian that day. And never should have allowed him to take Carlotta. The thought of her threat to Carlotta sickened her. How she could have said such words to her daughter seemed incomprehensible now. But she knew it was the fear of Leopold and his wrath if he learned of the betrayal. A thought suddenly crossed her mind. Would God also plague Leopold with an overpowering love for *her* if he were to take her life? But the thought was absurd and quickly vanished.

Years later Winthrop Palace received a visitor. The boy said his name was Maurice and that he had been informed he might find employment at Winthrop Palace.

Leopold was strangely intrigued by Maurice as well as who might have suggested he seek employment at Winthrop Palace. Maurice revealed that he had befriended a man some years back while in France. That the man had spoken often of the great Winthrop Palace. Through the years, he had lost touch with him, but the endless rumors flourished about the great Palace. Maurice told Leopold that he had been in the service of a family in Toulouse for several years. The head of the family had long since died, leaving only an elderly lady and her son. He continued by saying that the lady had recently died and her son had sold the estate. The son's departure had left him in dire need of employment. Leopold had not taken an outsider into his employment for centuries, yet he was finding himself entertaining the notion. After researching Maurice's story, satisfying himself of Maurice's credibility, he brought the boy into his employment.

As the months passed, Leopold grew more and more drawn to Maurice. Maurice was a beautiful boy in his early twenties with soft yet strong features. Beholding this boy was a disturbing sensation that Leopold could not quiet discern, and he found that he was becoming more and more distrustful of Maurice. Yet, he could not find it within himself to send the boy away. His obsession for Maurice had become too great. So great that the thought of this boy's beauty ebbing into decay caused an even deeper obsession. Knowing that it was only a matter of time before the decay of age would claim Maurice, he satiated himself with the young boy while watching his youth slowly yet determinedly leave his body.

Not understanding the rampant obsession he still bore for Maurice and overcome with grief and horror of what fifty-five years had done to this once beautiful man, he took Maurice into *The Chamber*. Leopold placed the Jaguar ring on Maurice's little finger, handed him the walking stick and told him to stand on the Winthrop crest and look into the mirror. But Maurice's eyes could not let go of the sight he beheld in the glass-top coffin. Leopold ordered Maurice to take his eyes from Tryn and into his own reflection. The sight sent Maurice staggering.

Leopold reached out and grabbed his arm. "Do you want to capture your lost youth forever?" he asked.

Maurice turned to Leopold with an incredulous glare.

"Do you!" Leopold raved.

Maurice looked back to the mirror. "Yes!" he answered. "Yes!"

Leopold handed Maurice the scroll, ordering him to read it with great passion. He then stood back in fear and with great anticipation as Maurice read. As the last words left his lips, Leopold stood, glaring into Maurice's face. Seconds passed, even minutes. Maurice looked back into the mirror with great trepidation. But the decaying form he had moments ago witnessed had vanished. Maurice again looked into the face of a fifty-five year old man.

Leopold bowed his head in defeat, though he knew his experiment was doomed to failure. How could he have expected otherwise. This evil *Gift* was designed only for a lineage of evils. Maurice was not of that ilk.

The years passed in rapid succession. It was now the early 1600's. Leopold and Madeline, along with most of their family decided to journey to their home in London at Nine Thornton Square. Leopold agonized over whether to take the coffin of his dead son with them. Madeline begged him not to leave Trynathian behind. So Tryn's body was transported from *The Chamber* of Winthrop Palace to *The Chamber* of Nine Thornton Square in London England. It was during that journey that one of Leopold's sons, Andrew, professed his desire to venture to the east coast of the New World and build a great mansion. He detailed to Leopold his vision of what this grand house would look like. That he would place it facing southeast and overlooking the mighty Atlantic where the great island of Atlantis had once stood. Andrew's wishes were eventually granted and he left for the new world with two of his sisters. He took Maurice as his servant. Andrew would build a magnificent structure. He would call it Winthrop House. And the Winthrop legacy would continue.

In 1790 Leopold and Madeline embarked on a long journey down through the Atlantic past the Canary Islands, the Brazil Basin, the Argentine Basin, around Cape Horn through Drake Passage and Northward into the Pacific toward the eastern coast of North America. After months and months of travel and treacherous seas they came upon the Farallon Islands and knew that San Francisco Bay was within reach. It was upon entering the bay that they spotted what they later would call, Belvedere (*beautiful to see* in Italian). This is where Leopold and Madeline would build a shrine to their son Trynathian. They would call it *DeLore House*.

The building of DeLore House was arduous. Only the finest materials were imported from around the world. This magnificent French and Italian piece of architecture took twelve long years to build. After completion, Madeline and Leopold occupied DeLore House, decorating it with lavish furnishings. One year later, Madeline gave birth to twin sons. Two years later a daughter. In 1834 they left their children and DeLore House to return to England. Leopold's departing words were that of caution:

"Stay true to your own kind and you will have a strong and everlasting lineage. Fall into the hands of mortal love and be destroyed. Guard DeLore House with your immortal souls."

Chapter Two
1835

adeline stood by the tall windows of Nine Thornton Square and watched the fog drift slowly past the lamplight below. How ominous, she thought, this eerie mass, churning and moving at will through the streets of London so utterly unattainable. How she longed to move like the fog, feel the joyous freedom as she walked through the busy parks, the lush gardens. She wanted to be seen. To be admired and worshipped. As it once had been. She wanted to be *Queen.*

Turning from the window, her mind still drifted. Leopold looked up momentarily from his writing.

"Daydreaming again Madie," he said smiling, though it appeared more of a smirk to Madeline. She glared at him with annoyance.

"Obsessed Madie. You are hopelessly obsessed."

"Obsession is my nature Leo," she said arrogantly. "Just as it is yours."

"I indulge in my obsessions, yours are unobtainable."

Madeline stood by the stone fireplace, her back to Leopold.

"Nothing is unobtainable," she countered, gazing heavily into the fire.

Soft laughter escaped Leopold's lips.

Madeline spun around, sending her long velvet skirt swaying. Her eyes were enraged. "You dare to laugh at my words," she shouted, clutching the carved mantel, her mane of red hair draped in curls down her back. "I have lived an eternity by your side, and you dare to laugh at me."

"I do," he said calmly, leaning back in his chair. "You have become amusing in your old age. Possibly you are tired? he questioned. "Tired of this life of eternal beauty?" Leopold folded his arms and sighed. "Pitiful."

"Be silent," Madeline ordered, and collapsed into a large tapestry covered chair. "Your sarcasm does not amuse me."

"No, but it amuses *me.*"

"I can see that it does," she replied, taking her gaze back to the fire.

Leopold resumed his writing.

"Why Leo? Why were we dealt with so cruelly?"

Again Leopold abandoned his writing. "And why is it," he said with exasperation, "am I presented with this absurdity century upon century?"

He then rose from his desk, walked across an ancient oriental carpet and onto the stone floor where a bronze cart stood holding decanters of wines. He poured two glasses and joined Madeline by the fire.

"Here Madie," he said, handing her a glass.

"I don't want any."

"Drink it Madie. God knows you need something."

"God?" she blurted, taking the glass. "It was GOD who took from me what I needed." She gulped half of her wine, then cast the remainder into the fire.

Leopold looked amused. "You are blaming Zeus for this?" he said. "Have you not the wisdom to know better?"

"With absolute certainty," she stormed. "Zeus was not our betrayer. Mortals were. We would have been a pure race, a divine race, untainted by ambition, greed, power. And we *were* that race until the seeds of mortal man grew and infested our souls."

"You know very well that we could not have been a divine race. There would not have been a race without mortal man. I must say, Madie, it amazes me how long you can hold onto this senseless grudge of yours. How many years has it been now, over eleven thousand?" Leopold sipped his wine calmly as he watched Madeline stir in her chair.

"The grudge has held fast to me, Leo, not I to it. Eleven thousand more years, and I will still be plagued with it." Abruptly, she flung herself from the chair. "Damn! That insipid little mouse of a woman will be crowned Queen of England in only a matter of weeks." Madie's face was now as red as her hair.

Leopold remained unaffected by her ravings. He had become quite used to Madeline's impossible obsession to reign as Queen of England. But they were progressively getting worse, and he feared what she might be considering.

There had been only three Queens of England since William I conquered Britain in 1066. In 1553, Mary I took the throne. For five long years Madie was impossible to be near. Her fits of jealously were common occurrences. Then, to make matters worse, Elizabeth I succeeded Mary. However, her reign was so lengthy that Madie began to occupy herself more with her family and less with her obsession. In the forty five years that Elizabeth reigned as Queen, Madie gave birth to twelve more children. Three girls and nine boys.

"Madie," Leopold said, "this obsession to rule England is running rampant. You know you are speaking of impossible things. We have been cast into the very depths of what we had become. The depths of obsessive greed and pleasures bound by heavy trepidation. Our existence is that of discretion. And must remain such. We must not flaunt ourselves among others as you are so possessed to do. It would be disastrous if we were known to possess eternal youth. Catastrophic. Learn to live with your evil *Gift* as I have. Why is it that you can not?"

Madeline slumped down into the tapestry chair and stared out into space. It's different for you than for me," she said not shifting her gaze. "You are obsessed with youth and beauty. Love is your nemesis so you indulge in your obsessiveness for sexual passion, money, possessions, anything you fancy. Except love."

"Yes," Leopold agreed. "Obsessions. I have found great pleasure in my obsessions. And love is by no means an emotion I will allow to destroy me." An anguished smirk then crossed his face. "May I remind you that love did not stand in the way of your incestuous deception with our son."

Madeline turned to Leopold with daggers in her eyes. "Do not dare to speak of that," and she turned back to the fire.

"The guilt still lingers, Madie. I can see it. It has failed to release you, even after all this time."

"I will never be free of it. Every time I look at you I am reminded of it."

Leopold rose from his chair with anguish caused by the very mention of his son. He, too, still bore guilt. Leopold's expression suddenly turned to anger. He reached out and grasped Madeline by the back of the neck.

"And our evil deeds have bound you to me. And I to you. In a passion that burns deep. A passion that has lasted for millenniums."

Madeline looked up into Leopold's piercing blue eyes, feeling that overwhelming love as her hatred slipped away. Just as Leopold's passion burned deep, so too her love. And she was doomed never to behold this love in return.

"Yes Leo," and she pushed away in bitter despair. "I am bound to you."

"You are *my* queen Madie. And *their* Queen. The Winthrop family. Why is this obsession of yours to rule all of England so great?"

Madeline looked up at Leopold briefly. "I told you, it's my nature," and she turned back to the fire as though preoccupied with it. "Just as it is your nature to leave my side and satiate your passion with our children. It tortures me, and time has not lessened my burden. My love for you only grows deeper."

"And I would flee to the ends of the earth to save myself from it," he proclaimed. "I can not conceive of losing my youth for the passion of such a foolish sentiment. Even the sound of it sickens me," and he stormed past her. "Tell me Madie," he said pouring another glass of wine. "You would relinquish your eternal beauty for my love or to reign as Queen?"

Madeline seemed hypnotized by the fire. "No," she answered. "And that, Leo, is my eternal damnation. That day," she scorned. "That wretched day. The horror of it will forever torture me. How could Zeus have destroyed Atlantis so completely and left Athínai in such devastation? We should not have been the ones to carry the blame for immorality."

"We knew the laws, Madie."

"The laws! Yes. Laws set for a divine nature, not the nature of ordinary humans. And that's what we had become. We were hopelessly influenced by them: cast into corruption." Madeline looked into Leopold's face with an accusing stare. "And lust." She lowered her head. "We had become incapable of divinity."

Leopold took Madeline by the arm. "Lust is what keeps me near you," and he touched her face with his fingertips, trailing gently down her flawless skin and across her lips. "Perfection," he whispered. "And it is you who strengthens my passion." He then pressed his lips to hers.

"My love," she muttered softly.

Leopold venomously ignored this.

Chapter Three
1878

Queen Victoria still reigned over all of Britain. Madie's hatred toward Her Majesty was vexing. She and Leopold would have violent arguments over this and Madeline would retreat to her bedchamber for days. Her obsession to reign as Queen was consuming her. So Leopold left her to her sequestered existence and indulged himself with his own obsessions. That of sexual fulfillment.

Though Leopold carefully guarded his family's secret vengefully, he was not solely unobtainable and entertained with discretion. He had a passion for music and commissioned some of the greatest masters of the time to perform at Nine Thornton Square. Because of his vast wealth, residing in a most magnificent dwelling, and while posturing an air of mystique, most were overjoyed when receiving an invitation from Leopold and Madeline Winthrop. However, Leopold and Madeline were rarely seen on these occasions, and then, only for brief moments. The guests, however, were lavishly attended to by the servants.

There were, and had always been rumors surrounding this eccentric family, but as the cycle of life and death played out its role for mortal man, old rumors faded while new ones brought a rebirth of speculation.

Who were these Winthrops? Where had they come from?

It was now 1881. Madeline, though still plagued with her infernal obsession to rule England, had once again occupied herself with her family and enjoying a more open display of social etiquette. Leopold had begun, at long last, to emerge from obscurity. And Madeline lavished in it. Their guests, as always, were selected with great care. Only the higher echelon of society were invited to the Winthrop Mansion, and then, only in small numbers. The Prince of Whales, Queen Victoria's first born, was a frequent visitor. His admiration toward Madeline was blatantly apparent. This was quite amusing to Madeline, thinking that the Queen's son was so taken with her, and all the while detesting the very thought that his mother, a pathetic mortal, was sitting on the royal throne.

It was then that Madeline began venturing into places that were foreign to her. She could not take the risk of being recognized so she chose the decayed slums of the East End known as Whitechapel for her playground. There she would most assuredly be noticed: admired for her beauty and sophistication. No one would have the slightest idea who she was or where she had come from. She would be discrete in her interaction with these people, reveling in the mystery she would create among them. What Madeline could not have known, though, was that these nightly adventures into the half world of London would only add to her obsessions. She soon became enamored with a young woman who played the piano at one of the clubs on Osborn Street between Wentworth and Whitechapel High. Madeline would sit for hours while the woman played, overtaken, not only by her talent but her extraordinary beauty. Night after night Madeline would sit off in a dark corner and listen to the woman play. Then one night, many months later, she inquired as to who the woman was. But her inquiry left her with an even deeper mystery. No one seemed to know her name or where she had come from. Not even Madeline was successful when, at last, she approached the woman and attempted conversation. And again, when she tired to follow the woman, in hopes of discovering where she lived. The woman had eluded her.

For two years Madeline listened and watched this woman at the piano. Until one night when she learned that the woman had gone. Madeline was frantic. No one could tell her of the woman's whereabouts. Endlessly Madeline searched the fog-draped streets and alleyways of Whitechapel. From one club to the other she searched.

While Madeline's obsession with this mysterious young woman grew, so was Leopold's passion for sexual fulfillment. He was now bringing young women into Nine Thornton Square. Mortal women. And this tortured Madeline. Once these women were brought to Leopold and into his domain, they were forbidden to leave. Groomed and pampered within their opulent prison, these women serviced, not only Leopold, but his family and selected guests. Guests of whom ranged from the Prince of Whales to earls, counts, lords and dukes. Nine Thornton Square was becoming a royal bordello. In exchange for services, Leopold was assured of complete discretion and anonymity from the outside world as well as discreet favors he might require. Besides, his guests would hardly relish the disgrace that such a scandal would cause them. They also did not want to lose the privileges that Nine Thornton Square provided. They had not only come to respect Leopold Winthrop and his family but learned to fear them as well. If the Winthrop family were ever discussed, it was done so with extreme caution and only among the selected few.

By now Leopold was indulging himself more and more in the sexual pleasures of mortal women. And Madeline was becoming even more obsessed with finding her mysterious woman. But the woman seemed to have vanished. No amount of inquiry had produced the least bit of information. So naturally it was a tremendous shock when one day the woman appeared at Nine Thornton Square. Her name was Bernadette Morland. It had been Mr. Oscar Wilde who had brought her to Leopold. A few years back Leopold had become interested in Mr. Wilde's work as well as his wit and controversial spin on Victorian England. He began indulging in long conversations with Wilde, and though Wild was not a particularly attractive man, his brilliance and charm had captivated Leopold. Their friendship soon developed into a sexual affair. Again, Leopold was not threatened by exposure with Wilde. Homosexual conduct was not tolerated in nineteenth century England, so fear of exposure assured Leopold of Mr. Wilde's discretion.

Bernadette Morland had now been coming to Thornton Square for several months. Madeline knew that Leopold had become as intoxicated with the woman as she had. Though Leopold's sexual appetite was strong, indulging in his passion among the sexes, Madeline had rarely been drawn to her own sex. And never with such intensity as she was experiencing now. She must find a way to approach this woman. But it was Bernadette who approached Madeline. It was Bernadette who was the seductress.

Madeline soon learned that Bernadette had an apartment in the slum-ridden Whitechapel where she lived with her invalid mother. And it was there Madeline would eventually learn the truth behind this mysterious woman, her eccentric mother and her obsession with Nine Thornton Square.

Leopold had now become more and more obsessive in his sexual pleasures with mortal women. Though he still hungered, and fed his passion for Madeline, the follies of seducing the imprisoned mortal women of Nine Thornton Square stirred his senses. He found pure ecstasy in these pleasures. He also found the offspring's of these women most suitable for subserviency.

Madeline, on the other hand, found his conduct repulsive. It did not matter to her that these women had been groomed, literally transformed. They were still the lowest form society had to offer. Nothing more than pathetic prostitutes and castaways, void of breeding. It sickened her to think of Leopold seducing these women. And every visit to Whitechapel reinforced her repulsion The streets were infested with them. And it was becoming painfully clear that Bernadette too enjoyed these repugnant creatures.

But Whitechapel fed Madeline's passion for admiration. These pathetic inhabitants of the east end were enamored with Madeline and in awe of her beauty and gentility. As so they were with Bernadette. But Bernadette was less flamboyant with her presence than Madeline. She entertained, with quiet discretion, the whores of Whitechapel, cared for her mother, and indulged in frequent trysts with Madeline while still visiting Nine Thornton Square on the arm of Oscar Wilde.

Leopold knew that Wilde was not the least interested in the beautiful and seductive Bernadette, for his sexual preferences lay elsewhere. Wilde had told him that he and Bernadette had become acquainted while at a small but elite gathering entertained by the great composer of operas, Léo Delibes. Bernadette had become one of Delibes protégés. But Bernadette remained a mystery to both Delibes and Wilde. They knew virtually nothing about the young woman. Her residence had never been revealed to them. Delibes, however, respected her secrecy and anonymity, accepting her eccentricity. Wilde, on the other hand, found the mystery intriguing and decided to follow her one night after depositing her at what he had come to find out, was not where she resided. Unlike Leopold and Delibes, Wilde was not capable of discarding such strange behavior. And he was equally incapable of discarding his bewilderment when, while laying in wait, crouched down by the edge of the cobblestone alleyway after depositing her at her supposed address, he witnessed Bernadette exit the building and enter a hansom. He cautiously followed the carriage on foot, darting in and out of dark buildings and alleyways to avoid discovery. To Wilde's amazement, the hansom pulled into the back alley of Nine Thornton Square. Wilde crept cautiously, following it toward the imposing rear gates. The gates opened as the hansom drew near. It was obvious that someone was awaiting their arrival.

Wilde contemplated whether to relay what he had witnessed to Leopold. But ultimately decided not to mention the incident. Possibly Leopold knew more about this beautiful creature than he was willing to reveal. Wilde found this intriguing, surmising that, like he with Leopold, the master of Nine Thornton Square was having a sordid affair with Bernadette behind his wife, Madeline's, back.

And how right Wilde was. Leopold was indeed rendezvousing with Bernedette. But it was upon Bernedette's insistence that no one know of this. Leopold agreed to the deception, finding the idea alluring. For he knew that Madeline had become enamored with Bernedette. What he did not know was the extent the two women had taken their relationship. Bernedette feigned repulsion of the idea of embracing another woman. She would become indignant when Leopold voiced his absurd suspicion that Madeline was obsessed in having her sexually.

Leopold was also ignorant of Bernedette's true reason for *their* nightly trysts. When it was time for Bernedette to leave, Leopold would have Bernie, his now faithful servant, whisk Bernedette through the dark corridors and down the back stairways to where her hansom awaited. But she did not enter her carriage, instead, with Bernie as her sentinel, she entered *The Chamber* of Nine Thornton Square.

As the story continues and 1888 approaches, Jack the Ripper's mayhem begins ∞

~About the Author~

Paulette Gaston Crain was born on October 18, 1942 in Sheffield, Alabama and raised in Jackson, Tennessee. She and her husband, Des, have two grown children, Steven Gaston Crain and Ashley Taylor Crain Cookus.

Paulette and her husband have enjoyed living in a number of cites throughout the US for the last twenty-eight years. She has worked for three airlines and had her own interior design business.

During the thirteen years in the San Francisco Bay area, Paulette worked for six years as Marketing Director for Rose Dust Designs. She left her position there to begin writing her first novel. Eight years and mounds of rewrites later Delore's Confession emerged.

Paulette and her husband now share their time between New Orleans and San Francisco. After finishing her new psychological thriller **FATEHUNTER**, Paulette will return to the Gothic world where she will complete the prequel to Delore's Confession.